"Well, aren't you going to invite me in?" Ross St. John's words were spoken mockingly, but his voice was hoarse and underlaid with a strange urgency.

"Are you crazy?" she whispered.

He shouldered past her and stepped inside, shutting the door. Jessica backed away from him, into the center of the room.

"Ross, what are you doing? This is madness. What if Jeffrey . . ."

"The hell with Jeffrey. You aren't right for him anyway. He hasn't got the guts to stand up for himself, to take what he wants. But I have."

He made no move toward her but stood slumped against the door, staring at her. His eyes glowed like coals in the lamplight.

"You're beautiful," he whispered hoarsely. "You're a woman made for a man, Jessica —for a real man. It's going to take a real man to tame you, to hold you, to satisfy you."

Reap the
Bitter Wind
Jill DuBois

BALLANTINE BOOKS • NEW YORK

Library of Congress Catalog Card Number: 85-90641

ISBN 0-345-32166-9

Manufactured in the United States of America

First Edition: July 1985

To Ray

Part I

The Ranch

Chapter 1

"There's the ranch house."

Jessica Howard, her hands braced on the pommel of her saddle, stretched tall so that she could see where her fiancé was pointing. Below her, the dusty strip of road wound down the mountain into the distance. She squinted beneath the broad brim of her sombrero. There. She could barely make out, at the far end of the valley, a tiny cluster of buildings nestled against the cascading forest. How frail this little outpost of civilization seemed underneath the vast turquoise sky. And how beautiful this surprise of green meadow ringed by pines, after the dry, wild hills which they had just climbed.

Jessica's pinto skittered restlessly beneath her as she eased herself back down into the saddle and stilled the horse with a firm tug on the reins. She had been pleased that she still remembered how to ride after all these years. Her old ease in the saddle had returned to her quickly. She was glad she had talked Jeffrey into renting horses at the livery stable in Bernalillo so they could ride up to the ranch by themselves instead of waiting for the buckboard. It meant that their luggage would not arrive until the day after they did, but she didn't care. It was such fun to be on a horse again and so lovely to be alone with Jeffrey exploring this beautiful rugged land. They had taken their time on the long, steep journey through the hills and into the mountains, relishing the silence and the fresh dry air after their many days on the train, soaking up the warmth of the New Mexico sun.

She turned to look at her fiancé, who had ridden up beside her on his rented hack, and her heart swelled with happiness. How handsome Jeffrey was, with his dark, wavy hair, his fine, aristocratic features, those dark blue eyes which regarded her with so much affection. He had changed from his city clothes, and his corduroy riding pants and open-necked shirt and vest were quite dashing. As Jeffrey pulled out his cotton bandanna to wipe the dust off his brow, Jessica noted that his face had already acquired a slight flush from the sun. He would soon lose his eastern pallor.

Jessica knew they made a handsome couple. She glanced down at her tailored riding suit, which had been made in anticipation of just such an occasion. It was severe in cut but molded tightly around her full figure, and it suited her perfectly. She had left her dark hair loose today, and it cascaded down from her sombrero and over her shoulders. Her cheeks were flushed with excitement and the intoxication of the sharp, dry air.

Feeling joyously alive and suddenly impatient with their brief halt, Jessica gathered up the reins.

"Race you to the bottom of the hill!" she cried, spurring her pinto forward down the dusty slope of road before Jeffrey could reply. She heard his laughing protests behind her, and then the slap of leather and the thud of hooves as he pressed his own mount to follow. Jessica's hair streamed out behind her as the pony threw itself into the race. She knew she was going much too fast, but she didn't care. She hadn't felt so free and unfettered for years. She could ride like this, like the wind, forever. Jessica laughed exultantly in the sheer overflowing of high spirits.

With her advantageous start and reckless riding, Jessica was easily the winner. She reined in her horse at the bottom of the slope, sending up a swirling cloud of dust around them. Dismounting, she flung herself into a patch of buttercup-studded grass at the foot of a stand of pines and lay there, trying to catch her breath. Jeffrey came up a moment later and reined his horse to a halt.

"You shouldn't have done that," he scolded as he dismounted and knelt down beside her. "That was a steep slope and that horse of yours is not very surefooted."

But Jessica's exuberance was infectious, and Jeffrey found himself smiling down at her in the middle of his lecture.

"Don't be stuffy, Jeffrey," she teased, wrinkling her nose. "We're out here on your father's ranch now, not at some concert in New York." She pillowed her head on her arms and sighed happily. "I feel so wonderful here. I'm glad we came."

Jeffrey reached down and rumpled her hair fondly. With another sigh of contentment, Jessica snuggled down against the grass. Even though it was only mid-May, and here and there patches of snow still nestled in the high peaks of the Sangre de Christo, the late afternoon sun was strong. The air was so clear here, she thought, not like the air back east where the summer was damp and heavy.

Jessica rolled on her side and gazed up at her fiancé. How lucky she was to be engaged to Jeffrey St. John and coming here to live on his father's ranch. And such a big and beautiful ranch it was, too—beyond her wildest expectations. Even from what little they had seen, Jessica had already fallen in love with it.

If only they could get married here, in the middle of these wild mountains, instead of going back to New York, she daydreamed. She could bring her mother out for the wedding. Her mother had sworn never to leave New York again, and especially never to return to the West. But if Jessica could explain how different the high desert and the fragrant pine and cedar forests of New Mexico were from the empty Texas plains of her childhood—maybe her mother would change her mind.

Jeffrey knelt beside her. His dark blue eyes smiled no

longer, but instead were filled with something that Jessica had only recently learned to recognize. It was a mixture of desire, longing, and something else. Awareness of her fiancé's gaze drew Jessica away from her own thoughts. Overcome by the languid warmth of the sun and the sweet scent of the grass, Jessica lifted her arms up toward Jeffrey. He hesitated a moment. Then, instead of yielding to her invitation, he grasped one of her hands in his, and, rising to his feet, pulled her up with him.

Jessica felt a little pang of disappointment, not the first she'd experienced in times spent alone with Jeffrey. She couldn't comprehend his restraint. After all, they were engaged. And it was a union that had the blessing of her mother. Isabelle Howard had been delighted to see her daughter betrothed to a young man who was not only the son of a wealthy rancher but also a charming and considerate Harvard-educated gentleman. It had taken a substantial burden off her mother's mind to know that her daughter would be provided for. Soon, if all went as planned, they would have the approval of Jeffrey's father, Ross St. John, as well. And yet, despite their engagement, despite all the time they had spent together, Jeffrey had never delivered much more than a chaste kiss to her forehead.

Well, she reflected as they remounted and set their horses trotting down the long road across the valley toward the ranch house, she really should be grateful. At least Jeffrey was a gentleman. Jessica thought of all the rough characters they had seen on their train journey west and at their stops in Albuquerque and Bernalillo. Gamblers, gunmen, adventurers, and other disreputable sorts were not individuals she would like to be alone with. She had been glad that Jeffrey's protective presence had prevented any attentions more bothersome than an occasional bold glance or muttered comment. And Jeffrey was such pleasant company, always even-tempered, even when faced with all the aggravations of a long journey.

The valley through which they were riding was bigger than it had seemed at first. Jessica had forgotten how deceptive western distances could be. The valley, a long fertile strip stretching between rugged mountain peaks, must have been ten to fifteen miles long, though from the road above it had seemed only three or four. And the ranch house lay a good halfway down its length.

Jessica was impressed by both the beauty of the valley and the wealth which it proclaimed. To their left ran lush meadows, dotted with a profusion of spring wild flowers. On the right a pine forest, shot with occasional dusty shafts of sunlight, radiated cool darkness.

As she thought of the man who owned all this, Jessica began to feel slightly apprehensive. How would he receive her? After all, Ross St. John was a wealthy and influential man. And she was . . . what? A respectable girl, certainly, but of no particular means or importance. Would Ross St. John see her as a fortune hunter who had latched on to the heir to a prosperous ranch? Jeffrey's descriptions of Ross had given her no clue as to what his reaction to her would be. As her mind began to create the image of an aristocratic and disapproving father, Jessica's exuberance began to lessen, and her good feelings of a few moments ago were tempered by the realization that her happiness was as yet by no means assured.

Her spirits picked up again, however, as they drew closer to the ranch house. The final stretch of their journey led them through a long strip of meadow. In the slanting rays of the late afternoon sun, Jessica could see horses grazing in the distance and her heart leaped at the sight. Jeffrey noted her interest.

"Those are just part of what the Running J owns," he told her. "Horses are my father's pride and joy. He has some really fine breeding stallions and brood mares in addition to the cow ponies. He'll be happy to provide you with your own mount."

"That would be wonderful. I can't wait!" Jessica's thoughts flew back to Sunny, the spirited little mare that had been hers to ride on the ranch in Texas. How she had loved that little

horse! And her love had caused her mother near despair, for
Jessica had taken to roaming freely on her horse, disappearing
for hours on end to explore creek banks, ravines, and wide-
open spaces. "No life for a young lady," her mother had
protested to her father. But to Jessica it had seemed the
perfect life. She hadn't feared Indians or rustlers or wild
steers as she ranged. She had enjoyed this so much more than
the years of schooling in New York, which had seemed dull
and confining by comparison. But then, she reflected, if they
hadn't moved to New York, she would never have met
Jeffrey and she would not be here now, riding through this
beautiful valley.

They turned off the main road and headed down the wide
track that led to the ranch house. On one side of them
stretched a field of new alfalfa, burnished green in the fading
light, and on the other side Jessica could see more horses
grazing.

A fence of split-pine railings surrounded the ranch house. It
was more decorative than functional, for there was no gate,
and they passed freely into the bare dirt yard and dismounted
in front of the long veranda. Roofed and supported by poles
of peeled yellow pine, the veranda ran the length of the south
side of the single-storied log structure. A rocker and several
crude pine chairs stood at inviting angles, and in a wooden
planter at the far end, a ragged clump of irises past the peak
of their bloom glowed purple in the shadows. Jessica could
see chintz curtains at several of the windows. The place had a
rustic but cozy look.

To the right of the house clustered a number of outbuildings, including a barn and a stable with an attached corral,
and behind the house tucked in the woods were several
commodious cabins, which Jessica took to be the bunk houses.
From the direction of one of these a man was hobbling toward
them. Aside from a few chickens scratching in the dust near
the porch, he was the only sign of life. As the man drew
closer, Jessica realized that his rocking gait was due to his
legs, which resembled wishbones, being severely bowed.
His clothes were faded and patched.

"Tom!" Jeffrey's greeting was joyful and affectionate.

The old man showed no change of expression at the sight of Jeffrey. As he drew closer, Jessica saw that a maze of fine lines crisscrossed his bronzed face and his eyes were black and bright above his high cheekbones.

"You're early." His speech was laconic. "Weren't expecting you till tomorrow."

"We thought we'd rent a couple of horses and ride up today. Dob will be here later with the buckboard and our luggage."

Tom continued to regard them impassively, his eyes giving no clue to his thoughts.

"I'd like you to meet my fiancée," Jeffrey continued. "Tom Mendoza, this is Jessica Howard. Tom has been with my father since before I was born."

Jessica started to offer her hand and then stopped, uncertain about the etiquette of the situation. Tom made no response to her interrupted gesture, but stared at her with a mixture of scorn and hostility.

What ails the old man? she wondered, beginning to feel annoyed.

Jeffrey, glancing around the ranch yard, had not noticed Tom's coldness.

"Things look pretty deserted," he remarked. "Is my father around?"

"Everybody's out at Castel Springs for the roundup," Tom replied. "Won't be back for a couple days." The touch of scorn in his voice implied that Jeffrey, the rancher's son, should have remembered what time of year it was.

Jeffrey flushed at the old man's tone.

"Of course," he replied quickly. "I forgot." He turned to Jessica and smiled. "Well, I guess we'll have the place to ourselves for a little while. That will give you a chance to get used to things before you meet everyone." He turned back to Tom and handed him the horses' reins. "Here, Tom, why don't you take these nags to the stable and look after them for us. I'll show Miss Howard around."

Tom spit eloquently into the dust, and then, almost reluctantly, he took the reins from Jeffrey's hands and shuffled off.

"He doesn't seem very friendly," Jessica commented when the old man was out of hearing.

Jeffrey laughed. "He's getting a bit old and crotchety," he admitted, "but he was a tough cowboy in his day. Used to rope and break wild horses. My father used to say you couldn't kill Old Tom. Someday he'll just shrivel up and blow away like a bit of desert dust."

He couldn't blow away too soon to suit her, Jessica decided, still piqued by the old man's unfriendliness. But then she felt ashamed of her thoughts. After all, he sounded like a valued hand. He was probably just slow to take to strangers.

Someone else had appeared while they were talking, and Jeffrey broke into a big smile when he spotted her standing in the shadows of the veranda.

"Donaciana!" In two bounds he was on the veranda beside her, giving the plump Mexican woman a loving kiss on the cheek. She endured his embrace but did not appear to return his warmth, and when she turned to him her voice was chiding.

"You're early, Jeffrey. We thought you'd come tomorrow." She spoke in strongly accented English, "Nothing is ready; nothing. Tomorrow I was going to cook all day, but today I have nothing."

Is everyone going to be upset with us for coming early? Jessica wondered. She was beginning to regret her impulsive plan to ride up ahead of the buckboard.

Jeffrey, however, paid no attention to the woman's scolding. He grinned down at her. "I'm sure you'll come up with something," he said. "We've been riding all day and have appetites like bears, so we won't be too fussy. With you in the kitchen, I've never starved."

She seemed to soften a little.

"Well, a little something maybe I can scrape up. There's some chile left, and a little venison. And I made last night a dried apple pie."

"You're making my mouth water already." Jeffrey had put

his arm around Donaciana's shoulder and was leading her toward Jessica. "Come over here, *mamacita*, and meet my fiancée, Jessica Howard. Jessica, this is Donaciana Valdez. She practically raised me, herself, after my mother died, and spoiled me, too, I might add." He gave the short woman's plump shoulders an affectionate squeeze.

This time there was no mistaking the hostility in the glance directed at her. The dark eyes regarding Jessica from beneath the braided coronet of hair glittered with dislike, and the downward turn of the tightly pressed lips clearly registered disapproval. Then, with a toss of her head, Donaciana turned her attention back to Jeffrey.

"I will go start supper," she told him. "It will be ready in an hour." She threw one more swift, malevolent glance at Jessica before plodding back down the veranda.

"Are our rooms ready?" Jeffrey called after her. "Miss Howard and I would like to wash up."

"I will send Serafina" was the muffled reply, and then the Mexican woman disappeared into a doorway at the end of the veranda.

Jeffrey did not seem disconcerted by Donaciana's curtness, but Jessica was a little shaken. Was no one happy at their arrival? she wondered. She was beginning to feel as if they were intruders, arriving unannounced and unwanted, rather than the heir to the ranch and his fiancée returning home. Puzzled and disturbed, she turned to follow Jeffrey to the house.

The ranch house was composed of several buildings, connected by roofed breezeways. The section at the far end of the house—into which Donaciana had disappeared—must be the kitchen, Jessica presumed. Jeffrey opened a heavy, iron-banded door and they entered what appeared to be the main part of the house, a large, cedar-paneled room filled with heavy wooden furniture. Bright woven rugs were strewn across the polished floor and hung from the paneled walls. A stone fireplace took up most of one wall, and the assortment of chairs pulled up close to its cavernous mouth proclaimed its importance as a source of warmth on chilly nights. Though the room was rustic, there was nothing haphazard about its arrangement. Here and there were touches that were surprising on a remote mountain ranch: a glass-fronted bookcase filled with gilt and leather-bound books, several framed watercolors along the back wall, and—most astonishing of all—a small grand piano tucked into the farthest corner of the room.

Jeffrey noticed her glance.

"It was quite a feat to move that up here," he laughed, gesturing to the piano. "It took several days to haul it—the road wasn't nearly as good then as it is now. And it cost a small fortune. But it was my mother's pride and joy. Father did it to please her. She was so fond of music. No one has played it since she died, though my father has kept it in tune." He looked down at her fondly. "Maybe now that you're here, we can have music again."

Jessica was warmed by his words. "Now that you're here." It sounded so settled. Well, this *was* to be her home from now on. The uneasiness she had felt with Tom and Donaciana began to dissipate. They would just have to get used to her, she decided. She was here to stay.

"How do you like it?" Jeffrey indicated the room with a sweep of his hand.

"I love it," Jessica replied sincerely. "It's so comfortable, like a refuge."

Jeffrey nodded. "It certainly feels that way in the winter, when the blizzards are blowing outside and the drifts are piling up against the door. But," he added, taking her hand in his and drawing it to his chest, "with any luck, we'll be spending this next winter, at least, in Europe, not here."

Jessica smiled fondly at him, but her feelings were mixed. That had been their plan—a honeymoon in Europe, visiting museums and art galleries and historic sites. There Jeffrey would begin to pursue his dreams of drawing and writing, surrounded by the inspiration of the European masters and European artistic society. They hoped to talk Ross St. John into lending his financial support so that they could spend at least a year abroad.

Most young women would be thrilled by the prospect of a honeymoon in Europe, and Jessica had been, too, at least at first. But as soon as they had ridden into the mountains of New Mexico, the romance of Europe had begun to fade and the prospect of spending her life on the ranch began to seem more and more enticing. Perhaps her trip west had rekindled her childhood love of the outdoors. Or perhaps New Mexico spoke to her long-held fascination with wild and faraway places. She had always loved to read accounts of exotic lands, books not approved of by her mother or her teachers at Miss Whitley's Day School for Young Women. Europe was beginning to sound too civilized, when compared to the adventures awaiting her on the Running J ranch.

"Come. Let me show you the rest of the house." Jeffrey was pulling her toward the dining room. It was clear that he loved the ranch, loved this house. His affection was obvious in his voice and in his eagerness to show it to her. Yet Jessica knew that this love was tinged with ambivalence. An ambivalence, she sensed, that had to do with his father, Ross St. John.

The dining room was dominated by an elaborately carved table in the Spanish style, with matching, velvet-cushioned chairs. An ornate but graceful, silver candelabrum cast its reflection in the table's polished surface. In a glass-fronted cabinet gleamed an assortment of fine china and other silver pieces. But what Jeffrey drew her toward was a gilt-framed portrait of a woman, which hung over a dark oak sideboard.

"My mother," he said simply.

Jessica gazed up at the framed face. It was a sweet face, beautiful but rather sad, set off by a black lace mantilla which descended in folds from an elaborate high comb. The mantilla, however, was a conceit of either the lady or the artist, for she was obviously not Spanish. Her hair was honey blond and her eyes the same dark blue as Jeffrey's. She was smiling wistfully, the corners of her mouth tilted slightly upward and her eyes gazing off into the distance. Jessica could recognize a little of his mother in Jeffrey—the eyes, the aristocratic lines of the nose and mouth, the softness around the chin.

And occasionally she had seen that same longing in Jeffrey's eyes, too.

"She's very lovely," Jessica said softly, unaware that she had spoken of Reina St. John in the present, although Jeffrey's mother had died when Jeffrey was ten, some eleven years ago. The painting had captured something so essential about the woman, it was as if she were still there in the room.

"Yes, she was a beautiful woman," Jeffrey replied sadly. "And kind and gentle, too. I don't remember her ever raising her voice. We were all grief-stricken when she died."

But especially you, Jessica thought. She had already sensed that Jeffrey had been much closer to his mother than to his father.

"How did she die?" Jessica asked, curious. "She must have been very young."

"Typhoid fever," Jeffrey replied shortly. "I had it myself and I was very ill, but I recovered. They didn't tell me she had died until nearly a week later."

Jessica laid her hand on his arm.

"I'm sorry," she said softly. "I didn't mean to bring up painful memories."

He folded his hand over hers.

"It's all right," he reassured her. "I don't mind talking about her. I only wish you could have met her. I'm sure you would have liked each other. And she would have been so pleased that I found such a lovely girl to marry."

"Jeffrey!"

They both whirled around at the sound of that joyful squeal, and Jessica saw a pretty Mexican woman of about her own age standing in the doorway of the dining room, a pile of linens in her arms. The linens tumbled on the table and the girl was flying toward Jeffrey, her arms outstretched.

"Serafina!" Jeffrey had moved from Jessica's side, and scooping the slender figure in his arms, he lifted her up in the air and planted a kiss affectionately on her cheek. As he set her down, she gazed up at him in delight.

"Serafina! It's so good to see you. You look so pretty.

You've really grown since I last saw you." He held her at arm's length and looked her up and down approvingly.

Jessica felt a little pang of jealousy. The girl *was* pretty, with a creamy dark complexion, sparkling black eyes, and dark hair hanging in a glossy braid down her back. She was obviously fond of Jeffrey—and he of her. He had never lifted her, Jessica, up in the air like that. Was this an old sweetheart? she wondered.

As if sensing her strained silence, both Jeffrey and Serafina turned toward her.

"Serafina"—his arm was still around her, Jessica noticed—"Serafina, I'd like you to meet my fiancée, Jessica Howard. Jessica, this is Serafina Valdez, Donaciana's daughter. Serafina and I grew up together. She's like a sister to me."

A sister? Jessica thought. The young woman's greeting had seemed more than sisterly. She braced herself for the same hostile scrutiny from the daughter that she had received from the mother. But Serafina rushed over to take her hand, her full, red lips curving into a pleasant smile.

"Oh, it's so lovely to meet you." Her English was perfect but there was a musical Spanish lilt to her voice. "I knew that Jeffrey was bringing his fiancée—of course he wrote us all about you—but he didn't tell us that you were so beautiful."

She gazed at Jessica in frank admiration, and Jessica suddenly found herself blushing. Serafina turned back toward Jeffrey, but kept Jessica's hand clasped in hers.

"They say you rode up here with some rented horses, which is why you are so early."

"Yes. It was Jessica's idea. She couldn't wait to get to the ranch and on a horse, so she talked me into riding."

Jessica was ashamed of her jealousy of a moment before. It was obvious that this warm, charming girl was to him just what Jeffrey said she was—like a sister and nothing more. She was foolish to have doubted him.

Serafina was regarding Jessica with approval.

"It is good that you ride. This is a big ranch. You will need to be skilled with a horse. And I am very glad that you are here early, which means we can have more time together.

Come.'' She picked up the linens she had tossed on the table. ''I am going to make up the beds. Then I will get you hot water for washing. Which will it be? One room or two?''

This time it was Jeffrey who blushed.

''Don't be silly, Serafina,'' he admonished her a little sharply. ''You know we aren't married yet. I'll take my old room, and Jessica can have the guest room down the hall.''

Serafina regarded him thoughtfully for a moment, and then she turned to Jessica and gave her an impish grin.

''Come along, then. If you insist on making more work for me, so be it.''

Jessica felt a little embarrassed, though she wasn't certain if it was on Jeffrey's account or her own. She avoided her fiancé's glance as they followed Serafina across the living room and down the adjoining hall to the next wing, where the bedrooms were located. Jeffrey's room was near the back of the house, facing the woods, and Jessica's was a little farther down on the other side of the hallway, with windows opening out onto the veranda. At the end of the hall, just past her room, was another doorway. Serafina explained that it led to a breezeway, on the other side of which was Ross St. John's room.

''He likes his privacy,'' she explained. ''And from there, he can come and go as he pleases.''

She led Jessica into her room, which was comfortably, if simply, furnished. There was a wooden bedstead, a dresser with a mirror, a large wardrobe, a small writing table with a chair, and a rocker. Chintz curtains in a faded yet cheerful flower print framed the windows. They were drawn, and Jessica pulled them back. Outside, the sun had disappeared behind the jagged mountains, and the sky was suffused with a soft pink glow.

Serafina lighted the oil lamp on the dresser.

''It's a lovely evening,'' she commented approvingly. ''You had a very nice day for your ride.''

''It was nice,'' Jessica agreed. ''Especially when we started climbing into the mountains. Here, let me help you with that." She moved toward the bed where Serafina was flipping the sheet over the mattress.

The other woman waved her away.

"No, no—that's all right. I work best by myself."

And she did work quickly. In no time she had made the bed and pulled several bright Indian blankets from the wardrobe to cover it.

"There. You should be warm tonight. It still gets a little chilly up here this time of year, once the sun goes down." She turned to smile at Jessica, and then a thought struck her and she frowned.

"You have no clothes to change into, do you?" she asked.

"I'm afraid not," Jessica confessed. "All I have is my riding habit. I left all my other things to be brought up on the buckboard."

"I'll lend you some of mine," Serafina said decisively, her eyes twinkling. "Then you will be all fresh and clean for dinner—and for Jeffrey."

"Oh no, I couldn't . . ."

"Please. I am happy to do it. After all, we are going to be like sisters, aren't we." She took Jessica's hand and squeezed it, and then moved toward the door. "I will take care of Jeffrey and then I'll come back with some hot water and something for you to wear."

After the other woman had gone, Jessica sat down on the bed to remove her boots. She ran her fingers through her tangled hair. Perhaps Serafina could find her a comb, too. She had to admit that it would be nice to change clothes. What a lovely person Serafina was. At least someone on the ranch appeared to have taken to her.

Serafina returned, carrying an enameled tin pitcher of hot water in one hand and a pile of clothing in the other. She set the pitcher in the basin on the dresser and laid the clothing across the bed. Then, after Jessica had removed her dusty riding habit and washed, Serafina combed the tangles out of her long dark hair.

"You should ride with your hair up, under your hat," she

scolded, working out a knot with the comb. "Your hair is beautiful, but it is very fine. It is like the nests of rats now."

"I know," Jessica laughed. "But it felt so good to ride like that today, with my hair loose and the wind blowing through it."

Serafina nodded understandingly.

"You have a free spirit. That is good, I think. Good for Jeffrey. He needs someone like you, to be free a little."

Jessica, puzzled by these words, wanted to ask Serafina what she meant, but she was uneasy about discussing her fiancé with a stranger.

Serafina had brought her a striped cotton skirt and a short-sleeved, white cotton blouse.

"These are just everyday clothes," she said. "Not like the things you are used to. But I think they will fit." She slipped the skirt over Jessica's head. "You are a little taller than I, but that will not matter too much. Jeffrey will not mind if he sees a little of your ankles. And you are bigger in the bosom than I, but the blouse is loose. It looks nice on you. Here." She adjusted the neckline. "That is just right. Now the rebozo. I will show you how to wrap it. It will be nice to have on this cool night." She took the long strip of red wool and wound it becomingly around Jessica's shoulders. "If you go outside, you can pull it up over your head—so." She demonstrated.

Jessica regarded herself in the mirror. Like Jeffrey's mother in the portrait, she was now dressed in Spanish style. But unlike his mother, she looked the part. Her Indian blood, inherited from her paternal grandmother, appeared to be especially prominent—the high cheekbones, the liquid dark eyes that gave her an exotic air, enhanced by the vivid red rebozo. What would Jeffrey think of her like this? she wondered.

Jeffrey was waiting for her in the living room. He looked up from his book as she walked in, and then rose and strode toward her.

"You're beautiful," he whispered, taking her hands in his.

"The New Mexican air must agree with me," she replied demurely, flirting with him with her long lashes.

"And so do those clothes. They look like they were made especially for you."

Jeffrey had also changed and was wearing a fresh shirt and a frock coat. They made an oddly elegant couple, Jessica thought as they went into the dining room. One end of the long table had been set, and the candelabrum was fully lighted to illuminate their dinner. Despite Donaciana's disclaimer, the meal was elaborate, with fresh trout, venison in sauce, fresh tortillas wrapped around highly spiced beef and beans, and several other unfamiliar but delicious dishes. Jessica had been afraid at first that the unfriendly visage of Donaciana would be hovering over them during dinner, but instead they were served by a smiling Serafina. Jeffrey invited the young woman to join them, but she politely refused.

"Since everyone is away on the roundup," she explained, "we have let the servants go home to visit their families for a while, and my mother needs me. Besides," she added with a wink, "it will be much nicer for you to dine alone together on your first evening here at the ranch."

Serafina had brought them wine, cooled in an earthenware jug. She poured some into their cut-glass goblets, then tactfully retired.

They lingered a long time at the table, enjoying the meal and each other. Jessica suspected that such moments would be rare, once the roundup was over and Ross St. John had returned to the ranch, so she savored the occasion.

After they had finished their meal, they strolled to the veranda to gaze at the splendor of the New Mexican sky. Jessica had never before seen so many stars. Maybe it was the clarity of the mountain air, or maybe simply having Jeffrey at her side on the ranch that would someday be theirs, that made the stars here seem so brilliant. Whatever the reason, Jessica felt dazzled and blessed, and later, after Jeffrey had kissed her good night, she fell into a profound and peaceful sleep, snug in her own room.

Chapter 2

Reno Hayden reined in his horse and paused for a moment while he rolled and lighted a cigarette. It was getting late; his side trip had taken him out of the way. It would be dark when he arrived at the Burnt Cedar ranch, but it had been worth it to take the extra time.

He wasn't exactly certain why he had so impulsively followed the young couple who had just plunged in a boisterous cloud of dust down the hill into the valley below. A kind of curiosity, perhaps—curiosity about anything affecting the St. Johns. He had recognized Jeffrey St. John as soon as the young man had stepped off the train in Bernalillo. And he had known immediately that the young woman with him was his fiancée. She was from New York, he had heard, but that was all anyone seemed to know about her. When they came into the livery stable to rent horses, he had been standing in a nearby stall, grooming Felicia, and he had decided to follow them. They were heading more or less in his direction anyway. It would be good to refresh his memory regarding the road to the Running J and good to observe, even briefly, two people whose lives might soon become tangled in his own.

They hadn't noticed him at all. Completely wrapped up in each other, busy viewing the sights along the trail, they paid no attention to the possibility that someone else might be sharing their mountain journey. It was careless of young St. John, Reno reflected. He wasn't even carrying a gun. But maybe being back East for several years had made him forget the need for caution. Or perhaps he was unaware of the extent to which New Mexico had become, especially since the coming of the railroads, a haven for the violent and the lawless. Reno appreciated the grim irony of his serving as an unknown guardian for the young couple, watching out for them where they had failed to watch out for themselves.

She was quite striking, St. John's fiancée—beautiful in a dark, exotic way. If he hadn't known she was from New York, he would have pegged her as native to the southwest, perhaps someone with Spanish or Indian ancestry. In any case, she was certainly one to make men turn their heads. But trust the St. Johns to always have the best—in land, cattle, horses— and women. He himself had never been drawn to beautiful women. He found them boring, especially when they were young. Nonetheless, there was something about this one that appealed to him. There was a spirit in her, almost a wildness. He could see it in the way she had galloped down the hill, laughing as her hair flew behind her in the wind. And she had quite a prize in Jeffrey St. John, a prize that was going to make many local women jealous. Even so, Reno thought, she wasn't quite fitted to him, however much they appeared to be in love.

He shrugged and turned his horse, carefully snuffing out his cigarette stub on the pommel of his saddle before he tossed it to the ground. Well, that part of the whole affair was none of his business. Still, he hoped that neither of them— especially the girl—would get hurt. . . .

Felicia took to the trail eagerly, apparently as glad to be going again as if she had not already made the grueling climb from Bernalillo. Reno gave the mare her head and let her pick her own way among the tangled undergrowth lining the creek they followed. They would come upon a clearer trail just over the ridge, the one he had bypassed earlier in favor of his little pursuit. It was best to let his horse choose her own pace. They could make time once they reached the trail. He hoped Kincaid had a good stock of oats in his stable. Felicia deserved a reward after her extra-long trip. Not that she hadn't made many more grueling runs. Reno's thoughts ran back to the day the vigilante posse had pursued him along the Mogollon Rim, a day that only the good horse under him had prevented from being his last. He was deep in reminiscences by the time Felicia clambered down a short, steep slope to the wide trail that wound through the piñon and juniper, toward the Burnt Cedar ranch. His mind had become as somber as the twilight, which had begun to deepen around him.

The last job, he had told himself. This would be his last job. Once this business was taken care of, he would quit it all, hang up his gun, maybe even return to that spread he had his eye on in northern California. He could almost see it when he closed his eyes—daisy and lupine-starred meadows stretched out in the shadow of Mount Shasta. His love for that remote place was second only to his love for the burned deserts and wild mountains of New Mexico. But he had no hope of settling in this territory, at least not right now. He had too many enemies. Punks with reputations in the making would seek him out, hoping that his fall would guarantee their fame. No, California would be his refuge—if he survived.

Bats flitted above the treetops, darting and squeaking. Somewhere deep in the woods, an owl hooted. There was just enough of the fading light left for Felicia to pick her way along the rutted road which stretched ahead of them through the woods. Then, when it was almost too dark to see, they emerged into an expanse of meadow scattered with sleeping cattle. Another short stretch of woods, and they arrived at the ranch house, a large clapboard building set on a hill above a stream. In back of the house, the tall trunk of a scorched tree was silhouetted against the pale night sky. Several horses were tied to the hitching rail in front, along with a buggy and a buckboard, and lights blazed in the windows, casting diamonds of yellow across the wide porch.

Big doings, Reno thought to himself as he dismounted. Kincaid really meant business.

Reno did not immediately make his way to the house. Instead, he led Felicia to the stable by the creek, unsaddled her, and rubbed her down. As he ascended the hill to the house, he noted the absence of guards and the fact that those inside were still oblivious to his presence. He mounted the steps and stood for a moment on the porch, just outside the door. Inside, voices were raised in argument, and a bottle clinked against a glass.

A careless operation, Reno thought. Or maybe Kincaid was so confident he felt that precautions were unnecessary.

He opened the door and stepped inside.

Ten or twelve men were sitting around a large pine table, illuminated by the smoky glare of an oil lamp. They all looked up, startled, as Reno entered and one or two half rose from their seats, their hands moving instinctively toward the guns at their sides. Reno shut the door behind him and stood with his back against it.

"Reno! Reno Hayden! I was afraid you wouldn't show." The speaker, a large, florid man with thinning, blond hair, had jumped up from the table and was striding toward Reno, his hand outstretched. He wore a rumpled frock coat and a black felt western hat.

Reno ignored the proffered hand and bent his head to light a cigarette, his face shadowed for a moment by the brim of his hat. He was aware that all eyes in the room were on him. He waved out the match and tossed it to the floor. Then he looked up.

"Howdy, Kincaid," he drawled.

Stuart Kincaid took Reno's arm and pulled him toward the table.

"Men, this here's Reno Hayden. You all heard of him. I told you I thought I could get him in on this deal with us. Once they hear he's on our side, all those greasers of St. John's'll be runnin' for the border."

"Hold it just a minute. I haven't said I'm takin' the job." Reno pulled his arm away from Kincaid's grasp and let his glance sweep deliberately around the table. He was fully aware of the impression he made. It was part of his stock in trade. It gave him a psychological advantage that put him one step ahead of the men he had to confront. At first glance, some who met him were almost disappointed. Given his reputation, they expected him to be bigger—six feet tall, he supposed, and breathing fire. At second glance, however, their disappointment vanished. While his drawl was soft, his eyes were hard and deadly, and his body compact and coiled like a spring. The deep lines that ran on either side of his mouth like scars confirmed the many stories about him, as did the gun resting low on his hip.

Kincaid's florid face turned redder at Reno's words.

"If you don't want the job, what're you doin' here?" he demanded. "I thought we had this all settled."

"I just want to see what the deal is—the whole deal—before I give you my hand on it," Reno replied easily. "Can't blame a man for wantin' to know what he's gettin' into now, can you?"

Kincaid's bluster subsided.

"Well, reckon you'll get your earful tonight, far as what this is all about. And action, too, later, if that's what you want. By the time we're finished, this could make the Lincoln County war look like a picnic."

A gray-haired man in a business suit and bowler hat raised his voice in protest.

"You said violence is a last resort, Kincaid. I thought we could work out most of this through the courts."

Another man nodded agreement. "A little pressure on St. John—we all go along with that. But a war—look what happened with that land-grant business in Colfax County. We don't want that here."

"Gentlemen! Gentlemen!" Kincaid raised his arms and patted the air soothingly with his hands. "Of course we'll do this as efficiently as possible. And if all goes well in Santa Fe next month, we'll have the power of the courts on our side. But you all know that this is a rough territory. Ross St. John's not going to bow down in front of a court order, lick our boots, and hand over his ranch. We've got to have a lot of weapons on our side if we're going to pull this off. And Hayden here is one of those weapons, just like Judge Denton in Santa Fe. We'll apply pressure, wherever it's needed, in whatever form it's needed." Kincaid's expression suddenly turned to a sneer. "Unless that's too rough for you gentlemen." He put a scornful emphasis on the last word. "You're free, any of you, to back out now, if you haven't the guts for what lies ahead. We don't want any lily-livered snivelers in on this. Anyone who doesn't think the rewards are worth our efforts can get out now." He paused and looked around the table. "Well, how about it?" There was shuffling of feet and several men averted their eyes, but no one spoke.

Kincaid turned back to Reno, who was still standing near the table.

"Here, Hayden, have a seat." He spun an empty chair out from the table and toward the other man. "Frank, go get a glass for our new partner here, and we'll have a little toast to our success."

Reno didn't move.

"Before I sit," he drawled, "I like to know who I'm sittin' with."

Kincaid's eyes glittered. Then suddenly he chuckled.

"You're a cool one, aren't you, Hayden. Well, we got no secrets here. Let me introduce you so's you can rest your feet."

He started at the left-hand side of the circle.

"This here's Reston Montague—he's a lawyer down in Las Vegas. And this's Charley Martin, his partner. Frank there is one of my boys. Joseph Reinhold there—the one who don't want no violence—he's a businessman from back east. Specializes in mining investments and equipment. Will Ryan, you already met—he's my right-hand man. . . ."

Each man nodded briefly as Reno was introduced. The glances of the businessmen and lawyers were cold. Reno knew they didn't like dealing with him but that they would be happy to have him do their dirty work if the time came. Kincaid's own men looked at him with guarded respect. They knew his reputation with a gun, and they were pleased to have him on their side, even if they didn't quite trust him.

Quite a crew, Reno mused. The introductions completed, he straddled the proffered chair and draped his arms across the back. He stayed a foot or so away from the table, just outside the circle, playing the observer, remaining aloof from the others and their plots. He accepted Kincaid's offer of whiskey but only sipped at his glass. It was a long-standing rule of his to never get drunk.

The disreputable deals that supposedly respectable folk conspire in, he reflected. He'd seen a lot of these in his time, but New Mexico topped them all. Land, water, gold, minerals— they were all the objects of underhanded deals. And if he'd understood Kincaid right when they'd talked in Bernalillo, this St. John business involved almost all of these. He settled in to listen.

"Gentlemen!" Kincaid, his glass raised high, was proposing a toast. "To our success! By the time the summer's over, the name of St. John will be no more than sand in the desert, and the riches of the Running J will be ours."

Glasses clinked and liquor splashed down thirsty throats. As the men around the table drew closer together in the circle of light to lay their plans, Reno could hear the night wind in the pines and, somewhere, deep in the rugged hills, a mountain lion's muffled scream.

Chapter 3

Jessica had forgotten to close her curtains, and when she awoke the next morning, shafts of dusk-speckled light were slanting through her bedroom window. She sat up in bed, stretched, and groaned. It had been a long time since she had been on a horse, and today she was paying for it. Every part of her body was stiff and aching. She stretched again, trying to relieve the soreness. One portion of her anatomy in particular bore the marks of the journey up the mountain.

"*Buenos días*, señorita. Did you sleep well?" Serafina breezed into the room, bearing a tray laden with several covered dishes and a pewter coffee pot.

"Very well." Jessica realized that despite last night's extravagant repast, she was ravenously hungry. The fresh mountain air must be giving her an appetite. She'd have to make certain to exercise in order not to get fat.

"Jeffrey is still not awake," Serafina told her, "so I thought I'd bring your breakfast in here. With the sun coming through the window, I knew you would be awake soon." She set the tray on the small table by the window and began to uncover the dishes. "I didn't know exactly what you'd like, so

I brought some hot chocolate and a little bit of everything—
eggs, beans, bacon, biscuits, some stewed apples, blackberry
jam.''

Jessica's mouth watered at the recital. She clambered out
of bed and tied Serafina's wrapper around her borrowed night
dress.

"It all smells delicious," she said, sitting down at the
table. The aroma of hot chocolate tickled her nostrils as she
poured the dark brew into a china mug. Then, uncertain
where to begin, she broke open a steaming biscuit and spread
it with fragrant jam.

Serafina began to make up the bed.

"Jeffrey really has become a lazybones," she laughed as
she worked. "He's forgotten that everyone rises early on a
ranch."

"I haven't done much better myself," Jessica confessed.
"After all, I grew up on a ranch, too. I should know the
routine."

"Well, you both have had a long, hard journey, and a long
ride yesterday," Serafina soothed her. "A good night's sleep
is probably just what you need." Then, suddenly curious, she
paused a moment in her work. "You said you grew up on a
ranch? But Jeffrey said he met you in New York. We all
assumed that was where you were from, even though you
obviously ride horseback very well."

"My father had a ranch in Texas," Jessica explained. "I
was born there and we lived there until I was twelve. Then
my father died and my mother and I moved back east. My
mother was happier there. She never liked the ranch and all
the work that went with it, but I missed it after we moved
away."

"Then you must be very happy to be here," Serafina
remarked. "This is the finest ranch, I think, in all of New
Mexico. Not the biggest, but certainly the richest, even if Mr.
St. John is not one to show off his wealth. We have good
water, good pasture, timber, lots of game. And it is so
beautiful here, even in the winter, when everything is buried
in snow."

Jessica noted the proprietary "we" and wondered at the way Serafina identified with the ranch. But, after all, why shouldn't she? She had grown up here and seemed to be considered almost one of the family. It was remarkable, Jessica thought, that Serafina did not regard her as an interloper.

"I have brushed off your riding clothes," Serafina told her, opening the polished walnut doors of the wardrobe. "So they are all ready should you wish to ride around the ranch today."

Jessica felt a little guilty. Her mother had a cook and a housekeeper but she had always cared for her own clothes. She wasn't used to being waited on like this.

"It's very kind of you to go to so much trouble for me."

Serafina shrugged.

"No trouble. I have little to do right now, anyway, with most of the hands on roundup. It's different when the men are here—much more cooking, more laundry, a million tasks I have to supervise. Though, of course, then we have servants to help—my mother's cousin Maria and several girls from the village. But while they are away, I do everything that needs to be done myself."

To her own amazement, Jessica had managed, while they were talking, to down three biscuits, two eggs, and a sizable portion of bacon and beans. She poured herself another cup of chocolate.

"Wouldn't you like a cup?" she asked Serafina, indicating the half-filled pot.

"Oh, no. I ate several hours ago, after I fed the chickens and cleaned up the kitchen."

Again Jessica felt ashamed of her own laziness. She would have to make herself useful around the ranch, she vowed. Her thoughts were interrupted by a clattering of hooves in the yard, accompanied by hoarse shouting and the cracking of a whip. The commotion drew both women to the window.

The ranch yard was filled with milling horses and clouds of dust. It took Jessica a moment before she was able to distinguish several horses with riders in the melee of moving bodies. Then, gradually, to the accompaniment of much shouting and slapping of flanks, the horses began to squeeze themselves into the corral, whinnying and stomping as they went.

"It's Riordon," Serafina said, a slight frown creasing her forehead. "I wonder why he's back."

"Riordon?"

"St. John's foreman. He's only been with us a year but he's very good with horses and cattle—and men." She wrinkled her nose. "Thinks he's good with women, too, but I don't like him."

Jessica was surprised by the distaste in Serafina's voice. She strained her eyes to try to distinguish the foreman in the swirl of horses and dust, but the figures of the three men on horseback were indistinct.

There was a knock at the door of the bedroom, and when Serafina went to open it, Jeffrey was standing there, wearing corduroy pants and an open-necked flannel shirt. He had obviously just shaved and he looked fresh and eager. He strode into the room and over to where Jessica was still standing by the window.

"Good morning, darling," he greeted her, stooping to kiss her on the cheek.

Jessica was pleased by both the kiss and the term of endearment. He really is mine, she thought. Any lingering suspicions she might have had regarding Jeffrey's relationship with Serafina quickly vanished.

"What are you watching so intently?" He peered over her shoulder and out of the window.

"Looks like Riordon, the foreman, is back with a couple of men and a string of horses," Serafina replied from the doorway.

"Is the roundup over?" Jessica asked. Maybe now she would have her long-awaited meeting with Jeffrey's father.

"I doubt it. They haven't been out more than a couple of days. Probably just sent some men back for fresh horses." Jeffrey glanced down at her half-empty breakfast tray. "Looks like you've already eaten. Why don't you get dressed while I grab a bite in the kitchen? Then we can go out and meet this new foreman of father's and see if he can pick out a horse for you. No point in your having to use that nag from the livery stable any more.'' He turned to Serafina. ''Do you know if Scotty's still around? I might saddle him up for myself.''

''I think so. He's probably out in the pasture somewhere. I don't think they take him to the roundup anymore. He's getting a bit old. But he'd probably enjoy a run.''

''Scotty was my horse before I left for college,'' Jeffrey explained to Jessica. ''He's a lovely little chestnut gelding— not very big, but gentle and good on his feet. I used to ride him all over the ranch.''

''I'd love to have a horse of my own again,'' said Jessica, thinking of Sunny. ''It doesn't have to be anything special. It would just be nice to be able to ride whenever I wanted to.''

''Well, then, let's find you something. One thing there's no shortage of on the Running J is horses. I'll meet you out by the corral in ten minutes.''

He turned to leave, and Serafina followed, carrying the breakfast tray.

In a flurry of excitement, Jessica took off her nightclothes and donned her riding habit. She pinned up her hair, and then, grabbing her hat and her leather gloves, made her way to the corral.

As she came up, Jeffrey was already standing by the peeled log fence, talking to a heavy-set man. Both men turned as she approached, and Jeffrey introduced her as she reached his side.

''Jessica, this is our foreman, Hugh Riordon. Riordon, this is my fiancée, Jessica Howard.''

''Pleased to meet you, Mr. Riordon.''

''Howdy.'' The foreman's greeting was laconic. He surveyed Jessica with a glance she could only describe as insolent, sweeping his eyes over her body with a slow deliberateness that made her blush. He was not a tall man, but he was solidly built, with a strong, wide-shouldered body. He was hatless, and Jessica noted that his dark brown hair was receding, a loss he made up for with a large moustache, which curved downward around the corners of a firm, cruel mouth. His sharp eyes were fixed on Jessica, not with the dislike she had encountered in the gaze of Donaciana and Old Tom, but rather with a kind of arrogant contempt. Jessica could understand why Serafina's lip had curled in dislike when she had mentioned the foreman. She herself felt somehow unclean under his gaze and repulsed by the heavy solidity of his body.

"How's the roundup going?"

The foreman shrugged in response to Jeffrey's question.

"Well as can be expected. Some losses this winter down near the canyon, but otherwise things 'pear to be runnin' pretty good. Loads of strong new heifers over in the upper meadows and no more losses to rustlers than usual."

"You have much cattle rustling around here?" It was Jessica's question.

Riordon turned his gaze on her contemptuously, and she realized she must sound like the typical Eastern tenderfoot.

"Ma'am, the day we don't have rustlin' is the day we don't have cattle."

"It looks like our days of Indian troubles are over, though," Jeffrey interjected.

"Not if Geronimo decides to kick up his heels. There's rumors about that. But I doubt it'll affect us. He's likely to strike south, down near the border." As if suddenly bored with the conversation, Riordon turned on his heel to go. "Now if you folks'll just excuse me, the boys and me need to round up some fresh horses and put these to pasture."

"Before you go, Riordon, I'd be much obliged if you'd pick out a good riding horse for Miss Howard. We rented a couple of hacks for the trip up, but they won't do for getting around the ranch."

The foreman turned slowly.

"Don't know as how I can do that without orders from the boss. These here are work horses, cow ponies. We need them for the roundup and don't have none to spare for pleasure ridin'."

His tone was insolent and Jeffrey grew dark. Jessica felt anger rise in her at the way the foreman was deliberately flouting Jeffrey's authority.

"Oh, come now, Riordon." Jeffrey's voice was husky with annoyance. "Surely there's one horse to spare. You must have something that's neither working nor worn out."

The foreman paused.

"Well," he drawled, "come to think of it, maybe there is something I could let you have. He's not the prettiest horse in the world, but he's sturdy and he ain't been worked too hard. Hardly worked at all, in fact. Guess I could spare him for you."

"I would appreciate that, Mr. Riordon," Jessica responded primly. "And I can assure you that looks mean less to me than other qualities."

"Well, we'll see about that," Riordon grinned at her. "Gonzales!" He called to one of the cowboys who was working inside the barn. "Go into the corral," he ordered the man when he appeared, "and rope me that tan mustang, the one in the far corner. Throw a saddle on him and bring him here." As the cowboy hurried off to do his bidding, he turned back to Jessica. "You done much riding?" he asked.

"Some." She wasn't about to explain to him her childhood days in Texas. This foreman of St. John's had definitely rubbed her the wrong way. Let him think she was a complete greenhorn if he wanted. She felt no need to try to win his acceptance. After all, he didn't even accept Jeffrey, the boss's son.

"Well, here he is. He'll give you a good bit of riding, this one will."

Both Jessica and Jeffrey stared at the horse that Gonzales was leading up to them, a wiry brown mustang whose shaggy coat looked as if it had never known a grooming brush. There was something tight and mean about its mouth and it jerked its head back against the reins. Its coal black eyes were those of an untamed creature of the desert, not a docile cow pony, and its feet danced a nervous tattoo against the hard dirt of the yard.

Jeffrey frowned.

"He looks a bit mean to me, Riordon. I don't think he's really what we want for Jessica. Don't you have something else?"

"This is all I can spare. But if the lady doesn't want him . . ." His eyes challenged Jessica.

If I say no to this horse, then Riordon will have thumbed his nose at me, and at Jeffrey too, Jessica realized.

"He looks fine," she said coolly. "Why don't you let me try him out?"

"Jessica!" Jeffrey's voice was sharp with fear.

"It's all right, Jeffrey. I can handle him." At least, I hope I can, she added to herself.

"Suit yourself." The foreman was grinning openly now. "He's all yours. Gonzales, help the lady up."

"I can mount by myself, thank you," she responded crisply. He's just waiting to see me get thrown on my posterior, she thought—or break my neck. She felt a small twinge of fear but forced herself to swing easily up into the saddle.

As she took the reins, the little horse snorted and tossed its head. Then it stood completely still for a moment. Jessica could feel the bony body trembling beneath her, as if with suppressed fear or rage. Gently, she urged it forward with her knees. It took a tentative step, as if trying to get used to the weight on its back. Then it exploded.

Jessica's ride almost ended right there, as the mustang landed on all four legs with a jolt that lifted her from the saddle. For a dizzying moment she thought she was going to be hurled across the yard. Then she fell back abruptly into her seat, the impact sending a bolt of pain running through her spine to the very top of her head. But before she could catch her breath, the horse had launched itself into the air again, bucking and sunfishing, so that her body snapped back and forth like a rag doll. As the horse careened around the yard she clung desperately to the pommel of the saddle. Fences, trees, and buildings were all a blur before her terrified eyes. She no longer cared about her horsemanship, and she made no attempt to try to control the animal writhing and jerking beneath her. Her only concern was to stay on, to keep from being thrown headfirst onto the hard-packed earth. It wasn't even a horse that she was riding now, but rather some nightmare creature, a beast determined only to kill her or to die in the attempt.

There were frantic shouts behind her, and she was dimly aware of a figure running nearby, trying to reach for the reins, driven away by the flying hooves. But she knew that no one else could stop the mustang. It would stop only when she herself brought it under control.

After what seemed like a jolting, pain-racked eternity, the mustang suddenly stopped and gave a violent shudder. It tossed back its head, as if to ascertain whether or not it still had its unwelcome rider. Jessica drew a painful breath. Her ribs felt as if someone had driven a million splinters of glass into her sides, and her knees and thighs ached with the effort of holding on. Gingerly, she felt to see if she had any broken bones.

But the horse was not finished with her yet. Whirling with a suddenness that caught her off guard, the horse took off down the yard, his wiry legs gathering speed as he thundered across the hard ground. Jessica struggled to remain upright in the saddle. Looking ahead, she realized in horror the nature of her mount's diabolical plan. Straight in front of them lay the barbed wire fence of the pasture, and the mustang was flying toward it, his head and neck stretched taut. Jessica knew that the wily beast had no intention of jumping barbed wire. More likely his aim was to throw her into it, either by halting abruptly so she would go somersaulting over his head, or by sideswiping it so she would become entangled in the barbs.

The house and outbuildings were speeding by in a distorted blur. Jessica's hat had long since flown from her head and her loosened hair was whipping across her face, blinding her and bringing tears to her eyes. With one hand, she tried to sweep the strands away from her face; with the other, she struggled with the reins. If only she could make the horse swerve in time, bring it around, then maybe she could force it to a halt, or even make it stumble and fall so she could leap free—anything to keep from being tossed into the fence.

The barbed wire drew nearer with menacing swiftness. Now. She had to bring him around now or it would be too late. You can do it, she told herself, exerting her will against the mustang's, increasing the pressure of her knees and thighs, pulling on the reins to bring the animal's head around, to make it turn, make it stop before they reached the fence. The weathered fence poles, the rusted strands of wire, and the blurred green of the pasture beyond loomed in front of her. Now, she thought. Now, you must turn. She heard her own voice, hoarse with fear and anger and determination, yelling at the wild beast beneath her. She had said she could do it and she would. She would show the mustang, the foreman, Jeffrey, everyone!

With her final, wrenching effort, the horse swerved, almost throwing them both to the ground, and stumbling from its abrupt change of course. Regaining its balance, it gathered its legs to resume its gallop, but Jessica continued to exert her newfound control. Gently but firmly, she brought the mustang to a halt. It stood there, its sides heaving beneath her, its breathing hoarse and heavy. She laid a hand tentatively on its neck and felt it shudder. It turned its head to look at her, as if trying to judge whether or not it should continue the fight. Then it turned away and shook its head.

"That's a good pony." Jessica spoke softly, trying to calm both the mustang and her own wildly racing heart. Her hand shook as she stroked the horse's mane, but she felt triumphant. She had stayed on! And she had brought this wild creature under her control. Maybe, just maybe the horse really would be right for her, as she had so confidently boasted to the foreman.

"Nice pony," she whispered. "You're going to do what I say from now on, aren't you? No more running off without me, no more bucking and jumping."

As if it understood her, the mustang tossed its head and snorted. Jessica nudged it gently with her knees, and it started down the yard at a walk.

Jeffrey and the cowboy Gonzales were running toward her, Riordon trailing behind them. They all slowed as they saw her turn in their direction, the mustang docile and under her control.

Jeffrey was raging at the foreman as she drew up, his usually calm face contorted with anger.

"You knew that nag was dangerous, damn you! You knew it and yet you deliberately had it brought out for her. I'll have your hide for this, Riordon!"

Riordon, unmoved by Jeffrey's tirade, merely shrugged, a sardonic smile playing around his lips.

"The lady said she could ride," he responded calmly. "It was her choice to mount. I didn't force her to do it."

"You knew that horse was dangerous, and yet you had it saddled for her. Wait till my father gets back here. I . . . I'll . . . ." His angry outburst sputtered to a stop as Jessica dismounted.

"Jessica, darling. Are you all right? I was terrified for you. That vicious animal could have killed you!" He searched her face anxiously.

Jessica smiled at him reassuringly. The wild pounding of her heart had started to subside, and although she still felt shaken, she managed to keep her voice calm.

"I'm all right, Jeffrey. No harm done." She turned to the foreman, who had come up alongside them. "I think this one will do fine, Mr. Riordon," she said matter-of-factly. "He's a little headstrong, but I believe I can handle him."

There was a kind of reluctant admiration in the foreman's gaze.

"I'm glad he pleases you, ma'am. And I'm certain the boss'll have no objection if I turn him over to your tender care."

"Does he have a name?"

"None that a lady'd care to use." The foreman grinned.

"Well, then, I'll call him Spur."

"He sure needs plenty of it, I'll say that for him."

"Jessica, you aren't going to keep this wild animal, are you?" Jeffrey protested.

Jessica turned to him.

"He'll do fine, Jeffrey, he's small and sturdy, just right for the mountains. He's got a little fight in him, but we'll soon get that out, won't we, Spur?" She stroked the muzzle of the mustang now standing mutely by her side, looking for all the world like the tamest of mounts.

"Well, if you really want him . . ." Jeffrey's tone was doubtful. "But I'm sure there are lots of other horses that are not only better-looking, but who won't try to break your neck when you mount them."

"I like this one," Jessica responded firmly. "Once he gets a little care, he won't look bad at all." The mustang nuzzled her arm and then gazed into her eyes as if to tender his agreement. It was almost as if he was saying, I had to try, didn't I? Now I'll behave. But Jessica saw a little spark still lurking there, and she knew she would have to be careful. Spur was not so easily tamed.

The foreman and hands went off to round up fresh horses, and Jeffrey went with them to locate his horse, Scotty. Jessica busied herself in the stable, giving Spur a rubdown and a badly needed brushing. She talked to the horse as she worked, and he seemed to respond to her words, shaking his head and making little snorting sounds. Recovered now from her terrifying ride, Jessica felt excited to have her own mount again, even one as wild and shaggy as this. It meant freedom, the exploration of distant and secret places. And she had developed an odd affection for the little mustang, a sympathy for its desire to be free, to shake off all constraints and run with the wind.

"We'll get along well, you and I," she whispered. "I'll give you your head and let you run, and you'll take me to strange and wonderful places."

Serafina joined her as she was combing the burrs out of Spur's tail.

"I saw you from the kitchen window," she said, her eyes wide. "I was so scared, my heart was in my mouth, but you were magnificent. Everybody had given up on that little horse, but you tamed him. You ride better than any of the men on the ranch, except for Mr. St. John himself."

"I think I just wore him out," Jessica replied modestly, patting the mustang on the back. "I also think he's taken a liking to me."

"That Riordon!" Serafina's face grew dark. "He could have killed you! How I hate that man."

"He was just having a little fun with me." Jessica's tone was mild, though inside she was still shaking. "I'm sure he didn't think I'd take him up on his challenge."

"Some idea of fun he has!" Serafina snorted. Then she smiled. "Well, I guess you showed him up. I'd better get back to the kitchen and get started on lunch. I'm sure Riordon and his crew will want to eat before they go back out. Enjoy your ride."

Jeffrey came back leading his horse Scotty, a lovely chestnut gelding whose gentle manner could not have been in greater contrast to Spur's wild display.

"We're quite a pair," Jessica commented when, after Jeffrey had saddled Scotty, they were both mounted and trotting down the lane from the ranch house.

Her fiancé looked down doubtfully at the mustang, now jogging along docilely, as if his earlier tricks were only a forgotten memory.

"I really wish you had picked another horse," he complained. "That mustang makes me uneasy. We have no idea how he's going to behave. You could get hurt, or he could run off and leave you without a mount."

"He'll be okay," Jessica reassured him. "He just needed a firm hand."

And indeed Spur behaved in admirable fashion, responsive to her every command, surefooted on narrow trails and up slippery slopes, not even breathing hard after long gallops and treacherous descents. He even seemed to enjoy the outing, holding his head high and sniffing the pine-scented air eagerly.

Jessica had told Jeffrey she wanted to see some of the ranch, so that she could acquire a feeling for her future home. So he took her further into the Sangre de Christo range, through rugged ravines cut by moss-lined streams, up steep mountain sides choked with piñon and manzanita, across meadows lush with new grass and rainbow clusters of flowers. It was a beautiful day, the sky brilliant, the air exhilarating. The only sounds were the sighing of the wind in the pines and the occasional echoing caw of a crow. It seemed to Jessica that they had journeyed to the end of the world, so far were they from the hectic, noisy streets of New York. Surely they had not simply arrived here by train and horse; they must also have been transported into another time.

On several occasions, they surprised grazing cattle, sheltered in ravines or along grassy streambeds, some of them cows with calves. Startled, the animals would lumber off, crashing through the undergrowth. Jessica could see the whimsical St. John brand, a J with little running feet, emblazoned on their flanks.

"We really have no idea how many head of cattle we have," Jeffrey remarked to her after one such encounter. "Even after the roundup there are always stragglers like these, which we never manage to find. Of course, this rough terrain makes it easy for rustlers, and there's simply no way for us to know how many head we lose that way."

Jessica could feel Spur straining beneath her whenever they sighted cattle, and she had to curb him from giving chase.

"I think he's a real cow pony," she laughed. "I'll bet he'd be a good worker. I wonder what made him so wild."

She would have liked to see the roundup. When she was a child, she had loved the excitement and activity, the noise and dust and the bawling of the calves, the scorched smell of the branding iron on cowhide. She suggested to Jeffrey that they find the roundup, but he was unenthusiastic.

"We'd just be in the way," he said. "Besides, they're a long way off at the moment. It would be a rough ride."

Jessica didn't press him. She sensed that Jeffrey was still

smarting from Riordon's snubs and didn't wish to risk another situation in which he might be treated as a useless outsider.

At one point along a rutted path that wound through a narrow valley between the hills, they came face to face with a herd of goats tended by a small grinning Mexican boy and two mangy collies. The goats, with shaggy coats of black and grey and tan, and intelligent, beady eyes, began to mill and bleat as they found their path blocked by the horses. Several attempted to bolt up the hillside, their bells clanging, but they were quickly rounded up by the dogs, who kept the herd together with constant circling and nipping.

Jeffrey edged his own horse and Jessica's to the side of the path to let the young shepherd pass. The boy waved his staff at them in greeting, calling a few words to Jeffrey in Spanish as he and his motley herd clattered by.

Jessica stared after them in surprise.

"There are several families of goat and sheep herders on our land," Jeffrey explained. "Usually it's just little kids like that who look after them all day, and nights, too, out in the mountains."

"And your father allows that?" Jessica knew that sheep and goats were anathema to most cattle ranchers because of the damage their hooves and close grazing did to the land and grass.

Jeffrey nodded. "Most of these families have been on the land for several generations. They're squatters, really, with no legal rights, but the land seemed so vast and unused, they just moved in. Some herd sheep and goats; others have little farms. When the land grants changed hands, the new owners kicked these people out, but my father let them stay on."

"Don't they cause problems for the ranch?"

Jeffrey shrugged. "Not really. They're quiet folk, mostly, and they leave the cattle alone. Any poaching of a cow here or there and they would be thrown out, pronto. And my father can always count on their support. It's one of the things that makes him such a powerful man around here. Besides"—there was a touch of bitterness in Jeffrey's voice—"my father enjoys playing the *patrón*."

He urged his horse ahead down the trail, and Jessica, following behind him, had no chance to respond to his words or to probe the meaning behind them. She still had a lot to learn, she realized, not only about life on the ranch, but also about her fiancé.

They stopped to eat beside a broad, clear stream which flowed along the floor of a wide, sheer-sided canyon. The descent into the canyon was steep, even treacherous in spots, but once they had arrived at the bottom, they were able to rest in the shade of the cottonwoods.

Serafina had assembled a picnic lunch for them and they dined sumptuously on fresh bread, crumbly goat cheese, cold sliced beef, fresh radishes and cucumbers, and pungent dried apricots. There was even a wineskin filled with some of the strong, dry red wine they had enjoyed the night before.

Plump, striped ground squirrels scampered boldly around their resting place while they ate, and Jessica tossed them some crumbs as Jeffrey got out his sketch pad and tried to capture their likeness with his pencil. Then, after they had finished their meal, Jessica removed her boots and thrust her feet into the clear, cold water of the stream. She wiggled her toes against the sandy bottom and watched the green eddies swirl around her feet. Jeffrey lay on his stomach beside her and pointed out a fat, speckled trout lurking in the shadow of a rock on the other side of the stream. Jessica drew up her knees and leaned back against a tangle of cottonwood roots stretching protectively down the bank.

"I could stay here forever," she sighed.

"You'd change your mind after a heavy rain, when the stream started rising." Jeffrey indicated the bleached, dead trunk of a tree, which had toppled partway into the water. "Looks like it was a victim of a flood."

But Jessica didn't care. At the moment, storms, flash floods, and fallen trees seemed remote and unreal. She rested her head on a root and closed her eyes. Surely, she thought, as she listened to the murmur of the stream, nothing could be more perfect than this.

And certainly nothing could be more perfect than being here with Jeffrey. After all, wasn't he the person she had always dreamed about—the handsome young man who was going to take her away from the city life she hated, a man like her father who was a born westerner and loved the land that nurtured him. It may have been Jeffrey's manners and sophistication which had won over her mother, but for Jessica, Jeffrey's appeal lay in his connection with the land. She remembered how hesitant Jeffrey had been, at first, to speak to her about the ranch, how pleasantly surprised he had been at her obvious interest, and then how happy he was that she was willing to travel to such a remote place to share a life with him. Little did he realize how she had pined to return to the Texas of her childhood, the only time and place she had ever felt truly happy. And little did he know how much she disliked the pale, dull city men who courted her, and how appalling the thought of a future as the wife of an accountant or a shopkeeper had been. Jeffrey, by contrast, shone with the promise of a new and exciting life. No wonder she had so eagerly welcomed his proposal.

Opening her eyes, Jessica saw her fiancé smiling down at her. She reached out to take his hand and he raised it to his lips and tenderly kissed her palm. "Are you happy, darling?" he asked her.

"Completely," she replied, and with a contented sigh, she leaned back and closed her eyes again.

It was with reluctance that, half an hour later, she let Jeffrey urge her from her perch. Beyond the peaceful walls of this little canyon, she imagined other, less tranquil, things awaited her. The thought passed like a shadow through her mind, making her shiver despite the bright afternoon sun.

Spur also seemed reluctant to leave, and Jessica had to guide him firmly, from his shady patch of grass, into the open, where she mounted. Jeffrey watched her as she adjusted the reins and pointed the mustang's head toward the trail leading out of the canyon.

"Father will be pleased that you ride so well," he remarked as he brought his horse up alongside hers.

Annoyance rose inside her. Ross St. John again! Everything around here seemed to center around that man. Jessica was getting a little tired of the way he dominated the lives of everyone on the ranch, even in his absence.

"Is it so important that I please him?" she asked, trying to hide her irritation.

Jeffrey gave a thin, rueful smile.

"Things will go more easily for us if you do. A lot depends upon his approving our marriage."

Including our getting married at all? Jessica wondered to herself. She was immediately ashamed of her thought. Obviously, Ross St. John was a difficult man, but she knew that Jeffrey loved her and would never let anything, including his father, stand in the way of their marriage.

"What sorts of things?" she said out loud.

"Well . . ." Jeffrey appeared reluctant to put his own thoughts into words. "If he approves of you, if he sees you as a suitable partner for me, then he is more likely to be agreeable to the rest of our plans—our trip to Europe, my plans to write and draw."

He paused for a moment and reined Scotty to a halt so that he could turn and face his fiancée.

"You remember what I said to you earlier about my father's wanting to play the *patrón*?" He hesitated, searching for the right words. "Well, that's exactly how he sees this ranch. It's like a fiefdom and he's the grand lord, with his retainers, his peasants, his allies. He inherited this place from his father, who brought it from the original Spanish land-grant family, the Valdezes. He sees himself in that grand tradition of passing the holding from father to son, so that the family of St. John continues to rule the land and the people on it. And I," he added bitterly, "am, of course, the next son."

"But don't you want the ranch?" Staggered by the wealth and magnificence of what she had seen of the Running J, Jessica couldn't imagine not wanting to be the ruler of this empire.

Jeffrey gazed at her a moment.

"I don't *not* want it, Jessica." There was almost a tone of reproach in his voice. "How could I not want it? I grew up here. I love these mountains, the house, all the things we've seen today. But I want other things, too. I want to travel, to write, to be a success as an artist. My work is good, but I need a chance to get on my feet before I can make it on my own." His glance lifted to the pine-rimmed canyon walls surrounding them. "I'm just not cut out to be a rancher, Jessica," he continued. "I've just never taken to it. I'd rather roam these mountains with a sketch pad than hunt heifers with a lasso. I'd like to live on the ranch for part of the year, I think. Spend summers here, maybe, then winters in New York or abroad. If the ranch were mine, I'd sell a lot of it, keep the house and a small amount of land to farm and run a few head of cattle. But I'd leave a foreman in charge so it wouldn't be too great a burden to maintain."

Jessica's heart sank at his words. In the last two days she had come to envision herself as the mistress of the Running J, helping Jeffrey to manage the vast holdings, being *patrona* of its many and varied inhabitants.

I'll manage the ranch for you, she wanted to cry. I know a lot about ranching already, and what I don't know, I can learn. I'll stay here in the winters while you go to Europe. I'll handle the cattle while you sketch and draw. I'll take care of the Running J the way your father wants.

But, of course, she said nothing. Jeffrey had urged his horse forward again, up the steep trail, and Jessica followed. There was time enough to change Jeffrey's mind, she told herself, time enough to discuss her plans with him. First things first: the most immediate obstacle was her meeting with Ross St. John. Like it or not, it was going to be necessary to convince him of her worthiness as a daughter-in-law before anything else could be accomplished.

When they reached the rim of the canyon where the trail widened and they could ride side by side, Jeffrey resumed their conversation.

"What my father refuses to recognize is that times have changed. The coming of the railroads has brought a lot of people to New Mexico. Things just aren't the same, anymore, but my father continues to live in the days of the *patrón* and the *hacienda*." Jeffrey made a sweeping gesture with his hand to indicate the forests and mountains around them. "He refuses to develop any of this, to let anyone use it for anything except cattle, sheep, and farming. He won't cut any timber except what we need for our own use or what's necessary to clear land for a field. And he hates mining. He claims it spoils the land and dirties the streams. He won't let anyone on his land survey for minerals, even though coal and copper and even silver have been found on neighboring spreads."

For the first time, Jessica began to feel sympathy for Ross St. John.

"Well, I can't blame him," she commented. "If I owned this land, I wouldn't want it torn up, either."

Jeffrey frowned. "I don't particularly like mining, myself," he told her, "nor do I like the kind of people it brings in—speculators, con men, people looking to get rich quickly, not to mention the riffraff who live off them. But the fact is when there's such a push for these things, it's hard to keep people out. Besides, I'm not sure we can afford to sit on this land forever without exploiting the minerals. The big cattle ranches have had their day. We're not going to be able to hold off change forever and still survive."

Jessica felt disturbed by Jeffrey's words and the tone of voice in which he spoke them. She had seen Jeffrey in a serious mood, before, but it had always been a sort of romantic, dreamy seriousness. Now, as he spoke of the ranch and its future, she saw a side of Jeffrey that was new to her.

It was a long ride back to the ranch house, but even though her body was weary from two days of riding, Jessica readily agreed when Jeffrey suggested a detour. Although she couldn't begin to see in a day everything the ranch had to offer, she was eager to absorb as much as possible.

Jeffrey took her to a high ridge, reached by a series of switchbacks up a pine slope. When they approached the top, Jessica understood why Jeffrey had wanted to bring her here.

The ridge fell away steeply beneath them toward the west. Beyond stretched the descending foothills of the Sangre de Christo range, marching in purple grandeur down to the floor of the high desert, itself a series of steplike plateaus unrolling into the distance. Here and there the gray expanse of desert was broken by what Jessica knew to be buttes, red-rock protuberances carved into fantastic shapes by wind and time, which from her perch appeared only as dots against the haze of the horizon. As she gazed, the mountains upon which she stood seemed to dwindle in importance, mere rocky accidents jutting out from the fundamental and overpowering presence of the desert. She felt drawn in some strange way toward that distant place where the pale blue of the sky and the purple-gray haze of the desert merged. She stood, transfixed, feeling for the first time the overwhelming power of some unnameable force.

Jeffrey stood close to her, and as she gazed across the distance, a strong awareness of him flowed through her body. She reached out to touch his arm. He looked down at her, his own thoughts distant.

"I used to come here often," he said softly, "especially after my mother died. I would lie up here for hours, gazing at the view. This is where I did some of my first sketches, too, after my mother started teaching me how to draw."

"Thank you for bringing me here," she whispered. She leaned her head against his chest and felt his arm steal around her. For a moment they stood locked together and she could hear the pounding of his heart.

"Jeffrey . . ."

He bent to kiss her on the lips, and Jessica pressed her body eagerly against him. His arms tightened around her as she surrendered to his embrace. Desire coursed through her body like rushing blood. Jeffrey's lips were warm and hard against hers. She could stay here forever, locked in Jeffrey's strong embrace, safe with him, wanting him. . . .

A twig snapped suddenly behind them. Startled, they broke apart. Jeffrey glanced around nervously. But it was only one of their horses, grazing at the edge of the woods. Jessica waited for Jeffrey to take her in his arms again, but he held her at arm's length, staring down. She tried to read the expression in the blue depth of his eyes.

"We'd better get going," he said brusquely, and turned away. "We still have a long way to go, and it will be dark soon." Feeling disappointed and oddly shaken, Jessica trailed slowly behind him as he strode toward the waiting horses.

Chapter 4

Jessica was awakened the next morning by a light but persistent knocking on her door. As she struggled to rouse herself from sleep, Serafina pushed the door open with her foot and breezed in, carrying, as she had the previous morning, a tray from which wafted the tantalizing fragrance of hot chocolate. Jessica glanced at the enameled brass clock beside her bed, a parting gift from her mother, and noted that it was not yet six o'clock. Outside the window, only the faintest gray light illuminated the yard.

"Excuse me for waking you so early," Serafina said, setting the tray down. "But I am making a trip today to visit my grandfather, and I thought you might like to come with me. For that, we need an early start."

"Your grandfather?" Jessica sat up in bed, stretched, and groaned. She felt even worse today than she had yesterday, for in addition to the stiffness resulting from two full days of riding were bruises from all the jolts in her taming of Spur. Her body was one vast ache. She was certain that if she stood up, she would be unable to move. In fact, she wasn't even sure she could stand up.

Serafina watched her sympathetically.

"I should have thought, last night, to give you some of my mother's ointment. It's marvelous when you're sore. And I could massage you like I do my mother when she gets stiff from standing in the kitchen all day." She sat down on the bed next to Jessica and began to knead her shoulders with expert hands.

"That's not where I'm most sore," Jessica told her.

Serafina laughed but continued her ministrations, and gradually Jessica began to feel better. The relaxation in her shoulder muscles seemed to flow into the rest of her body, and the stiffness began to melt away.

"My grandfather lives near the village," Serafina explained to her as she worked. "He has a large garden and he spends all his time working on it. Because he is further down the mountain, where it's warmer, he has fruits and vegetables earlier than we do here, and my mother wants me to fetch some things from his garden for dinner tonight. We want to go early, before the sun is too high, so the vegetables don't wilt. So that we don't, either," she added.

"Do we ride?" Jessica asked. She wasn't certain she wanted to get back up on a horse for a while.

"We could ride, but it is longer that way. There is a footpath we can take which is a shortcut, but it is too steep and narrow for a horse." Serafina moved her fingers up to work on Jessica's neck for a moment, pulling aside the tangled, luxurious mass of dark hair, and then, finishing her massage, she jumped up. "I think the walk will be good for you after all that riding, and the trail is really very pretty. Wear a sturdy skirt and shoes, and bring a hat."

When she had left, Jessica realized that Serafina had not even waited for Jessica's assent to the proposed expedition but had simply taken it for granted. Well, that was all right. Spending some time in Serafina's lively company would give Jessica an opportunity to see more of the ranch.

When she had finished her breakfast, she put on a heavy loden-green serge skirt, cut short for walking, and she donned thick stockings and a pair of sturdy leather shoes. A long-sleeved, linen blouse went over her chemise. Although the morning air was on the chilly side, Jessica decided against a jacket. She would warm up quickly once they began walking, and the afternoon sun would later make the extra clothing uncomfortable. She had just picked up her sombrero, the one she had purchased in Bernalillo, and placed it on her head, when Serafina reappeared.

The Mexican woman nodded her approval.

"That is good," she said. "I am glad you have brought clothes for a ranch, and not just pretty dresses."

"I feel somewhat silly with this hat." Jessica was peering at her reflection in the mirror.

"You'll be glad you have it when the sun is high." Serafina herself was wearing a black wool skirt and cotton blouse. Her feet were clad in fringed moccasins, and the inevitable re-bozo, this one striped in red and blue, was wrapped around her shoulders and looped over her head. In her hand she carried a straw hat.

"I must go through the kitchen to get a basket for the vegetables," Serafina said as they headed down the hallway. Jessica noted that Jeffrey's door was still closed. She had the feeling he had been up late, for the light had been burning under his door when she herself had gone to bed. He had probably been writing in the journal in which he religiously kept an account of his thoughts and experiences. What would he say about yesterday? Jessica wondered.

The tiled kitchen was dim and still cool. Copper utensils gleamed on the walls and the shelves held rows of earthen-ware vessels. A pot of bubbling coffee stood on the huge cast-iron stove. Donaciana was kneading bread on a large pine table. She nodded to her daughter as Serafina selected a basket from the assortment stacked near the fireplace, but she pointedly ignored Jessica. However, Jessica seemed to feel the older woman's hostile gaze burning into her back as she headed out the door.

"Your mother doesn't seem to like me much," she re-marked to Serafina as they clambered down the creek bank behind the house to the trail. She tried to keep her tone light, not wanting to reveal how disturbed she was by Donaciana's hostility toward her.

Serafina shrugged in a gesture that Jessica had already learned was characteristic.

"You mustn't mind her," she replied. "She is just an old woman grown sour with age. Besides," she added, "for her, you are an interference in her plans."

"Her plans?"

"Yes, she had big plans for me. You see, I was to be the bride of Jeffrey St. John when we both grew up. She had planned this, I think, from the time we were children together."

Jessica was suddenly overcome with embarrassment.

"I . . . I'm sorry," she stammered in confusion. "I didn't realize . . . I had no idea . . ." All her earlier suspicions came flooding back. Serafina and Jeffrey, promised to each other as children . . .

Serafina ignored her confusion and, giving a tug on her arm, urged her to continue on the trail.

"Don't worry," she said cheerfully. "It's my mother's plan we are talking about, not mine—or Jeffrey's. I have no desire to be the wife of Jeffrey St. John. We grew up together, we played together as children, we took lessons together from his mother Doña Reina. Jeffrey is like a brother to me. He is a very nice person, very kind, very sensitive. We have much affection for each other, and I am glad to have him for a brother. But love—as man and wife—no, that we do not feel." She paused. "Besides—and I do not mean this against Jeffrey; I just tell you very frankly my feelings—he is not my type, not *simpático*. I prefer someone more . . . more *macho*."

"Pardon?" Jessica did not understand the word Serafina had just used.

"Someone—how should I say it?—someone who is *muy hombre*, more manly, more forceful, someone stronger, someone—don't laugh at me if I tell you this; again I speak frankly because we are going to be like sisters—someone who can take me in his arms and sweep me away."

Serafina had been walking ahead of Jessica, speaking over her shoulder. Now she turned and laid a hand on Jessica's arm.

"Please understand," she said kindly. "Jeffrey will make a fine husband. He is just not for me."

Jessica felt as if she had been criticized in some subtle fashion.

"Doesn't your mother know all this?" she asked crossly as they continued their walk. It seemed unfair that Donaciana should hate her for preventing a marriage that Serafina—and Jeffrey, too—did not even want.

Serafina threw out her hands.

"My mother! Oh, yes, she knows it. But she has her plan, her big plan, and she is determined to succeed in it, no matter what."

"I don't understand." Serafina had lengthened her stride as she spoke, and Jessica found herself having to hurry to keep up. "What is this big plan you speak of," she asked, a little breathlessly, "besides having you marry Jeffrey?"

"It is her dream that once again the Valdezes will be masters of the Running J, just as we used to be, and not simply servants, living off the charity of the St. Johns."

"But you're not . . ." Jessica stopped, embarrassed. Suddenly she felt like an interloper, stepping into a place that should rightfully have been Serafina's.

"It doesn't matter much to me," Serafina continued. "After all, I don't remember the old days like my mother does. My father wasn't the Don Octaviano who was once one of the most powerful landowners in the territory. These are just old stories to me. And Don Octaviano is just an old man, my grandfather, who lives near the village and raises grapes and apricots. But my mother—it's different for her. It's become an obsession. She spent her childhood first as the daughter of a great *patrón*, and then later in the household of the St. Johns. You see, she missed her own chance, so she is determined that I won't miss mine, that she will make up for her own mistakes with me."

"What do you mean? What mistakes?" Jessica's curiosity was aroused now.

"Well, my mother was, I think, in love with Mr. St. John—Ross—Don Rosario, they call him around here. Or maybe she was just in love with the idea of being the mistress of the Running J. I don't know. But I think from the time she was a girl, when she and my uncle were taken in by the St. Johns, she hoped to marry him."

"That's hard to imagine." Jessica was thinking of the dumpy, hostile-eyed woman bent over the kitchen table. "I mean it's hard to see her as young and in love."

"She was a beauty in her day," Serafina countered. "Maybe it was not unreasonable to hope. I don't know. Now she is lumpy and sour—like sourdough. Anyway, she had hopes. But while Don Rosario was away in the war—he joined the Union Army right after Fort Sumter fell, but he came back here when his father died, in '63—anyway, while he was away, my mother let herself fall in love with one of the cowboys, and—what can you expect?—she got pregnant."

"What happened then?" Jessica was somewhat shocked by Serafina's confidences, but also flattered that her companion was revealing her family's history to her so frankly.

"Mr. St. John—Jeffrey's grandfather—made the cowboy marry her; this was just before he died. When Ross—Don Rosario—came back, she had already had the baby, my brother Miguel."

"What did Ross St. John think?"

"*Quién sabe*? Maybe he didn't care. Maybe he was never in love with my mother, anyway. Or maybe he was. In any case, he got married himself, almost right away, to Doña Reina, a beautiful woman who was the daughter of another rancher. Maybe he had made a promise to her even before he went away. If so, my mother didn't know about it. One year later, Jeffery was born, and the year after that, my mother had me. Then my father left and we never saw him again. Don Rosario let us stay on in the house. He was very kind to us. Whether it was because he really had loved my mother, or just because we were the children of Don Octaviano, I don't know. So my mother is still in the house, but not as mistress, as she had dreamed.'' Serafina shrugged again. ''My mother is not very smart. She had plans, but she thinks here''—Serafina laid her hand across her heart—''not here.'' She tapped a long slender finger against her forehead. ''Me, I have plans, too, but I will not let passion make me foolish.''

Jessica felt a lively curiosity as to what plans this beautiful young woman might have, but she felt too inhibited to ask. Instead, she turned to something else Serafina had mentioned.

''You have a brother? Where is he?''

''Dead. He was killed in a fight over a dance-hall girl in a saloon in Las Vegas. He was like my mother, ruled by his heart, not his head.'' She spoke with a scorn that shocked Jessica.

They walked in silence for a while, Jessica digesting what she had just heard. She felt a strange uneasiness seeping through her, and she was conscious of how much an outsider she was in the tangled family history Serafina had related.

As if sensing the other's mood, Serafina stopped and laid a hand on Jessica's arm.

''You and I, we'll be friends, all right?'' Her eyes seemed green as a cat's in the thick light of the forest. ''I've never had a friend my own age—a female friend, I mean. It will be good to have you here.''

Jessica found it hard not to respond to the other's apparent sincerity, although she had the unsettling feeling that there was much Serafina still hadn't told her. And in her mind was a faint lingering doubt regarding the young woman's feelings for Jeffrey.

''I'd like to be friends,'' she replied with a smile that was only slightly forced. Somehow she felt that her position with Serafina had suddenly changed. Though her own age, the other woman now seemed more worldly, more sophisticated. She spoke easily, and with no apparent embarrassment, of matters that Jessica's mother had told her were never discussed. And she had a firmness of purpose which Jessica envied. As they continued their journey, she resolved to learn from Serafina, to not let her own plans be overturned by passion and doubt.

Whereas the trail at first had followed the course of the stream, as the terrain began to descend, the trail grew steeper. The stream plunged into narrow ravines with sheer rock sides where they could not follow. They had to clamber up steep banks and along rocky ridges, always keeping the roaring of the water within hearing distance, even when the stream itself disappeared from sight. Jessica was grateful for her sturdy shoes, and she wondered how Serafina in her soft moccasins could tolerate the washboard of flinty ridges which criss-crossed long sections of the path. The Mexican woman, however, seemed unperturbed by the terrain, and clambered up steep slopes and slid down precipitous paths with an ease which Jessica envied.

The sun, while not yet high, was already hot, especially when they traversed some brush-choked, airless canyon where no wind stirred. Several times Jessica paused to bathe her face in the refreshing coolness of the stream and to clear the dust from her parched throat with the snow-fed water. She began to dread the trip back, when they would have to make their way up the mountain, in the heat of midday.

Finally, when Jessica was certain her sore, tired feet could take her no further, they emerged from the mouth of a canyon and found themselves in a small river valley, fed by both the stream they had been following and another which joined it further down. Nestled in the high end of the valley was a cluster of adobe houses, and along the river's edge, small fields and neat rows of fruit trees joined the native cotton-woods and oak to make a long, wide fringe of green. Jessica could see the tiny figures of women, their skirts hitched up and their feet bare, laboriously hoeing in several of the fields. A mangy, yellow dog ran up and started barking furiously at them as they made their way along the valley.

"Who lives in the village?" Jessica asked, curious, as they skirted the settlement and made their way toward the far end of the valley.

Serafina shrugged. "Just peasants—shepherds, farmers,

laborers—people who've lived here for centuries, from even before my grandfather's time, I think.''

''What do they do?''

''They farm a little, keep a few sheep and goats. Some of the men work for St. John whenever he needs extra help, like at roundup, or for the cattle drive to the railroad. Some go to work in the mines. The women come help us at the ranch house whenever we have a fiesta.''

A gang of small boys playing by the stream stopped and stared at them as they passed. One of the bolder ones called a greeting in Spanish, to which Serafina cheerfully replied, adding something which set them all laughing. Jessica was struck by their white teeth and the luminous brightness of their dark eyes, which contrasted with the ragged poverty of their clothing.

Serafina's grandfather lived at the very end of the valley, where the walls steepened and narrowed, and the stream, placid in its passage through the valley, began to rush and foam again, gathering energy for its next plunge down the mountains.

They crossed a small footbridge and found themselves at the foot of a steep, terraced hill. Each terrace was shored with a wall of adobe bricks, and meticulously planted. Jessica noted fruit trees, grape vines, beans, the bright green shoots of young corn, and a number of other plants which she did not immediately recognize. A series of cisterns was arranged so that water could be pumped from the stream and used to irrigate each miniscule field. The entire slope faced south, and it was obvious that here in the sheltered warmth of the canyon, the crops received an advantageous start, for already there were little green fruits forming on the trees. At the top of the hill stood a small adobe house, and a steep path, set with flat river stones to form steps, led up to it.

Serafina's grandfather emerged from the doorway of the house and stood watching as they toiled up the path. He was a tall man with a lined, weathered face and sharp, dark eyes. Despite his patched, faded clothing and the humbleness of his surroundings, his bearing was aristocratic.

"*Buenos días*, Don Octaviano," Serafina greeted him formally and then walked over to give him a dutiful kiss on his wrinkled brown cheek. He held her hand between his for a moment and spoke to her rapidly in Spanish. She held out her basket and swept her free hand toward the fields below them. He nodded and then turned to regard Jessica. She forced herself to not turn away under his piercing scrutiny. Serafina addressed him in another rapid-fire burst of Spanish, and then they both walked over to where Jessica was standing.

"I was explaining to him who you are," Serafina told her. "He says he is very pleased to meet Señor Jeffrey's fiancée."

"Please tell him that I am very honored to meet him." Jessica felt uncertain as to how to greet this dignified old man. Should she shake hands? He solved her dilemma by reaching out his hand to take hers in a firm grip, speaking to her in deep, musical Spanish.

"He says that you are very lovely and look like a strong woman, who will make a good wife for Jeffrey and give him lots of children." Her eyes twinkled as Jessica blushed. "Grandfather knows English," she went on, as an aside, "but for many years now, he has refused to speak it."

The old man bent closer to Jessica, transfixing her with his glittering, dark eyes and lifting up her chin with a long, leathery finger. Jessica felt acutely uncomfortable, but didn't move. There was something about this scrutiny, which made it difficult to turn away.

Don Octaviano dropped his hand, turned, and spoke to Serafina. The young woman listened intently for a moment, and then translated for Jessica.

"He says he feels that you are already part of this land," she told her. "He thinks that maybe you are part Mexican or Indian, that you are not like most *gringos* he has met, that there is something different about you."

Jessica felt a little confused by the old man's words. She was surprised that he had guessed her ancestry—though perhaps that was not hard to see—but she herself was not certain that she felt the kinship hinted at by his words.

"I . . . I am part Indian," she stammered. "On my father's side. His mother was a Cherokee who came west as a girl with her parents from North Carolina to Oklahoma on the Trail of Tears. But I never knew her. She died before I was born."

Serafina repeated what Jessica had said in Spanish, and Don Octaviano nodded sagely. Then he picked up the basket that Serafina had brought and ducked his head inside the doorway of the adobe hut, uttering a sharp command, "Annunciata!"

Serafina turned back to Jessica and grinned.

"Don't mind the old man," she said. "He sometimes rambles on about things. All this nonsense about Indians, belonging to the land, and being one of us—you don't know all the things that the Mexicans and the Spanish did to the Indians. We only feel close to them with the coming of the *gringo*, who has been a sort of common enemy."

"Including the St. Johns?" Jessica said uncomfortably.

Serafina shrugged.

"Times change," she replied enigmatically. "Each people has its day here. Each has to live with the newcomers."

And we are punished by the past, Jessica thought. Her mind flew suddenly to an incident that occurred when she was a child in Texas. A boy her own age, son of a neighboring rancher, had called her a half-breed. When her protests that she was only one-quarter Indian had failed to stem his taunts, she had punched him, taking him by surprise and sending him sprawling in the dust. Even now, she could recall the taste of rage in her mouth as she continued to beat him with her fists until he was screaming and the blood ran from his nose, and their horrified parents had come running to separate them. A faint smile played across Jessica's lips as she recalled the incident. She had never apologized to the boy, who from then on had accorded her wary respect.

A plump, young Mexican woman appeared in the doorway of the adobe hut. She had a soft, round face and a thick braid of hair which hung past her waist. She smiled shyly at Jessica, revealing several gaps in her rows of white teeth.

Don Octaviano spoke to her curtly in Spanish and she ducked back inside the house, reappearing with a tray of split willow upon which she had placed goat cheese, tortillas, dried apricots, and an earthenware jug of cold water. Don Octaviano motioned for his guests to sit on the weathered wooden bench by the door, and Annunciata placed the tray between them before disappearing once again into the house. Then the old man headed down the path toward the terraced fields below, with Serafina's basket slung over his arm.

The simple food tasted good, and the water, cooled by evaporation, tasted even better. Jessica took a deep draught and then munched on the crumbly, acrid cheese as she watched Don Octaviano picking beans, his tall, bony body stooped low over the neat rows of plants.

"He won't let anyone else touch his garden," Serafina told her, breaking off a piece of tortilla and stuffing it thoughtfully into her mouth. "It's his domain and he takes care of everything in it, just as if it were his *hacienda*, and all the plants and trees, his cattle and cowboys."

Jessica, her eyes on the shabby figure working below her, suddenly put together all the things Serafina had been telling her. Don Octaviano. The title was no mere courtesy to an old man. Serafina's grandfather—her family—had once been the owner and master of the Running J ranch. And now this dignified aristocrat tended vegetables on a tiny farm, a mockery of his former estate.

"How did your grandfather come to"—She searched for a tactful way to ask her question, but could not think of one—"come to lose the ranch? Did he sell it to the St. Johns?"

Serafina nodded.

"Yes, he sold it. He had to sell, though he didn't want to, of course. The ranch was one of the original land grants in New Mexico, from the king of Spain, and it had been in the Valdez family for generations."

"Why did he have to sell?"

"It was very sad, really. You know that in '46, after the United States won its war with Mexico, this became American territory. Some people left for Mexico, but my grandfather and his family stayed, and their claims to the land were honored. But soon after that, there were people who plotted the overthrow of the new American rule, and in one uprising, in Taos, some *gringos* were killed by a handful of Mexicans and Indians. The uprising spread to a few other places but it was soon put down.''

''And your grandfather was involved in this?''

''No. He may seem fierce and proud, but underneath he is a gentle soul, who would not plot to kill people. And he knew that such a plot would lead to no good end. Besides, I don't think he really cared that much whether his government was that of the United States or Mexico. All he wanted was to be left alone on his ranch with his family and his people.''

''Then what happened?''

''Well, somebody claimed he *was* involved in the plot. There was no proof and all his friends knew that he was innocent. But one night a group of men—nobody knows who they were, but they all were *gringos* and masked—attacked the ranch house, which stood near Don Rosario's house, but further up the creek. They attacked it and set fire to it. His wife and several servants were killed in the attack. After that, well . . .'' Serafina's eyes rested on the tall figure toiling below them. ''Don Octaviano was never the same after that. He loved his wife, I think, very, very much, for even though he still had his ranch, after he lost her he lost interest in everything else, even his children. He began to drink, to gamble, to neglect the ranch. He got very much in debt. Of course, there were many people greedy for his land—it is some of the finest in the territory—and they were nipping like dogs at his heels, ready to take over.''

''Was St. John one of these?'' Jessica was beginning to see the St. Johns, who had seemed in her eyes so established, as interlopers on this land, whose traditions extended further back than she had thought.

''The St. Johns? Yes, they were there. But Randall St. John, Ross's father, was not one of those greedy ones. He was a merchant who had made a small fortune in the Santa Fe trade. In a way, I suppose, he was our savior. He bought out

my grandfather's holdings, and debts, at a good price, but
promised that the family could stay on the land. He loved
New Mexico like one of us and had long planned to settle
here. He didn't know much about ranching but he was a
good businessman and he was good to all the people who
lived around here—the cowboys, the villagers, the other
landowners—and they helped him out.''

"So your grandfather stayed?"

"No, he left, he left at first." Idly, Serafina tossed tortilla
crumbs to the chickens foraging among the weeds at the edge
of the house. "Nobody knows where he went. He just disappeared. St. John took in the children—my mother and her
brother—and raised them in his house. Then one day, many
years later, my grandfather showed up. He had nothing—no
horse, no gun, no money—just the clothes on his back. He
didn't tell anyone where he'd been. But Mr. St. John gave
him this place—it was all he wanted, my mother says—and
built him this house and bought him a few chickens and
goats, and he's been here ever since. He never comes to the
ranch house, just stays here with his garden. Lots of people
think he's crazy, but he's not, really. He says strange things
sometimes, but he's sharp. His mind's still alive." She grinned.
"I guess he's still alive as a man, too." Serafina nodded
toward Annunciata sweeping the stoop of bare earth with
a ragged straw broom. "She moved in with him a couple
years ago."

"You don't mean . . .'' Jessica halted, embarrassed.

"Men!" Serafina winked at her. "I like the ones that stay
lively as they get old. I hope to marry somebody like that.
Besides, young men are boring."

Jessica was saved from having to reply to these risque
remarks by the reappearance of Don Octaviano, who set a full
basket of fresh beans, radishes, and lettuce beside the bench.
He called an order to Annunciata and she quickly ducked into
the house, her long braid swinging, and emerged a few
moments later with a large hunk of goat cheese and a moistened linen cloth to spread over the vegetables to keep them
fresh.

They said good-bye, Serafina giving her grandfather another kiss on the cheek, the old man bowing before Jessica in a courtly, old-fashioned manner as they departed. As they descended the steep stone stairway, Jessica reflected that it would be hard to find a more complete contrast to the rustic luxuriousness and wealth of the Running J ranch house than this tiny adobe hut with its narrow, terraced garden. And yet she had felt a certain peace at Don Octaviano's. She wondered if he had not perhaps found a kind of contentment there that would have been lacking for the wealthy owner of a large ranch.

Despite the fact that much of the going was uphill, the return trip seemed shorter to Jessica than their journey down had been. Still, she was glad when they reached the final stretch of trail—the shady path along the stream behind the house.

"I think maybe we could both use a bath after this morning's work." Serafina, who was in the lead as they toiled up the bank, had glanced back over her shoulder to make the remark laughingly to Jessica. Then, as she reached the top, she stopped suddenly. Jessica, coming up behind her, peered over the other woman's shoulder to see what had caused her to halt so abruptly.

Five men on horseback had just reined up in front of the house. Jeffrey stood beside the porch, facing them, his back slightly turned to the two women on the path. Even from where she stood, Jessica could see the tenseness in his shoulders, and she could hear the rough challenge in his voice as he spoke. But what alarmed her most was the rifle cradled meaningfully in the crook of his arm. She noted that Old Tom had come up along the porch to stand, armed with a shotgun, behind Jeffrey.

"Who are those men?" Jessica whispered to Serafina, heeding the other's unspoken admonition that they remain where they stood. She was puzzled by the scene before her, for the men seemed respectable enough. One looked like a prosperous rancher, another like a cowboy, and the others were dressed like businessmen, in dark suits and felt bowler hats.

"That man in front, the blond one with the red face, is Stuart Kincaid," Serafina whispered back. "He owns the ranch next to the Running J."

"But why . . ."

Serafina signaled her to silence. Jessica could hear the men arguing about something, or at least Jeffrey was arguing, in a tone of voice that Jessica had never heard before. She strained to hear, but she could make out only a few words against the background of the rushing stream below them.

". . . know perfectly well . . . at the roundup . . . come to threaten . . ."

The man whom Serafina had referred to as Kincaid was responding in a tone which was not so much placating, it seemed to Jessica, as mocking. The men with him said nothing, but watched the scene with an alertness she found menacing. She was suddenly acutely conscious that they were alone at the ranch house—three women, an old man, and Jeffrey. At that moment, even the presence of the foreman Riordon would have been welcome.

Suddenly Kincaid laughed and wheeled his horse around. As if that were a signal, they all turned and galloped out of the yard, the pounding hooves raising lingering clouds of dust as they disappeared down the road. Jeffrey stood watching, not relaxing his defensive pose until they were well out of sight. Then he turned and saw the two women coming up the path toward the house. He smiled in greeting, but Jessica noted that a frown remained between his eyes. She thought she was seeing another unknown side of Jeffrey—Jeffrey as protector of the ranch. He seemed—what was the word Serafina had used?—more *macho*, more a man, than he had seemed to her before.

"What did Kincaid want?" Serafina's voice was indignant.

"Hard to say, really." Jeffrey spoke evenly, but Jessica sensed the tension in his voice. "I think he just came over to show his face so we wouldn't forget he's around and up to more mischief. He made some show of asking for my father but he knew quite well that everyone's out on roundup."

"What did you tell him?"

"Just that—that father wasn't here, and if he wanted him, he could probably find him somewhere over near Castel Springs or Sandy Meadows. Then he told me some nonsense about the land grant and a court decision coming up and how I shouldn't be so cocky, because this place might not be ours for much longer. I have no idea what he was talking about, but I told him to get off the ranch."

Serafina looked thoughtful.

"Yes, we had heard some rumors that he was going to try to challenge the land grant in court. Did you know he offered to buy Ro . . . your father out last winter?"

"Yes, he wrote me about it. Seemed to find it funny. Apparently Kincaid offered him some ridiculously low sum of money."

"Your father finds Kincaid and his cattle company merely annoying, like a big horsefly buzzing around our heads. I think he is dangerous."

Jessica was feeling very left out of this exchange, a feeling heightened by Serafina's use of the term "we" and the way she seemed to assume she had an equal interest in the matter she was discussing with Jeffrey.

"Who exactly *is* Kincaid?" she interrupted somewhat petulantly.

"Kincaid bought the Burnt Cedar ranch a few years ago," Serafina explained, "just before Jeffrey went away to college. Then he formed the Burnt Cedar Cattle Company with the backing of several businessmen from Las Vegas and, rumor has it, a couple of big shots from back east. The Burnt Cedar is not a bad ranch, though it hasn't been kept up properly, but it's not very big, and Kincaid would like to get his hands on all or part of the Running J."

"And," Jeffrey added, "I suspect he's not very fussy about how he does it."

"You mean . . . you mean he might try something illegal? But what about this court case he mentioned?"

"Lots of these Spanish land grants are very old but very murky. The Spanish crown gave sweeping grants in areas which were often unmapped, so that claims and boundaries were never very clear. It's made for a lot of litigation, out of which a lot of lawyers have gotten fat."

"I don't think he can challenge the grant for the Running J," Serafina scoffed. "It's been in the Valdez family for generations, and no one has ever questioned it."

Jeffrey frowned. "I hope you're right. What worries me is that Kincaid and some of his friends have a few of the judges around the state in their pockets. And they're tied in closely with the Santa Fe Ring."

"The Santa Fe Ring?" Jessica was feeling more and more confused.

"It's a group of rather disreputable individuals who have been a power in New Mexican politics for many years. A lot of questionable people in search of patronage positions have attached themselves to the group, and a number of people in high places are their associates. The chief justice of the county of San Miguel, where Las Vegas is located, is one of them. They may be hoping that he will give them a favorable decision. It's happened before."

"Pooh! It will take more than a crooked judge to make Ross St. John turn over the Running J to someone like Kincaid," said Serafina.

"I know. That's what worries me. It wouldn't be the first time that violence has erupted over land grant claims. Look at the Colfax County War."

"I think that Kincaid should be snuffed out"—Serafina snapped her fingers—"like a rattlesnake, just like that."

"That's exactly what we don't need," Jeffrey told her sternly. "We've had enough violence in this territory."

"That's the only thing people like Kincaid understand." Serafina was not intimidated by Jeffrey's tone. "The barrel of a gun—that's the way to deal with it. They say he's hiring gunfighters. We should do the same. Get this all over with and not wait for some silly court decision by a crooked judge."

Jessica was listening in growing alarm.

"Serafina! Surely you can't mean that!"

The other woman shrugged.

"This land wasn't won or kept by being lily-livered." Then, suddenly, she smiled. "Come! Enough of this. I must take these vegetables to my mother, who is probably already cross with me for taking so long. Then I will heat water for baths for both of us. Otherwise, Señor Jeffrey will not want either of us in the house with him." She bustled off, leaving Jessica and Jeffrey standing together on the porch.

Jeffrey gave his fiancée a wry smile.

"I'm afraid Serafina's a little hotheaded at times. She's also as proud of the ranch as if it were her own. In a way I almost feel it is. The way my father has treated her, she really is one of the family." Then, seeing the worried expression on Jessica's face, he put his arm around her. "I hope you're not too upset by all of this. Kincaid's out to cause us trouble, but we can handle him."

Jessica knew that Jeffrey meant to be reassuring and protective, but there was a troubled note in his voice that did nothing to allay her own uneasiness.

Soaking later in the big tin tub that filled most of the tiny bath house behind the kitchen, Jessica felt some of the tension from the scene in the yard melt away. She leaned back, shutting her eyes, and sank up to her chin in the warm water. The aches and pains began to ease as the warmth seeped into her stiff and tired muscles. She let her thoughts wander to the many natural wonders of her ride the day before, to all of the nooks and crannies and surprising vistas the ranch had to offer, to the trek to the village with Serafina and the encounter with Don Octaviano. What did that old man really think of her? she wondered. Did he resent her, as did Donaciana, because he had hoped his granddaughter would marry Jeffrey? Or, perhaps, resent her because, had he not lost the ranch, it would be his own grandson getting married, a grandson who, had he been heir to the vast magnificence of

the Running J, probably would not have been shot and killed
in a saloon brawl? It was, after all, the old man's own fault
he had lost the ranch. But would he have behaved in such an
irresponsible fashion if he had not lost his wife? He must
have loved her very much, Jessica thought. It was hard to
imagine that dignified, weathered old man passionately in
love—or maybe not. There was a certain power in his eyes, a
hint of fires that had not quite dwindled. And sparks seemed
to have been passed on to his granddaughter, to judge by
Serafina's remarks about Kincaid. Yet Serafina swore she
would live her life with her head, not her heart.

Jessica sighed. How strange and complex were these people with whom her life had suddenly become entwined. How
much simpler everything had seemed when she had met the
handsome young rancher's son at a concert in New York,
when all she thought she had to do, once her mother was won
over, was to meet the approval of his father. Now she realized that if she were to be happy here, she would have to be
accepted by a number of people, people who seemed almost
as integral a part of the Running J as Ross St. John himself.
And yet, resentful as she was of some of the scrutiny she had
been given, she almost didn't mind.

Jessica reached for the soap which lay on a wooden shelf
near the tub and began to lather herself with suds, rubbing the
soap luxuriously over her smooth skin. One of her secret
pleasures was derived from contemplating her own body. She
knew that she was beautiful—the looks she got from men told
her that. But no man, not even her fiancé, had ever seen her
body in its full nakedness, as she herself had. The long
tapering legs, the rounded but slender hips, the narrow curve
of waist, the full, firm breasts—these things were only hinted
at under the voluminous costumes of the day. Jessica cupped
her breasts in her hands and lifted them above the level of the
water, watching the wet, rosy nipples grow hard in the cool
air. She sighed. Perhaps if Jeffrey could see her like this, he
might . . . might what? She wasn't entirely sure. Might take
her in his arms the way she wanted, might kiss her in the
deep passionate way she yearned for.

Guiltily, she stopped her thoughts from running farther. This was all wickedness. Some things were permitted between husband and wife, she knew, but were sinful outside of marriage. Surely a man seeing a woman naked was one. Still . . . Jessica sighed again and began to rinse herself. It was time for lunch, and once again, she was ravenously hungry.

Chapter 5

Dearest Mother,
 I hope this letter finds you well and that you are enjoying good weather. I am fine and am adjusting well to life here on the ranch.

It was late afternoon. Jessica sat at the table in her bedroom, trying to catch up on her correspondence. She had been at the ranch a week, and it had already begun to seem like home. New York was very far away, and she had difficulty recalling the crowded streets, the close-set buildings, the constant noise and bustle. They all seemed unreal in view of the scene outside her window. Her mother's face, however, was not unreal. Jessica felt a twinge of guilt as she thought of Isabelle Howard sitting by the window in her home near Washington Square, sewing or reading her Bible, or perhaps just gazing outside, wondering what was happening to her daughter. Except for a hastily scratched note to let her mother know they had arrived safely in New Mexico, Jessica had not

written since she left home. She had been so busy here on the
ranch—talking to Serafina, exploring the valley in which the
ranch house lay, training Spur so that the little horse would
now come trotting up to her when she appeared at the pasture
fence. Of course, none of this excused her dereliction, and
she knew that the real reason she had not written was that she
did not know exactly what to say. How could she write of
Serafina and Don Octaviano in a way that her mother would
understand? Or speak of the mingled feelings of excitement,
uneasiness, and longing alternating in her since she arrived?
How could she tell her mother that she did not want to return
to New York for the wedding and persuade her to make the
long journey to New Mexico instead? As for the encounter
with Kincaid, her taming of Spur, the troubles that seemed to
be brewing over the land grant—of course she could say
nothing about these. Her mother had been nervous enough
about Jessica's returning to the Wild West. No need to alarm
her further.

All of this made writing the letter a matter of slow delibera-
tion, and Jessica often found herself staring out of the window at the sky, where big, fluffy piles of cloud cast the
meadow and the pine woods into alternating sun and shadow.

But it was more than just the uncertainty of what to say and
how to say it that bothered her. Jessica was also suffering
from steadily mounting anxiety. The roundup was over, and
part of the herd was on its way to the railroad head with the
foreman in charge, while the rest had been driven to summer
pasture. Today was the day that Ross St. John would return to
the ranch. At last Jessica would encounter Ross St. John—
Don Rosario—proprietor—no, *patrón*—of one of the largest
ranches in the territory. Tyrant in his own kingdom—the man
upon whom her future and Jeffrey's seemed to rest. Would he
like her? The question kept pounding in Jessica's brain, sometimes filling her with anxiety, at other times filling her with
anger that so much depended upon this man's opinion of her.

"Of course he'll like you," Jeffrey had reassured her the
night before. "You're beautiful. You're intelligent. And besides, you grew up on a ranch; you know horses and cattle, so

he can't look down on you for being a tenderfoot. And you're charming and educated. He'll have to agree that I couldn't have made a more perfect choice for a wife.''

Jessica couldn't tell him it was precisely because Jeffrey had chosen her that she feared his father would disapprove. Ross St. John apparently had his son's life all mapped out. Suppose Ross St. John, like Donaciana, had hoped that Jeffrey would marry Serafina? After all, she knew the ranch better and was passionately committed to it. Jessica tried to shake off these thoughts. What did it matter, after all, what Ross St. John wanted? He couldn't force his son to marry anyone. Resolutely, Jessica took up her pen again and tried to resume her letter.

> . . . *covers miles and miles of beautiful country, with lovely forests, clear streams, and spectacular mountains. It is nothing like Texas, which I know you found rather flat and forbidding. New Mexico is truly lovely, at least up here in the mountains, and I know you would enjoy the scenery, wildflowers, and the clean, dry air.*

Jessica paused to gaze out of the window again. Strange that both she and her mother had traveled west to be brides. But how different their circumstances were. She herself was eager and happy and in love with the man she was to marry, and had fallen in love with the land once she arrived. Her mother, one of numerous progeny of a poor Methodist minister, had come west to marry a stranger, known only by the recommendation of a mutual friend. Hating the Texas plains—blazing hot and windswept in summer, blizzard-bound in winter—she stayed because she had come to love the man who became Jessica's father. When her husband died, the profitable sale of the ranch had been the widow's only consolation, because it allowed her to return to the New York she loved and to live there, not lavishly, but in modest comfort with her daughter. What a sacrifice it must have been for her,

Jessica reflected, to give her blessing to her daughter's marriage to a man who would take her so far away.

I have met several interesting people since coming here. There is a Mexican family, the Valdezes, who used to own the ranch, and who now work for the St. Johns. The daughter, Serafina, has been very friendly and helpful and has done much to make me feel at home. I have not yet had the opportunity to meet Jeffrey's father, Ross St. John, for he has been away at the roundup. However, we have heard that he will be returning sometime today and I am looking forward to getting acquainted.

With a sigh, Jessica laid down her pen. It was so hard to concentrate on her writing, especially when she couldn't reveal her real feelings. She gazed out of the window again. The clouds were marching closer together now, obscuring the remaining patches of blue. She wondered if they were going to have rain. Jeffrey had told her it was badly needed. It had been a rather dry spring and there was a strong danger of forest fires.

So many worries. So many responsibilities in running a ranch, Jessica reflected. Her mother had hated it. She had greatly preferred a life in the confines of the city to the riskier but freer life they had on the ranch in Texas. But Jessica could sympathize with the Valdezes. She knew what it was like to lose a place one loved. How often had she fantasized that one day their ranch would be restored to her and she would once again enjoy the freedom of her childhood. Now, it seemed, her fantasies were finally going to be realized, on a scale she had never even dreamed.

She turned back to her letter and was trying to frame the next sentence when she heard something that caused her to jerk her head up and lay down her pen again. Wasn't that the thudding of horses' hooves, the sound of riders coming down the road to the house? She stood up to see better, and moved around to the side of the table, pressing her face to the window. Yes, she could see the cloud of dust and barely make out the forms of horses and riders. It must be Ross St. John. Hadn't the cowboys said, yesterday, it would probably be late afternoon when he arrived?

Jessica paced across the room nervously and then returned to the window. They were closer now, but still she could make out nothing.

I'm not going to stand here watching, she told herself firmly. No need to gawk out of the window. I'll meet Ross St. John soon enough.

She flung herself on her bed and picked up the book she had been reading, *Middlemarch* by George Eliot. She fluffed up the pillow behind her, removed her bookmark, and tried to read. But the hoofbeats were growing closer, and it was difficult to focus on the lines of the page in front of her. After a few minutes she realized that she had just read the same sentence twice, and she tossed the book aside and returned to the window. To her disappointment, she found that during her attempt to distract herself, the party of riders had pulled in behind the stable so all that was visible was a haze of dust in the darkening afternoon air.

She pulled out the chair and sat down again at the table to resume her letter. She could hear the whinny of a horse and a muffled voice shouting orders from the direction of the stable. In the distance thunder growled and then resonated off the mountains. A blue-white fork of lightning flashed briefly across the distant clouds, and Jessica paused for a moment, waiting for the roll of thunder. It came, faint and threatening, across the valley. Still far away, she thought. The damp fragrance of wet earth wafted through her open window, and a faint, cool breeze stirred the curtains. Somewhere it was raining. Would they get any of it, she wondered. In New Mexico, inches of rain could fall in one location in the space of half an hour, while a few short miles away it could be bone-dry.

She heard voices. A group of men emerged from behind the stable. They conversed for a few moments, and then all but one headed toward the bunkhouses. The remaining man shut and barred the stable door, and then, with a glance at the ominous sky, headed toward the house. Jessica did not need anyone to tell her that this was Ross St. John. She stood up to observe him better, hoping he would not notice her at the window. Her heart was pounding and she put her hand on her breast as if to still it.

He was a big man, not only tall but broad-shouldered, and his stride was purposeful, almost arrogant. Other than that, Jessica noted in disappointment, he could have been any other cowboy. Huge bat-wing chaps covered his legs and he wore a dirty flannel shirt, leather vest, and large, black sombrero, now gray with dust. All that Jessica could see of his face was the hard line of jaw, dark with several days' stubble of brown beard. So this was the great Ross St. John, looking like the dirtiest and hardest-worked of his wranglers. Yet she had to admit that despite his attire, he was an imposing figure. Just the size of him, she thought, would inspire respect. He disappeared from her sight, heading toward the kitchen, and she heard him calling for Donaciana. Probably he wants a bath before dinner, she thought. Who wouldn't, after all those days on the roundup.

Dinner. There was no question now that she and Jeffrey would be having dinner with his father. Serafina and Donaciana had been cooking all day in anticipation of the event. What was she going to wear? Jessica had been devoting much of her thought that day to this question but had not managed to come to a decision. She swung open the door of the wardrobe and surveyed the dresses hanging there. She and her mother had planned a variety of clothes for her to bring on this trip, clothes to cover every sort of occasion, from traveling, to horseback riding, to a dress ball. But no dress had specifically been designated as the most appropriate for the first meeting with a future father-in-law.

For the tenth time that day, Jessica rummaged through the assortment in front of her. She had already rejected the pink flowered muslin with its lilac sash. It was a cool, pretty dress for a summer day, but she wanted to look like a woman tonight and not like a girl. The cream satin, on the other hand, was much too elegant for dinner at the ranch. Perhaps a plain dark skirt and high-necked, ruffled blouse—simple, but dignified. No, she would look like a dowdy schoolteacher in that. She pushed aside several more outfits until she came to the end of the rack and then worked her way back and pulled out the dress that seemed, by default, to be her best choice. It was a midnight-blue watered-silk, the fabric elegant but the cut plain, with short puffed sleeves and a neckline cut low, but not provocatively so. The neck and sleeves were laced with narrow, black velvet ribbon. With her cameo on a matching ribbon around her neck, she knew she would look pretty and, she hoped, appropriate. She laid out the dress across her bed and glanced at the clock. There would be several hours before dinner—no use getting dressed just now. She sat down to finish her letter to her mother but, instead, spent the time gazing across the yard, where rain was now pounding on the bare, red earth.

It was still raining when Jessica, dressed for dinner, her hair coiled smoothly at the nape of her neck, stood at the window of the living room. In the dim twilight she could barely make out the pasture and the fringe of trees beyond, but she could see the yard and the outbuildings, slick and gleaming in the rain. Inside, Serafina had lighted the oil lamps, and a fire of pine logs crackled in the fireplace.

She was alone. Earlier, Jessica had heard Jeffrey in the living room talking to his father, but when she came out they were gone. The table had been set in the dining room and Jessica could smell the aroma of roasting meat as it drifted from the kitchen across the breezeway. Everything was very cozy, but Jessica was ill at ease. She wanted the evening to begin.

"Well, I reckon you must be Jeffrey's intended."

The booming voice startled Jessica. She jumped and then swung around to face the man in the doorway. Ross St. John had changed into dark pants and a white cotton shirt which heightened the bronze of his sun-tanned face. He wore an embroidered Mexican vest, and a silk scarf was knotted around his neck. He was eyeing her boldly, his glance sweeping over her from head to foot, lingering on the lush curves of her body.

"Mr. St. John? I'm Jessica Howard, Jeffrey's fiancée." To her embarrassment, her voice was squeaky with nervousness. "I . . . I'm very pleased to meet you."

"Pleased to meet you, too, young lady." His eyes, an almost startling shade of gray, regarded her with mocking amusement, and his teeth flashed underneath a sun-lightened moustache. He strode into the room and leaned carelessly against the mantel, watching her. He seemed even bigger than he had when she had seen him outside. He was a very handsome and imposing man.

"I must say, my son has good taste in women," Ross St. John continued. Jessica realized that she was becoming uncomfortable under his scrutiny. "I confess I had my doubts when I heard he'd become engaged. Figured he'd pick some pale-faced, mealy-mouthed little city girl who'd read him poetry and feed him bonbons. But you certainly are a looker. In fact you look like you might even be a bit of a handful for Jeffrey."

Jessica's cheeks burned at the impertinence of his words. She lowered her eyes in sudden confusion, uncertain as to how to respond to these sallies. No one had ever spoken to her that way before!

Ross was still regarding her from his position by the mantel.

"No answer, eh? Don't know whether that's a good sign or bad." He laughed suddenly at the expression on her face. "Now don't get your feathers ruffled. Didn't mean to offend you. I'd just like to know a little about the wench my son thinks he's going to be walkin' to the altar."

Jessica was further incensed by his choice of words.

"I suppose Jeffrey needs your permission to get married," she responded stiffly. Her initial anxiety was beginning to give way to indignation. What a horrible, crude man Ross St. John was! And to think she had been so concerned with winning his approval.

"No, Miss Spitfire. My son's of legal age and doesn't need anyone's permission to make his own decisions—or mistakes."

"Are you implying that you consider me one of his mistakes?"

"Hard to say who's makin' a mistake," he said, eyeing her thoughtfully, "you or him."

"I don't know what you mean."

"You'll both know soon enough, I reckon." He strode over to the bookcase where a decanter of whiskey stood, and poured himself a glass. He raised it to her. "Want a drink?"

It was on the tip of Jessica's tongue to refuse. She seldom drank anything stronger than sherry or a glass of wine with dinner. But she decided she was not going to let her future father-in-law intimidate her.

"Yes, please," she replied coolly. "I'll have a glass."

He poured a large tumblerful and handed it to her. Then he raised his glass to her again in a mock toast and downed the contents in a single gulp. Jessica tried to hide her amazement. She had never seen anyone drink like that before. She sipped her own potion carefully, attempting unsuccessfully to keep from choking as the fiery liquid trickled down her throat.

Ross St. John watched her in amusement for a moment and then turned back to the decanter to pour himself another drink. This one he consumed more slowly, resuming his former place against the mantel.

"Better learn to drink whiskey," he advised her. "Winters are long and lonesome around here, and there's only two things worth doing to while away the time. Though with all this time alone together," he added, grinning, "I'll bet you and Jeffrey haven't been waiting till winter to have a little fun. And I don't mean drinkin'."

Jessica's cheeks began to burn again. Really, this man was impossible! She lowered her eyes to her glass to avoid his gaze.

"So, how do you like the ranch so far?" Ross continued.

Jessica seized upon the change of subject.

"It's beautiful," she responded sincerely, raising her eyes

again. "I've never seen anything like it. It's so vast and so
. . . so varied. And I know I've seen only a small part of it."

Ross St. John seemed pleased.

"It's my life's work," he said simply. "And it will be
Jeffrey's when I get too feeble to run it. And yours too, if you
decide to stay. Jeffrey tells me you grew up on a ranch?"

"Yes, sir, in west Texas. My father started ranching just
before the Civil War, and then after the war, when the cattle
business began to boom, he did quite well. Unfortunately,
after he died, we had to sell the spread and move east."

"Was your father Ben Howard?"

"Why, yes." Jessica gave a start of surprise.

"I think I may have met him. I bummed around in Texas
before the war, and then afterward I was often down there on
cattle business. I think I met him through Loving and Chisolm.
I was doing business with them back then."

"Yes, he was friends with Chisolm." Jessica felt more at
ease now. The idea that Ross St. John might have met her
father made that part of her own past seem more real. And it
made St. John seem more human.

"Never met Ben's family. 'Course you would have been
just a squirt then and wouldn't have remembered me, any-
how." He swept her body with a meaningful glance and
grinned. "I reckon you've changed a bit since then."

Mercifully, Jeffrey entered the room at that moment, and
Jessica was saved from having to reply to any more of Ross's
suggestive banter. Jeffrey refused his father's offer of a drink,
glancing quizzically at the glass in Jessica's hand. She had
managed to down only a small portion of the liquor, but she
could already feel its warmth in her veins.

Oh, dear, she thought, I hope I don't get drunk. However,
from what she had seen of him so far, she was not certain that
getting drunk would necessarily lower her stature in her future
father-in-law's eyes. How could someone like Ross St. John
have a son as well-mannered and sophisticated as Jeffrey, she
wondered, as they moved into the dining room. As they sat
down, she glanced up at the portrait on the wall. It was
probably his mother's influence that had a civilizing effect on

Jeffrey. He must have had something to counteract his father's crudeness.

Ross St. John followed her glance.

"My late, lamented wife. But I suppose Jeffrey's already told you all about her." He raised his glass to the gilt-framed portrait. "A beautiful woman. More beautiful and sensitive than I deserved. Maybe even too beautiful and sensitive for this world." There was a mocking undertone in his voice.

Jessica saw Jeffrey cringe. What an unfeeling brute, she thought. Whatever his own feelings toward his wife, he ought to know that his son had loved his mother dearly. She was beginning to develop a definite dislike for Ross St. John and wished that the dinner facing them were already over.

As soon as they had seated themselves, Serafina came bustling in carrying large bowls of hot bean soup, and for a few minutes they were absorbed in eating. It was obvious that Ross St. John was ravenous, for he polished off his bowl of soup quickly and then called Serafina to bring him a second. She followed the soup with roast beef, fresh bread, cooked greens, stewed dried fruit, steamed new potatoes, hot tortillas, and stewed, canned tomatoes with corn.

"My compliments to Donaciana," Ross told her. "You don't know how good this grub tastes after two weeks with the chuck wagon."

"How did the roundup go?" Jeffrey asked his father after Serafina had left.

"Seems like a good year." Ross paused to scoop up some gravy with his bread. "Williams and I didn't have too much trouble sorting our stock, and we split the mavericks fifty-fifty. But we lost a lot to rustlers, more than any other year."

"That seems to be more and more of a problem these days, doesn't it?"

"Well, what can you expect," Ross growled. "Look at the kinds of people who are pouring into the territory. It's now the most lawless place in the country, they say. The problem is there's no civil authority to speak of because the federal government doesn't give a damn about us. They don't see any use for New Mexico. I bet a lot of people in Washington wish we'd never taken it from the Mexicans in the first place."

"Isn't there anything you can do about the rustlers?" Jessica asked.

"We try, but it's not easy. This place is full of more hidey-holes and out-of-the-way nooks and crannies than a wasp's nest—and just as dangerous. And to add to it all, many of the lawmen are as crooked as the men they're supposed to catch. Vigilante justice—that seems to be the only thing that works. Or people think it works, anyway, to judge by how many they've already hung in Las Vegas this year."

"Speaking of crooks," Jeffrey interjected. "Did Serafina tell you that Kincaid paid us a visit while you were gone?"

"I heard. But I already knew that he'd been here. Rode into our camp, bold as brass, with his bunch of cronies."

"What did he want?" Jeffrey asked.

"Same as when he came here, I guess. Made a few more threats about a court case. Brought some Scotchman with him. Said the fellow was willing to buy the place, weak legal claim and all. Don't know whether he was trying to con me or the Scotchman, but I told him to get the hell off my land and said I'd blow his face off next time I saw him around here."

Jeffrey frowned. "Was that wise? Making threats, I mean. There's no point in letting all this erupt into violence."

Ross snorted. "Violence is all those skunks understand. I hear he's even gone and hired himself some gunslinger. Reckon he thinks to scare me. But with Riordon and the boys and all the men from the village, I can hold off an army. And if I give the word, which I intend to do, it won't be safe for Kincaid or any of his gang to set foot on our land. I can count on the loyalty of my men."

"What chance do you think this court case has?"

Ross shrugged and reached for a second helping of roast beef.

"Who knows? These old land grants are as tangled as a mare's tail. And in court, anything can happen. However, if I know Kincaid, he's not going to rely on the legal merits of his case but on gettin' a judge to sit in his back pocket.''

"I have to admit, that's got me a little nervous.''

"Don't worry.'' Ross refilled his wine glass from the earthenware jug. "The Santa Fe Ring's on its way out, I hear. They got beaten badly at the Republican convention back in early May. I think they're going to be losing their grip on this territory, and none too soon.''

"I hope you're right.''

Ross grinned.

"Buck up, Jeffrey. It's going to take more than a court order to get me off the Running J. I'll fight if I have to, and Kincaid knows it. That's why there's all this talk of gunfighters. That's why he keeps coming over here trying to intimidate me. But I intend to stand up to him, with guns if need be. Right, Jessica?'' He turned to her, still grinning, challenging her to agree.

Caught between father and son, knowing that Jeffrey hated the idea of violence and feared the destruction a range war would bring, Jessica mumbled something noncommittal and stuffed a large piece of potato in her mouth.

"Glad to see your fiancée has such a good appetite,'' Ross laughed. "At least you didn't pick some wimpy thing who eats like a bird. I never could stand skinny women.''

Jeffrey, ignoring his father's sally, was frowning again.

"I was wondering if there's something more behind Kincaid's sudden push.''

"Like what?''

"Well, do you suppose he's found the mine?''

Ross St. John looked thoughtful.

"I doubt it. The whole thing's more likely some silly Indian legend. I've certainly been all over the ranch and never stumbled across it.''

"What mine?'' Jessica questioned.

"An old Spanish gold mine,'' Jeffrey explained to her. "It's supposed to be somewhere on the ranch, but nobody knows where—except maybe Don Octaviano, and if he does, he's never told anyone.''

"Is it very valuable?"

"Probably not, if the Spaniards abandoned it."

"Unless they were chased away by Indians," Ross interrupted. "That's supposed to be the story, anyway. But the mine probably wouldn't be of much use, in any case."

"Why is that?"

"Most of the gold rushes in New Mexico have been a bust. The Spaniards were the first to come here looking for gold, and the Indians soon learned they could always get them to move on by telling them that in the next village the streets were paved with it. That's the story of gold here—it's always over the next mountain."

"But they have found some gold here, haven't they?" Jessica asked.

"There've been some strikes, and New Mexico's had its share of gold rushes. But most of the veins peter out fast and don't yield much. Placer mining would work best, but there's not enough water around here to run sluices."

"Then why do you think Kincaid's looking for the gold mine, if it's not worthwhile?" Jessica persisted.

Ross shrugged.

"Men aren't exactly sensible when it comes to gold. It's like an itch that's gotta be scratched. Everyone hopes the next find will be the big one, and Kincaid's no exception. But I don't think he's found the mine, assuming it exists in the first place. What he wants most is the range and the cattle—and the other minerals on the land, maybe, but not gold."

Jeffrey shook his head stubbornly.

"He thinks he's on to something regarding the gold. I can feel it, somehow."

Ross St. John smiled at his son in a way that Jessica found patronizing.

"Well, I'll take the artist's word for it. You're like your mother. You have more intuition than I do."

Despite her annoyance at St. John's manner, Jessica was entranced by the story of the lost Spanish gold mine. What a romantic addition to the ranch's already colorful history.

The rest of the dinner conversation centered on affairs of

the Running J. Jessica listened intently, determined to learn all she could.

After he had finished his coffee and dessert, Ross St. John stood up and stretched.

"Think I'll turn in for the night," he said, yawning. "I've had a long, hard day and I'm not used to these late evening hours you city folks indulge in. I'll leave you two lovebirds to enjoy each other's company. Not, I suppose," he added, flashing Jessica a meaningful grin, "that you've had any shortage of that the last week or so."

Jessica sat for a moment after he left, staring into her coffee and listening to Ross's heavy footsteps as he made his way down the hall toward his room. The dining room suddenly seemed very quiet.

"Well," said Jeffrey breaking the awkward silence, "what do you think of him?"

"I . . . He seems like a very forceful man."

Jeffrey laughed and placed his hand affectionately over hers.

"I'm afraid he tends to be a little overbearing at times, but I definitely think he likes you. And you didn't seem to have any trouble getting along with him."

He hadn't heard the earlier exchange between herself and Ross in the living room, Jessica thought to herself.

Aloud she said, "Well, maybe at least we won't have any trouble with him over our plans."

Jeffrey sobered. "I haven't mentioned anything to him about that. I think he's still set on my staying here permanently and running the ranch with him. We'll have to try slowly to bring him around to our way of thinking. I'm counting on your help in that." He smiled and squeezed her hand.

Jessica returned his smile, but inside she was feeling torn, for she knew that whatever Ross St. John thought of her and she of him, her own greatest desire was to become mistress of the Running J.

Chapter 6

Jessica was awakened the next morning by a pounding on her bedroom door. Reluctantly she opened her eyes and twisted her body so she could see the clock by the bed.

Why were people always waking her up at such early hours? It was still too dark to see the clock face. And it was cold outside the covers, she discovered as she sat up.

"Come in!" she called, trying to shake the sleep from her voice. What in the world could Serafina want at such an early hour, she wondered.

The door flew open and Ross St. John stood there. He was fully dressed and carried a rifle in his hand.

Shocked at the intrusion, Jessica drew the blankets up across the frilled front of her linen nightgown.

"Can you shoot?" he demanded abruptly before she could say anything.

"I used . . . I mean . . ."

"Answer yes or no."

"Yes." Jessica stuck her chin out. If this was a challenge of some sort, she wasn't going to back down.

"Good. Donaciana said if I can bag some rabbits for her,

she'll make her famous rabbit stew tonight. You have fifteen minutes to get dressed. I'll meet you at the stable.'' He tossed her the rifle.

Without even thinking, Jessica somehow managed to catch it. She sat up in bed, open-mouthed, the rifle clutched in her hand, as Ross St. John slammed the door behind him.

The nerve of him, barging into her room like that! And to awaken her at such an early hour to go hunting. She stared doubtfully at the rifle. She hadn't held a gun in her hand since she left Texas, and even then she had only begun to learn how to shoot. But, she remembered, her father had said she was a natural markswoman. And this gun, though new and elaborate, with flowers and curlicues etched into the brass trim on the stock, was basically a Winchester.

She laid the rifle across the bed and slipped out from under the covers. Last night's storm had caused the temperature to fall, and the floor was icy beneath her feet. She pulled the curtains aside to glance out of the window. The sky was pale gray, but clear. At least it would be a nice day. But Jessica wasn't quite certain that she wanted to begin it with a hunting expedition in the company of Ross St. John. Well, she had to go through with it now. She groped in the wardrobe for her riding habit, slipped out of her nightgown, and dressed quickly, her teeth chattering. Then, sombrero in hand, she tiptoed out of the house and crossed the dirt yard to the pasture fence.

She whistled softly. Spur came trotting over to the fence, his hooves leaving dark tracks in the wet grass. He nuzzled her arm, looking for a treat.

''No apple this morning,'' she laughed as she slipped the bridle on and then opened the gate to let him out. ''But we are going riding.''

As if he understood, the little mustang tossed his head and gave a joyful snort.

Ross St. John came across the yard as she was leading Spur to the stable for his saddle. He had in tow a magnificent strawberry roan with a large, white blaze across one leg. St. John stopped abruptly when he saw Spur and stared in amazement.

"Is that your horse?" he demanded.

She nodded.

"How did you end up with him? He's the meanest horse in the whole *caballada*."

Jessica shrugged.

"Oh, he just looked as if he would be tough and have a lot of endurance. I thought that might be important around here," she said casually.

"You must be kidding. Nobody can ride that beast. He was left behind by a puncher who moved on to another spread. He should've paid us to take him. I was going to have him shot."

"No need." Jessica rubbed Spur's muzzle affectionately, enjoying Ross's astonishment. "I've ridden him all over the ranch. We get along just fine."

Ross St. John regarded her doubtfully.

"I can't believe you actually get up on that beast. He's ugly as hell, too. Why don't you just put him back in the pasture and I'll find you a real mount. We've got no shortage of good horses on the Running J. There's no need for you to ride a flea-bitten nag like that."

"Hush. You'll hurt his feelings and then he really will be mean." She gave Spur another pat on the muzzle and then left him standing docilely in the yard while she went for his saddle. Ross St. John watched in disbelief as she mounted. As if to help her show off, Spur was on his best behavior and didn't even nip at her as he was sometimes prone to do.

"Well, he certainly seems to behave for you," Ross commented reluctantly.

"It's all in knowing how to handle a horse properly," Jessica replied primly. If it was important that she impress Ross St. John with her horsemanship, as Jeffrey had suggested, she undoubtedly had made a good start. Now if only Spur would not throw her as he had done just the other day while she was exercising him in the pasture.

Ross St. John fastened a rifle scabbard to her saddle, she settled her hat firmly on her head, and they were off, trotting down the muddy lane along the pasture. The sky was the palest of grays, with not even the faintest tinge of pink showing in the east. They rode in silence, which suited Jessica, for she suddenly found herself feeling ill at ease. Here she was riding alone in the early morning with a man who was a virtual stranger to her; a man whose rude comments to her the night before had caused her to redden in embarrassment. Yet it was imperative that she impress him.

What would impress Ross St. John, she wondered. What did he really want in a daughter-in-law? Everything, perhaps. Weren't all parents like that when it came to their children's prospective mates? In St. John's case, she sensed that he would have been particularly disappointed if she had been homely. A beautiful woman, on the other hand, met with his definite approval. At the same time, beauty was obviously not enough. Had she been some frail flower, as he hinted his wife had been, he probably would have treated her with scorn. Beautiful and tough—that was obviously the combination he wanted. A daughter-in-law who could hold her own in a rough-and-tumble life of the ranch in a way he felt his son, perhaps, could not. Already in various ways—with the offer of a drink, the lewd comments, this early morning hunting expedition—Ross was testing her for some of the qualities he found lacking in Jeffrey. The thought disturbed her, for it seemed unfair to her fiancé. If Jeffrey didn't want to carry on the traditions of the Running J in the way his father had envisioned, it wasn't because he was incapable, but because he had other ambitions. By expecting her to behave like a man, Ross seemed to be casting doubts on his own son's manhood.

Jessica shivered in the chill air. She had donned an old flannel shirt of Jeffrey's beneath her riding jacket, but the cold air still penetrated. Ross St. John noticed her discomfort and grinned.

"You'll warm up a bit when we get to walking," he told her. "I know a little ravine not far from here, where the rabbits like to come out for an early morning nibble. We can leave the horses behind and go in on foot."

Jessica nodded, afraid to speak through her chattering teeth.

Ross looked her up and down.

"That's a mighty handsome outfit you're wearing, but it's going to get torn to bits the first time you tramp through a mesquite thicket. You'd be better off with a good pair of trousers. Jeffrey probably has some old ones you could wear."

"These have been fine so far," Jessica retorted. Trousers! Her mother would be appalled. She had thought Jessica's riding habit risqué enough as it was.

"Suit yourself. But there's no point in being stylish out here in the middle of nowhere. Come on. Let's move the horses and get the blood flowing." He urged his roan into a canter and Jessica followed suit. They were on the same road she and Jeffrey had taken from Bernalillo, and they had just finished climbing the steep section out of the valley. The road stretched before them in a long, winding descent through the mountains.

Spur was no match for the long-legged roan, and Ross St. John soon left her behind and disappeared around a bend. When she caught up with him, he had dismounted just above a small, brush-choked gully which descended the hillside to the left of the road.

"As I said, you should let me pick you out another horse," he called to her as she came up alongside him. "You'll never win any races on that stringy thing."

"Maybe not." Jessica laughed as she dismounted. The short brisk run had exhilarated her. "But I'll match my mount against yours on any good uphill climb."

"Well, at least your little nag has a loyal rider." Ross St. John was regarding her strangely. Unaccountably, Jessica found herself blushing under his gaze.

Drat the man! she thought. Is he always going to make me feel awkward and uncomfortable? She turned away and pretended to be adjusting her saddle girth.

"We walk from here." Ross St. John had pulled his rifle from its sheath and was leading his horse toward a clump of trees lying just below a rocky overhang. "We can leave the horses here where they'll be out of sight of the road."

Jessica followed him. They tethered their horses to some manzanita, and she pulled out her gun.

Ross came over to stand beside her. "Ever fire one of those?"

Jessica shook her head. "My father taught me to shoot with a Winchester when I was a kid, but it was an older model. I haven't done any shooting since then."

"Well, you shouldn't have any problem. They haven't changed much. Here, let me load it, and you can take a couple practice shots before we tackle the rabbits." He took the rifle from her, loaded it quickly, and handed it back. Jessica rested the gun tentatively against her shoulder, sighting down the barrel. Ross St. John rested a rotten hunk of pine on top of a log.

"Go ahead. Take a shot at it. Let's see how you do."

Jessica tried frantically to remember her father's instructions. His voice, affectionate but firm, seemed to ring in her ears. "Slowly, now. No hurry. Hold the gun steady. Got your target lined up? Now, *squeeeeze* the trigger." She remembered how she had been knocked backward by the rifle's recoil during that first lesson, and how she had picked herself up out of the dust, humiliated but determined to try again until she mastered it.

This time she didn't get knocked down but the stock jarred bruisingly against her shoulder. And the hunk of pine didn't move.

"Try again."

Again, she missed. Jessica bit her lip in frustration. True, it had been some time since she had done this, but the target was so big, it should be easy to hit. And St. John was watching her, undoubtedly scornful of her poor marksmanship.

"Aim lower. I think that gun shoots a little high."

She followed his advice, and her next shot blew splinters from the top of her target, while the following one sent it spinning off the log.

"Good. You shouldn't have any problem—at least as long as the rabbits sit on logs and don't move for the first couple of shots."

Jessica's pleasure at her successful shots soured at Ross's words. But then she looked up and saw that he was smiling approvingly at her. She felt pleased but also a little annoyed with herself for being pleased. After all, why should this man's opinion matter to her? But she knew it did.

"Come on. Let's go get dinner." Ross headed down a narrow trail that wound through the brush, following the course of a boulder-strewn creek. Jessica hurried to keep up with her companion's long strides.

Their pace slowed as St. John cut away from the trail and plowed through the thick undergrowth, working his way up the side of the ravine. Jessica had to pause frequently to disentangle the edges of her long, divided skirt from the grasping branches, and she began to wonder if the suggestion of trousers wasn't a good one. She also wondered if any rabbits would be awaiting them at the end of their trek. All this crashing through the brush would surely scare off the game for miles.

Finally, the undergrowth thinned, and Ross St. John signaled for caution. Almost on tiptoe, she followed him as they emerged at the edge of a grassy strip running along the rim of the ravine. They skirted the strip until Ross stopped abruptly, gesturing to Jessica to move up beside him. There, near the middle of the grassy patch, was a rabbit, gray as the morning light and dappled as the landscape against which it fed. Sensing their presence, it ceased feeding and raised its head to listen, its ears twitching. Jessica hardly dared to breathe. Then, reassured, the little animal took several short hops and began to nibble at the grass again.

"He's all yours," St. John whispered to Jessica, moving her in front of him. "Remember, aim low."

Nervously, Jessica raised her rifle. The rabbit, vulnerable and unaware, came into line. She could feel Ross St. John's breath on the back of her neck and his hand resting on her shoulder. She shivered and then steadied herself.

She missed her first shot. The rabbit leaped in panic and then bounced off. Feeling foolish, Jessica lowered the gun, but then immediately raised it again. She was in luck. The rabbit had zigzagged in fear for a few yards and then sought shelter under a bush near the rim of the ravine. It stood, frozen and alert, its nose twitching, feeling secure in its camouflage against the gray leaves and branches. Jessica sighted again, waited until she was certain that she had the outline of the rabbit's body in full view against the shadows of the bush, and squeezed the trigger. The rabbit bounded from its hiding place, seemed to fall from midair, twitched a moment on the grass, and then lay still.

Ross St. John thumped her on the back.

"Good shot! Thought you'd lost him there for a minute, but rabbits aren't very smart. Think they're well hidden when sometimes they're in plain sight." He hurried forward to pick up her trophy.

Jessica's feeling of triumph was somewhat dampened when she saw her victim swinging from St. John's grip by its long, velvet ears, its soft fur bespattered with blood. However, her companion seemed pleased by her feat, and Jessica was determined not to reveal any signs of squeamishness.

That first rabbit, however, turned out to be Jessica's only kill. She and Ross St. John worked their way cautiously along the edge of the ravine, seeking to surprise more prey at breakfast. Jessica had several unsuccessful shots, but these did not undo her initial triumph. Ross had several misses, too, although it was he who bagged the rest of their morning's take. They had half a dozen victims when they decided to call it a day.

"We've probably scared all the rabbits from here to Santa Fe," St. John said. "Besides, it's gettin' on. They'll be goin' undercover again till their evening feed."

The sun had risen, and it was already quite warm, as they trudged back through the thickets. Jessica removed her jacket and flung it over her shoulder. Her feet were sore from walking in boots made more for riding than for tramping over rough terrain, and rivulets of sweat formed under her hat and ran down her dust-streaked face. It was hard to believe that only a few short hours before, her teeth had chattered as she dressed.

The horses were grazing peacefully when they arrived again at the head of the ravine. Ross St. John tossed the canvas bag with their kill across the back of his saddle, quieting the roan as she shied away from the scent of blood. Glad to be off her feet, Jessica mounted Spur. As they trotted down the road toward the ranch, she realized she had left without eating breakfast and that once again she had worked up an enormous appetite. Sometimes it seemed as if she had done nothing since her arrival but eat. But the food was so good, and the mountain air and the exercise made her so hungry. She glanced down at her slender waist. Well, at least she didn't seem to be gaining weight.

"What are you grinning at?"

Ross St. John had pulled his horse alongside hers so that they rode knee to knee. Jessica smiled up at him, suddenly happy to be riding through the mountains on such a lovely morning. She was even enjoying Ross's company. After their adventure this morning, he was beginning to seem less intimidating.

"I'm just thinking that I'm so hungry I could eat all those rabbits right now," she laughed.

"Well, in that case, maybe we'd better get a move on. Wouldn't want you to die of starvation on the road—or have you deprive Donaciana of the ingredients for her stew." He urged the roan forward, and before she could nudge Spur, he had taken off too. This time Ross held in his mount so that they arrived together back at the house, breathless from their run.

Despite her protests, Ross insisted on helping Jessica down from her horse. She swung one leg over the saddle and then found herself in his arms. He lowered her to the ground, his strong hands lingering a moment on her waist. Jessica was acutely aware of the nearness of his body and the strong masculine scent of him, a scent compounded of sweat, horses, and tobacco. She broke away as Old Tom came hobbling toward them from the direction of the stable.

"Guess I'd better rub down Spur," she murmured, burying

her face in the mustang's mane and stroking his lathered neck
to hide her sudden confusion.

It was too nice a morning to eat inside, Ross decided, and
he ordered Donaciana to set up a small folding table on the
porch. After he had polished off a large breakfast of steak,
eggs, and sourdough biscuits, he excused himself to attend to
various chores around the ranch. Jessica lingered on the
porch, enjoying her coffee and the fresh clean air of what had
turned out to be a beautiful day. She had brought out the
novel which had proved so unsuccessful a distraction the day
before, and propped it up in front of her by her cup.

"Good morning." Jeffrey, clean-shaven and wearing a
red-checked flannel shirt, sat down opposite her in the chair
his father had just vacated.

Jessica laid down her book and smiled at him. How good-
looking he is, she thought. His gentle presence always made
her feel warm inside.

"I understand you went hunting with Father this morning."

She nodded. "I'm afraid he woke me up at an ungodly
hour," she laughed. "If I hadn't been so muddled with sleep,
I don't know that I would have agreed to go."

"Well, it was better that you went than I. One of Father's
disappointments in me, I suspect, is that I never could see any
point in running around the countryside shooting helpless
animals."

"You have better things to do," Jessica observed affectionately. "Like drawing animals." She pushed a plate half
full of biscuits toward him. "Here. These are very good this
morning. There's blackberry jam, too."

"No thanks. I've already eaten. And I've even been out to
do a little sketching. I did several drawings of a blue jay I
think are particularly lifelike."

"If you keep this up, you'll become the Audubon of New
Mexico."

"Or of some place, at least, I hope." He paused a moment. "I'm glad to see you're getting along so well with

Father. I told you he'd like you. Asking you to go hunting is
proof.''

"Oh, I think he just wanted me to prove I was a real
daughter of the West and not just some namby-pamby New
Yorker.''

To herself, Jessica was thinking that indeed Ross St. John
did like her. Why, then, did she feel so uneasy?

Chapter 7

The next few days drifted by pleasantly but uneventfully.
Jessica found herself settling gradually into the routines of the
ranch. Ross St. John did not invite her on any more hunting
expeditions, but he did make her a gift of the rifle with which
she had shot the rabbit. His presentation of it had been as
abrupt and unceremonious as the rest of his attentions to her.
One afternoon, as she was doing some mending in a rocking
chair in the breezeway, he strode up to her, carrying the rifle.

"Here," he said, tossing it into her lap. "This is yours.
Reckon you know how to use it."

He waved aside her stammered thanks.

"Consider it a wedding present. Not quite as traditional as
china and silver, but a hell of a lot more useful out here."
And he stalked off.

Jessica was oddly touched by the gift, even though she did
not really see what use she was likely to have for it. Certainly, she had no particular desire to go hunting again. She
still remembered the limp, bloody carcasses of the slaugh-
tered rabbits, and decided that hunting was not a sport she
would ever really enjoy.

But Serafina disagreed with her about the rifle's utility.

"You'll see," she said. "It's a good thing to have. A woman living out here should know how to shoot. This is dangerous country, and you can't always rely on having a man to look after you."

Although she made no reply, Jessica was not convinced. There were dangers here—the sinister visit of Kincaid and his men had brought that home to her—but after all, she had Jeffrey to take care of her, and Ross, too. Surely she need not worry about having to defend herself.

Nonetheless, she was proud of her gift. She had Jeffrey put some pegs on the wall of her room so that she would have a place to hang it, and she frequently admired the rifle as it hung there, the sun glinting off the brass plate of the stock.

Although they didn't go hunting again, Ross did take Jessica with him when he attended to various tasks around the ranch. Since they were still waiting for the return of the foreman and his crew from the railhead at Bernalillo, Ross had time to instruct her in all matters pertinent to the daily functioning of the Running J. Determined to learn all she could, Jessica was an avid pupil. He took an obvious delight in her interest in every detail, from the mending of fences to the calculations for winter feed to the logistics of feeding a large crew of cowboys. She rode one day with Ross to watch two cowboys rescue a calf from a *ciénaga*, one of the deceptive green bogs scattered around the ranch. On another occasion, she accompanied him to negotiate with a shepherd who wished to herd his sheep on a high pasture, usually the exclusive domain of the Running J cattle. Rain had been so scarce that year, Ross explained to her as they rode back, that some of the lower pastures, which normally provided early summer grazing, were already dry and sparse. Jessica also enjoyed the negotiations with the traveling mule dealers, an Indian family who raised mules and burros and traveled around from ranch to ranch in the early summer, selling their stock. She especially loved the furry little burros, the first she had ever seen. Ross sent several mules, laden with supplies, to the line camps, the cabins high in the mountains where cowboys were stationed to keep an eye on the cattle in the summer pastures.

But Jessica's favorite activity was the breaking of the colts. She delighted in the sleek, frisky young horses, and privately cheered their resistance to the rope and bit. But she turned down Ross St. John's repeated offers to exchange Spur. He made fun of her loyalty to the mustang but seemed pleased that she came to watch the cowboys work. They did not seem to mind her presence, and Ross joked that they worked twice as hard when she was there. Jessica suspected that her taming of Spur had served as a kind of passport. She had succeeded with the mustang where they themselves had failed. "Old Ass Breaker," the cowboys used to call the little horse, Serafina laughingly confided.

She and Serafina were rapidly becoming close friends. Jessica discovered that the other woman was an avid reader, and she eagerly devoured the small library Jessica had brought from New York. Serafina was especially fond of romances and other works of a kind she had never been allowed to read when she attended the Sisters of Loretto Academy in Santa Fe. In return for the loan of the books, Serafina promised to teach Jessica Spanish, and they devoted a half hour or so each morning to this task.

Jeffrey and his father also seemed to be getting along well, although there were occasional tensions. Jeffrey had still not broached the matter of their future plans, despite Jessica's urging. The subject of their wedding and Jeffrey's hopes for an artistic career hung in the air like an unacknowledged presence between the two men. Jeffrey maintained that the time was not yet ripe for a discussion of these matters. He and his father needed time to get used to each other, and his father needed to get to know Jessica before the volatile topic of their future was addressed. But Jessica could not help wondering if the time would ever be ripe. Jeffrey was intimidated by his father and preferred to postpone confrontation. She herself would not be so hesitant, she thought. And yet she had to admit that Ross St. John was a formidable individual. He was not a person one wanted to anger or offend. How much more intimidating he must seem to someone who had grown up as his son.

Every evening after dinner, Jessica, Jeffrey, and Ross would gather together in the living room. Ross was not particularly sociable on these occasions. He immersed himself in the stockmen's association newspaper, looking up only occasionally to comment, usually in disgust, upon some item he had read. Jessica and Jeffrey would read or play cards together, and sometimes Jessica played the piano. Jeffrey would listen raptly to the music, but Ross paid only polite attention. He would compliment her on her performance, but Jessica had the feeling that his interest was more in watching her than in listening to her play, and the realization made her uneasy.

She was also a little uncomfortable in her curious position between the two men. She sensed that each expected her to be his ally in winning over the other to his plans. Jeffrey hoped that her growing friendship with his father would make Ross more amenable to supporting his ambitions, while Ross seemed to feel that Jessica's involvement with the ranch would have an effect on his son. Although the conflict was muted and subtle, the depth of feeling which lay behind it became clear one evening, several weeks after Jessica's arrival.

She was sitting alone in the living room in front of the fireplace, with a book on her lap, its delights abandoned in favor of contemplating the snapping logs. Even now, in June, it was cool enough at night to make a fire welcome. Lost in her own thoughts, she hardly noticed Ross's entrance. He crossed the room with long strides and plopped himself abruptly in the chair beside her. And then, in a rare burst of candor, he began to talk to her about his plans for the ranch and for his son, and to divulge his hopes for her own role. He spoke seriously, with none of the bantering tone he often used toward her. Jessica could hear the voice of the *patrón* speaking, the man who saw himself as the inheritor and transmitter of a dynasty.

"I see all of us as heirs to the Valdezes," he told her. "They were a noble family, fallen into bad times in part because of what we, the *gringos*, did to them. I hold this land in trust, to keep it as they kept it. I intend that there will always be St. Johns on this land.''

Jessica found herself somewhat uncomfortable with these confidences and the intensity with which they were imparted.

''Why do you tell me all this?'' she asked.

''Why? Because it will be your heritage, too.'' He stared at her for a moment, the firelight playing on the bronzed planes of his face. ''Yours and your children's, and their children's. I want you to feel the way I do about the Running J, about this territory. But more than that''—he paused again, searching her face, searching for words—''more than that, I fear that without you, or someone strong like you, Jeffrey will never be able to hold this place. He is a nice boy, intelligent—I sent him away to college because I think it's important he be well educated. The world is changing; he'll have to know more than just ranching to survive. But I always intended he would come back here, take over from me someday. I fear, however, there is a certain weakness in him. I don't know if he can handle the Running J. I feel him leaning away from it.''

''But Jeffrey loves this ranch as much as you do,'' Jessica protested.

''As much, maybe, but not in the same way. I would die to defend what is mine, but it is not the same for him. I need you, Jessica''—he leaned toward her, his eyes hard and intent—''I need you to persuade Jeffrey to stay. Even though you weren't born here like he was, the blood of New Mexico runs in your veins in a way it never will in his. You can make him stay, I know it. He would do anything for you. He wouldn't leave if you were determined to stay.''

''Maybe Jeffrey needs to decide things for himself,'' Jessica ventured. ''Maybe he has his own plans for his life.''

''Bah!'' Ross St. John jumped up and began pacing in front of the fireplace. ''Jeffrey doesn't know what he really wants. And what about *my* plans? I've devoted my life to this ranch. I'm not going to see it fall into the hands of strangers. There will always be St. Johns on the Running J, do you hear?'' His voice had risen, and Jessica was afraid that Jeffrey, ensconced in his own room down the hall, might hear.

"Shh!" She gestured to Ross to sit down again, but he ignored her and leaned over her chair, gripping her arm so tightly that it hurt.

"Always!" he hissed. "Do you understand?"

A little frightened, Jessica nodded. He released her and stalked out of the room, leaving her shaken and disturbed. She wondered if she would ever understand this man with all his pride and violent changes of mood.

One evening in early June, Jessica decided to go down to the stream that ran behind the house, to a place where she could curl up between the exposed roots of a tree and read in undisturbed quiet. It had become her favorite spot when she wanted to be alone. On this particular evening, the ground was slightly damp from a brief rainstorm that had swept across the valley the night before, and to protect her skirt, she spread her wool shawl between the roots before she sat down. The forest was cool and pleasant and the waters of the brook provided a soothing background to her reading. The book, H. Ryder Haggard's *King Solomon's Mines* (her mother definitely would not have approved!), absorbed her thoroughly and it had grown quite dark by the time she reluctantly put it down, leaving the wilds of Africa to return to the less exotic setting of her own life. She stood up and stretched, and then, folding her shawl, started back toward the house. Jeffrey would begin to worry about her, she knew, if she were gone too long.

She clambered up the bank and then headed down the path. The pine needles cushioned her steps so that she made only the faintest crunching sound as she walked. How peaceful it was, she thought. Only the squeal of a bat high above her in the trees broke the stillness.

Suddenly she stopped in her tracks and cocked her head to listen. No, there was something else, some other noise, muffled but urgent, in the evening air. The rushing of the stream and the breeze in the pines suddenly drowned out what she was trying to hear. She strained her ears. There. She could hear it more clearly now. It was the pounding of hoofbeats on hard earth. Riders were coming from somewhere, and coming fast.

Puzzled, Jessica hastened her footsteps toward the house, wondering who could be approaching with such speed. Jeffrey and Ross St. John had gone fishing, downstream from the house. They would probably be returning about this time, but they had gone on foot. Had the cowboys returned from the railhead at Bernalillo? They weren't due for another day or so. And besides, why would they gallop so urgently?

Jessica hurried around a bend in the path. The clearing where the ranch house stood lay directly in front of her. She could hear the horsemen coming closer now, and they were definitely heading for the house, but they were still blocked from her view by the dark rectangles of the stable and barn. Beginning to feel alarmed, Jessica ran the last few steps to the end of the path. What she saw froze her abruptly at the edge of the woods.

A band of horsemen had just swept into the yard and in a flurry of milling hooves and jangling harnesses, jerked their mounts to a halt in front of the house. Although the light was dim, Jessica could see that the men were all masked and armed. With an almost military precision, they dismounted and scattered swiftly and purposefully across the yard, spreading out toward the outbuildings and the porch of the house. Pine torches blazed suddenly in the darkness, and while Jessica gazed in horror, one of the raiders flung a flaming brand onto the shingled roof of the house. Two others leaped onto the veranda, and with a crashing of glass, thrust their own torches through the windows. The smell of smoking pitch permeated the night air, and orange flames leapt inside the house, reflecting crazily off the jagged fragments of the window. Other men were flinging open the doors of the barn and stable, and Jessica heard the frantic whinny of a horse. The men themselves, however, did not speak but moved with a swift, deadly precision.

Where is everyone? she thought in panic. Were these raiders going to burn everything to the ground with no one to stop them? How she wished she had her gun, the weapon she had

been so confident would be of no use to her. Where were
Ross and Jeffrey? Where were the cowboys? They would
never get here in time. What could she, a lone, unarmed
woman, do against all these armed men?

Horror-struck, she remembered Serafina and Donaciana.
They would be in the house at this time of evening. What if
they were trapped there, unable to escape the burning building? What if they were afraid to come out for fear of being
shot? She must do something. She couldn't just stand there
while her friend was in danger.

Resolutely, Jessica gathered up her courage. Hugging the
protective edges of the forest, she began to move stealthily
toward the back of the house, glancing nervously over her
shoulder at the melee of men and milling horses outlined
against the leaping flames.

She almost succeeded. She had managed to put the far
wing of the house between herself and most of the raiders,
when one of them, moving away from his companions and
toward the pasture fence, spotted her. Their eyes met for a
moment, his mere glinting slits above his mask. Then he
turned and strode purposefully toward her.

Panic-stricken, Jessica spun around and ran back toward
the woods. Her pursuer quickened his pace, and Jessica could
hear the heavy thud of boots and the clink of spurs behind her
as she plunged down the path. He was gaining on her; she
could tell by the sound of his steps, but she did not dare turn
around. Her spine tingled, as if she could already feel the
bullet in her back. But he did not fire. He was trying to run
her down instead. Terrified, Jessica tried to run faster, her
breath coming in hard, heavy gasps. Her long skirts caught on
protruding bushes, and pine boughs slapped her in the face.
Behind her, the sounds in the ranch yard grew dim, swallowed by the denseness of the forest. All she could hear now
was the pounding of her pursuer's footsteps and her own
labored breathing.

A protruding tree root sent her sprawling, and before she
could struggle to her feet, the man was upon her, pinning her
to the ground with the weight of his body. Desperately,

Jessica struggled to free herself, pushing futilely against his chest with her hands. All she could see of her attacker was a pair of glittering eyes above his mask. Although her terror gave her strength, she was no match for him, and his powerful hands pressed her shoulders to the ground. Jessica desperately tried to snatch away the bandana that concealed his face, but the man was too quick for her. Grabbing her wrists, he pinned her arms above her head with one hand, fastening the other in the front of her blouse, ripping the fabric with violent fingers. Jessica felt the cool night air on her bare breasts. She screamed and tried frantically to twist away. But her struggles only caused her assailant to press against her more forcefully with his body. As she opened her mouth to scream again, he slapped her hard across the face with his free hand. While her head reeled from the brutal blow, he stuffed the torn fragments of her blouse in her mouth. Gagged and dizzy, Jessica was barely aware of the hard calloused hand exploring the contours of her breasts, rubbing roughly across the erect nipples. She could smell the mingled odor of sweat and lust and the acrid scent of her own fear. Now he was hiking up her skirts, his hand sliding underneath her petticoats, fumbling with the fastenings of her drawers. She could feel his fingers against the smooth surface of her thigh, probing the intimate places of her body.

Oh, God, no! Jessica moaned to herself. This couldn't be happening to her. She could feel the man fumbling with his trousers, and then something hard was pressing against her bare leg. With the sharp pressure of his knees, he began to force her legs apart. Weakened by terror, Jessica no longer had the strength to resist. She closed her eyes. If she lay still and didn't look, maybe this nightmare would soon be over. She could feel the pounding of her own blood in her temples and hear the heavy breathing of the man on top of her as he prepared to enter her. She held her breath.

Suddenly she was aware that the man had stopped and that her hands were free. She opened her eyes. Her attacker was sitting up, his head turned toward the house, listening. Then Jessica heard it, too, the sharp crack of rifle fire, accompa-

nied by hoarse, urgent shouts. It was not the raiders firing,
she guessed from the sudden attentiveness of the man above
her. Some of the Running J cowboys must have returned.

"Damn!" he muttered. He staggered to his feet, fastening
his pants. He paused a moment to gaze down at Jessica,
sprawled, half-naked and too stunned to move, on the ground
at his feet. His eyes shone malevolently above his mask. "I'll
get to you later," he hissed. Then he turned and ran off
toward the house.

Jessica lay there for a moment, listening to the crunching
footsteps of her attacker fading into the night. The sounds of
the forest had momentarily ceased, and all she could hear
were sporadic shots and shouting from the direction of the
house and then the distant tattoo of hooves.

Slowly, she pulled the gag from her mouth and sat up. She
tugged at her skirts, trying to cover herself. Then she stood.
Her knees were weak and her whole body shook so that she
had to lean against a tree for a moment to maintain her
balance. Numbly, she pulled the torn fragments of her blouse
across her bare breasts. Her hair, loosened in the struggle,
tumbled around her shoulders. She couldn't go back to the
house like this, she thought confusedly—not so bedraggled,
half-naked. She would die of shame. She needed her shawl.
Where had she left it? She knew she had it when she'd been
running.

She found the shawl lying in the bushes, near the spot on
the trail where she had tripped. Picking it up, she wrapped it
around her shoulders to conceal her nakedness. Then she
paused, listening to the sounds from the yard.

Would he come back for her, she wondered, shivering as
she remembered her attacker's threat. Although she could see
orange flames still dancing somewhere near the edge of the
yard, the noise seemed to have abated. There was no more
gunfire, and the sound of hoofbeats had grown faint in the
night air. Maybe the raiders had been driven off; maybe the
nightmare was over. She took a deep breath and mustered her
courage. Whatever was happening, she couldn't stay there
cowering in the woods.

As she emerged from the woods, Jeffrey came hurrying toward her, his face pale and tense with worry. He had a black smudge on his cheek and smudges on the front of his shirt, but he seemed unharmed. Jessica felt a great wave of relief flow through her at the sight of him. She was safe now. No danger could threaten her with Jeffrey there to protect her. Behind him, the yard was empty of masked riders, and, mercifully, the ranch house was not ablaze. But the barn was still a mass of flames, and black shadows of men with buckets moved urgently across its face, seeking less to put the fire out than to prevent its spread.

Jessica walked toward the porch on shaky legs, and then waited, leaning against the railing, as Jeffrey reached her side.

"Jessica!" His voice was hoarse with anxiety. "Where have you been?" He gripped her by her shoulders and gazed intently into her face. "Are you all right?"

Jessica nodded weakly, unable to speak. His eyes swept over her. As they took in her disheveled appearance, her torn clothes, and the fear written across her face, they widened in alarm.

"Jessica! What's happened?"

"One . . . one of them attacked me." She wasn't going to cry. She was determined she wasn't going to cry—at least not yet. She steadied herself against the porch railing, biting her lower lip.

"Are you all right?" Jeffrey repeated, shaking her gently by the shoulder. "He didn't hurt you, did he?"

She shook her head, tears stinging her eyes, and then buried her face in her fiancé's shoulder. He wrapped his arms around her protectively, and she closed her eyes for a moment, drinking in the comfort of his body. Then abruptly she pulled away.

"Serafina! Is she all right? And the house? What happened to it?" Her own fright suddenly receded as she recalled the concern that had led to her own pursuit and attack.

"No one was hurt," he reassured her. "Serafina and Donaciana were in the kitchen and they hid in the woodshed when the attack came. And the roof was too wet from last night's rain to burn well. Tom and Serafina managed to put out the blaze inside before it had a chance to spread. They did get the barn, though. Last winter's hay was stacked there and it was pretty dry.''

"Who were they?"

Jeffrey's jaw tightened.

"Whoever they were, they weren't interested in fighting, just in doing as much damage as they could. They left pretty fast when all of us showed up.''

Barely in time to save me, Jessica thought, and she shivered. Jeffrey tightened his arms around her again.

"It's all right now. They won't be back, at least not tonight.''

"Was it Kincaid?"

Jeffrey shrugged.

"I can't imagine who else would pull a pointless raid like that. No way we can prove it, however; they were all masked.''

Ross St. John strode up, a rifle clutched in his hand. He took in Jessica's appearance at a glance.

"What happened? Don't tell me one of those bastards dared lay a hand on you.''

Numbly, Jessica nodded.

"One of them saw me and chased me into the woods. I couldn't get away. I fell. He . . . he tried to . . . to . . .'' She couldn't say the words and her voice dwindled to a whisper as the shame of her experience washed over her.

But her meaning was clear. Ross St. John's face grew dark.

"I'll have Kincaid's hide for this,'' he growled. "And I'll take it off him personally!''

"We don't know for certain that it was Kincaid.'' Jeffrey's voice was mild, but Jessica sensed the tension of suppressed anger underneath.

"Who else could it be? Who else would pull a cowardly, sneaky trick like this?''

For a moment, Jessica felt warmed, sheltered, and defended by the anger and concern of the two men beside her.

She was safe now. The helpless rage, the fear, and the sense of humiliation that had overwhelmed her in the woods began to fade. The lust and violence that had pursued her there could not touch her here. But then she looked up into the faces of her protectors, one flushed with anger, the other white and drawn, and she suddenly became aware that something stronger and more disturbing than indignation burned in their eyes. Confused and a little dismayed, she stepped back. For what she saw, fierce, unmistakable, intense as the flames reddening the sky behind them, was a desire, a passion so focused upon her that it imprisoned her as surely, as breathlessly as the most violent embrace. They stood there a moment, the three of them, lit by the wavering glow of the fire, frozen in a strange erotic tableau, and Jessica was dizzy with the sudden knowledge of things she would rather not have known. Then Serafina came hurrying across the yard toward them, and the spell was broken.

Jeffrey explained tersely what had happened, and Serafina, murmuring sympathetically, ushered Jessica toward the house. Behind them, Ross St. John's voice boomed, calling orders to the men at the barn.

Inside, the house was permeated with the smell of wet, burnt wood. Serafina led Jessica into her room and lighted the oil lamp. Then Jessica was promptly and humiliatingly sick in the basin by the bed.

"It's all right," Serafina soothed her, pressing a cool wet cloth against her forehead as Jessica bent over the basin. "You're safe now. Everything will be all right."

She helped Jessica remove her clothes, brought her a glass of brandy, and then put her to bed. After Serafina had blown out the lamp and left, Jessica lay huddled under the covers, watching the last dying flames from the barn make strange patterns through the curtains. It was a long time before she was able to fall asleep.

Chapter 8

Patience. If there was one thing Reno had learned in his life it was an almost infinite patience with horses, with people, with himself, and, most of all, with events. Everything unfolded in its own good time. You had to learn to wait. Then, when the time was ripe, you had to act quickly, instinctively. For Reno, this was the key to survival.

Patience was certainly not one of Kincaid's strong points, Reno reflected as he lay beneath the pale sky of early dawn, listening for the sounds of Kincaid's men returning from their night's work. The rancher was always straining at the bit, trying to force things when events didn't move fast enough for him. In the end, that might not prove a bad thing—for Reno.

Reno had spread his bedroll beneath a stand of pines at the top of the creek bank. The pine needles made a soft resting place and he was concealed from view by the low branches. It was his habit to sleep outside whenever possible. Not only were the fresh air and open spaces preferable to the stuffy confines of cabin or bunkhouse, but there was less likelihood of surprise when he slept in the open. He could change his

resting place nightly if he wished. Such caution had more
than once saved him from ambush. Felicia usually grazed
tethered nearby.

This particular night he had slept lightly, his senses alert
for the return of Kincaid's men. This business of the raid
bothered him. If only Kincaid had told him about it earlier.
But the rancher had sprung it on him and the other men only
the night before.

"Just a little jaunt to shake up Ross St. John," Kincaid had
told them. "We'll make him jumpy. He won't know where
we're comin' from next."

Later, Reno had drawn Kincaid aside to tell him he wanted
no part of it.

"Rustling stock and midnight raids aren't my kind of
fighting. It's not what I was hired to do and it's a waste of my
time."

Kincaid's face darkened with anger.

"Well, if you're afraid to go . . ." he sneered. Then he
stopped, noting the glint in the other man's eyes, and quickly
backed down.

"No need for you to go, really. This is just a little skir-
mish. No point in having you along. I'm saving you for
bigger and better things."

"Better things." Reno gave a bitter little laugh as he
recalled the rancher's words. Maybe gunning down another
man in a fight was better than rustling cattle—but barely.

The whole raid was a foolish idea, anyway, part of Kincaid's
impatience. Such petty harassment wouldn't make a dent in
the defenses of the Running J and would serve only to put
Ross St. John on his guard. Better for Kincaid to bide his
time and then strike swiftly and with all his strength, when
the time was right.

The clatter of hoofbeats from the direction of the trail
alerted Reno to the return of Kincaid's men. He parted the
branches which screened his resting place, and peered out.
The stable was directly below him, across the stream from
where he lay, and he saw the riders as they rode into the yard
and then disappeared around the side of the building. He

could hear the clink of harnesses, tired voices, and an occasional curse as the men unsaddled their horses. He gathered from the general tone of their remarks that the raid had not been entirely successful and that they were not looking forward to reporting to their boss.

Kincaid had not accompanied his men on the raid. He had felt it prudent to provide himself with an alibi and so had engaged himself in a poker game in town. Reno heard him ride in shortly after his men returned and there was a murmured consultation in the stable. Curious to learn what had happened, Reno slipped from his hiding place and edged cautiously down the creek bank to position himself behind some stacks of hay at the rear of the stable. He could hear two men talking inside the building. One voice was Kincaid's; the other was that of a stranger.

"You really made a mess of it." Kincaid's voice was low but tense with anger.

"Hell, everything would've gone just like we planned if it hadn't been for that rain." The other man spoke in a rasping voice, and his tone was belligerent. "There was nobody around when we got there and we went right for the house and the stable, just like you said. But the stuff was too wet to burn well, and we only got the barn. Then the St. Johns and a couple of hands showed up. You said not to fight it out, so we hightailed it."

"Maybe if you hadn't gone running after that girl, you would've done a better job."

"She was sneakin' around the house to fetch the St. Johns, so I chased her off, that's all." The other man spoke sullenly. "No harm in that. Besides"—there was a leer in his voice—"you ain't seen her yet. She's quite a piece, pert as a filly, and a body a man could really get his hands around. I just thought I might have a little fun."

"I don't care if she's the Queen of Sheba. Your skirt-chasing is going to get you in trouble one of these days. I don't want any more attacks on women. Is that clear?"

There was a muttered response from the other man, which Reno did not catch. Then, more clearly, "Well, at least we grabbed some horses, including that stallion St. John is so proud of.''

"And what am I supposed to do with it, ride it into town? Everybody in the territory knows the St. John stock. I couldn't take those horses for a drink of water without someone recognizing them. They're worthless to me.''

"I can drive them south, sell them down by the border. No one knows them there and that stallion will fetch a good price.''

"You'd better get back to work instead, I need you here, not gallivanting around the countryside with stolen horses. I'll get Ryan to hide the horses in that arroyo south of here. And you'd better get going. I don't want anyone else seeing you.''

As the two left the stable, Reno stepped out cautiously from his hiding place, hoping to catch a glimpse of Kincaid's companion. But all he saw was a powerful, heavyset body and a brief view of a still-masked face as the man mounted his horse and set off toward the woods. Kincaid stood for a moment staring after him, and then made his way toward the house. Thoughtfully, Reno returned to his sleeping place and began to fold up his bedroll.

He had no doubt that the girl the two men were referring to was young St. John's fiancée. It looked as if she'd ended up right in the middle of all the troubles that were brewing, just as Reno had feared. He hoped she'd had nothing more than a bad fright. From what he'd overheard, it sounded as if Kincaid's men had fled before anything too serious happened. Maybe this whole incident would serve as a warning to the St. Johns, and they would send the girl someplace where she would be out of danger. That's what he'd do if she were his woman.

His woman. Reno paused a moment and shut his eyes in sudden pain at the memories that phrase evoked. How easy for him to say what other men should do, but how careless he had been with the one thing in the world that had been most precious to him. He opened his eyes and shook his head as if to dispel his painful thoughts. He couldn't think of that, mustn't think of that, or the old insanity would return. As for the girl . . . well, there was nothing he could do for her now.

It was the St. Johns' responsibility to protect her. As Reno untethered Felicia and led her to the creek to drink, he thought briefly of the girl he had seen riding down the hill, so full of life, and he hoped the St. Johns would be equal to their task.

Chapter 9

"Of course you hate him." Serafina was on her hands and knees, scrubbing soot from the baseboards in the living room. She was slightly breathless from her efforts, but her tone was matter-of-fact.

"But I want to kill him!" Jessica had paused a moment to push several damp strands of hair off her forehead. She leaned back on her heels and surveyed the wreckage of the living room. All the fire-damaged furniture had been removed and the rubble swept away, but soot covered everything, and the heavy shutters that had been placed temporarily over the broken windows made the once cheerful house dank and gloomy.

Serafina gazed at her companion sympathetically.

"Who could blame you for feeling as you do? I could strangle him with my bare hands, and it wasn't even me he attacked."

Jessica rubbed her eyes with the back of her hand, as if to wipe away the images which possessed her. She had worked feverishly all day at cleaning up the wreckage left by the raid, hoping to take her mind off the events of the night before.

Yet in the midst of her scrubbing, scraping, and sweeping, she would find herself gripped by a sickening spasm of anger as the memory of the attack in the woods flooded over her. Her only relief was to pause for a moment and relive the scene. But this time she was not helpless. This time, instead of lying passively on the forest floor, pinned under the lustful weight of her assailant, she struck back. She shot him. She shot him again and again, watching him double up in pain, watching him die bloodily at her feet.

Shocked by the violence of her own feelings, Jessica had never dreamed her mind could harbor such gruesome fantasies. And yet, such thoughts were her only release.

Opening her eyes, she could hear the sound of sawing and hammering outside. Ross had put his men to work clearing away the rubble of the burned barn and already they were busy on a new building. Above the noise of the yard rose the voice of Ross St. John as he called orders to his men. Jessica could almost see him as he strode among them, seeking in work some outlet for his sense of helplessness and anger, just as she did. She knew that his mood had not been helped that morning when it was discovered that in their retreat, the raiders had managed to make off with three of Ross's most prized horses—two mares and a stallion.

Ross had sent Donaciana to the village to recruit some young men to be posted as extra guards around the ranch. News of the raid would soon spread through the vast territory beyond the Running J.

"Ross will also tell the horse thief," Serafina said.

"The what?"

"Amadeo Lopez. He is our official horse thief. Everyone knows he is the best. He could steal a horse right out from under you, and you wouldn't even know it was gone."

"I don't understand," Jessica responded. "What does he have to do with this? I thought Kincaid's men were the ones who took the horses."

"It's a matter of honor," Serafina explained patiently. "Lopez's *and* St. John's. Nobody steals horses from St. John. That's understood around here. And nobody but Amadeo steals horses. It's a kind of unspoken agreement. So he will be very angry when he finds out that somebody took St. John's horses."

"What will he do?"

"Bring them back."

"Bring them back? But how can he?"

Serafina shrugged.

"*Quién sabe?* All anyone knows is that if you want your own horse back, or someone else's, you call on Amadeo Lopez."

"But doesn't he ever get caught and put in jail?"

Serafina smiled enigmatically, but made no reply. Jessica had returned to her scrubbing, a little confused. Obviously there was much she still had to learn about life here in New Mexico.

At mid-afternoon, the chuck wagon rolled into the yard, accompanied by the rest of the cowboys and their strings of horses. They were led by Doan, the second in charge, a tall, thin, blond man who explained that Riordon had left them the day before to check on some cut fencing reported by Mexican sheepherders. With the return of all the men, everyone on the ranch seemed to breathe more easily. The Mexicans from the village, who would normally have headed home to tend their own farms, now that the cattle drive was over, were easily persuaded to stay on at the ranch. Though the extra wages were obviously attractive, Jessica could see that there was more to their willingness than extra pay. A ripple of indignation had spread over the outfit when they heard the tale of the events of the night before and saw the damage inflicted on the ranch by the raiders.

What St. John had said was true; if he mobilized his men, it would be difficult to drive him off the ranch. The events of the night before, while still vivid in Jessica's memory, no longer seemed an intimation of darker things to come. Rather, they were an aberration, which had occurred only because they'd let themselves be caught off guard. Well, that would not happen again. Ross had posted permanent guards, and he planned regular patrols. The ranch would be protected from future attack.

A short time later, Hugh Riordon rode in, and Jessica saw him consulting earnestly with Ross St. John as they surveyed the house and damaged outbuildings. There was still something about the man she didn't like, but she had to admit that he seemed capable, and his presence was reassuring. Ross had told her that Riordon had a minor reputation with a gun and was a good organizer of men—two qualities useful in time of trouble. The Mexicans hadn't liked him at first, but eventually they came to accord him a grudging respect. If he ran the outfit with a somewhat heavy hand, he was tough and he got things done, and that was what counted—with boss and hands, alike.

Toward evening the sheriff arrived from Bernalillo. He took a brief stroll around the ranch yard to survey the damage, and then St. John invited him to join them for dinner. Sheriff Pete Towers was tall and lanky, with reddish sandy hair and a flourishing moustache. He had a lean toughness about him, but it was overlaid with a pleasant, humorous manner. Jessica found herself enjoying his company, though she sensed that he was a man who could be ruthless if need be. He shared Ross St. John's indignation over the events of the night before, but agreed with Jeffrey that confrontation with Kincaid was not the answer.

"Not that there's any doubt Kincaid's behind it, Ross, no doubt at all. But we got no proof. We need to bide our time a bit, wait for him to tip his hand. Give him enough rope, and a man like Kincaid'll hang himself easily enough."

"So how many more burned barns and stolen cattle before I can nail the bastard?"

"No need to swear in front of the lady, Ross." The sheriff cast a fatherly glance at Jessica, who had heard far worse from Ross St. John. She smiled warmly at the sheriff, and with a certain reluctance, he turned his gaze back to Ross. "Judgin' by the guards you got posted out by the road, and the number of Mexicans crawling all over the place, 'tain't too likely he's gonna surprise you again."

"Then he'll try something else."

"Let him, and we'll get him. Besides, I got a few men workin' on it, too. We'll nail him, you'll see."

"It better be soon," Ross growled, but he seemed mollified by the sheriff's words.

The next morning, three Mexican boys arrived from the village, carrying rifles that were almost too big for them and swaggering with importance. Ross St. John sent them to the far end of the pasture to guard the horses. Jessica saw them traipsing down the road, chattering to each other in Spanish, as she crossed the breezeway into the kitchen where Serafina and Donaciana were supervising the heating of water for laundry. Large tin tubs, filled with shirts and pants and long underwear, filthy from weeks on the roundup, stood near the back door of the kitchen. Though one of the results of the raid on the ranch had been the breakdown of Jessica's status as honored and idle guest, Serafina still balked at letting her help with the heavier chores. Unwilling to be completely idle in the face of so much to do, Jessica had brought a book to read to Serafina, while she worked.

Donaciana's cousin Maria, a shy, pleasant-faced woman, had returned from her sojourn in the village and the two older women chatted and busied themselves with preparations for the midday meal while Serafina instructed the young girl heating the water in the stone fireplace. She smiled as Jessica entered and then turned to empty the last bucket into the iron kettle set over the flames. Her face was flushed from the heat.

"Sit down for a minute," she suggested. "There's coffee on the stove and some bread fresh out of the oven on the table. Here, I'll join you. This water's not ready yet."

She seated herself opposite Jessica at the pine table and cut several slices of bread from the still-warm loaf. The two young women chatted for a while, and Jessica reflected how nice it was to have a friend of her own age to work with and confide in. She had never felt as close to any of her New York schoolmates as she did to Serafina. She hoped that their relationship would not change when she became Mrs. Jeffrey

St. John. Although Jessica would then be mistress of the ranch, she knew she would continue to rely on Serafina's advice and expertise.

The water began to boil and Serafina turned her attention back to the fireplace. Jessica rose and went to the back doorway. The climbing roses were in full bloom and their scent lay heavy in the air. Jessica breathed deeply and stretched. Then she paused, startled by the sight before her in the yard, and called Serafina to the door.

A man with his shirt off was standing near the pump, splashing water over his head and shoulders. He had his back to the doorway but from what Jessica could see, she judged him to be Mexican, about medium height, with a broad, thick-set body. His entire torso was covered with a crisscross mass of scars and welts which ran from his shoulders down the broad length of his back, disappearing into the baggy folds of his pants. The lacerated flesh did not resemble anything human but, instead, the hellish surface of some grotesque desert landscape.

"Who is that?" Jessica whispered to Serafina.

"Oh, him. That's my uncle Manuel, my mother's brother." Serafina's response carried an undertone of scorn.

"But his back! What happened to him? Who did that to him?"

"He did it to himself, mostly."

"What do you mean? How could he do it to himself?"

"He's a *Penitente.*"

"A *Penitente?* What's that?"

"*Los Hermanos de la Luz* they call themselves—Brothers of the Light. They believe that one must do penance for one's sins. During Holy Week before Easter, they march in processions, flagellating themselves until the blood flows. They say that by experiencing Christ's sufferings, they bring themselves closer to God."

Jessica stared in fascinated horror at the man standing by the pump.

"Your uncle does that?"

"He and others like him. There are lots of them, the

Penitentes. Nearly everyone in the village is one, except maybe my grandfather. He has no patience with things like that. But," she added, placing her arm on Jessica's, "don't underestimate the *Penitentes*. They may be a little crazy, but it's not only the common folk who belong. Some very powerful people are *Penitentes* and they have a lot of political influence in the state. They stick by each other and even have their own courts and system of justice. Fortunately for Ross St. John, they have given him much support. Things here would be very difficult for him without it."

"And you—what about you?" Jessica turned suddenly to her companion. "You don't belong to these . . . these *Penitentes?*"

Serafina shook her head.

"Me, I am a good Catholic. I believe in Christ and our gracious merciful lady, His Mother. But I don't believe that God likes to see people suffer. There's enough of that in the world already without our having to go around whipping ourselves. But," she added with a shrug, "it's none of my business what others choose to do. My uncle Manuel's a good man. If he wants to do such crazy things, that's between him and God." And on this note of religious tolerance, she turned back to the kitchen and her work.

Since Serafina again refused her offers of help, Jessica left the stifling kitchen and returned to her own room to write letters. Then she went outside to call Jeffrey to lunch. Her fiancé was working on the new barn. She had just started across the yard to fetch him when she came face to face with Manuel Valdez, who was untying the reins of his horses from the hitching rail. Startled, she stopped and stared at the man whose back had so repulsed and fascinated her. A rough cotton shirt now covered his torso, but he was almost as formidable from the front as from the back. His face was broad, deep brown, with sharp, dark eyes set under bushy brows. His cheeks were pitted with pockmarks and his lips were wide and hard. It was a rather frightening visage, and Jessica felt uneasy under his scrutiny.

"You're Jessica Howard, Señor Jeffrey's fiancée." It was

a statement rather than a question. He spoke with a slight but distinctive Spanish accent.

She nodded.

"And I'm Manuel Valdez, Serafina's uncle. But I suppose you already know that." He gazed at her for a moment and then nodded, as if to himself. "Señor Jeffrey makes a good choice. Someone like you is needed on the ranch. But"—his eyes seemed to be drilling into her—"I think that maybe the ranch is not what you yourself need, and in the end you will not stay." There was a note almost of disappointment in his voice.

Indignation rose in her. Why did everyone, from Serafina to Don Octaviano to Ross St. John himself, feel they had the right to pass judgment on her suitability as the next consort of the St. John dynasty? Jessica's annoyance overcame the momentary fear Manuel Valdez had aroused.

"Well," she said sarcastically, "I'm so glad to know that you approve of me. Why don't we just line up all the ranch hands and get their approval, too, while we're at it."

She stopped, afraid that in her anger she might have offended him, but to her surprise Manuel laughed. She caught the flash of a gold tooth, and laugh lines crinkled outward from his eyes. His face suddenly seemed transformed, no longer threatening.

"You must excuse us Valdezes," he told her. "We're a proud, old family. Even though my father managed to lose our inheritance, we still take an interest in the land and those who affect it. I'm now just a wagon driver hauling sacks of flour and beans. But every now and then I come up to the ranch to check on things. And my sister—look at her. She took back her name of Valdez after her husband left, and she'd rather stay here as a cook than live anywhere else." He gestured with his hand toward the mountains around them. "All this used to be the Rancho Valdez, and we can never really let go." He winked at her. "Pay us no mind. We say crazy things that mean nothing. Just listen to Serafina. She's the only one of us with any sense."

Jessica was not deceived by his bantering tone of voice.

She sensed a deep seriousness underneath his words, and she knew that Manuel Valdez was a man to be reckoned with. Fortunately, he seemed to be well disposed toward her and she was relieved that Donaciana's unremitting hostility did not seem to be shared by other members of her family. She managed to return his smile. He gave her a courtly bow, and the gesture did not seem incongruous, despite his faded, baggy clothes. Even with little overt physical resemblance, there was nonetheless a touch of Don Octaviano in the son. Then Manuel mounted his horse and trotted off down the road.

That evening after dinner Jeffrey proposed a walk.

"It's a nice night," he said casually. "We could go just a short distance down the creek."

Jessica knew Jeffrey had been waiting, since the evening of the raid, for a chance to be alone with her, but all the activities around the ranch had kept them busy and tired. Readily agreeing to his suggestion, she ran to get her shawl, and together they headed down the path to the stream. Lights glowed in the bunkhouse, and Jessica could hear laughter and the clinking of poker chips and bottles. Somewhere someone strummed a guitar, and the music was romantically melancholy in the soft night air.

They made their way to the edge of the stream, not far from the place where Jessica had so unsuspectingly curled up to read, just two short days ago.

She sat down on the mossy bank and Jeffrey sat down beside her and put his arm around her shoulders. She leaned against him, grateful for his affection.

"You don't know how worried I've been about you," he told her, burying his face in her fragrant hair.

"There's nothing to worry about," she said gently. "It's all over. Nothing more is going to happen to me." But suddenly, like a dark shadow, the memory of her attacker's whispered threat passed through her mind. She shivered. What if he *did* come back. What if . . .

Jeffrey drew her closer.

"You're my life, Jessica," he whispered. "I love you. I would die if anything happened to you."

"I love you, too, Jeffrey." She lifted her face up to his and their lips came together in a long passionate kiss. Jessica felt herself weaken and her limbs seemed to be melting. She wrapped her arms tightly around her fiancé's neck and pressed her body against him. Gently, he lowered her against the mossy ground, and she pulled him down beside her.

"Jessica!"

He held her head between his hands, running his fingers through her hair. Her long dark tresses came loose from her pins and tumbled around her face. He kissed her forehead, her eyelids, her cheeks, and then again her lips. She let herself sink into him, almost dizzy with the passion that surged through her. How she wanted him! Now she felt her own body, urgent with desire, arching up against his. He had one leg flung across hers and she could feel him grow hard against her thigh.

His fingers caressed the silken skin of her neck and then moved lower, probing at the edge of her blouse. He fumbled with the buttons, and then pulled at the ribbons of her chemise, releasing the full globes of her breasts to the exploration of his hands. Her nipples grew hard at his touch and she moaned as he squeezed the firm rounded flesh, and then lowered his face to kiss the tops of her breasts.

"Jeffrey! Oh yes, yes!"

How different this was from what had happened here two nights before. What had been terrifying and painful with her unknown attacker was the fulfillment of her heart's and body's most passionate desire with her fiancé. As if to erase the memory of that earlier nightmare, she pulled Jeffrey further down against her.

His hand moved across her thigh, exploring the contours of her legs and hips beneath the fabric of the skirt. Warmth coursed through her body, and she parted her legs expectantly as he pushed up her skirts, his hand moving gently, probing toward the center of her desire.

"Jessica! I love you so much!" His urgent words were

muffled in the overwhelming warmth and abundance of her
flesh. She pressed her hips against his and closed her eyes,
surrendering herself in ecstasy and expectation.

"Jeffrey!" she murmured between lips swollen and ripe
from his kisses. How she wanted to have him take her, to be
his, to be bonded to him through the coming together of their
flesh.

Abruptly, he rolled off her and sat up. Startled, Jessica
opened her eyes. Jeffrey sat beside her, his back to her, his
body rigid, no longer touching her. Jessica lay sprawled upon
the bank, her bare breasts gleaming in the moonlight, feeling
stunned and abandoned. A horrible sick feeling washed over
her. What had she done? She had been on the verge of
surrendering herself to Jeffrey, of giving her body to him
totally, just as she had already given him her love. She had been
ready, eager to do this, even though they were not yet man
and wife. She had lost control of herself completely. Now
Jeffrey would know what she was really like. He had seen her
true character, her sinful, lustful nature. Surely, after such a
shocking display, he would no longer want to marry her. She
could tell that he was angry at her by the way he was sitting.
Well, she could hardly blame him. He had just learned that
his fiancée was little better than a common wanton. Jessica
sat up and began to button her blouse, tears of shame and loss
springing to her eyes.

Jeffrey turned at her movement and looked at her. His blue
eyes were a dark violet in the moonlight. He reached out and
touched her face tentatively with his hand.

"Jessica . . ." She braced herself for his reproaches. "Jessica, I'm so sorry. You must think I'm a heartless brute. How
could I have done that to you after what you've just been
through."

"Oh, Jeffrey." The waiting tears began to course down her
cheeks, as if to confirm his self-reproach. His words took her
aback and she could think of nothing to say.

He wiped away the tears with his handkerchief.

"I don't know what got into me. I've just been thinking
about you all day, wanting to take you into my arms. I think

maybe everything that's been happening around here has made me a little crazy and has made me realize how precious you are to me." He gathered her in his arms. "You know I'd never do anything to hurt you, darling."

"I know that, Jeffrey." Her voice was muffled against his chest. She felt curiously deflated, even a little annoyed. A moment earlier she had been worried that he would despise her for her passionate responses. Now, it seemed, her own desire had gone unnoticed and he blamed only himself for what they had nearly done. Was it wrong for a woman to want a man?

"I promise, it won't happen again" Jeffrey was saying. "Much as I want you, I'll control myself until we're married, until I can really and honestly claim you as my wife."

Jessica pulled her head back and looked up at her fiancée.

"Jeffrey," she pleaded, "let's get married now, soon. Let's not wait until the end of the summer like we'd planned. Let's do it now."

He smiled down at her tenderly.

"You know I'm as anxious as you are, darling, but we can't just rush off and get married. You deserve to have everything done right—a proper announcement of our engagement, a beautiful wedding. Don't worry, sweetheart," he added reassuringly. "I won't take any more chances. What happened tonight won't happen again, I promise. I can wait until we're married."

But I can't, Jessica thought as she leaned against him. What is the matter with me?

"Shall we go back?" Jeffrey stood up and began to brush the pine needles from his clothes. Numbly, Jessica nodded and let him help her to her feet. She straightened her clothing and tucked her blouse into the waistband of her skirt. Then she tried to rearrange her hair, which had fallen from its pins and hung in disheveled wisps about her face. Despite her efforts, she knew it was embarrassingly obvious what she and Jeffrey had been doing. Certainly Serafina noticed them when they returned to the house. She glanced curiously at Jessica but only wished them a brief good night as they headed down the hallway toward their rooms. Ross St. John, however, was not so diplomatic. He grinned meaningfully at them as they came down the hall.

"Spoonin', eh? Hope you had a good time."

Humiliated, Jessica stumbled into her room. Shutting the door, she threw herself on the bed and burst into tears.

Chapter 10

Jessica turned as she heard the hoofbeats coming up behind her, flashing her eyes at Ross above her bandanna as he drew alongside, letting them carry the laughter the bandanna hid.

"You look like a little *bandida*," Ross teased her. His spirits seemed as high as Jessica's today. Maybe it was the glorious weather, or the scenery through which they rode—the forests alive with impudent jays, the meadows quilted with vivid patches of summer flowers. Or maybe it was just the trip itself, being on horseback, being outdoors.

Jessica glanced down at Ross's mount. Undoubtedly, one reason for this good mood was having his favorite stallion back. The stolen horses had mysteriously turned up in the pasture several days ago, their return as surreptitious as their theft.

"You look like you're ready to protect the whole caravan." Ross eyed the rifle mounted securely in its leather sheath. "I would certainly think twice about tangling with you."

Jeffrey had also teased her about the gun, but Jessica had decided that she would never again go unarmed, even when

127

riding in such protective company as this. She turned a
moment to look back. She and Ross rode well ahead of the
caravan. Behind them were four of the Running J cowboys,
all armed, followed by the chuck wagon, loaded with tents
and luggage, as well as three days' supply of food. The chuck
wagon was driven by the cook, Bart Adams, a rather grizzled
and surly man of middle age. Serafina, however, seemed to
get along well with him. She rode on the high seat of the
wagon, chatting gaily and ignoring the gruffness of his responses. Even Jeffrey, riding alongside the wagon and ex-
changing occasional remarks with Serafina, seemed in good
humor, less preoccupied and withdrawn than he had been for
the past few days. Ever since their walk in the woods, Jessica
felt he had been avoiding her. Perhaps he felt embarrassed by
his behavior (or maybe, now that he had a chance to think
about it, by hers). Or perhaps he chose to be alone with her as
little as possible in order to avoid further temptation. Jessica
was unhappy about his withdrawal, but she did not know
what to do to bring him close to her again.

If Jeffrey had been deliberately avoiding her, the opposite
was true of his father. Jessica glanced up at the tall man
riding so confidently beside her. From the occasional amused
glances with which he favored her at times, she knew he was
convinced that she had lost her virginity in the woods with
Jeffrey. It was galling to be thus tacitly accused, when
nothing—or at least nothing worth mentioning—had happened. Yet she could hardly confront Ross and inform him
that, against her own inclinations, she was still chaste.

Jessica could not help contrasting her growing friendship
with Ross St. John with the distance between herself and
Jeffrey. And yet it was natural that she should keep Ross
company, for her avid interest in, and excitement about, the
ranch gave them a strong bond in common. And after all, she
was his daughter-in-law to be, and, perhaps, in some ways,
the daughter he never had. And that was how he treated her,
she told herself, though occasionally his gray eyes rested
speculatively upon her in a manner which she found disturbing.

For this trip, the excuse was that they needed to visit Las

Vegas to buy supplies for the big fiesta. But more than that it was defiance on Ross's part. He was determined to show his enemies that he could do what he pleased. Jeffrey had protested the trip, arguing that it afforded too many opportunities for ambush, and he had become even more concerned when Ross told him he was thinking of taking Serafina and Jessica along.

"For Christ's sake, Jeffrey," Ross burst out, after listening in growing exasperation to his son's objections. "I swear that raid on the ranch has made you into an old lady. We'll go armed and take several of the men. I'm not going to let Kincaid and his riffraff keep me penned up on my own ranch. A trip to town will give me a chance to see a few of my friends and let them know what's up. Kincaid's not the only one with strings to pull in high places. Besides—" Ross reached over and gave Serafina a pat on the bottom as she bent to pick up the plates—"I'll bet Serafina would like a new dress and I'm sure Jessica could use a few things from town."

Jessica had expected Serafina to protest such familiarity but the young woman didn't seem to take offense. She responded to the gesture with an impudent wrinkle of her nose as she carried away the full tray of dirty dishes.

"What is this fiesta?" Jessica had sought to smooth the troubled waters with a change of subject.

"It's a Fourth of July celebration, really," Jeffrey had explained to her. "Traditionally, it's also the time for a big festival at the ranch. Everyone from the village is invited, and all the hands, and people from town. It's one of the two big fiestas we celebrate around here every year. The other is the *Cinco de Mayo*, the Fifth of May, held in the village, but that took place before we arrived."

"A Fourth of July fiesta—it sounds like fun!"

"Maybe I'll invite Kincaid. Hell, wouldn't that be something if he came! He'll see what kind of support I can draw, and he won't be so cocky about driving me off my land."

"Father, you wouldn't!"

Ross laughed at his son's consternation. Jessica was certain he was joking, but she wouldn't have put it past Ross to make

such a defiant gesture toward his enemy, challenging him to a
meeting on Ross's own ground.

They had spent several hectic days getting ready for the trip
and making arrangements for the protection of the ranch
while they were gone. The day of their departure had dawned
clear and fresh. The sky behind the peaks of the Sangre de
Christo mountains was barely light when the caravan rolled
out of the ranch yard. Jessica, mounted on Spur, and with her
jacket tightly buttoned against the morning chill, felt as if
they were part of a wagon train heading west, like the
pioneers—except that they were heading east and had only
one wagon.

The first leg of their trip took them farther into the valley,
continuing along the road which led up to the ranch from
Bernalillo. Then they climbed a short distance, descended,
and climbed again, following the curve of the road through
the mountains. The day grew rapidly warmer. Jessica shed
her jacket, and then, as the fine reddish dust stirred up by the
chuck wagon began to choke her and sting her eyes, she
wrapped her bandanna around her mouth and urged Spur
ahead of the caravan. Ross joined her and after his initial
bantering remarks, they trotted side by side in companionable
silence until one of the cowboys came riding up to say he'd
just spotted a deer. Ross pulled out his rifle, and the two men
galloped off on an impromptu hunting expedition. Jessica fell
back to join the wagon.

Their first day's journey was uneventful. At midday they
stopped by a clear, narrow stream, stretched out luxuriously
on the grassy bank, and enjoyed Donaciana's delicious cold
lunch. And that night they camped in a stand of yellow pine
by a meadow thick with marsh marigold, mountain iris and
dog-toothed violets.

While several of the men busied themselves pitching the
tents, Jessica watched the cook prepare dinner. She was
fascinated by the chuck wagon. It was Bart's little kingdom.
He ruled supreme in all its doings and wouldn't even let
Serafina help him as he worked. He lowered the back of the
chuck box, which was in the rear of the wagon, and this

unfolded to form a cooking table, supported by a swinging leg. Above this table, neatly arranged for the cook's convenience, was a multitude of shelves and compartments filled with utensils and supplies. After he had built a fire and put on a pot of coffee, Bart began the task of making sourdough bread. He worked the dough on his cooking table, adding flour, soda, water and a little lard. He then formed egg-sized balls of dough and set them in a cast-iron Dutch oven to rise, while he prepared the rest of the meal. Shortly after their arrival, they all sat down to a plain but delicious meal of fried steaks, sourdough biscuits, syrup, and stewed dried peaches, washed down with the strongest coffee Jessica had ever tasted. It was not Donaciana's fine cooking, but it seemed just right after a day on the trail.

Although Ross posted a rotating guard throughout the night, Jessica felt no sense of danger in their encampment. Sharing a tent with Serafina, she slept soundly, and awoke to the pungent smells of woodsmoke, coffee, and frying bacon, and to the sounds of camp being broken.

The next day they began their descent down the mountains. The narrow road wound down the slopes of the Sangre de Christos, then crossed a wide flat plateau which ended abruptly in another steep descent to yet another plateau. The horses had little difficulty, though in places they had to be reined in to avoid too precipitous a descent, but the chuck wagon had to be eased down the steep incline with plentiful use of rein and brake. Its painful progress slowed the party considerably, but when Jessica contemplated the delicious meals the wagon had produced the night before, she realized it was more than worth the trouble it caused.

The country through which they now rode was very different from the mountains. The stands of yellow pine gave way first to piñon and juniper and then to open land which stretched dry and flat before them, a semi-desert upon which the sun beat fiercely. Jessica found herself beginning to wilt in the heat. Ross St. John showed her how to wet her bandanna from her canteen and wrap it around her head under her hat so that the evaporation would provide some measure of coolness. Despite this and the protection of her hat's broad brim, Jessica was grateful for the occasional opportunities to stop and rest in the infrequent patches of shade. Ross insisted she drink at each stop, warning her that even if she did not feel thirsty, she could quickly suffer from dehydration in the hot climate.

Even the heat, however, could not dampen Jessica's enjoyment of the trip and the sense of freedom she felt as she rode knee to knee with Ross St. John. He pointed out interesting landmarks, and she was constantly amazed by his intimate and extensive knowledge of the land, a knowledge which reached even beyond the vast boundaries of St. John holdings. Ross knew the mountains and deserts the way some people know the streets and buildings of a city. Jessica began to understand that for Ross St. John the land upon which he lived was an extension of himself.

The day was beginning to fade and the sun cast long, sharp shadows over the desert when they reached the beginning of the last steep descent. Ross decided not to risk the narrow, twisting road in the dying light and ordered them to camp on the plateau's rim. The chuck wagon and the tents were set up near the edge of a small arroyo, which cut across the desert floor and down into the steep face of the cliff. A tiny stream, almost dry, ran through the arroyo and then disappeared over the cliff's edge. It appeared to be their only source of water, so they had to clamber down the rocky sides of the arroyo to fetch it. While the cowboys busied themselves carrying up water for the other horses, Jessica led the sure-footed Spur down the eroded trail to the stream's edge. Here and there his iron-shod hoof rang on the stones, but he never lost his footing, and Jessica was proud of her little mount.

The stream itself was not deep enough to drink from directly, but one of the cowboys had dug a deep hole in the sandy bank and it gradually filled with murky water. Jessica waited until the hands had filled several buckets from this man-made pool, and then she let her mustang drink. Like a true veteran of the desert, he drank sparingly, and she did not have to pull his head away to keep him from gulping too much water too quickly. As she waited for Spur to slake his thirst, she heard a shower of pebbles clattering up above her. She looked up to see Ross St. John sliding down the precipitous trail. He joined her at the bottom, kneeling a few feet upstream to dig his own drinking hole in the sand. Then he splashed water on his face and slicked back his hair.

"Water!" he exclaimed as he stood up. "You don't really appreciate it till you get out here where it's in short supply." He turned toward her and smiled. "Men have tramped all over deserts and mountains looking for gold, but to my mind this muddy water is worth more than any precious metal. It's what keeps us all alive. And," he added, glancing up the arroyo, "there's been too damn little of it this year."

Jessica knew that he had been worried by the many low and dry streams they had encountered, especially on the latter part of their trip. Ross gazed down at the barely moving trickle at his feet.

"Too damn little or too damn much—that seems to be the usual state of affairs. You wouldn't believe it to look at it now, but I've seen this stream when it was a raging torrent almost up to the top of the bank."

Jessica glanced at the edge of the plateau high above her. It was hard to imagine the now dry arroyo filled with rushing water. But she had already heard many stories about the fury of desert storms and flash floods they can bring. Suddenly, she felt a little uneasy standing at the bottom of the canyon. She pulled Spur back toward the trail. Ross St. John followed her, and, in companionable silence, the two of them climbed up toward the camp.

Later that evening, after they had finished supper, Jessica felt restless. Excusing herself from the company, she wandered away from the flickering circle of campfire around which her companions had gathered, and headed toward the rim of the plateau. Here, from the shelter of a lone twisted piñon which clung to the edge of the precipice, she could view the shadowy desolation of the desert. From the campfire came muted voices, the strumming of a guitar, Serafina's silvery laughter floating on the night air—sounds strangely distant in the face of the scene spread before her. The sky was even more vast, the stars more brilliant than in the mountains, perhaps because no trees or mountain peaks intruded between her and the far circle of the horizon. Jessica marveled at the great expanse of darkness—even the lights of Las Vegas were too far away to be visible—and at the silky perfection of the night air on her skin.

Just as when she stood with Jeffrey on the high ridge of the Sangre de Christo range and gazed westward across the hills and mountains, the desert aroused a longing whose object she did not know, and her soul seemed to yearn for some distant place. What could be the source of such a longing, she wondered, when all she could possibly want in her life—a loving husband-to-be, a fine ranch of which she would soon become mistress, a land she loved on which to live—lay so close at hand?

A twig snapped behind her. Startled, Jessica spun around and then relaxed when she saw the broad shoulders of Ross St. John outlined against the night sky.

"This is one of my favorite views, too," he remarked as he joined her under the piñon. The sardonic tone of voice he often adopted when he spoke to her was missing tonight and his voice was soft, as if he too were affected by the peace and vastness of the night-shrouded desert.

"Kind of has a way of making you feel small, doesn't it," he went on, gesturing toward the scene before them. He leaned back against the gnarled tree trunk, his fingers hooked casually in his belt. "You know, sometimes I think about how hard I fight for what I have. Seems like I'm always struggling—against people, the weather, the land itself. And sometimes it all seems so useless. Like now. When I stand up here and look out like this, I figure we're all just tiny specks on a land that doesn't give a damn about us. It was here long before we were, and it won't care when we're gone."

Gazing out across the plateau below them, noting the dark splotches of trees against the silvered desert floor, she heard the soft hooting of an owl. She had her back turned to Ross, but she was acutely aware of his presence. She paused a moment before she replied. "But even if the land doesn't care—that doesn't matter does it? What's important is the way you care about the land." For some reason she didn't turn to look at him but kept her eyes on the scene before her.

"This land is my life's blood," Ross replied simply. "I couldn't live anywhere else. I'd die if I tried."

Jessica nodded.

"I know how you feel. Ever since I came here, I've loved everything about New Mexico—the desert, the mountains, the ranch—everything. If you lived here all your life, it must become a part of you."

She sensed that Ross had moved away from the tree. He laughed softly; his voice was almost in her ear.

"And to think how worried I was when Jeffrey wrote he'd gotten himself engaged. I figured you'd be some lace-covered lady, all prim and proper, someone who'd scream if she saw a lizard, and hate horses because they smell bad, and hate the ranch because it was stuck in the middle of nowhere. Little did I know my son had found himself a real daughter of the desert. The ranch means much more to you than it ever will to him. We're two of a kind, you and I." He bent closer. She could feel her heart pounding at his nearness and the sudden intimacy of his voice. "Two of a kind, Jessica. You know that, don't you?"

Jessica could think of no reply, and they stood there for a long moment, locked in companionable silence, bonded by their sharing of the beauty and wildness of their surroundings— bonded by something else too, something which made Jessica shiver.

"You getting cold?"

Jessica seized upon this excuse to break the moment.

"Yes, a little," she replied quickly, though the night was in fact quite warm. "I'm afraid I left my jacket back at camp. I'd better go get it."

She turned to leave, but Ross stepped in front of her, barring her way. He reached out and gripped her arms, and she could feel the strength of his hard fingers through the fabric of her shirt. With an effort she lifted her eyes to his.

"I can keep you warm, Jessica," he whispered. His voice was soft, persuasive. His gray eyes were veiled with a strange light. He bent his face toward hers.

"No!" she burst out in a shocked whisper. "Please, no." She tried to pull away, but his hands held her in a firm grip. He pulled her to him and held her against his chest, wrapping his arms around her in a strong embrace. She could feel the rapid beating of his heart beneath the flannel shirt. He smelled of wood smoke and the outdoors. Jessica tried to pull away. Then, realizing that her struggles were futile, she ceased to resist and let herself lean against him, the pounding of her own heart matching his. She could feel his lips pressing against her hair as he bent to kiss the top of her head. She lifted her face to his.

"Ross, please," she pleaded, her voice a low, tense whisper. "This is wrong. What if Jeffrey were to see us?" She could hear the desperation in her voice. She was afraid, not just of Ross, but of the tumultuous feelings that his touch had aroused in her.

He smoothed her hair back from her face and then gently caressed her cheek with his hand.

"You and Jeffrey—you're not really suited for each other. You know that, Jessica. You're too hot-blooded, too strong-willed for my son."

"That's not true! I love him. I'm pledged to him. I promised . . ." Her protests sounded weak in her own ears.

"A promise made before you came here," Ross interrupted. "A promise made in another world, before you saw what life could really hold for you here in New Mexico."

"What . . . what are you saying?" Jessica faltered. "What is it you want from me?"

As if in answer to her question, Ross bent his face to hers and kissed her fully on the lips. She pressed her hands against his chest as if to push him away, but his arms held her firmly, and as they tightened around her waist, she found her own arms reaching up to wind around his neck. She returned the kiss, hesitantly at first, then pressed her mouth firmly against his until the stiff bristles of his mustache rubbed her upper lip. His lips were hard against her own, his teeth sharp behind them. His tongue probed the edge of her trembling mouth. Without thinking, she curved her body against his, and he responded, pressing into her. The blood was pounding in her ears and her limbs felt weak and weightless. She knew that if she showed willingness, Ross St. John, unlike his son, would not pull back. The knowledge terrified her, and in a sudden burst of strength, she broke from Ross's embrace and stepped away.

He did not try to stop her but stood staring at her in the starlight. He was breathing heavily. For a long moment they stood there, neither of them speaking. Then Ross reached out and gently touched her cheek. She felt something in her go out to this man she had thought so crude and unlikable when they had first met. Through his veins flowed the same passion for life, for the land, for love, that flowed through hers.

Ross is right, she thought, we are alike. Only a few short weeks before, she would have scorned such a suggestion, but now she had a momentary wild desire to throw herself into his arms again, and follow him to wherever he would lead. But, with an effort, she held herself back.

Ross dropped his hand and then, wheeling abruptly on his heel, stalked off. She could hear the faint crunch of his boots on the rough ground as he made his way back toward the camp.

Jessica sagged against the twisted trunk of the piñon, her knees suddenly weak, her heart pounding, her mind in a tumult. How dare Ross accost her like that! How dare he say such things to her and take her in his arms and kiss her with such demanding passion. He must be mad to take such liberties with his son's fiancée.

And yet . . . and yet as the pounding of her heart began to subside, Jessica had to admit that it should have been clear to her for some time that Ross St. John's attentions to her were something more than the interest a man might take in a prospective daughter-in-law. His pleasure in her company was that which any man might take in being with an attractive woman. But it had never for a moment occurred to her that Ross would try to talk her out of her impending marriage. It was almost too shocking to contemplate. Even now, Jessica could not really believe it had happened.

And what of her own feelings? A hot wave of shame washed over her as she recalled how she had pressed her body hungrily to his. How could she have done that? Was she, a woman happily engaged to the son, now falling in love with the father? Was she really any less to blame than Ross for what had happened?

Slowly, Jessica made her way back to camp, pondering these bitter questions.

Chapter 11

"*Señor Hayden!*"

Annoyed by the loud voice hailing him, Reno paused deliberately for a moment at the doorway of the saddlery shop before he turned around.

The man hurrying toward him across the street was attracting a considerable amount of attention. As a self-proclaimed *bandido*, Pablo Ruiz did his best to look and act the part. Even in the rough and colorful crowds of Las Vegas, New Mexico, he cut a striking figure. A variety of suggestive scars marked his broad face, and gold teeth flashed beneath a bushy, drooping moustache. A leather cartridge belt was slung across his chest and he sported two large revolvers in elaborately tooled, leather holsters.

He acted the part too well, Reno reflected, as Pablo hoisted his formidable bulk onto the sidewalk and swaggered toward him. Reno did not mind the *bandido*, but Pablo was really too flamboyant a figure for Kincaid's purposes; the rancher had made a mistake in hiring him. He was also prone to giving long, boring, and probably fictitious recitals on his exploits, as Kincaid, and those unfortunate enough to be cornered by the Mexican, had discovered.

Reno did not like being accosted so noisily. He was uneasy in town, as it was.

"What is it, Ruiz? I have some errands to run and don't have time to chat."

The Mexican was unoffended by the other's tone.

"I'll wait out here till you finish," he replied cheerfully in his heavily accented English. "It's good to have someone on guard while you're inside, eh?" He favored Reno with a conspiratorial wink, enjoying his association with a notorious gunman. "Then we go on together to Señor Kincaid's mysterious meeting, okay?" he continued.

"It's a little early, still. Kincaid doesn't expect us till five or so."

"We take our time. It's a nice day for a little stroll. We watch the young ladies, maybe go down to the plaza and see who they have hanged today. Okay, as long as it's not us." He laughed and winked again.

Resigned to the inevitability of the other's company, Reno entered the saddlery shop and made his purchases. The *bandido* was waiting for him as he emerged, lounging with elaborate nonchalance against the side of the building, his bright eyes darting back and forth across the passing throng. He straightened up as Reno joined him, crushing the remains of the thin cigar he'd been smoking beneath the high heel of his boot.

"This meeting," he went on, continuing their previous conversation, "what's it all about?"

Reno shrugged.

"I have no idea. Sometimes Kincaid likes to play things close to the vest."

"Meetings," the Mexican grumbled. "Meetings and more meetings with all Kincaid's fancy friends. I came here for a little action—not for all this sitting around."

"You'll get action soon enough,"

"We've both missed some of it already. I—*I* could have shown them a raid. Why, when I was with . . ."

"I don't think Kincaid will try a stunt like that again," Reno interrupted, seeking to forestall the recital of another one of Pablo's exploits. "All he accomplished by that was to get St. John's guard up. He's not a man to turn tail and run."

As if to confirm his words, a wagon accompanied by a party of horsemen pulled to a halt in front of the Grand View Hotel, just across the street from where the two men stood. Despite the dust they stirred up, Reno had no trouble recognizing the tall powerful figure of Ross St. John. So the rancher was in town. That was interesting. Was he showing his face here just to show he was determined to fight, or did he have business? There were women with him, though. That made it look like an excursion. Reno watched with interest as the members of the party dismounted. The wagon was quickly unloaded and then it rumbled off, followed by the cowboys with the horses. Reno had a clear view of Jessica as she paused on the boardwalk in front of the hotel, gazing around in fascination.

"A beautiful señorita," Pablo exclaimed, his dark eyes gleaming.

She *was* beautiful, Reno reflected, even though dusty and tired from the long ride. And apparently she was already a close member of the St. John family. Both men seemed very attentive toward her, and Ross St. John even tucked his hand lightly under her elbow as he escorted her into the hotel lobby. It looked as if she had won over the father, just as she had the son. But that was hardly surprising. She could probably win most men over, and it was rumored that Ross St. John had a weakness for a pretty face.

"That young St. John, he is a lucky man," Pablo interrupted Reno's thoughts. "But I wonder now"—he turned toward Reno and winked again—"if he is man enough to hold her. A lovely thing like that—she is a fine armful for a real man's bed, is she not?"

"Let's get going. Kincaid's going to be waiting." Reno turned abruptly on his heel and strode down the street, leaving the Mexican hurrying to catch up with him.

Why had the man's words annoyed him, Reno asked himself. After all, Pablo, in his own crude way, had said no more than Reno himself had been thinking—that things didn't seem quite right for Jeffrey St. John's fiancée. Perhaps she was simply disturbed by the events of the past weeks. She probably had not expected such troubles in the little kingdom into which she was to marry.

He shrugged off his thoughts. It was no concern of his. Right now he had other things on his mind. Although he had too often shed blood to share Pablo's itch for action, he, too, hoped there would soon be an end to these meetings with Kincaid and his friends. Reno took no enjoyment from the many distractions which Las Vegas offered. There were too many people here to suit him, too many chances for his own past to turn up unexpectedly. Better the solitude of the mountains than this noisy, crowded town.

Sensing his companion's somber mood, Pablo maintained an uncharacteristic silence until they reached the Davis Building, where Kincaid's meeting was to be held. As if by mutual signal, both men stopped to survey the street before climbing the outside staircase to the second floor. Reno ascended cautiously, his senses alert, his hand never far from his gun. Like a shadow, the Mexican followed him, mimicking his every move. They paused at the door at the top of the stairs, and Reno knocked.

"Come in!" Kincaid's voice boomed into the hall. Not waiting for his words to be obeyed, the rancher flung open the door. The two gunmen entered a smoke-wreathed room, dimly lit by the fading light of late afternoon. A large baize-covered table dominated the center of the room, its neatly stacked chips and cards awaiting the poker game that would begin later in the evening. This floor of the Davis Building served as an annex to the Exchange Hotel, just across the street, and the rooms often accommodated the high rollers who thirsted for a little private action. Reno knew this evening's game would go far into the night, just as it had the night before.

"Where've you been?" Kincaid growled. He wore an elaborate brocaded frock coat and his thinning hair had been freshly slicked back from his face. "You knew I wanted you both here before the others came."

Reno merely favored the other man with a cold stare. He knew that he and Pablo were early. The only other person there was Kincaid's new hired gun, Jack Rutledge, a vicious-looking, young man with a pinched, hard face. Reno knew that Rutledge was someone to reckon with, and that sooner or later he would probably have to kill him. He did not look forward to the task.

Kincaid, growing nervous at Reno's silence, suddenly became conciliatory.

"Well, guess we're all here. I feel more confident, Hayden, with you here to back me up. And Jack and Pablo, too," he added hastily. "Here, have a seat."

Reno moved over to the window. He noted that Kincaid seemed ill at ease. The rancher was chewing nervously on a large unlit cigar. Rivulets of sweat trickled down his neck and under his tight, starched collar. It was stuffy in the room and no breeze stirred the grimy curtains at the open window. From the barroom in the Exchange Hotel across the street came sounds of revelry.

"St. John's in town," Reno remarked.

Kincaid jerked around in his chair.

"St. John? When did you see him?"

"About fifteen minutes ago. St. John, his son, his son's fiancée, and some Mexican woman all stopped at the Grand View."

Reno leaned casually against the wall on the opposite side of the window from Rutledge and began to roll a cigarette. Neither he nor the other gunman had taken a seat; both stood facing the door. Pablo, lacking a strategic place to position himself, was reduced to pacing back and forth at one end of the room.

"For God's sake, will you sit down," Kincaid snapped at the *bandido*. Pablo jumped at the other's tone and sank into a chair in the corner. He seemed a little subdued in the rancher's presence, though he flashed Reno another wink as if to deny that he could be intimidated. Reno ignored him.

Kincaid stood up, and now he began to pace.

"Ross St. John!" he practically spat out the name. "He's

got a nerve, showing his face like this. Thinks he owns the territory, that he's some sort of big man around here. But he's just a pompous bully, like his father. Everyone knows that St. John got the Running J by running off the old Mexican who owned it. He's got no more right to that place than a squatter has. Well, he's not going to be king of the Sangre de Christo much longer.''

Kincaid's tirade was interrupted by a discreet knocking, and he sprang toward the door. Three men entered. Reno recognized two of them, the lawyers Reston Montague and Charley Martin. The third man was a stranger. Kincaid ushered him in and shut the door.

''Afternoon, gents—or evenin', as the case may be. Please have a seat.'' Kincaid's voice was a little too loud and cordial as he gestured expansively at the chairs around the table. Reston Montague had picked up a cut-glass decanter and several glasses from the dresser before he sat down. The other lawyer introduced their companion.

''Kincaid, this here's Hoyle Holt. He's a cattle buyer out of Kansas City, and he might—just might—be interested in throwing in with us.''

Kincaid extended his hand. ''Pleased to meet you, Mr. Holt. I know you won't be sorry to get in on this deal once you hear the latest developments.''

Hoyle Holt was a large, florid man dressed in a somewhat travel-stained suit. He grunted in response to Kincaid's greeting and then lowered himself rather ponderously into a chair, setting his bowler hat on the table beside him. Reston Montague passed the decanter and the others helped themselves generously to its contents.

''All right, Kincaid, what's this all about? You said you wanted us here early to show us something special, so show us.''

''Looks like St. John's in town,'' the other lawyer interrupted. ''Saw him heading for Montero's just a few minutes ago.''

Kincaid settled back in his chair and filled his glass with whiskey.

"St. John's probably stirring up his friends. Maybe he thinks with their backing he can wiggle his way out of this."

"You don't seem too concerned."

"As long as we keep up the pressure and make sure our friend Judge Denton doesn't stray from the straight and narrow, we'll have St. John over a barrel and he knows it. That's why he's runnin' scared."

"You sure it ain't Denton who's runnin' scared?" Reston Montague seemed a little annoyed by Kincaid's overconfidence. "I heard he took off somewhere. That's going to delay this land-grant case some, isn't it? Or did he leave because he wants to back out of the deal?"

"Denton won't back out, and the delay will only work to our advantage, *if* we use the time to gather our support."

Reno watched Kincaid as he talked, knowing that despite his air of assurance, the rancher was worried. Reinhold, the eastern investor, had dropped out of their venture, and the Scotchman who had been looking for ranching investments had decided against joining the Burnt Cedar Cattle Company. In addition, several of Kincaid's local backers were growing doubtful about the outcome of Kincaid's fight against St. John.

"We can get even more support than we have now," Kincaid said. "Once the right people learn what I just learned today."

"Cut the mystery, Kincaid, and level with us. What the hell are you talking about?"

"Just be patient, gentlemen, just be patient. In a few minutes, I can show you something that will make your eyes pop, I guarantee it."

Though Kincaid's voice sounded confident, Reno noted that his glance kept darting toward the door.

"This better be good, Kincaid," Montague growled. "My time's valuable and I don't appreciate having it wasted."

"It's good all right. Good as my word. Good as gold." Kincaid chuckled, and then jumped, as a light, almost timid knock sounded at the door. He sprang up, but the door was already open. The men at the table turned to stare at the person who entered.

He was an unimposing figure, hardly seeming to warrant such intense interest. Part Indian, with a thin, weathered face and long, lank hair, he wore faded cowboy garb and elaborate but dusty, tooled leather boots.

"Lupe, come on in." Kincaid pulled the other man over to the table. "Have a seat and help yourself to the booze. Did you bring the stuff?"

The Indian nodded, but made no move to sit.

"Well, then"—Kincaid turned impatient—"why don't you let these gentlemen see what you found?"

Slowly Lupe reached into his pocket and pulled out a small leather sack. He tipped it upside down and a stream of gold nuggets tumbled onto the green table top, glinting in the dusty rays of the dying sun.

The men around the table stared for a moment. Then one of the lawyers reached out and tentatively fingered a nugget, turning it around in his hand. Kincaid lighted the oil lamp in the center of the table to give them more light, and then stood watching, a smug smile on his face. The men's eyes matched the shine of the gold as the nugget was passed from hand to hand.

"One hundred percent pure and genuine," Kincaid announced triumphantly. "And it all came from the Running J ranch."

"That's impossible." Charley Martin tossed the nugget back on the table.

"Not at all. I had it assayed this afternoon, and there's no doubt about it."

"Not that," the other returned impatiently. "I'm sure it's the real thing. But you know there's no gold on the Running J. We had that surveyor go over the place with a fine-tooth comb. Almost got caught a couple of times surveying right around the ranch. Didn't find as much as a flake."

"Its a big spread, got some rugged places. An old mine could be lost and never found, even by an expert."

"Are you claiming these nuggets are from that old Spanish

mine that's supposed to be on the Running J?'' Reston
Montague demanded.

"Well, I ain't sayin' they're right from the mine itself, but
I'm bettin' they're near it. 'Specially since we ain't found no
other sign of gold anywhere else on the ranch.''

"Where *were* they found?'' Hoyle Holt, who had been
following the conversation avidly, spoke for the first time.

Kincaid's face took on a crafty expression.

"Well, now, that's between Lupe and me. Let's just say he
found them washed down into a streambed somewhere on the
Running J, and we're both bettin' that the mine isn't too far
away.''

"How come he came to you instead of going to St. John?''

"Well, Lupe was engaged in, shall we say, not quite legal
activities involving some Running J cattle, when he stumbled
on this. He figured I might be interested and might pay him a
little better for his time than St. John would.''

"All that could be a hoax, a plant, either by you or the
Indian.''

Kincaid seemed undisturbed by the accusation.

"You can think what you want,'' he replied, "but I believe
Lupe's story, and, what's more, I'm convinced that this gold
came from the old mine. Here.'' He handed each of the men
a small nugget from the pile on the table. "Take these. I'm
sure each of you can think of someone to show them to. Once
the right people know there's gold on the ranch, we'll find
ourselves getting all the help we need.''

"I still think it's a hoax of some kind. It's just another one
of those legends about lost mines. They're a dime a dozen
around here. Nobody's ever seen it, nobody knows for sure
where it is.''

"There's somebody who knows.'' The old Indian spoke
for the first time. A surprised silence fell over the room, and
all eyes turned toward him. "They say the Valdez family has
always known,'' Lupe continued. "The knowledge passes
from father to son. Old Don Octaviano knows where the mine
is. Everyone knows he knows, but he's never told anyone his
secret.''

Hoyle Holt was growing impatient, his florid face drawn into a scowl. "Who the hell's Don Octaviano?"

"He's the old man who sold the ranch to the St. Johns," Kincaid explained. "The place was in his family for generations before that."

"Him? He's just a crazy old man." Charley Martin's voice was scornful. "I hear he wandered off for a couple years after he sold the ranch. When he returned, he'd completely lost his mind. Putters around with his goats on a bit of land St. John gave him. I wouldn't believe a thing he says."

"And if the Valdezes have known about the mine all these years, why haven't they done anything about it?" the other lawyer demanded.

The Indian shrugged. "They say there's a curse on it. That it brings only death."

"I never heard such a bunch of horse shit!" Reston Montague gulped down the rest of his whiskey and slammed down the glass.

But the men's eyes kept returning to the pile of nuggets in the center of the table. Kincaid had baited his line well, and though the fish might not know it, they were already hooked. The fools, Reno thought. They'll tear the land and each other to pieces to get that useless metal.

Heavy footsteps resounded on the stairs, and Kincaid hastily scooped up the remaining nuggets, stuffed them into the leather pouch, and tossed the pouch back to Lupe. The other men pocketed their samples.

"Remember," he warned, as loud rapping sounded on the door, "not a word of this to anyone."

The rest of the poker party burst into the room, and the gathering got down to what was for most of them the serious business of the evening. The Indian, Lupe, slipped quietly out of the room, and Reno followed, turning down Pablo's invitation for a drink. The happenings in the upstairs room had amused him, but now that Kincaid's secret meeting was over, Reno felt impatient with the people who surrounded him and restless from his long, enforced stay in town. He wished he could talk to Pete, but that would have to wait till he could return to Bernalillo. Maybe after that, he'd ride off into the desert for a few days. Kincaid wouldn't be needing him for a while. Nothing much was likely to happen until the court case was decided, and that wouldn't be for another few weeks.

Darkness had fallen when Reno reached the street, and, as usual, the Las Vegas night was raucous and lively. Laughter, light, and music spilled out onto the sidewalk from the saloons. But these had little appeal for Reno. His restless steps carried him down the boardwalks and into the New Town area—East Las Vegas it was now called. As he passed the doorway of another saloon, he spotted a familiar figure. Quickly he turned and stepped back into the shadows. Ross St. John strode boldly across the boardwalk and entered the swinging doors of Close and Patterson's dance hall.

Reno had to admire the man's courage—or at least his arrogance. True, Ross had a gun strapped to his hip, but he was alone and otherwise unprotected in a town full of enemies. Yet he walked as if he owned the streets. Reno watched as the doors of the dance hall swung shut behind the rancher, and then, on impulse, followed him inside.

He paused a moment to let his eyes adjust to the brightly lighted interior, then glanced about him with his customary caution, before moving toward a far corner of the bar. He ordered a double whiskey from the bewhiskered bartender and sipped it slowly as he watched the crowd of patrons standing up at the bar and thronging the tables and dance floor. A large sign over the bar proclaimed: EVERYONE ENTERTAINED IN THE BEST POSSIBLE MANNER. All the girls of Close and Patterson's were doing their best to make certain this promise was fulfilled. A tall, blond woman in a blue satin dress spotted Reno as he came in, and detaching herself from a knot of her sisters, she sauntered toward him, a professional smile carefully arranged on her face. But as she neared the bar, she stopped, disconcerted by the coldness of his glance. With an exaggerated shrug of nonchalance, she turned away and moved on to more promising prospects.

Reno observed that Ross St. John had no objections to the companionship the dance hall offered. The rancher was standing at the other end of the bar, engaged in animated conversation with a dark-haired beauty for whom he had just ordered a drink. The woman leaned seductively against him, revealing the tops of her generous breasts above the low, red-lace bodice of her dress.

Reno wondered why he had bothered to come in. The cheap whiskey burned his throat, and he felt distant from the festivities around him. He was overwhelmed by a sudden feeling of loneliness. Somewhere in the past he had chosen to walk a trail apart from other men, and while for the most part he had few regrets, there were times, like tonight, when the consequences of his decision came to haunt him. As he watched St. John, he felt a bitter stab of envy. The man seemed so confident, almost arrogantly at ease in whatever surroundings he found himself. What would it be like, Reno wondered, to have the power and wealth that someone like St. John commanded, to be a man to whom other men deferred, and to whom women gravitated like moths to a flame. He himself commanded the respect of other men only through his gun. And as for women . . . Reno gazed coldly at the bright moths of the dance hall, fluttering around their customers, swaying in time to the music. How long had it been since he had enjoyed the company of a woman? Not since Sarah, and that now seemed very long ago.

He gulped down the rest of his drink. Then, unable to bear the bright lights and gaiety any longer, he left. Ross St. John's hearty laugh rang out behind him as Reno strode into the night.

Chapter 12

After their two-and-a-half-day journey through the wilderness, life in Las Vegas was something of a shock. Jessica could hardly imagine a greater contrast to the peace of the mountains and the vastness of the desert than the rawness, noise, and crowds of town. Yet Las Vegas was fascinating in its own way, with its stores, restaurants, saloons, and dance halls. Many businesses stayed open into the night. Indeed, Las Vegas seemed even more lively after dark than it did during the day, and sometimes Jessica found it difficult to sleep.

Both Jessica and Serafina enjoyed Jeffrey's company as they made their rounds of the stores, purchasing supplies for themselves and the ranch. It was good to have masculine protection in the jostling crowds, especially when they passed the saloon, where the mostly male, generally drunk clientele never failed to notice the passage of two attractive women. Much to Jeffrey's annoyance, Jessica would try to peek into these establishments as they walked by. He thought her curiosity improper, but Jessica was fascinated by the raucous life within and by the gaudy ladies who lounged against the bar.

She even thought of asking Ross St. John to escort her into such a place. She suspected that Ross might find it amusing, but she knew Jeffrey would be angry, especially if Ross decided to humor her whim.

Jessica had no need to buy anything in Las Vegas, but she enjoyed browsing through the stores with Serafina and helping to select material in the dry goods store for dresses for the fiesta. Serafina persuaded Jessica to order a pair of tooled, Mexican, leather boots, and Jessica almost bought a broad-brimmed black felt hat with a silver and turquoise band. At the last minute she decided that her faithful sombrero was more practical for riding, and reluctantly set the more dashing hat aside. She and Serafina also visited the book store in search of fresh reading matter. They were delighted to find that the store had just received a shipment of novels from the East. Jessica also bought two books in Spanish, which Serafina assured her she would soon be able to read if her progress in that language continued to advance as rapidly as it had been doing.

Although shopping had been one of the major purposes of their trip, it proved to be the least time-consuming of their activities. To Jessica's surprise, their social life in Las Vegas was quite lively. Many of the St. Johns' friends had not seen Jeffrey for some time and they were eager to meet his fiancée. Although everyone was polite and friendly to her, and English was always spoken in deference to her still-limited Spanish, Jessica still felt left out occasionally as Ross and Jeffrey exchanged news and local gossip over leisurely luncheons and lingering dinners. She tried to listen carefully to everything that was said, determined to learn all she could about this world which would very soon be hers.

Jessica became especially fond of the Monteros, an old established family of Mexican descent, who owned a dry goods store and several buildings, and lived in the Old Town area. They had three beautiful daughters, ranging from ten to eighteen, and Jessica admired the grace and elegance that all of them, even the youngest, displayed. At first, they greeted her with shy reserve, and then, as they warmed up to her, plied her with questions about life in New York. The Monteros' son, who was Jeffrey's age, had gone with some friends on a fishing trip in the mountains just before they arrived, much to Jeffrey's disappointment.

During dinner at the Monteros' modest but tastefully furnished house, conversation ranged over a wide variety of topics. Jessica listened in fascination, but she was somewhat shocked when, after dinner was over, Señora Montero and the other women present joined the men in smoking thin, dark cigarillos.

Ross recounted to his host their troubles with Kincaid, and Señor Montero listened intently. His face was calm, but his dark eyes flashed with anger as Ross told him about the raid on the ranch.

"He has grown even bolder than I thought he would, this Kincaid," he commented when Ross had finished. "He himself is nothing, really, a man of no consequence, not even a very good rancher, from what I hear. But he has managed to collect some powerful friends who wouldn't mind using him to gain control of the Running J."

"Well, they'll have a fight on their hands, I promise you that," Ross responded grimly. "Even with all his friends and hired guns, he won't find it an easy task to drive me out."

"No one doubts your courage or your determination, my friend, but it won't hurt for us to see what other help we can bring to your side. I have many friends, some of them in high places, who are not happy with the way Kincaid and his sort are trying to run the territory."

"What chance do you think this court case has?"

Señor Montero considered the question carefully, stroking his neat, dark moustache with one hand.

"It is hard to say. Certainly Denton is as crooked a judge as ever sat on a bench, but the power of the Santa Fe Ring has grown weaker in recent months. Do not worry. Even if Kincaid gets a favorable ruling, we will appeal and seek delays."

"If Kincaid waits for that. I have a feeling this whole affair is more likely to end in gunplay."

Señor Montero nodded sadly.

"It may be as you say. Yes, it may very well be as you say. But let us hope otherwise."

From there the conversation turned to corruption in territorial politics. As Señor Montero pointed out, in certain counties, it seemed, even the sheep were voting. Then, they discussed the latest finds of Adolf Bandelier, the Swiss-born archaeologist who worked for the American Archaeological Institute. Bandelier had made some fascinating discoveries of ancient Indian ruins—whole cliffs lined with the remains of dwellings built right into the rock walls, deserted villages tucked in remote mountain canyons. Jeffrey was excited to learn that the Monteros had met Bandelier the year before in Santa Fe, and he quizzed them further about the archaeologist's finds. Jessica became excited, too, recalling her father's many tales of Indian ruins and legends of lost peoples. Later, she and Jeffrey discussed the possibility of organizing an expedition to some of the ruins so that Jeffrey could sketch them.

Jessica kept busy with other activities, as well. She and Jeffrey saw a performance of Gilbert and Sullivan's *Pirates of Penzance* at the Opera House and attended a dance at the Montezuma, a resort hotel a few miles outside Las Vegas. The hotel, built by the Atchison, Topeka, and Santa Fe railroad, had been completed only a few years before, but had already attracted many wealthy vacationers from both the East and abroad, who came to enjoy the famous hot springs located nearby. Jessica was glad she had brought a few evening dresses, for she found herself in glittering company. She met several members of the European nobility, including an English earl and a German countess, and chatted with a senator, a famous author, and several other notables from the East. As she danced with Jeffrey to a lilting Viennese waltz, Jessica glanced around the spacious ballroom filled with whirling, stylish couples, and found it hard to believe that only a few days earlier she had been camping in the desert.

But life in Las Vegas also had a wild side. There were several shootings during their stay, one of them fatal. Such incidents, Jessica learned, had come to be regarded as normal, and each morning, people would routinely inquire how many men had been shot the night before. Sometimes the citizenry took justice into its own hands. Mobs had been known to storm the jail, demanding that notorious lawbreakers be released to them. Such criminals then met a speedy and unceremonious death by hanging in the plaza. Jessica was appalled by these stories, but she could see how people might be driven to such desperate measures. Since the arrival of the railroads, Las Vegas had been overrun with gamblers, gunmen, and thieves, and had acquired a reputation that rivaled that of any other town in the Wild West.

Jessica had little opportunity to be alone with Ross St. John during their stay, a situation for which she was grateful. The memory of that night on the plateau lingered, vivid and painful, and she could not banish it from her mind. When she closed her eyes, she could still taste Ross's lips on hers and feel his strong hands around her waist. But she also missed Ross's company. He was very busy with his own affairs in town, and Jessica saw him only for dinner at the houses of his friends, or in brief encounters when they passed each other in the hallway of the hotel. Ross declined Jeffrey's invitation to come to the dance with them, thus saving Jessica from a situation both exciting and painful to contemplate, of having Ross hold her in his arms again.

Ross seemed to be drinking a lot, more than Jessica had known him to do on the ranch. She did not know if he drank because of her, or if he simply found more opportunities in town. In any case, it disturbed her. Liquor intensified Ross's sarcastic manner, sometimes to the point of ugliness.

Though she saw little of Ross, Jessica found that he was constantly in her thoughts, and she wondered if she really had fallen in love with him. If so, she must be a very wicked and fickle person to feel this way about the father of her fiancé. Jeffrey loved her so deeply, and she had been certain she loved him in return. How could she so quickly turn away from the man to whom she had promised herself, and be drawn to someone else instead? And yet she knew that Jef-

frey, handsome and gentle as he was, did not strike sparks
from her the way Ross did. With Jeffrey she had the vague
sense of something missing, of a gap between them, which
seemed to have widened in the last few weeks. But she did
still want Jeffrey, didn't she? After all, that night in the forest
when they . . . when she had almost . . . she must indeed be
wicked if she could transfer her desires so easily from one
man to another.

She tried to persuade Jeffrey to have a quiet wedding while
they were still in Las Vegas.

"Are you in such a hurry?" He smiled at her fondly,
obviously mistaking the source of the urgent appeal.

Jessica nodded, unable to say more, not wishing to lie
about the reason for her haste. He drew her to him, flattered
by her impatience.

"You know we can't do that, Jessica," he told her gently.
"It wouldn't be right to wed in such haste. Just be patient. It
won't be long. I'll ask father about announcing our engagement at the fiesta. Then, come September, we can go back to
New York and be married properly, as you deserve. Time
will pass quickly. You'll see."

She clung to him.

"I'm so afraid."

"Afraid? But of what? Nothing can harm you." His arms
tightened around her.

"I'm afraid something terrible will happen and I'll lose
you."

"Nothing will happen. I won't let anything happen. I love
you so, Jessica. If I lost you, I would die."

Ashamed and miserable, Jessica said nothing. If Jeffrey
only knew what she was really like, she thought, he would
never want to marry her. But she would never let him know.
She would resolutely crush whatever desire she felt for Ross
St. John and carry her feelings of guilt buried deep inside her.
She would work hard to be the good wife Jeffrey deserved.

The night before their return to the ranch, Jessica had
difficulty settling down to sleep. Her bags were packed and
waiting by the door, her traveling clothes laid out across a

chair. There was nothing further for her to do, so Jessica changed into her nightclothes and stretched out on the bed with a book. Maybe if she read for a while, she would become sleepy.

She had been reading for about half an hour when she was startled by a knock on the door. She glanced at the little clock by the bed. It was late, almost midnight. Who could be disturbing her at this hour?

Rising from her bed, Jessica padded barefoot across the carpet and cautiously opened the door. Ross St. John loomed in the doorway, outlined against the dim light of the gas lamp in the hall. He wore evening clothes, and although he seemed steady on his feet, she could smell whiskey on his breath. They stared at each other a moment before he spoke.

"Well, aren't you going to invite me in?" His words were spoken mockingly, but his voice was hoarse and underlaid with a strange urgency.

"Are you crazy?" she whispered, terrified that someone would see him standing outside the door. "What are you doing here? What if Jeffrey comes by?"

Ignoring her protests, Ross pushed the door open further.

"Well, if you won't invite me in, reckon I'll just have to invite myself."

He shouldered past her and stepped inside, shutting the door. Jessica backed away from him, into the center of the room.

"Ross, what are you doing? This is madness. What if Jeffrey . . ." She tried to remain calm but was rapidly becoming alarmed.

Ross made an impatient gesture.

"The hell with Jeffrey. You aren't right for him, anyway. He hasn't got the guts to stand up for himself, to take what he wants. But I have. And when I know what I want, I don't let anything stop me."

Jessica was frightened now. Ross must be very drunk to be speaking to her like this. She remembered that night on the desert plateau and suddenly felt very vulnerable, acutely conscious of her own state of undress and of the silence of the hotel around her. She backed a few feet farther into the room, but found her passage blocked by the bed. Uncertainly, she tried to edge around it, toward the window, away from Ross.

He made no move toward her, but stood slumped against the door, staring at her. His eyes glowed like coals in the lamplight.

"You're beautiful," he whispered hoarsely. "You're a woman made for a man, Jessica—for a real man. It's going to take a real man to tame you, to hold you, to satisfy you."

"Please go away," Jessica urged, her knuckles white as she clutched the brass railing of the bed for support. "This is madness for you to be here like this. Please. Please leave."

Ross gazed at her a moment without speaking. Then, abruptly, he straightened up. He swept off his hat and made Jessica a mocking bow.

"Excuse me for disturbing you like this, ma'am," he drawled. "I reckon I must be a little bit drunk."

He left before Jessica could respond, shutting the door softly behind him. She could hear his heavy footsteps on the carpet as he strode down the hallway toward his room.

The return trip to the ranch was somewhat subdued. The cowboys were more exhausted from their excesses in town than from a week of hard work on the range. Even Bart Adams was gruffer than usual. The wagon was laden with purchases, and their progress was slow as they toiled under the fierce desert sun up the steep inclines to the plateaus and then climbed the rugged slopes of the mountains. Nonetheless, Jessica was glad to leave Las Vegas. The town and the crowds had begun to oppress her and it was good to be outdoors again. As she rode she recalled an incident that had occurred just as they were leaving. Crossing the crowded boardwalk to the hitching rail, she had collided with one of the passersby. Strong fingers gripped her arm briefly to steady her, and Jessica looked up into a lean, hard face with deep lines running like scars on either side of the mouth. A pair of cold, gray eyes regarded her intently for a moment before the man, murmuring an apology, released his grip and moved on.

His gun, deadly low on his hip, brushed against her as he passed, and Jessica shuddered. It was with relief that she had mounted Spur and joined the Running J caravan, heading away from that violent town.

Jeffrey, on the other hand, had enjoyed their stay in Las Vegas and he rode now with Serafina, the two of them chatting happily together.

Perhaps Jeffrey would really be happier with Serafina, Jessica reflected. This thought, which several weeks earlier would have aroused jealousy, now suggested a solution to her dilemma. For a brief moment, Jessica fantasized herself with Ross St. John, and Jeffrey with Serafina, all living happily on the Running J. But then, ashamed, she suppressed the idea. Jeffrey's feelings for the young Mexican woman were nothing more than what he had told her they were—that of a brother toward a sister. As for herself and Ross—she let her thoughts go no further.

Ross St. John did not take any pains to avoid Jessica on the trip back, nor did he seek out her company as he had before. Now and then he drew up alongside her to exchange a remark or two, his manner self-consciously casual.

For the most part, Jessica rode alone, wrapped up in her own gloomy thoughts. A part of her questioned whether she could really go through with her marriage plans, full of doubts and questions as she was. But if she called off the wedding, what would she do? She could hardly turn to her fiancé's father. Obviously, the best thing to do would be to return to New York. But the idea filled her with despondency. To be once again dependent upon her mother, confined by the city, instead of becoming mistress of the Running J and enjoying the power and freedom such a position offered—such a vision of her future was painful to contemplate. Besides, she loved the wild beauty of New Mexico, and she loved these two men who loomed so large in her life, though each in a different way. Her heart and her future were here. She could not leave it all now and return to the East.

And what of Jeffrey? He loved her and had told her he would die if he lost her. How could she leave him? She was being selfish to think only of her own feelings; she had other people to consider.

As they climbed into the pine-scented mountains, the clear, cooler air seemed to lift everyone's spirits. Then, late in the afternoon of the third day, they descended into the valley where the ranch house lay. Seeing the fenced pastures, the cozy cluster of buildings set against the pines, and a thin spiral of smoke rising from the kitchen chimney, Jessica felt she was truly coming home. The events of the past days began to fade into the background and her hopes began to rise again. Surely, things would work out somehow.

Upon their arrival, the ranch yard burst into a flurry of activity. Donaciana bustled out of the kitchen to help unload supplies, and Old Tom, the foreman Riordon, and several of the hands came striding from the bunkhouse to greet them and hear the news. Jessica led Spur into the stable to unsaddle and groom him. She preferred to perform these chores herself rather than entrust them to one of the cowboys. He was happiest when she did it and had occasionally tried to nip when other people touched him. Jessica hummed softly as she worked, contentment stealing over her. The little mustang stood docilely under the vigorous brushing, enjoying the attention. After she finished grooming him, she would tend to herself. Jessica looked forward to the luxury of a long, hot bath to melt away her aches and the dirt of the trail.

So absorbed was she in her thoughts that Jessica did not even hear Ross St. John coming into the stable until he was right behind her.

As soon as she turned, she knew something was wrong. Ross's face was dark with anger and his eyes flashed. Jessica felt a cold, hard knot forming in the pit of her stomach.

"I just talked to Jeffrey." Ross spoke evenly, but it was obvious that he was struggling for control. "He took the opportunity of our homecoming to inform me of his—your— plans."

So that was it. Jessica waited, not saying anything, striving to stay calm.

"You two must have had a really good time plotting

behind my back," Ross continued, his voice beginning to rise. "Getting married in New York, going to Europe, Jeffrey following his ridiculous notions of being an artist. You must have had a good laugh to yourselves every time I talked about the ranch, my plans, how you would someday run the Running J."

"That's not how it was at all," Jessica protested. "We never thought of it that way; we never made fun of your plans. We aren't leaving the Running J forever. It's just that Jeffrey . . ."

Ross ignored her.

"To think I pinned my hopes on you. I saw you as the daughter I never had, someone like me, who would love the ranch as I love it. I thought you were on my side, but now you turn around and betray me."

"Jeffrey's my fiancé. It's my duty to support him." Jessica spoke with more calmness than she felt.

Ross stared at her scornfully.

"Well, you needn't worry. I won't stand in the way of your plans," he sneered. "You'll get your wedding announcement and your trip to Europe. I won't force you to stay here. In fact, I'd just as soon get rid of both of you."

"It won't be forever, Ross. Please be reasonable." Jessica, trying to be placating, laid her hand on his sleeve. "We'll be back. Jeffrey loves the ranch, just like I do. We aren't deserting you or the Running J. Just give Jeffrey a chance to do what he wants to do. It won't be for that long. He'll want to come back here in the end. I know he will."

Ross shook off her hand.

"I should have known better than to trust a woman," he responded coldly. "Conniving little bitches, all of you. Well, I hope you're satisfied. I hope you've gotten what you want."

Stung, Jessica stepped back.

"It's not . . . not what I want," she murmured. "It's Jeffrey who . . ." She stopped, afraid of revealing too much of her own feelings and doubts.

Ross leaned forward, placing his arms against the stall

behind her, imprisoning her with his body. He didn't touch her but his closeness was palpable. His eyes bored into hers.

"And you, Jessica," he hissed. "What is it that *you* want?"

Their gaze met and she knew that in hers he could read the answer to his question. She let out a long shuddering breath and closed her eyes. When she opened them, he was gone.

Mechanically, she put away the grooming brush and comb, and led Spur to the stable door. She felt numb and drained, her peace of the moment before totally shattered.

As she turned Spur loose in the fenced pasture, she saw Riordon watching her from the doorway of the stable, his gaze bold and calculating. How much of her exchange with Ross St. John had he seen and heard, she wondered uneasily. She gave Spur a pat on the rump to send him foward, and closed the gate. As she walked toward the house, she felt the foreman's eyes burning into her back. But when she turned, he was gone.

Chapter 13

Jessica had little time to brood over her confrontation with Ross, for they soon found themselves with more important matters on their minds. While they were at breakfast the following morning, one of the line riders galloped into the yard, clutching his bloody arm. He almost fell from the saddle as he reined up, and as they helped him into the kitchen to wash and bind his wound, he gasped out a tale of a midnight raid on one of the line camps. Several masked men had attacked while he was asleep and driven off several dozen head of cattle. He had been wounded when he shot at them with his rifle, and they returned his fire. While Serafina doctored the cowboy, Ross sent for the buggy to take him to the doctor in Bernalillo, and then he dispatched several armed men to the line camp to track down the rustlers and stand guard over the remaining cattle. He also sent men to the other line camps, along with several supply-laden mules. They were to remain there until further notice. Obviously, one man at each camp was no longer sufficient.

"You think Kincaid's behind this?" Jeffrey asked his father as the men rode off.

Ross shrugged.

"Hard to say. Rustling goes on all the time, though this is bolder than petty rustlers usually get. And these seem to be pretty well-informed about where we're grazing and where my men are—and aren't. If we could track this bunch down, maybe we could get some kind of proof to hang on Kincaid's door. But I'm afraid they've got too much of a head start. And we've had so little rain, the ground's hard as a rock. I doubt Doan and the boys are going to be able to find much."

But the cattle rustling was not the most disturbing piece of news they were to receive that day. Not long after the buggy bearing the wounded cowboy left for Bernalillo, a young boy came running up the trail from the village, breathless from his exertions and pale-faced with the horror and importance of his news. He sat in a chair on the porch while the members of the household listened in shocked disbelief to his tale.

It's Don Octaviano, he told them, his words coming in hoarse gasps as he tried to catch his breath. Just that morning, shortly after daybreak, a young woman of the village, Maria Felicia—Don Rosario knew her—a cousin of Pedro, the muleteer, had gone to inquire whether Don Octaviano had fresh eggs. She wanted them for her mother who was ailing again. When she'd arrived at the cottage, she hadn't seen Annunciata or the old man anywhere, which was strange for they were both usually up early—Don Octaviano liked to work in his garden in the early morning, while it was still cool. The girl had called Annunciata's name, and then, receiving no answer, she had stepped inside the doorway of the hut. Just inside the doorway—here the boy paused a moment—just inside, sprawled across the dirt floor, was Annunciata, dead, and beyond, barely visible in the dim light of the hut, was the old man, also dead, his body tied to a chair, his face streaked with blood. Panicked by the sight, the young woman fled back to the village. Several of the village men had armed themselves and set out for the hut. Don Octaviano, they found, had been brutally tortured before he died, and Annunciata had been beaten and raped.

Before the boy had finished his recital, Donaciana burst

into tears. While Serafina tried to comfort her mother, Ross gave orders for several of his men to join the villagers in their search for the killers, and arranged for the buckboard to carry Serafina and Donaciana to the village.

"Tell them I'll be there shortly," Ross told Riordon as the foreman and his small posse made ready to leave. "Just as soon as I can get things in order here. And tell them there's a good reward for the first man who finds the tracks leading to the murderers."

Numbly, Jessica helped Serafina pack clothing for herself and her mother and food for the *velorio*, the wake which would be held that night, and they loaded the buckboard. It was hard to comprehend that the gentle, aristocratic Don Octaviano, an old man interested only in his garden and his chickens, could have died such a violent death. And the shy, plump Annunciata . . . Jessica's mind recoiled in horror from contemplating the young woman's death. Would that have been her own fate if the outlaw who attacked her had not been interrupted in his act?

Once the buckboard had departed with a driver and an armed guard, the ranch suddenly seemed very quiet. Jessica was glad when Ross St. John, preparing to depart for the village, curtly refused Jeffrey's request that he be allowed to go along.

"No, you need to stay here with Jessica and guard the ranch. We're spread too thin as it is. I'm not sure all this isn't just a plot to draw us out. You need to double the guards at the pastures. And Jessica," he turned to her, his face grim, "you get out your rifle and keep it ready."

She nodded, too frightened to speak.

"Kincaid again, then?" Jeffrey's tone was sober but calm.

"Could be, though I would've thought that torturing old men and killing girls would be a bit beneath him. Guess with skunks like that you just never can tell."

"But why?" Jessica burst out. "Why would anyone want to kill Don Octaviano?"

Ross shrugged.

"To get at me, maybe—to intimidate the villagers so they'll

be afraid to give me their support. That's why I have to go down there now, to let them know I'm not just going to stand by when something like this happens.''

"The gold mine." Jeffrey spoke suddenly.

"What are you talking about?" Ross stared impatiently at his son.

"It must have something to do with the gold mine. It's always been rumored that Don Octaviano knew about the gold mine but he would never tell anyone. That's probably why he was tortured—for information about the mine.''

Ross snorted. "You've got that gold mine on the brain.''

"Nothing else makes sense," Jeffrey insisted quietly. "Somebody—Kincaid or somebody else—wanted to know the location of the mine. There's no other explanation.''

Jessica stood on the veranda at Jeffrey's side as Ross rode away. He put his arm around her and drew her close. The day was clear, and the mountains shone in the distance. Despite the warmth of the sun, Jessica shivered.

"Do you suppose they found what they were after?" she whispered.

"Who knows? Perhaps. Don Octaviano was a tough and courageous man, but if they threatened Annunciata . . .''

"Maybe there really is a curse on the mine." Jessica recalled what Jeffrey had said the night of their first supper with Ross St. John.

"I know there is. Don Octaviano is not the first to die for it, nor will he be the last.''

Jessica did not question the accuracy of Jeffrey's prediction. As she gazed down the road at the rapidly disappearing figure of Ross St. John, a deep sense of foreboding crept over her. The woods and mountains, normally so inviting, now appeared dark and sinister. The Sangre de Christo—the Blood of Christ—the name suddenly took on a new and menacing significance.

Despite their determined efforts, Ross and his men were unable to pick up any clear trails. The rustlers seemed to have vanished into thin air. They did find some hoofprints in the

creek below Don Octaviano's house, but they were those of a
lone rider, which seemed odd if the murder had been carried
out by Kincaid or his men. Other than this, there were no
clues, since the murderer's trail disappeared abruptly in the dry
hills, and no amount of patient circling enabled them to pick
it up again. Ross St. John returned from the search, dusty and
grim, and sent one of his men to report the crimes to the
sheriff.

"Not that Pete can do anything," he growled, "but it
should keep him busy for a while. Two murders, a shooting,
and cattle rustling, all in one day and all on the Running J."

Later that night as she lay in bed, Jessica pondered the
paradox of her experiences in New Mexico. For every moment of happiness and delight in the land had also come pain
and disappointment, violence and fear. It was as if one had to
pay, and sometimes dearly, for the riches the land had to
offer. As she drifted into uneasy sleep, Jessica dreamed of a
distant land, a clean, free place, unspoiled by violence and
greed. Somewhere such a place existed, floating on the pe-
riphery of her vision. But before she could arrive, she was
asleep.

The next morning, Jessica was up early. She washed and
then donned the gray traveling suit she had selected for the
funeral the night before. She carefully brushed her hair into a
chignon, and then put on the matching hat.

She and Jeffrey would accompany Ross St. John in the
buggy, escorted by several heavily armed villagers who had
arrived early that morning to do them the honor of providing
protection. Jessica knew that Ross was pleased by their arrival, both because it indicated the respect in which he was
held and because it would allow him to leave more men to
guard the ranch while they attended the funeral.

When she emerged, Ross and Jeffrey were waiting for her
in the living room, somber and handsome in their black
broadcloth suits. With the troubles which had recently descended upon them, any animosity or ill-feeling which Ross
St. John might have harbored toward her seemed to have

dissipated. He was sober but cordial as he offered her his arm. They went outside and he lifted her into the buggy. Accompanied by their rather formidable armed escort, they set off down the road toward the village.

The road provided a less precipitous approach to the village than the path Jessica and Serafina had taken the morning they visited Don Octaviano. It was also longer. Jessica could see why the Mexican girl had preferred to make her journey on foot. The bells in the tower of the little adobe church were already beginning to ring as the buggy rolled into the village square. In addition to the entire village, other mourners had come to pay their respects, and the crowd overflowed the church, spreading out from the carved wooden doors into the square. They left the buggy under a large oak at the far end of the square and made their way to the church.

When they saw Ross St. John, the crowd parted, leaving a passage for the three of them to enter. Inside the church, more people moved aside, and room was cleared for them at the wooden pew in the back. But since most of those gathered in the church had no seats, Jessica and the St. Johns remained standing so that they could observe the services over the sea of heads.

Jessica had never attended a Catholic service—the mournful cadences of the Latin mass, the heavy scent of incense and candle wax, the huge wooden statue of a gaunt and bloody Christ which dominated the altar—all these created a somber mood. Her eyes were drawn to the two flower-draped caskets. It was hard to believe they contained the remains of two people who had so recently been vitally alive. All around her, women clad in black were weeping openly and loudly. Jessica had never before seen such a violent public display of emotion. Almost despite herself, she was drawn into their grief. She had to blink back the tears forming in her eyes. Jeffrey noticed her emotion and gently squeezed her arm. Pressed against the back of the church by the crowd of mourners and overwhelmed by the alien mysteries of the Catholic ceremony, Jessica was grateful for his reassuring presence.

After the service, the caskets were borne in solemn proces-

sion to the small, weed-choked cemetery behind the church.
There they were lowered into shallow graves scraped out of
the hard earth. As the first shovelfuls of dirt rattled on the
caskets, several of the women broke into loud wailing, and
Jessica was struck by the heavy finality of death. She saw
Serafina on the other side of the graves, supporting a weeping
Donaciana. As the grave diggers continued their somber shov-
eling, Jessica turned away and followed Ross and Jeffrey
through the chipped and tilting headstones to the village
square.

Manuel Valdez was leaning against a tree in front of the
church, as if he had been waiting for them. He wore a dark
suit, shiny and faded from age but carefully cleaned and
pressed. Ross St. John strode up to him and clasped his hand.

"I can't tell you how grieved I am at your father's death,
Manuel. You know I thought of him as my own family. I
won't rest until we track down the killers."

Manuel's gold tooth flashed briefly as he returned the other
man's handshake.

"Don't worry, Señor Ross. They won't get away. We'll
take care of that."

Jessica wondered to whom his confident "we" referred,
but Ross St. John seemed to understand.

"Well, you know that all the resources of the Running J
are at your command."

"I know that, Señor Ross, and I thank you." Jessica
sensed a slightly mocking note in Manuel's voice, but if Ross
noticed it, he gave no sign. A strange equality existed between the well-dressed prosperous rancher and the shabby
Mexican wagoneer.

Manuel Valdez gave Jessica a courtly bow as she and the
St. Johns moved away, his dark eyes regarding her speculatively
from under his bushy brows. She responded with a nod and
an uncertain smile. She never knew how to behave with this
man whose relationship with the St. Johns was filled with so
many contradictions. In addition, Manuel seemed to take an
inordinate interest in her. She was not certain why, and his
interest made her uneasy.

From the square, they made their way to the small adobe house of Donaciana's cousin, Maria. There a composed Donaciana, along with Serafina and other relatives of the deceased, served food and drink to those who had come to pay their respects. Jessica felt out of place among these people who had known each other all their lives, and she stayed close to Jeffrey as he moved easily through the room, shaking hands and offering his condolences in Spanish. She had no opportunity to speak to Serafina, who moved busily among the guests, carrying a tray laden with small glasses of brandy, but the young woman caught Jessica's eye as she paused and gave her a quick, friendly wink. The reassuring gesture warmed her and made her feel less a stranger in these ceremonies of death.

It was midday by the time they climbed into the buggy for their journey back to the ranch. The complement of armed villagers resumed its position as escort and the cavalcade headed out of the village. Neither Ross nor Jeffrey seemed inclined to converse, and Jessica was glad of the opportunity to sit quietly with her thoughts.

What would come of all this, she wondered. Where would all this violence and tragedy lead them? Underneath the obvious horror were ominous undercurrents she did not comprehend. She recalled Manuel Valdez's remark to them at the cemetery. "We'll take care of that," he had said. Who were the "we" of whom Manuel spoke? What would they do, and to whom? Part of her wanted to know more, to penetrate these mysteries, but part of her was afraid of such knowledge.

She glanced toward her fiancé, handsome and serious in his dark suit, staring out over the dusty landscape. She had seen the young patrón in Jeffrey as he circulated among the mourners at the funeral. And the events of the day seemed to have drawn Jeffrey and his father close together, bringing out their common interest in the ranch and its people. Perhaps out of this horror and tragedy would eventually come some peace and resolution. She felt a surge of optimism for the future, and began mentally composing a letter to her mother. It would be full of the plans for the fiesta and the wedding, but would say nothing of the events of the past two days.

Jessica had feared that the fiesta might be canceled or made less elaborate because of Don Octaviano's death, but Ross seemed determined to make it more lavish than ever. In this he had the wholehearted support of Donaciana and Serafina, if not his son. Jeffrey felt the festivities to be inappropriate now, but Ross St. John insisted that to curtail or cancel the traditional fiesta, an event to which so many of the St. Johns' friends and retainers would come, would be a sign of weakness. Both Donaciana and Serafina backed Ross in this matter, and he pointed out that with their support, no one could view the festivities as indicating any disrespect for Don Octaviano.

"Besides," Serafina confidingly said to Jessica during a now rare moment they had alone in the kitchen, "it is what the old man would have wanted. 'Never show you are afraid,' he used to tell me, 'because that only invites attack.' He always spoke of courage and strength, but I think underneath he felt he was weak and a coward because of the way he behaved when my grandmother died and because that lost him—and his children—the ranch. I only hope that at the end—when they did to him what they did—he had a chance to redeem himself in his own eyes." It was the first time that Jessica had heard the Mexican girl speak with any emotion of her grandfather's death. In fact she had been rather shocked when, after Serafina had returned to the ranch with her mother and Jessica had offered her condolences, Serafina had shrugged and replied, "He was an old man. He had a long life, and he spent his last days in peace. It was time for him to die."

"But the way he died . . ."

"Ah, yes." Serafina's jaw hardened. "That was unnecessary and someone will pay."

The expression and tone of voice reminded Jessica of Manuel Valdez. The Valdez family, though loyal to friends and *patrón*, were obviously not a family to be crossed. Although Donaciana appeared subdued and depressed and occasionally burst into tears while she worked, Jessica detected no signs of grief in Serafina. Perhaps, like her uncle, she channeled her grief into other forms, so that thoughts of revenge substituted for her tears.

As the shock of events wore off and no new violence disturbed the ranch, Jessica became engrossed in preparations for the fiesta, now looming only a week away. The entire house had to be cleaned, and large amounts of food prepared several days in advance, including carcasses of beef set roasting in their stone-lined pits. Pavilions were set up in the yard, and tents and wagons were arranged for the guests who would be staying overnight. Jessica had already decided on her dress for the occasion. She would wear the cream satin gown she had rejected as too elegant on the night of her first dinner with Ross St. John. It would be appropriate for a future *patrona*. With few personal preparations to make, she was free to help Serafina with her dress, constructed from yards and yards of pale blue watered-silk purchased in Las Vegas.

Jessica looked forward to the fiesta not only as a festive occasion but also as a decisive point in her own life. Her engagement to Jeffrey would become official. She was certain that once that happened she could turn her mind away from Ross St. John, knowing that anything more than a father-daughter relationship would be impossible. The fact that Ross was so busy with preparations for the fiesta that she saw little of him helped her to convince herself that her new status would remove any romantic thoughts of him. Although occasional memories of his lips on hers and the strength of his arms as he embraced her that night on the plateau crept unbidden into her mind, she resolutely pushed them away. On the Fourth of July, Independence Day, she would be bound to Jeffrey, and she would be free.

Chapter 14

Reno was taking his time in saddling Felicia. The mare was too well-behaved to fidget, but he could sense her impatience in the way she tensed the muscles under her sleek brown hide and by the way she kept turning her head to gaze at the mountains in the distance, as if longing to be on the trail again.

Well, who could blame her. Too much time in town, too much time indoors. It was good that they were finally underway, that he could wake up in the morning to the scent of dust and pine and desert air instead of the stale smokiness of the hotel. Still, there was no point in hurrying. Though the sun was already well above the horizon, Kincaid's men had barely begun to stir in their campsite by the stream. Behind him Reno could hear the crack of sticks being broken for the fire, the clink of harness, and an occasional groan as a stiff cowboy stretched his joints. Although they had stopped just after dark, most of the party had stayed up late, playing cards and passing around the bottle, unable to give up the habits of town life.

As he bent to tighten Felicia's girth, Reno heard footsteps

moving across the hard ground behind him. He knew by the sound, or perhaps by some highly developed instinct, that the person approaching him was the gunman, Rutledge.

"Mornin', Hayden. Or should I say afternoon? Looks like another early start."

Reno slowly straightened up and stared coldly at the other man, not bothering to reply. He checked the saddle once more to make certain it was secure, then pulled his tobacco pouch from his pocket and began to roll a cigarette. Rutledge slouched against the trunk of a piñon tree, watching with a mixture of wariness and sardonic amusement. Reno was not deceived by the other's apparent friendliness. He knew that Rutledge had his eye on Reno's reputation, as a hunter eyes a trophy buck. Except for Pablo Ruiz, Rutledge was the only one of Kincaid's men who would come near him.

"You sure nailed that fellow Evans the other night," the younger man continued, ignoring his companion's silence. "Reckon I never seen such a draw. From the look on his face, I bet he didn't even know what hit him."

And I bet you were watching every move, Reno thought to himself, measuring just how fast I really am, trying to figure out your chances of beating me.

"It's my job. That's what I was hired for."

"I can't believe Kincaid let himself get into a jam like that. Accusing Evans of cheating, and Evans with all his men there."

Reno said nothing. Perhaps it really had been stupidity on Kincaid's part. If so, he had been lucky that Reno was there. Reno had the uncomfortable feeling that Kincaid was in fact not so stupid and that he set Reno up, like a dancing bear, to perform for the benefit of the onlookers. He was Kincaid's pet hired gun, and while everyone knew him by reputation, no one had actually seen him in action—until last night. But news of the shooting would spread, and Reno had the feeling that was exactly what Kincaid wanted. Such reports would strengthen Kincaid's own hand through the fear they excited in those who opposed him.

Well, what did he expect? Reno asked himself bitterly. He

was a hired gun; his job was killing people. At least he hadn't killed the man last night, only given him a shoulder wound that would keep him out of action for a while. Still, he didn't like it, for a number of reasons. Who knew what rats would start crawling out of the woodwork when they heard Reno Hayden was back in action?

"Reckon Kincaid plans on your takin' on St. John when the time comes?" Rutledge's query interrupted Reno's thoughts.

"St. John?" Reno spoke with calculated scorn. "He's no gunman."

"Still, for a rancher, he's said to be pretty mean with a gun," Rutledge persisted. "Shot someone in a fight over in Las Vegas a few years back, I hear tell."

"He doesn't worry me."

St. John didn't worry him. Some other things did, though, but he could hardly discuss them with the young gunman.

The others had joined them now, and Kincaid greeted Reno effusively. There was no doubt that Reno's actions in Las Vegas had confirmed his worth in the rancher's eyes, and also added to his mingled feelings of fear and respect. Reno noted the all too familiar way that Kincaid's men were eyeing him, and the unobtrusive manner in which they moved to keep their distance as they mounted. A heavy, sour depression settled over him as once again he felt the gulf that separated him from others.

They were a somewhat reduced party from that which had originally ridden into Las Vegas. Several of the men had already returned to the ranch, in the company of the foreman Ryan. Pablo had joined them, complaining of the lack of action in town. What action he expected on the ranch, Reno didn't know. Perhaps he hoped to be able to indulge in a little rustling.

The red dust rose around them in a choking cloud and Reno drew his bandanna up over his nose and mouth. Trust Kincaid not to get started until the heat of the day. Reno eyed the sun beating down cruelly on the plateau. The sky was absolutely clear, a pale, hot blue. It would be dark before they arrived at the Burnt Cedar. But that was typical of the way Kincaid ran

things. Though he claimed an extensive background in the
cattle business, acquired from years spent in Texas, Kincaid
seemed to have little interest in the actual running of the
ranch. Will Ryan, the foreman, one of the few men in Kincaid's
hire for whom Reno had developed any respect, had complained to him bitterly about the way that the Burnt Cedar
was being run. The ranch had not been in very good condition
when Kincaid had acquired it, and it was declining steadily.
Reno wondered what Kincaid would do if he ever actually
succeeded in getting his hands on the vast holdings of St.
John's. The man was no rancher. Perhaps he would attempt
to realize a quick profit, selling off all the cattle except for a
few he could use to "seed" the place in order to palm it off
on some naive eastern buyer. And then there was the gold
mine. But Kincaid didn't really take that seriously. Did he?

They began their climb from the plateau, and the men fell
silent as the horses toiled up the steep path and the heat grew
more intense. By the time they reached the pine forests of the
Sangre de Christo, it was already mid-afternoon. As they
headed up the valley, the shadows of the mountains grew
long across the trail.

Reno's thoughts turned briefly to what lay further down the
road. What were the St. Johns doing now? Ross St. John
gave some big fiesta every Fourth of July. They were probably getting ready for it. Reno was certain that many of the
people invited would come out of curiosity—to see the girl
who was going to marry the heir to those vast acres and to
see how the St. Johns were bearing up under the attacks
against them and their domain. And those who came would
see displayed the vastness of St. John's wealth and power.
His enemies would go away impressed, and his friends would
be reassured. For a moment, Reno toyed with the idea of
going disguised, but he quickly rejected it. Amusing as that
would be, it would also be too dangerous.

As they neared the turnoff for the Running J, Kincaid grew
visibly more nervous. While he had insisted on taking this
route when they set out from Las Vegas, he seemed to be
losing some of his bravado now that they were so close to the

stronghold of his enemy. Reno wondered if the rancher now regretted having allowed so many of his men to return early. Several of the other riders kept looking around, and one or two pulled their rifles from their sheaths.

Their uneasiness increased when they spotted a rider galloping rapidly down the road toward them. Kincaid pulled his horse to a halt and drew his gun. The others followed suit, drawing close together in a protective knot. The tension abated somewhat as the horseman drew nearer and they saw that it was Ryan, Kincaid's foreman. Kincaid sheathed his gun, but there was a worried look on his face as Ryan reined his mount in beside them.

"What's up?" he asked gruffly. "Trouble at the ranch?"

"Trouble, all right," Ryan replied, wiping his sweat and dust-streaked face with his bandanna. "Don't know what, if anything, it's got to do with us, but thought I'd better come out and warn you anyway."

"Warn us about what?" Kincaid's voice was impatient.

"Somebody murdered old Don Octaviano yesterday. The St. Johns just got back from the funeral. If you'd come a little earlier, you'd have run right into them, along with what looked like half the Mexican army, armed to the teeth."

"Don Octaviano? Oh, yeah, isn't that the old guy who used to own the Running J, way back when? But who'd want to kill him? And how's that trouble for us?"

Ryan shrugged.

"Who knows who would've had it in for him. Seemed harmless enough, far as I know. But the St. Johns are up in arms about it, and I sure wouldn't want to get in Ross St. John's way right now."

"Hell, what's he think, that I did it? He thinks I got nothin' better to do than go runnin' around murdering old men!" Kincaid was genuinely indignant about this slur on his character, Reno noted with amusement.

Ryan shrugged again.

"Don't know what he thinks. I just figured it might be a good idea to avoid runnin' into St. John today, and I thought I'd ride out and see if you were comin' and suggest you might

want to take the back route—'specially,'' he added shrewdly,
''seein' as how you're shorthanded and all.''

Kincaid seized upon the excuse.

''Well, I ain't afraid of meetin' St. John, and I wouldn't
mind tellin' him I know nothin' about this murder he's so
fired up about, but I suppose this might not be the best time.
We're short and we're tired and there's no point in trying for
a showdown right now.''

Rutledge smiled, but the others looked relieved, and they
willingly followed Kincaid as he turned off the main road and
headed up the slopes to seek the back trail through the woods.
It was dusk by the time they picked up the trail, and they had
to proceed slowly. Reno enjoyed the quiet of the night,
broken only by the jingling of spur and bridle and the occasional rustling of small creatures in the brush, and as the
outline of the tall Burnt Cedar came into view, he was sorry
their journey was over.

Both the bunkhouse and the ranch house on the hill were
dark as they rode up. Reno wondered where Pablo was. Was
he engaged in finding some ''action'' as he put it, or had he
gone to drink himself into a stupor at a local *cantina*. The
bandido's drinking exploits had acquired a certain notoriety,
even in this wild country.

After they had dismounted, Reno led Felicia down to the
stream to drink. As she slaked her thirst, he gazed up at the
clear night sky. There should be no trouble sleeping outside
tonight, he thought. There was no sign of rain.

Most of the others had unsaddled their mounts and were
straggling up the hill toward the house as he led Felicia
toward the stable. Reno hoped there was still some food left
in the cookhouse. Meals at the Burnt Cedar were anything but
elegant, but tonight he was so hungry he didn't care and
could easily have eaten anything Rickard, the cook, chose to
put in front of him.

A light flared in the windows of the house as someone
lighted one of the lamps, and a long rectangle of light shot
out across the porch. A few seconds later a horrible scream
rent the still air of the night.

Reno's response was automatic and instantaneous. He dropped Felicia's reins, and jerking his gun from the holster, he ran, crouching low, moving rapidly from tree to tree, up the hill toward the porch. The rest of the men, upon hearing the screams, had charged in a disorderly fashion up to the house, several of them drawing their guns. They stood huddled in a knot at the doorway, none willing to venture inside. Kincaid bounded up the stairs and shouldered his way through the crowd. Reno was right behind him and sheathed his gun as he strode through the door, sensing no immediate threat.

He almost bumped into Kincaid, who had stopped abruptly just inside the door. The rancher stood staring in horrified fascination at the table in the center of the room. Illuminated in the sickly yellow light of the oil lamp, the head of Pablo, the *bandido*, lay severed at the neck. His eyes bulged with the horror of his own death, and beneath the ferocious bristle of his moustache, his mouth was twisted in a mocking grimace, the gold teeth winking in the flickering light. From the severed neck, the blood, still fresh, crept in a crimson ribbon across the pine boards, dripping in a low macabre cadence onto the floor. In the corner, the man who had lighted the lantern was retching quietly.

"My God!" The exclamation, coming from one of the men in the doorway, was as much prayerful as profane. Several men crowded into the room to stare in grim fascination at the severed head.

"Who could have done it?"

" 'Tweren't long ago. The blood's still fresh."

"Somebody had it in for him."

"Where's the rest of him?"

"Jesus Christ, I ain't staying here tonight." The last speaker, a young cowboy with lank, reddish hair and a sunburned nose, glanced nervously around the room. "If they did it to him, they're gonna be back for the rest of us."

Several of the men stirred in uneasy agreement.

"Stop it!" Kincaid's voice cut sharply through the hubbub.

His usually ruddy complexion was waxen, but Reno had to admire his composure.

The man's no coward, he thought to himself. It was something to keep in mind.

"I want everybody to take lanterns and fan out, two men together at all times. Keep your guns ready and look for the body and for any tracks," Kincaid continued. "If you hear anything, shoot first and ask questions later, but try not to shoot each other. And somebody fetch a burlap bag from the stable."

Muttering nervously, the men clustered at the doorway withdrew. Reno could hear them clattering down the steps of the porch. Lights flared up in the darkness as lanterns from the stable and bunkhouse were lighted. Little pools of light moved off into the woods around the house.

"Hayden, Rutledge, you stay here," Kincaid ordered. "Let those idiots crash around out there. I want a couple of cool heads to stay with the house."

Reno suddenly felt uneasy under the lamplight, and he moved toward a corner, placing his back toward the wall. Rutledge remained staring in frank fascination at the head placed so rakishly in the center of the table. He was the only one of all the party who seemed unaffected by the gruesome sight.

"Who do you suppose did it?" he speculated. "Old Pablo was a bit of a show-off, but he wasn't a bad sort."

"I don't know," Kincaid replied grimly, "but if this is someone's idea of a joke, I sure as hell ain't laughin'."

"St. John? I understand he was pretty ticked about that old greaser gettin' killed. Maybe this is his idea of revenge."

Kincaid shook his head. "This isn't St. John's kind of game. He doesn't pull things in the dark. If he's got a grudge, it's more like him to come ridin' up to my door bold as brass."

Rutledge seemed about to say more but a shout from outside told Reno that Pablo's body had been found. They rushed onto the porch and looked down toward the creek. Two men were kneeling over something on the bank, as the lantern beside them sent high, distorted shadows wavering among the trees. Kincaid and Rutledge hurried down the steps. Reno glanced around cautiously before he followed. His hand stayed near his holster and his body was tensed and ready. The thought once more crossed his mind that Kincaid ran a careless operation. Guards should have been posted while they were gone. And the men converging on the creek were leaving themselves open for an ambush. He stood back from the crowd bent over the bank, his back against a tree, his body masked by shadows.

The headless body was sprawled across the bank in a manner that at first seemed the careless reflex of death but at second glance revealed itself as unnatural and posed. The arms were flung wide on either side and the legs spread slightly apart. The cartridge belt, the brightly colored scarf, and the elaborate leather boots that the *bandido* had sported in flamboyant conceit were all grotesquely intact, and the body was unmarked—unmarked, that is, except for the bloody stump where the head had been, and a bloody dark hole in the middle of each hand.

"Madre de Díos!" one of the Mexican cowboys had come up beside Reno and stood staring at the body. *"Penitentes!"*

Kincaid heard him and spun swiftly around.

"What did you say?" he demanded.

"Penitentes, señor. It looks like their work to me. You see his hands? They crucified him, I think."

"Who the hell are the *Penitentes*?" It was Rutledge who spoke.

"A group of religious fanatics," Kincaid explained. "They have some sort of weird rites where they do penance for their sins."

"And they punish and revenge their own," the Mexican added. "Fanatics, maybe, but powerful people belong to the *Penitentes*. It is not good to cross them."

"But that doesn't make any sense. Pablo wasn't a *Penitente*, was he? Why the hell should they care about him?"

"Maybe he offended one of them," the cowboy shrugged. "But I would swear this is their work."

"Don Octaviano!" Kincaid exclaimed.

Rutledge stared at him. "Who the hell you talkin' about? That old greaser who got killed? What the hell's he got to do with this?"

"It wouldn't surprise me at all if he belonged to the *Penitentes*," Kincaid continued. "It's well known that his son does. And if the old man didn't, the son would still try to avenge him and probably bring his friends in to help."

"You mean, Pablo killed the old man?" Rutledge was puzzled. The other men had drawn closer to listen, keeping their eyes on the dark woods behind them. "But why would he do that? He didn't even know him. And the old guy was poor as a church mouse. He wasn't even worth robbing."

"The mine." Kincaid spoke under his breath so that only Reno, Rutledge, and the Mexican could hear him. "He heard us talking about the mine and Lupe said the old man knew where the mine was. So Pablo thought he'd steal a march on us and wring the information out of him." He swore softly. "That double-crossing son of a bitch. He went right behind my back. And what's more"—he glanced over at the body— "he's pulled us into this mess with him."

"Well, whoever they were, they got him. And it looks like it was him they were after, so I don't see why they should bother us."

"I still don't like it. I don't like it at all." Kincaid's forehead was creased with worry. "This was to be a straight-forward kind of deal, just us and the St. Johns. We don't need this kind of complication."

Kincaid ordered double guards posted, knowing that none of his men would be willing to stand duty alone that night. He set the rest of the men to work digging a grave for the body, and had the head, wrapped in a burlap bag, carried down from the house to join it. The cook had brewed coffee and was preparing supper, and Kincaid ordered the meal served to everyone on the porch. No one, Kincaid included, was eager to return to that room of death. Reno, hardened as he was to bloody sights, knew he would long be haunted by the image of the *bandido*'s head grinning grotesquely in the lamp-light, much more frightening in death than it had been in life.

After supper, Kincaid brought a bottle and several glasses onto the porch, and poured himself a stiff drink. Reno declined the offer to join him, but Rutledge helped himself. Unlike Kincaid, Reno noted, the young gunfighter did not seem to be drinking to steady his nerves. Rutledge's only reaction to the gruesome events of the night seemed to be curiosity. There was no doubt he would prove a formidable opponent—that is, if he could shoot, and that was something Reno knew nothing about, at least not yet.

"Do you suppose he found out?" Rutledge mused as they sat on the porch, listening to the sounds of the cowboys as they settled down—or tried to—for the night.

"Who found out what?" Kincaid demanded. Now that the tense moments were past, he appeared truculent and a little shaken.

"Pablo. I wonder if he got the old man to tell him about the mine."

"Who knows? If he did, the secret's gone now, in the grave with both of them. And Lupe—that little rat—has skipped out on me. Said to leave any messages with his relatives. But they say they don't know where he went."

"But you don't need him, do you? You know where he found the gold."

"Maybe I do, and maybe I don't," Kincaid replied evasively. "But one thing's for sure, the whereabouts of that mine—if it exists—is still somebody else's secret."

"Think any of the other Valdezes know where it is?"

"Manuel, maybe. But I wouldn't go tangling with him. He's one tough *hombre*."

Reno stared into the darkness of the forest, listening to the two men talk. Tonight he would select his sleeping place with special care. It would not surprise him if they were being watched. Whoever had carried out the gruesome act of revenge against Pablo had obviously waited until just before they came back to do it. The freshness of the deed was evident in the dripping blood seeping across the table. Whoever had done it might very well still be out there in the woods.

It was definitely time to go away for a while. Kincaid would not like it, especially after tonight. But Reno had been too much in the company of men lately and needed to be alone. He would leave for a week, or two, however long he needed to regain his equilibrium. Nothing important was going to happen here until Kincaid's friend, the judge, returned. And then—then there would be action. And he'd be ready for it. Reno's hand brushed gently against the barrel of his gun. He thought of the blood of the *bandido* dripping on the floor and he knew the killing had just begun.

Chapter 15

The day of the fiesta dawned under a sky heavy with dark clouds. The members of the St. John household watched the heavens anxiously, torn between the rancher's desire for much needed rain and the wish for a clear bright day for the festivities. However, after producing a few distant rumblings over the mountains and splashing a handful of tantalizing drops in the dust of the ranch-house yard, the clouds parted and gave way to a sky as clear and dazzling as anyone could have wished.

Aflutter with anticipation of the day's events, Jessica had slept little the night before. Although the Fourth of July fiesta was an annual event and would have occurred even if she'd not been there, she knew that on this occasion she occupied a central place in the festivities. Serafina refused Jessica's offer to help with the many last-minute preparations, ordering her to relax and prepare herself for the evening ahead.

"You must look rested and beautiful, for everyone will be looking at you and will want to meet you," the young woman told her.

"But what about you? You will be so busy today. You'll

185

want to look your best, too. Surely there will be many young
men here who will be interested in you."

Serafina laughed.

"Don't worry about me. I have plenty of help today. And
this evening I will enjoy myself—you'll see. But as for young
men," she added enigmatically, "I have no interest in them."

Frustrated in her desire to help, Jessica returned to her
room to read and rest. She wondered, not for the first time,
why the attractive Serafina had no beaus. Several of the
cowboys had tried to woo her, but Serafina, while never cold
or unfriendly, had a way of keeping men at a distance and
discouraging intimate attentions. Only with Jeffrey and Ross
St. John—and with her uncle Manuel—did she seem affectionate and open.

As the day progressed, Jessica grew increasingly restless.
She gave up trying to read, and paced back and forth across
the room, pausing every now and then to open the doors of
the walnut wardrobe and touch the shimmering folds of the
cream satin gown. Then for the hundredth time she turned to
peer at herself in the mirror, gazing at her reflection for
reassurance. The high-cheeked oval face seemed the visage of
a stranger. Indeed, Jessica often felt, lately, that she no
longer knew herself. Her future, so simple and so assured
when she first arrived at the Running J, no longer seemed
certain in its promise of happiness. Like a chip of wood on
the surface of a swiftly moving stream, she was being borne
along by forces beyond her control.

Unconsciously, Jessica straightened her shoulders. Whatever her doubts, whatever her innermost desires, she must
face the fact that she had made certain promises and decisions
she could not back out of now. She was determined to be a
worthy wife to Jeffrey and a worthy mistress of the Running
J. It was up to her to carry on the traditions established by the
Valdezes and the St. Johns, and for this she must be strong.
She would not let Ross St. John's stubbornness and selfish-
ness interfere with her plans, nor would she waste time
longing for things that could not be.

Jessica glanced at the mirror again, her chin tilted resolutely. Tonight she would show everyone, including Ross St. John. She would be beautiful; she would be regal; she would make both Jeffrey and his father proud of her.

Although it was only mid-afternoon, many of the guests had already arrived and were setting up tents and wagons and sampling the cold lunch which had been laid out under a pavilion in the ranch yard. Jessica and the St. Johns were not to make their appearance until later, and then, after everyone had feasted on the barbecued beef and the many other dishes prepared by Donaciana and Serafina, there would be dancing on the wooden platforms set up beside the new barn. Before the dancing began, Ross St. John would make his traditional welcoming speech to the assembled guests. It was at that time he would announce his son's engagement and propose a toast to the young couple. Jessica could already hear, in the distance, the strains of violins and guitar, as the musicians practiced their pieces for the evening. She found her foot tapping to the rhythm, and excitement began to rise inside her. Whatever else this day brought, it would be a time of festival, a time to dress up and be gay and to enjoy herself to the fullest, without worry about the future.

Jessica called one of the servant girls to heat water for her bath. As she sank into the pleasant warmth of the water, scented with the fragrance of the French soap her mother had given her, she felt the last remnants of worry and anxiety melt out of her. She luxuriated for a while in the suds, and then scrubbed herself briskly with her long-handled bath brush, concentrating on the silky curves of her back and shoulders, which would be revealed by her gown.

Back in her room, Jessica slipped on the voluminous lace petticoats that went under her skirt. Her naturally slender waist had never known the confines of a corset; she wore only a beribboned chemise, cut low to fit under the deep neckline of her gown and laced tightly around her full breasts. She carefully dabbed perfume behind her ears and on her wrists, and, after a moment's hesitation, between her breasts. She was very conscious of the voluptuousness of her own body, and intoxicated by the heady scent of the perfume. A sense of expectation arose in her. She felt as if something could happen—something *must* happen—to her tonight. She didn't know exactly what that something might be, but her heart and body ached with longing.

Serafina knocked at the door, and throwing on her wrapper, Jessica went to let her friend in. They had allowed ample time for Serafina to fix her hair and arrange the elaborate coiffure they had devised—a coronet which would encircle Jessica's head with shining black loops. It was an old-fashioned hairstyle, but one which would accentuate her lustrous dark eyes and high cheekbones, making her look both exotic and regal.

Serafina chatted gaily as she worked, telling Jessica about the preparations that still needed to be made and discussing those guests who had already arrived and those who hadn't. Happy to be spared the necessity of talking herself, Jessica listened avidly to Serafina's gossip and tried to memorize the names that were rattled off. When Serafina had finished, they both stood back from the mirror to examine her handiwork.

"It's beautiful." Jessica's admiration was purely a comment on the other woman's skill and carried no conceit.

Serafina shrugged nonchalantly, but she seemed pleased.

"I had a friend at the convent school whose cousin worked as a hairdresser for a lady in Santa Fé, and she taught me."

"What about your own hair? How do you intend to wear it?"

"Oh, I will go to no trouble." Serafina flipped her long, lustrous braid over her shoulder. "Perhaps I will just wear it down and loose. That will do, I think, for me. I am not like you, almost the lady of the house."

If there was any resentment in the words, Jessica could not detect it. Yet she suddenly felt uncomfortable at this reminder of the difference in their status. She thought of Serafina as an equal, as the descendant of Don Octaviano, once the proud owner of one of the largest ranches in New Mexico, and she forgot sometimes that the other woman's position in the household was not the same as her own.

As if sensing Jessica's embarrassment, Serafina turned away

and went to the wardrobe to pull out the satin dress. She laid it out on the bed, nodding approvingly.

"It is perfect. Very stylish. No one else will have anything like it. It takes so long for new things from the East to arrive. Your mother has very good taste."

"My mother did not order that one," Jessica laughed. "She's never seen it. I had the dressmaker copy it for me from a fashion book. I don't think Mother would have approved of the way the neck is cut."

"Ah, yes, there is much of you that will show in that dress. I think the men will be pleased, even if the women are not." Serafina gave Jessica a conspiratorial wink, and their eyes met in mutual feminine understanding.

"Come," Serafina said briskly. "I will help you into the dress and then I must go get ready myself. Señor St. John has forbidden me to work any more today, and I am to dress and join you when you greet your guests."

Jessica doubted that any order from Ross St. John would cause Serafina to completely abandon her overseeing the day's events, but she was glad the rancher had insisted that Serafina not be confined to the kitchen. After all her work, she certainly deserved to be part of the festivities.

The dress was even more dazzling than when she had tried it on at the dressmaker's. Its shimmering, cream-colored fabric highlighted the warm tones of her skin and contrasted with the dark beauty of her hair. It was cut lower than she remembered, and for a moment she blushed at the expanse of shoulder that was revealed by the curved neckline. The rounded tops of her breasts gleamed tantalizingly above the lace edging, a promise of what lay beneath. Could she really wear this in public, she wondered, momentarily panic-stricken. But Serafina was approving and supportive.

"It is very lovely. Just right for such an occasion. You will be the most elegant person here, as well as the most beautiful."

"You are very kind," Jessica murmured, grateful for this generous praise from someone who could so easily and naturally have been jealous instead.

"Don't worry," Serafina continued reassuringly. "Everyone will like you, I'm sure. And if they don't''—she laughed, with a flash of white teeth—''it does not matter. After all, you are to be the wife of Jeffrey St. John, and there is nothing anyone can do about that.'' She turned toward the door. ''I must go now, if I am to be ready. Ross St. John does not like people to be late. Sometimes I think he would be angry at the sun if he thought it had not risen on time.''

After the Mexican girl had left, Jessica sat staring at the mirror, thinking about what Serafina had said. ''You are to be the wife of Jeffrey St. John, and there is nothing anyone can do about that.'' It was true. She *was* engaged to Jeffrey and they were going to be married. As Mrs. Jeffrey St. John, it would be she who would set the styles, arrange the fiestas, invite the guests. She did not have to be concerned about seeking others' approval; it was they who would have to seek hers.

As she sat at her dressing table, lost in these thoughts, there was a knock at the door. It was not Serafina's delicate tapping, nor did it sound like Jeffrey. Jessica felt a sudden wave of excitement, mixed with apprehension.

''Come in,'' she called, trying to keep her voice steady. She did not turn around as Ross St. John entered the room, but watched his image in the mirror. Their eyes met and she realized her heart was pounding.

Ross was dressed for the evening ahead. He wore the same outfit he had worn the night they met—open-necked white shirt, embroidered vest, silk scarf knotted at the neck—and over these he had donned a dark frock coat. His boots were new, of softly tooled leather. He looked extraordinarily handsome.

Neither of them moved for a moment as they regarded each other in the mirror, and then Ross strode across the room to stand behind her. She noticed that he held a flat, velvet box in his hand.

''You look lovely, even more so than usual, if that's possible.'' His voice was husky. Even though he was standing behind her, Jessica could smell the whiskey on his breath, and while he did not seem drunk, there was a faint flush of things to come under the bronze of his skin.

"Thank you," she murmured, cast into confusion by his compliment, the first attention he had paid to her in many days. She was acutely and uncomfortably aware that from where he stood, Ross could look down the smooth slope of her shoulders into the lace-edged front of her decolletage.

"I have something for you." He laid the velvet box on the dressing table. "Go ahead, open it," he urged as she hesitated, her fingers resting lightly on the plush surface.

The box opened easily on gold hinges to reveal a necklace of turquoises set in silver filigree and a matching pair of ear studs, resting on a white satin lining.

"I bought them for you in Las Vegas."

"Thank you. They . . . they're beautiful." Jessica was touched that he had been thinking of her during their trip to town and had found the time to shop for such a gift.

"My wedding present to you from me. I was going to give you some of my wife's jewels, family heirlooms, but I thought you deserved something of your own. Besides"—he plucked the necklace out of the box and held it up to the light—"these are more appropriate for you than anything my wife owned. These are New Mexico, like the desert sky, as beautiful and dazzling as you are."

Before Jessica could protest, he had looped the necklace around her neck and his strong fingers were fumbling with the clasp. To distract herself from the feelings his touch provoked, Jessica picked up the matching earrings and fastened them in her ears. Then she gazed into the mirror, entranced by her own image.

Ross St. John was right—the necklace and earrings were perfect. The turquoises, small and lightly veined, contrasted with the luxurious darkness of her hair and glowed against her skin. A single turquoise in a pearl-shaped pendant rested just above the rich cleavage of her breasts. Ross St. John could not have chosen better. And Jessica knew instinctively that his gift was not that of a father to his future daughter-in-law, but of a man to a lover.

Ross was standing close behind her and his hands moved from the back of her neck to her bare shoulders. His fingers burned her flesh as they slid down to touch the tops of her breasts above the lace-edged neckline of her gown. His eyes met hers in the mirror, and Jessica held her breath, afraid to speak or move. The blood pounded in her temples and her skin was flushed from Ross's touch.

"They're beautiful. It was a perfect choice." Jeffrey's voice from the doorway startled them both, and Ross quickly dropped his hands and stepped back. Jessica felt a blush sweep over her shoulders. What would her fiancé think, finding them together like that?

She turned as Jeffrey came over to the dressing table, and he bent to place a brief kiss on her forehead.

"You look so lovely, Jessica. Father showed me the necklace and earrings earlier today and I knew they would suit you."

Jessica managed a brief, tremulous smile, trying to banish her feelings of guilt. After all, what had she done? Ross had simply presented her with a gift and helped her to put it on. But in her heart she knew there had been more involved than that. And Jeffrey's lack of suspicion only made her feel worse.

Ross had left the room when Jeffrey entered, but he returned a moment later, bearing an open bottle of champagne and three crystal goblets.

"Here!" he cried, setting the bottle on the dressing table. "I think before we join our guests we should have a little private toast, just the three of us."

Jessica tried to demur, sensing that Ross had already had enough to drink, but Jeffrey seemed pleased by the idea and was already filling her glass.

"To the evening! To your wedding! To our futures, to all our futures!"

Ross raised his glass in an exaggerated toast before downing its contents in a single gulp. Jessica and Jeffrey sipped theirs more slowly, and Jeffrey gazed down at her fondly as they drank.

How handsome he is, Jessica thought to herself, and how much in love. She could never do anything to hurt him. She smiled back, this time with more assurance. Ross, who had already poured himself another glass of champagne, was watching her, and Jessica knew she looked both elegant and desirable. As the champagne bubbles started rising to her head, she felt both excited and overwhelmed by the intensity of the masculine attention directed at her. For a brief moment she was reminded of the scene by the burning barn when desire had flickered like flames in the eyes of both men who now stood before her. The room began to sway, and for a terrifying instant, Jessica thought she was about to faint. Then she caught herself and took a deep breath, and the room became steady again. As if from afar, she heard Jeffrey's voice suggesting that perhaps it was time they joined their guests. Setting her glass on the dressing table, Jessica gave her image in the mirror one last reassuring glance, and then, taking the arm that Jeffrey offered her, she let herself be led out to the fiesta.

The yard was overflowing with color, movement and noise. The three of them paused for a moment on the veranda to drink in the scene. People had been invited to the fiesta from as far away as Las Vegas and Bernalillo, and the crowd of guests was large and varied. There were cowboys from the Running J and from neighboring ranches, all dressed in their most colorful garb. There were ranchers and businessmen, members of the Mexican aristocracy and people from the local village. There was a priest and a sprinkling of Indians from the nearby Jeméz pueblo, and some colorful Navaho. Liberated from the watchful eyes of adults, small children ran everywhere, shrieking and laughing. At first it was difficult for Jessica to distinguish any familiar faces in all the confusion. But then she spotted the tall, lanky figure of Pete Towers, the sheriff from Bernalillo, and noticed one of the Montero girls flirting with a cowboy, under the watchful eye of her mother. Several of the people she had met at Don Octaviano's funeral were also there. Jessica took another deep breath and then, her arm linked with Jeffrey's, she descended the steps to play hostess.

The next several hours were a blur. Jeffrey led her from one group of people to the next. Jessica chatted gaily with the guests she already knew, was introduced to others, and listened intently to the conversations around her, soaking up gossip and information about the St. Johns' neighbors.

". . . found his yearlings all right. Clever bastards—covered right over his brand with their own. If he hadn't had a sharp eye, he never would've noticed. . . ."

". . . one of Kincaid's men, gunman by the name of Hayden. Nailed Evans right in the arm during a poker game. Claimed Evans was cheating. Wouldn't doubt it myself. Why I remember a time when . . ."

". . . she couldn't have been more than fourteen. And right out of convent school. They say the nuns never even knew about it, though I can't believe . . ."

". . . not a drop for a month now. I'm losing head, right and left. I tell you, unless we get some rain soon . . ."

Gradually, Jessica began to shed her nervousness and enjoy herself. Although she was regarded with considerable curiosity, and occasionally a certain amount of envy, everyone was friendly and seemed eager to make her feel welcome. Jeffrey's obvious affection and regard, as well as her own beauty and charm, did much to make people take to her, and her unfeigned love of New Mexico and genuine interest in the ranch quickly opened up doors of conversation. As the afternoon progressed, Jessica began to feel more and more as if she belonged. She could see herself and Jeffrey, growing old together, moving among the guests at many more such Fourth of July fiestas, their own children running in happy abandon through the crowds. She was certain that once they had a family, Jeffrey would be willing to settle on the Running J and give up his ideas of travel. She could even take over some of the responsibilities of running the ranch so that he would have time to write and draw. As she mingled with the guests, Jessica's future stretched before her, comfortable and fulfilling.

In spite of herself, however, every now and then her
fingers strayed to the turquoise and filigree necklace, and she
recalled the burning weight of Ross's hands on her shoulders.
After they left the house, she only caught occasional glimpses
of him through the crowds. Once she saw him talking with a
handsome Mexican woman, laughing boisterously at something she had just said. She noticed the flirtatious light in the
woman's eyes and felt a sudden, irrational stab of jealousy.

Ross continued to drink heavily, although only someone
who knew him well would have guessed that he was drunk.
Jessica marveled at his capacity for liquor. One glass of
champagne had gone to her head enough to make her refuse
another, and the noise and movement of the crowd were
themselves intoxicating.

Serafina seemed to be obeying Ross's orders to enjoy
herself. Jessica saw her moving through the crowds, laughing
and talking. Her blue dress, with its full skirt and tight
bodice, suited her slender figure perfectly. Despite her casual
response to Jessica's query about her hair, she had put it up in
an elegant chignon that made her look older and more beautiful. Several young men had already approached her, but their
efforts at flirtation were met with a lack of seriousness, which
was its own kind of distance and reserve.

Toward dusk, the barbecue pits were opened. The smell of
roasting meat drew the guests toward the long tables set up in
front of the veranda. Lines formed as people began to help
themselves to the bounteous array of food. Jeffrey solici-
tously seated Jessica in a chair near the end of the porch,
away from the crowds, while he went to fill their plates.
Serafina joined her, flipping open an elaborate ivory fan to
cool her flushed cheeks.

"Did you ever see such a crowd!" she laughed. "I didn't
expect so many people. I hope we have enough food."

"I can't imagine that we wouldn't have," Jessica replied,
thinking of the days of preparation in the kitchen which had
preceded the fiesta.

"Well, when they stop eating, they can drink. No shortage
of *that* around here when Ross St. John lays in the supplies."

Serafina did not seem perturbed by the idea, even though an argument between two drunken cowboys had already erupted into blows.

"That's a lovely fan," Jessica remarked.

"This?" Serafina held out her fan for a moment to contemplate its intricate ivory carvings. "It was my grandmother's. It came from Spain, or so they say. It's hard to believe, isn't it, that people came from so far away to settle in this barren land. To think that anyone would want it. Yet everybody fights for it." She stared thoughtfully across the valley to the mountains, growing dim in the rapidly approaching darkness.

Their reverie was interrupted by Ross St. John. He strolled over and leaned against the porch railing, eyeing them speculatively. As if they were fancy women, Jessica thought, and he was trying to make his choice.

"Evenin', ladies," he drawled. "I hope you're having a good time."

"How could I not, Señor Ross," Serafina returned lightly, "when you have so explicitly ordered me to do so?"

"That's what I like," Ross grinned. "A woman who follows orders." He made a mocking bow. "See you both later at the dancing—and that's an order, too." He sauntered off.

Serafina stared after him, her forehead creased in a frown.

"He drinks too much," she stated flatly. "And over the years it gets worse."

Not knowing what to say, Jessica made no reply.

Then Serafina jumped up, her serious mood shed as quickly as it had appeared.

"I must get back to the kitchen for a minute. My mother is not as young as she used to be and she finds it hard to be everywhere at once. I need to check to be certain that everything is being done right." Her silk skirts rustled as she moved off down the porch.

Her place was almost immediately taken by Jeffrey, who appeared balancing two plates and two glasses of fragrant red wine. He sat down on a bench beside her and set the plates between them. Jessica ate cautiously, careful not to soil her

gown. She had been ravenously hungry only a short while
before, but she found that with all the excitement of the
evening, it was hard for her to eat much. Sipping the strong
wine, she inhaled the fragrance, which spoke to her of the
dusty earth of the vineyards near Bernalillo.

"I hope all this isn't too much for you," Jeffrey asked
anxiously, noting her uncharacteristic lack of appetite, "We
are used to such fiestas but it must be hard for you to meet so
many strangers."

"It's fine," Jessica reassured him. "I'm enjoying myself
very much. And I want to meet everyone—your friends and
the people who are important to the ranch." Despite her
words, however, she realized that she was glad for this brief
opportunity to sit down and to escape, for a moment, being
the center of attention.

The scraping and tuning of the fiddles announced that the
dancing was soon to begin and gradually people began to
gravitate toward the platforms. Jeffrey and Jessica left their
sheltered anonymity and emerged from the porch to mingle
with the crowd. Jessica spotted Ross heading toward the
platform and she and Jeffrey moved closer to join him.

Ross jumped up on the wooden floor and raised both arms.
Slowly the crowd fell silent with expectation. With his tall,
powerful figure and his arrogant confidence, the rancher made
a commanding figure. Jessica tried to imagine Jeffrey bringing this large crowd under his spell as his father did, but she
could not.

Ross was speaking now, his voice booming out over the
yard. Lanterns had been strung between the buildings and
trees, and their light cast a festive glow over the scene.

" . . . to welcome all of you to the Running J. As most of
you know, this is an annual event, one in which we celebrate
the coming together of all the peoples who make up this
wonderful territory of New Mexico." A small chorus of
cheers and applause rippled through the crowd. "As you
know, the last few years have brought us many blessings and
many troubles. The coming of the railroads has led to more
prosperity for most of us but it has also brought us certain

elements which have been a somewhat less than desirable addition to our population. The lack of effective and decent law enforcement—our friend Pete Towers here excepted"—there was a murmur of laughter—"has meant that sometimes we have to take the law into our own hands. In recent weeks there have been several incidents—including the tragic and brutal murder of our beloved Don Octaviano—which represent an attack on everything that decent, hardworking people like yourselves stand for. But I know that if we stick together and show that we intend to fight for what belongs to us—our lives and our land and our families—in the end we can drive the scum out of our territory so that New Mexico will once again be safe for law-abiding folks."

There were more cheers and applause and St. John was forced to pause for a moment before he could continue. Jessica could see that, underneath the seriousness of his demeanor, he was pleased at the effect he was having, and he was enjoying his own showmanship. He raised his arms for silence and a hush fell once again over the crowd.

"Just as serious, and even more difficult to remedy in the long run, is another problem that this year has come to plague us especially hard. I am speaking, of course, of drought. Here again I urge that we all pull together, helping each other, sharing water when we can, and not selfishly guarding what little we have while our neighbors watch their sheep and cattle die. I have already opened some of my high pastures to people who are in need. While the rest of you must follow your own conscience in this respect, let me remind you that we are all partners in this great land and that ultimately our neighbors' fortunes, good or bad, will be our own."

The response from the crowd was mixed this time, and Jessica heard mutterings from several of the ranchers. She knew that considerable tension existed between ranchers and sheepherders in the area. Ross St. John's policies of letting sheep run on his range and of helping out the Mexican herders who lived on his land were not entirely popular with his neighbors. Her heart swelled with pride, though, at Ross's courage in expressing his convictions. He is right, she thought, we must all pull together. The things that divide us will only make it easier for Kincaid and others like him to get their lawless way and take over the land.

"But I did not get up here tonight to speak only of troubles," Ross continued. "As many of you already know, I also have happy news to impart. My son Jeffrey, whom some of you may remember only as the little skinny-legged kid who used to run wild here around the ranch, has returned from the East where he has not only finished his schooling but has found a very lovely, intelligent, and spirited young woman to be his bride. I am honored to announce their engagement and to welcome Miss Jessica Howard as my daughter-in-law and the future mistress of the Running J."

Jessica, who had been anticipating Ross St. John's announcement with some anxiety, was moved and flattered by his introduction. She could detect in it no trace of the expected mockery or sarcasm, and she was blushing as Jeffrey helped her onto the platform. They took their place by his father's side, in front of the cheering crowd.

Ross raised his arms for silence again.

"I would like to propose a toast. Those of you who have glasses, please fill them. Those who don't will just have to wait till later." A small burst of laughter issued from the crowd. As if on signal, Serafina had mounted the platform with another bottle of champagne and several glasses. She handed one to each of them and filled them while Ross made his toast.

"To the future happiness of my son and his bride. May their children be many"—Jessica found herself blushing again—"and may the Sangre de Christo always be their home." Jessica wondered how Jeffrey felt about this last remark, but there was no change of expression on his face as he cheerfully raised his own glass in response.

To the accompaniment of further applause, Ross downed his champagne and then signaled the musicians to begin to play.

"Come on! Enjoy yourselves!" he urged the people gathered by the platform. "The night is young, the musicians are fresh, and we've got plenty of food and drink." As the musicians swung into a spirited waltz, couples began to form and the wooden platform began to shake with the pounding and stomping of dancers' feet.

Jessica turned to find Ross standing at her side, eyeing her boldly.

"I think, as future father-in-law, I should have the honor of the first dance." His voice was a challenge rather than a request. Momentarily panicked by the thought of finding herself in his arms, Jessica glanced around wildly, hoping for a rescue from Jeffrey. But her fiancé merely smiled at her encouragingly. As Ross took her in his arms, Jessica saw Jeffrey offer his own arm to Serafina. They whirled away, the Mexican woman's full skirts flying as they disappeared into the crowd.

"You're not afraid to dance with me, are you?" Ross was grinning down at her. Jessica realized he was holding her much too close, but there was no way she could pull away.

"Of course not," she murmured in confusion as he moved her easily across the dance floor. "Why should I be?"

"No reason in the world." He drew her still closer and she glanced around nervously, afraid that someone would notice the impropriety of their embrace.

"You really do look beautiful tonight," Ross continued. She could feel the hard muscles of his thighs through the fabric of her dress as he guided her through the intricate steps of the dance. Her breasts, pressed tight against his chest, swelled even further above the lace-edged neckline. She felt dizzy from his embrace, and the strong masculine scent of him. "But you know that, don't you," he went on. His teeth gleamed in a brief smile beneath the sun-streaked moustache. "You know the effect you have on men, don't you, you little witch. And that dress—why I'll bet there isn't a man here tonight with any blood in his veins who wouldn't like to take it off you."

She felt the blood rush to her cheeks. "How dare you!"

"Don't get all prissy with me, now!" He laughed. "You can't pretend you don't know what I'm talking about. Women don't wear things like that by accident. And I'm sure you and Jeffrey haven't been waiting for your wedding night. I've seen you go off in the woods together."

Jessica started to protest, but then stopped. She would not lower herself by discussing the subject, and Ross St. John would certainly never believe her protestations, anyway. She stuck her chin out stubbornly. Ross was deliberately trying to provoke her, but he was not going to succeed. She only wished his physical closeness did not make her feel so dizzy and so weak.

Ross noticed the resolute tilt of her chin and chuckled.

"That's what I like—a woman of spirit. And you have plenty, my future daughter-in-law." He tightened his grip and pressed her closer.

Jessica tried to pull away again, but to no avail. Rather than make a scene, she surrendered herself to his embrace, and they finished the dance in silence.

After the first dance, Ross turned her over to Jeffrey and made no further attempt to claim her, to Jessica's mixed annoyance and relief. She danced several dances with Jeffrey, and then her partnership was requested by other guests. She made small talk with her partners, all the while trying to catch a glimpse of Ross. But he had disappeared into the crowd. She saw him later by the food tables, drink in hand. She danced with several of the cowboys, and then Hugh Riordon, the foreman, cut in. The cowboys had all flirted with her madly and she found the obviousness of their attentions amusing, but the foreman made her uncomfortable. She was very conscious of her bare shoulders and breasts and of the suggestive way he looked down at them. His powerful, stocky body made her strangely uneasy, and she was glad when the dance was over, and, pleading fatigue, she could break away and seek out Jeffrey.

As the evening progressed, Jessica lost track of time, of the number of dances she danced, of her partners. Sometime during the evening, the musicians took a break, and everyone moved down toward the pasture to watch the fireworks display. Jessica stood by the fence next to Jeffrey and watched as the sky was brightened by burst after burst of multicolored cascades of stars. The night was punctuated with the explosion of the fireworks, the shrieks of the children, and the appreciative *ooh*'s and *ah*'s of the adults. Jeffrey moved close to Jessica in the darkness and put his arm around her waist. She could feel his breath on her neck. She knew that he had been drinking a little more than usual, but she didn't mind. The liquor seemed to make him amorous. Perhaps they could slip away for a while. . . . But then she realized there was no way they could do so without being conspicuous. Still, it would be nice. . . .

The other festivities resumed after the fireworks display, but some of the guests had already begun to drift away. Knots of cowboys wandered over to the bunkhouses for impromptu poker games. Children began to nod off to sleep in their mothers' arms and were carried away to buggies and wagons to be tucked into bed. Several young couples slipped away from parental chaperonage and into the woods. A loud political discussion, fueled by the plentiful liquor supply, was underway near one of the pavilions. But there were still enough dancers to keep the musicians busy, and the night continued to resound with the lively strains of reels, schottisches, and waltzes.

Jessica danced a few more times, and then, as the musicians struck up the notes of *El Chinche*, "The Bedbug," a stomping Mexican dance which she did not know, she pleaded fatigue and joined Serafina and the women of the Montero family on a nearby bench, content for the moment to be a spectator.

Finally, long after midnight, the crowd on the dance floor thinned, and Ross St. John dismissed the weary musicians, presenting them with a liberal tip in addition to their regular fee for the night. They departed for the village, laden with some of the excess food, which, despite Serafina's fears, was left over from the night's feast.

Gradually the party began to break up, although several knots of diehards still lingered by the tables of food and drink. Some families loaded their buggies, intending to make their way home by moonlight. Others, with destinations more distant, retired to wagons and tents set up in the pasture, postponing their departure till the morning. Some, like the Monteros, would be staying for several days. A small party of cowboys clattered down the road, whooping and shouting, obviously happy from the effects of the long day's partying. Jessica hoped they would manage to make it home. It seemed strange that the fiesta, which had taken so much time and effort to prepare, was now over. The evening, which had been so long anticipated, and which was so full and exciting while it lasted, seemed in retrospect to have flown by.

Serafina went to supervise the clearing away of food and the Monteros retired to their tents. As Jessica sat contemplating the wreckage of the evening's festivities, Jeffrey came and sat down beside her. He took her hand and held it affectionately.

"Tired?" he asked.

"A little." She leaned her head against his shoulder.

"Did you enjoy it? After all, it was in your honor."

"And in yours, too." She laughed. "I could hardly be engaged by myself. Yes, I did enjoy it—very much. I liked meeting all those people, and I love to dance."

"We'll have dancing at our wedding in New York. And when we travel in Europe. I have several friends living abroad, and I'm sure they'll be able to introduce us into society there."

Jeffrey's words cast a chill over Jessica. In her enjoyment of the fiesta, she had allowed the more immediate plans for their future to slip from her mind. Well, they would only be away for a while. And when they finally came back, they would stay. She was determined about that.

"I think I'm going to go to bed now. Shall I walk you back to the house?"

Jessica stood up, suddenly aware of how tired she was. Jeffrey took her arm and they started toward the house. Jessica could see Ross St. John near the far end of the porch, talking with a small group of men.

"Father is probably trying to get a poker game going,"

Jeffrey laughed. "He always hates the festivities to end and tries to keep things going as long as he can."

The house was quiet when they entered. Someone had lighted the lamps in their rooms, and they shed a soft welcoming glow into the hallway. Jeffrey paused outside her door and rested his hands on her bare shoulders. She closed her eyes expectantly, but he merely brushed her forehead gently with his lips.

"Good night, darling," he whispered. "See you in the morning."

"Good night, Jeffrey," she murmured in response, lingering at the doorway of her room, reluctant to go in. Jeffrey, seeming not to notice her hesitation, smiled affectionately at her, and, entering his own room, quietly shut the door behind him.

With a sigh, Jessica turned into her own room. It was very late, and certainly it was time to go to bed. And she was very tired. But as she pulled the curtains shut and turned down the covers on the bed, she realized that she felt restless and knew that she would not be able to sleep—at least not yet.

She pulled a shawl from her wardrobe, and draping it over her bare shoulders, she opened her door and slipped out into the hallway. Jeffrey had already blown out his light, for the crack under his door was dark. She turned right, down the hall to the breezeway which joined Ross St. John's room to the rest of the house. His room, too, was dark. Had he gone to bed, she wondered, or had he succeeded in drawing his companions into a poker game, as Jeffrey had predicted.

She made her way down the steps at the back of the breezeway, and headed toward the stream which ran behind the house. She could see lights glowing in the windows of the bunkhouses and heard sounds of laughter and the strumming of a guitar. Not everyone, it appeared, was ready to call a halt to the night's festivities.

She kept her distance from these sounds of revelry and made her way to the bank of the stream. It was steep at this point and she made no effort to find her way down in the dark, but instead leaned against a tree by the edge, listening

to the faint rushing of the water far below. Its soothing
sounds relaxed her and helped to still the restlessness that still
churned inside her. She could hear the muffled scurrying of
nocturnal creatures in the woods, and the sounds were reassuring. They were part of a separate orderly world that cared
nothing for her own life. But then, as the breeze stirred the
pines into a whispering chorus above her, a darker thought
assailed her. She remembered the man who had attacked her,
the glittering eyes above the mask and the whispered threat,
"I'll get you later!" and she shivered in sudden fear. It
wasn't true, was it? He couldn't get her now. No one could.
She was to be Mrs. Jeffrey St. John, daughter-in-law to Ross
St. John. Together they would protect her.

But the night no longer seemed so soothing, and drawing
her shawl more closely about her, Jessica turned back toward
the house.

As she mounted the steps to the breezeway, she noticed the
yellow light of the lamp behind the curtains in Ross St.
John's room. He must have returned while she was by the
stream bank. She wondered if he had brought his poker party
to the room. But no sounds of merriment came through the
open window. Surely, a party with Ross and his friends
would not be silent.

The door to the room opened as she entered the breezeway.
Ross stood there in his shirt-sleeves, silhouetted against the
light. He crossed his arms and leaned against the doorway,
his eyes as predatory as a cat's.

"Out for a little walk?"

"I couldn't sleep," Jessica replied shortly. She hesitated a
moment near the steps, feeling uneasy in Ross's presence,
and then moved to pass him. He stepped out and blocked her
way.

"Not so fast. Why, you haven't even said good night."

"Well, good night, then." Jessica tried to move around
him, toward the doorway to the house. "It's late, Ross. I
think I'll be going to bed."

"What's your hurry?" He reached out to detain her, laying

his hand on her arm. "The night's still young. Plenty of time for a little chat."

"Please, Ross, I have to go." She tried to withdraw her arm, but he tightened his grip.

"Is this any way to treat your future father-in-law? I've gone to a lot of trouble for you, my dear. Bought you that nice jewelry you're wearing so bewitchingly around your neck. Had all these festivities in your honor. At least you can be nice to me."

"Ross, please. Please let me go. What if someone should see us?"

"That's easy enough to take care of."

Tightening his grip on her arm, Ross pulled her into his room and locked the door behind him. Jessica freed her arm and stepped back.

"You're drunk," she said flatly as he leaned against the door, watching her. She retreated several more steps into the room. "You've been drinking all evening and you're drunk."

"Not too drunk to know what I want."

He stepped toward her, and before Jessica could turn to flee, he pulled her into his arms, crushing his mouth against hers. She could taste the liquor on his breath, but she also felt the remembered hardness of his lips and the warm strength of his body. He slid his hands down her back, encircling her waist.

"Ross, please!" She wrenched her lips away from his but he still held her tightly. "You can't do this! This is crazy. It's wrong. Please let me go."

"The only thing that's crazy and wrong is that I didn't do it sooner." Ross sank his fingers into the elaborate coronet of her hair and tilted her head back so that she was forced to gaze into his eyes. "I told you, I take what I want," he whispered fiercely. "And that includes you."

"No!" Jessica twisted her face away as Ross bent to kiss her again. He grasped her chin between his fingers and turned her face back to his.

"Don't fight me, Jessica." His voice was coaxing now. "You know you want it as much as I do, so why struggle?"

His fingers still gripping her chin, he kissed her on the lips and then pressed kisses on her eyes, her forehead, the tip of her nose, moving down to bury his face in the pulsing curve of her neck. She was no match for the skillful assurance of his touch or for his all-too-certain knowledge of the weakness of her flesh. Ross bent lower to plant his burning kisses on her bare shoulders, pulling at the lace-trimmed edge of her dress to expose more flesh for his lips. Almost involuntarily, Jessica arched her body against him. His arm tightened around her while with one hand he worked at the bodice of her dress, continuing his rain of kisses to silence her weakening protests. Skillfully he undid the ribbons of her chemise, freeing her full breasts for the explorations of his fingers. Her nipples hardened against the roughness of his palm as he stroked the soft flesh. No longer did she try to turn away. Her lips now sought his eagerly, her body moving against him as she responded to his touch. She no longer cared that Ross was Jeffrey's father, that she was his daughter-in-law to be. They were simply a man and a woman. All that Jessica knew, all that she cared about at this moment, was her overwhelming desire to be possessed, to quench the passions of her body in Ross's powerful embrace. With trembling fingers she fumbled with the buttons of his shirt as his mouth bore down on hers, probing, demanding, sucking her breath away. She made no protest as Ross scooped her in his arms, and, carrying her to the large corner bed, laid her down gently on the brightly colored blankets.

He flung off his shirt and lay down beside her, the muscles of his chest gleaming in the lamplight. Impatiently he ripped at her bodice, exposing her breasts completely to his gaze.

"You're so beautiful, Jessica," he whispered hoarsely, gazing down at her.

She blushed at her nakedness and instinctively sought to draw the tattered remnants of her dress across her bare breasts. But he gripped her wrists firmly and pulled her hands away, lowering his head to kiss the exposed flesh.

"No, please, no!" She was moaning from pleasure now, not protest. As his lips touched her stiffened nipples, she moaned again. She felt the gentle nip of his teeth against her skin, and her body arched uncontrollably against his. Their legs were entwined, his knee between her thighs, and she could feel his demanding hardness pressed against her. She wrapped her arms around his bare back, his flesh a shock beneath her hands. His heart pounded against her own and she could smell the sweaty, intoxicating, masculine odor of his body.

Ross's hands moved lower, down the curve of her waist, across her thighs, pulling up her skirts. Her fingers joined his in undoing the ties on her petticoats and the lacy garments slithered in a heap upon the floor. Impatiently, Ross pushed her skirt up around her hips, exposing her smooth thighs to his exploring fingers. Jessica moaned again as his hand moved between her legs, probing her wetness.

"Jessica, Jessica!" Ross's voice was hoarse with urgency as he knelt above her. His hands fumbled with his pants as he gently pushed her legs apart with his knees, and his own garments quickly joined hers on the floor.

Seeing him naked, Jessica had a moment of panic. What was she doing here? This couldn't really be happening. She struggled briefly to sit up, her lips forming a protest, but then Ross was on top of her, his body pressing her to the bed, then inside her, pushing slowly as he entered her moist, intimate warmth. Her protests died as she arched her body to ease his passage. Her hands slid down his back, feeling the long, hard, naked length of him, resting against the rippling muscles of his flanks as their bodies joined in fluid, pulsing motion. Delirious now with wanting him, she closed her eyes, surrendering to Ross's passion and her own.

Suddenly pain stabbed deep inside her and she cried out, struggling to pull away. Ross, mistaking her movement and her cry, tightened his embrace and thrust even more deeply. Then the pain was past and all she felt was Ross, moving within her, and the movement of her own body in response, as the two of them climbed together in steadily mounting passion. Suddenly Ross groaned, gave one final thrust, and

lay still, his body now inert and heavy across hers. Jessica
clung to him, numb and drained, the pain inside her a dull
ache. Tears formed at the corners of her eyes. She reached up
to wipe them away, and then gave a little gasp as Ross rolled
away from her.

He propped himself beside her, leaning on one elbow, the
other arm curved around her waist. He contemplated her for a
moment, his glance both affectionate and amused. Then he
reached up and gently touched her tear-stained cheek with his
finger.

"My apologies, little one. I guess my son's not as much of
a man as I thought. I certainly didn't expect to find you still
intact. I would have been a little gentler had I known."

Jessica, her passion spent, her pain subsiding, began to
feel indignant at the casual way Ross was treating what he
had just done. "Intact" indeed!—as if she were a package he
had just unwrapped!

"Doesn't it matter at all to you that I'm engaged to your
son?" she demanded. "Or that he should have been the first,
not you?"

"Not at all," Ross replied calmly, tracing the high curve
of her cheek with his finger. "I told you once I was determined to have my way. And I meant every word of what I
said."

Yes, he *had* told her, Jessica reflected bitterly. She should
have taken warning from his words and realized how dangerous his passion—and hers—could be.

"Besides," Ross continued, "you and Jeffrey are obviously not meant for each other. Deep in your heart you know
that, even if you won't admit it. You're a woman ready for
love, Jessica, a peach ripe for the picking, and my son didn't
even reach out to pluck you."

"Jeffrey's a gentleman," Jessica protested. "He wouldn't
. . . He's not . . ."

"Not like me," Ross finished for her, laughing again.
"That's what my wife used to tell me, but I never saw that
being a gentleman got me anywhere. And it's not really a
gentleman you want, is it, Jessica? You want a man."

As he spoke, Ross's hands were busy freeing the disheveled coronet of her hair from its last remaining pins. As the tangled locks tumbled around her bare shoulders, he bent to kiss her again, his hands moving down to caress her naked breasts. Then, one by one, he began to remove the tattered remnants of her dress, bending to kiss each spot that he exposed. Jessica tried to protest, but her voice was weak, and soon the burning pressure of his lips on the intimate parts of her body brought her to a frenzy.

"Please. Please," she whispered. It was no longer a protest but a plea.

"Please what?" he teased, his probing fingers sending a flush of warmth through her body.

"I want you."

"How do you want me?"

She showed him, and he slipped inside her.

He moved slowly at first, with long purposeful strokes that caused her to moan in ecstasy, then faster, bringing her, stroke by stroke, to a fevered pitch of desire that suddenly and shatteringly exploded, washing over her in wave after wave of body-and-soul-shaking release.

She lay afterward in Ross's arms, her head buried on his shoulder. He nuzzled her hair gently, and as if from a great distance she thought she heard him murmur, "I love you, Jessica." A great peace settled over her, and her exhausted, satiated body sank into the welcome oblivion of sleep.

When Jessica awoke, the oil lamp had burned low and was casting guttering, smoky shadows on the wall. For a moment she lay still, uncertain where she was. Every limb of her body felt weak, and a dull pain throbbed between her legs. Then, as consciousness gradually returned, she became aware of Ross's leg entwined with hers, and heard his heavy breathing beside her. Panic clutched her, and it was only with a great effort of will that she kept from springing out of bed.

What had she done? She had betrayed the man she was to marry and given her virginity to someone else—and that someone else was Jeffrey's father! Lying there in bed with her lover's heavy, inert body sprawled beside her, Jessica wanted to die of shame. It was all her fault—she had no one else to blame. She had wanted Ross St. John, and she had done her best to entice him, not even admitting to herself what she was doing. The cream satin dress—now in shreds on the bedroom floor—she had not worn it that evening for Jeffrey. It had been for Ross, for Ross alone. And it had worked all too well. And now that she had succeeded in her wicked designs, what was she going to do?

Carefully, Jessica disentangled herself from Ross's legs and slipped out of bed. For a moment the room whirled around her, and she clutched the edge of the bedside table to steady herself. Glancing down, she saw dark streaks of blood against her thighs and she cast a resentful glance at the figure in the bed. How could Ross have taken her like that, not caring whether or not she was a virgin, overpowering her with his embrace, ignoring her protests. He had taken advantage of a weakness she did not know she had, but which he knew all too well how to exploit. But then she remembered her own passionate response and her intoxicated surrender, and she knew that whatever Ross had done, he had acted with the knowledge that her own resistance was no more than token and that his desire was equaled by her own.

Jessica quickly shook off her thoughts and her self-reproach. What had happened had happened. Whoever was at fault, the result was the same, and nothing could be undone. What was important now was to decide what her own course of action should be.

The first thing was to get out of Ross's room before she was discovered. Dawn could not be far away, and with the daylight, people would be stirring. Not bothering to put on her undergarments, Jessica donned the ragged remains of her dress, and then, scooping up her petticoats and chemise, she tiptoed to the door and cautiously pulled it open.

There was no one in the hallway, and no sound from the rest of the house. Quickly, Jessica slipped across the breezeway and down the hallway to her room.

The lamp had long since burned out and Jessica lighted a candle. Stripping off her gown, she stuffed both it and her undergarments into the far corner of the wardrobe. Then she poured water into the basin on the dresser and, taking a towel, gently wiped away the crusted blood between her legs, trying not to think of how Ross had touched her there, or how he had felt inside her. She could not think about that now. She must not ever think about that. What had occurred between them was wrong—it was wicked—and it must never happen again.

Jessica wrung out the stained towel and shoved it in the wardrobe with the dress. Then she unclasped the filigree and turquoise necklace and laid it on the dresser. It would serve as a message for Ross St. John, the only message she would leave him.

For it was clear there was only one course of action she could take—she must leave the ranch. It might be a cowardly thing to do, but Jessica could think of no other way out of her unbearable situation. She could never face Jeffrey or his father—not after what had happened last night. And as for going through with her marriage—the idea was unthinkable. Not only was she no longer the pure bride Jeffrey deserved, but also to have Ross as her father-in-law now would be intolerable. It was better that she leave, and leave without telling Jeffrey the true reason for her desertion. It would break his heart to learn that he had been betrayed by both his father and his fiancé. Better that she leave him puzzled and hurt by her departure than burdened with such awful knowledge.

But she would not leave with no word at all. Jessica donned her riding clothes and boots and then, brushing the tears from her eyes, she sat down to compose a letter to her fiancé.

Dear Jeffrey

The letters wavered in the unsteady light of the candle.

> *Please forgive me for leaving you like this, in the middle of the night, with no word of explanation or*

*good-bye, but something has occurred which makes it
impossible for me to go through with our marriage.
This is in no way your fault, only mine. I am unworthy
to be your wife. To marry you would be to deceive you,
for you expect and deserve a decent and honorable
woman for your wife, and I am neither of these. I know
that my departure will be painful for you at first, but I
am certain that in time you will recover and find someone more worthy of you, a woman who will be the
decent, loving wife you deserve.*

*I am going away. Please do not come after me. Try
to erase the memory of me from your mind. I will be all
right.*

I will always hold you in the deepest affection.

Jessica

Grimly, Jessica arose and folded the letter. She hesitated a
moment, glancing around the room. There was little for her to
take. She picked up her sombrero, and then, snuffing out the
candle, she headed for the door. Halfway there, she paused
again. Her rifle, her gift from Ross St. John, rested against
the wall, its brass plate gleaming faintly in the light from the
window. Jessica strode over to lift it from its pegs. She would
take with her this one memento of the ranch, and nothing
more. Shutting the bedroom door behind her, she tiptoed
down the hall, pausing at Jeffrey's door to slide the folded
note over the sill. Then she made her way outside to the
stable.

The yard was deserted, in striking contrast to a few short
hours ago. The contrast was appropriate, Jessica decided. Just
as her own life had been rich and full of promise, it now
loomed bleak and empty.

Jessica took her saddle and a canteen from the stable, and
crossed the yard to the pasture. She would ride as far as she
could in what remained of the night. She would head for
Bernalillo, or maybe Albuquerque—which was further away.

She would wire her mother for money and take the train back to New York. Or perhaps she could find a job in Albuquerque. No matter. She would think about all that later. What was important was to get away—as far away as she could—from the Running J.

Spur came immediately to her soft call, obviously eager for a ride. She saddled the little mustang and led him into the yard, closing the gate behind her.

Here she faced a dilemma. It would be easiest to take the main road, and she would make better time. But Ross had posted continuous rotating guards at all the entrances to the ranch. The guards were changed frequently, so that no one would have to miss the festivities, and Jessica had no doubt that the ones by the road would still be alert. She couldn't go that way. But where could she go?

Then she thought of the path to the village. It had not been guarded because it was too rugged for horsemen to travel. Also, for the past few days it had been heavily traveled by villagers going back and forth from village to ranch, preparing for the fiesta. But now, at this hour of the night, it should be deserted. It would be impossible to ride Spur, but if she led him until they reached the road branching off to the village, they should be able to manage. In any case, that seemed to be her only choice, so she would have to try it.

Cautiously, Jessica circled the back of the ranch house, Spur following willingly behind her. She glanced up at Ross St. John's window. The lamp had finally gone out and the room was dark. What would Ross think when he woke up to find her gone? Would Jeffrey show him the note she had left, and if so, what would he think of it? Would he care that she had gone? Now that his passion was spent, would he find her an embarrassment he was well rid of? Had he really whispered "I love you" as she drifted into love-exhausted sleep, or had she only imagined those tender words?

These questions were too painful to contemplate, and Jessica concentrated, instead, on finding the path ahead of her, a difficult task in the dark. Then, before descending the bank to pick up the trail by the stream, she paused a moment and turned to look back.

In the predawn darkness, the ranch was a jumbled mass of buildings, barely visible against the trees. Tears burned in Jessica's throat at the thought that she would probably never see this beloved place again. Resolutely, she choked them down, and gathering Spur's reins firmly in her hands, she headed down the trail.

Part II

The Desert

Chapter 16

Jessica squinted as she gazed across the desert. The bare horizon shimmered in the heat, blurring her vision. Above her, the sun was fierce, and despite her sombrero, Jessica could feel the harsh rays burning her scalp. Her head throbbed painfully and her skin was tight and dry. She shook the canteen before raising it to her lips to draw out a few more precious drops of water. Almost empty. She had carefully filled it before leaving the mountains, but that had been many hours ago. What a fool she had been to bring only one canteen with her. But then she had not planned to spend today wandering in the desert.

Shielding her eyes with her hands, she once more scanned the horizon and saw no familiar landmarks. As she lowered her gaze, she could no longer keep back the despair lurking at the edges of her mind, and it rushed in to overwhelm her. She was lost—thoroughly, hopelessly, and maddeningly—lost.

Fighting back tears, Jessica tried to think clearly about her dilemma. She cast her mind back over the terrain she had covered since she left the ranch. When she had passed the village just before dawn, the adobe houses were still clusters of shadow in the narrow valley, and only a lone dog had been awake to note her passage. His frantic barking echoed after her as she continued down the canyon. She had been fearful of turning onto the main road lest she be overtaken and had continued, instead, past Don Octaviano's garden. The steep terraces were already crumbling and weed-choked, and Jessica had hurried on, not wanting to linger near the boarded house with its gruesome memories. The path continued down the mountain, steep and narrow at first, then widening sufficiently so that Jessica was able to mount Spur and give her own weary limbs and feet a welcome rest.

Shortly after the rim of the sun rose above the edges of the dry hills, Jessica had pulled her mount to a halt and lay down to rest under a stunted piñon tree. She was awakened later by Spur's restless nuzzling, and looked up just in time to see the shaggy back of a bear disappearing into the scrub-lined hillside. Its tracks were sharp in the mud by the water's edge where it had been drinking at the stream. As she knelt to fill her canteen, the indentations filled rapidly with muddy water.

As the path wandered lower through the foothills, Jessica had become less and less certain of her direction. When she had set out, the path seemed to parallel the road. She had planned eventually to cut south to join it, heading for Bernalillo. But then the path turned north, following the meanderings of the stream. Jessica had finally decided to cut through the hills in the direction in which she thought the road would lie. Her shortcut proved rough going, and she had to twist and turn across the broken terrain and through a tangle of mesquite and cactus, which sought to bar her way. Though still low in the sky, the sun was already hot, and her passage through the brush stirred scores of noxious biting insects, which plagued both her and Spur. The little horse ploughed on patiently, and she tried to spare him as much as possible, dismounting to lead him through the more difficult places. She would need his strength later.

Finally, tired of her trailbreaking, Jessica turned into a dry streambed at the bottom of a broad canyon and followed this easier passageway out of the hills and toward the open country beyond. She paused at the canyon's mouth, scanning the sky, trying to establish some sense of direction. Then, mounting Spur, she turned in the direction she thought the road would lie. Even if she did not immediately come upon the road, surely she would see some familiar landmark, or pass a ranch or other habitation where she could ask for directions. If she could just get to Bernalillo, she told herself, as her body sagged wearily in the saddle, she could take the train to Albuquerque, or at least find someone to accompany her on the road.

But the desert seemed to stretch on forever. Perhaps her path through the hills had brought her out of the mountains farther west than she had thought. Or perhaps she had mis-judged the direction of the sun. As she left the foothills of the Sangre de Christo, no landmarks of any kind appeared before her searching eyes, and the only sign of human life was a collapsing clapboard and adobe building, ominously aban-doned to the blowing sand. Finally, as the mountains faded to a hazy line in the distance behind her, Jessica's hopes began to dwindle, and she finally admitted she was lost.

The sun pressed upon her like a weight; even Spur's head was drooping. Her mouth was dry, her lips cracked. Jessica longed to do what Ross had showed her—soak her kerchief in water and wrap it around her throbbing head, but she did not dare use too much of the water in the canteen. Better to save the precious fluid for drinking.

The desert here was so much more barren than the desert they had traveled to Las Vegas. There were no trees at all in the sun-blasted expanse which stretched before her, and little or nothing grew between the dusty clumps of sage. No cool mountains beckoned in the distance, and no green-fringed canyons told of water. Perhaps the desert only seemed more grim and hostile because she was alone and lost. Jessica recalled the day she had stood with Jeffrey on the edge of the mountains, feeling the magic pull of the desert. But there was no magic in the arid land before her, and if it called her, it was only to her death.

She could not go on in that merciless sun. She must have

shade, must have water. But the desert gave no promise of either, and Jessica squinted in vain across the horizon.

Finally, after several plodding miles of emptiness, she saw something ahead, a tiny lump against the dusty blue sky. She had no idea what it might be, but at least it was a marker in this otherwise unmarked land. As she drew closer, she saw that it was a small butte, one of the many carved out of the red rock by the forces of the desert, standing like a sentinel against the horizon. Jessica's heart contracted in disappointment. The butte offered no comfort; it was as stark and inhuman as the desert which surrounded it. But as she drew nearer, she realized that it did have one welcome feature, for at its base stretched a long sliver of shade. Here at least they could find a little respite from the glare of the afternoon sun.

Jessica unsaddled Spur and then carefully poured a little of the precious water into her hand. The mustang slurped it greedily and then nuzzled her hand for more. She hated to deny him for he had served her so faithfully. If she ever managed to leave the desert alive, it would only be with his help. But she knew that for both their sakes she would have to ration what little water they had.

Wearily, Jessica stretched out in the shade at the foot of the butte, her head pillowed on the saddle. Spur turned to nibble in desultory fashion at some tough clumps of dusty grass that clung stubbornly to the hard ground. Trying to make herself comfortable, Jessica reflected on how unprepared she was for such a journey. Not only did she lack water, she had brought no blanket or extra clothing, and now she also felt the pangs of hunger beginning to gnaw at her stomach. She had eaten nothing since the evening before, and not very much then. Her stomach contracted as she recalled the plates heaped high with barbecued beef, the stacks of fresh tortillas, the bowls of hot spiced beans, all the food, both savoury and plentiful, which had graced the St. Johns' tables. Her qualms about hunting would have vanished instantly, she knew, if she had seen a rabbit cross her path at that moment. And she would not have hesitated to eat her victim raw.

Eventually, Jessica fell into an exhausted but restless sleep.

Strange scenes and images rose to haunt her. She saw Don Octaviano bending over his garden, but he was much younger now, and when he stood up, he smiled at her invitingly, white teeth gleaming in his handsome, tanned face. Then, gradually, his face began to transform itself, becoming fierce and shaggy, with a large bristling moustache. Jessica could see blood running from his mouth as he opened it in a hideous grin. His teeth were blood red. Suddenly Jessica realized that he had no body, only a head, which was floating away through the forest, with a young woman running after it. It was Annunciata, or was it Serafina? She was screaming as she ran, and the screams still echoed in Jessica's ears as she suddenly awoke and sat up, her heart pounding.

She lay there a moment, listening to Spur's peaceful, rhythmic chomping, afraid to go back to sleep. Nearby, a dust-colored lizard stood posed on top of a rock, regarding her with jeweled eyes. Then it suddenly flickered away. Jessica turned over, the hard ground bruising her ribs. Somewhere near her ear an insect buzzed as she drifted into sleep again.

Now it was Ross who was with her. She could see him coming across the desert, his broad shoulders outlined against the blue sky. She ran to him as he dismounted and he took her tenderly in his arms, holding her tight and whispering endearments as she clung to him. She could feel the hard strength of his chest, the reassuring warmth of his breath. He led her to the bank of a stream which flowed along the base of the butte, and she wondered how she had failed to notice it before. Pulling her down on the cool grassy bank, he began to make love to her, slowly and gently, kissing her smooth flesh, running his hands slowly over the curves of her body. She surrendered joyfully to the comfort and ecstasy of his embrace.

Then she was awake again, and the long shadow of the butte stretched before her. She was alone. Her empty arms seemed to bear the warmth of Ross's body and she could still feel his flesh pressed against hers. Tears started at the corners of her eyes. Never before had she felt such loneliness and desolation.

Spur stood gazing at her expectantly, and Jessica sat up, trying to muster her courage. If she gave way to despair, she knew, she would never survive the desert. Part of her wished only to lie down right there and die, but she struggled against it, forcing herself to her feet.

The shadow of the butte stretched out, well into the desert now, and she could tell that the sun, invisible behind the mass of carved rock, was very low. The moon, when it rose, would be nearly full tonight. In its light, she could continue her journey, free from the sun's fierce power.

She would head back, she decided, toward the mountains. If she skirted their edge, instead of striking out across the desert as she had done earlier, she would surely come to something—a road, a town, a village. And in the mountains there would be water, at least.

Jessica saddled and mounted Spur and rode out from behind the butte. The glaring red ball of the sun squatted on the horizon, about to slip away. She must fix her directions. If she started off with her back to the west, to the setting sun, she would be going roughly the right way. But she would have to then fix the moon as it came up, and not lose her direction as it tracked across the sky. Resolutely, Jessica started forward, the long shadow of herself and her mount stretched before her like a pointer.

After several hours of riding, Jessica found her way blocked by a narrow canyon, which ran like a dark gash across the desert floor. Although she had not passed the canyon earlier, she did not feel alarmed. She had zigzagged so much in her wanderings that stumbling upon this canyon did not necessarily mean she had once again lost her way. But the canyon was a serious obstacle, for it stretched in both directions as far as she could see.

Jessica dismounted and cautiously approached the canyon rim, peering into its depths to gauge its steepness. Though the moonlight was deceptive, the canyon did not appear to be very deep, and on its floor, something gleamed with a pale silver light. Jessica's heart leapt in excitement and hope. Water! Was that water she saw below her? If only she could get down to it. Eagerly, she explored the canyon's edge, looking for a path.

About a hundred yards away, Jessica found a narrow track, which snaked down the canyon face. It looked like a path made by animals, though she couldn't imagine what animals could live in this barren wasteland. But whatever they were, if they descended to the canyon floor habitually, it must mean there was water. The trail was much too steep for Spur, however. She would have to leave him tethered to bushes by the rim.

The moonlight proved almost as much a hindrance as a help, lighting some portions of the path but casting others into deceptive shadows and causing Jessica to miss her step. She had several heart-stopping falls and was dusty and bruised by the time she reached the bottom.

She stumbled eagerly toward the stream, her dry throat already contracting at the thought of water. But there was no water—only the sandy surface of a dry streambed gleaming in the moonlight. Tears sprang to Jessica's eyes as she realized that her exhausting descent had been for nothing. Then she remembered the trip to Las Vegas and the way they had obtained water from the stream at the edge of the plateau. Falling on her knees, she began to dig frantically in the sand with her hands. At first her efforts were in vain, but gradually, the sand grew moist between her fingers and a small murky pool formed in the hole she had dug. Jessica scooped up the tepid water, trying not to gulp it as she carried her hands to her lips. She rolled the water around inside her parched mouth before she swallowed and then did the same with the next mouthful. She dug farther, trying to hold back the collapsing sides of the pool, and then lowered the canteen into the water to fill it.

How was she going to get water to Spur? She pondered that question as she looked back up the steep trail she had just descended. She thought of carrying water in her sombrero, but she was certain she would spill most of it in such a precipitous climb. She could carry the canteen up, but that would hardly suffice to quench Spur's thirst. After that, of course, the canteen would have to be refilled before she continued her journey. Reluctantly, Jessica concluded that the only thing to be done was to make several trips up and down the canyon side.

Jessica didn't know how long it took her to make those trips. It might have been an hour; it might have been several hours. All she knew was that at the end she was staggering from her exertions and from lack of food and sleep. And the canyon, despite its life-giving gift of water, became more oppressive and ominous with each descent. The shadows underneath its walls were menacing and impenetrable, and Jessica had a sense of eyes watching her. The canyon itself, with its steep walls, seemed a trap, and Jessica uneasily recalled the many warnings of flash floods. Was it thunder she was hearing now, somewhere in the distance? She strained her ears but could detect only the vast silence of the desert. Then something rustled in the bushes behind her and she jumped. Hastily, she finished filling her canteen and scrambled back up the steep path, grateful to be able to continue her journey.

She had to travel several miles along the canyon's rim before it became shallow and sloping enough to cross. As she headed once more across the desert, Jessica realized that she had become confused about her position. The moon was high, now, and useless for determining direction. How long had she been in the canyon? How long had she been traveling? She peered worriedly ahead, hoping to catch a glimpse of the dark line of the mountains across the horizon.

Spur, seemingly refreshed by the water Jessica had so laboriously carried up to him, moved briskly, but Jessica found her eyelids growing heavy, and her head began to nod. At one point, she sat up with a jerk and realized she had dozed off. She looked around, still slightly dazed, wondering in what direction they had been traveling while she was asleep. She tried to keep herself awake after that, afraid that Spur would stop or double back if she slept. Her body ached with weariness and she longed to lie down on the hard floor of the desert. But she knew that she had to keep going; once the sun rose, any further travel would be too difficult.

The journey became a blur. Jessica lost all sense of direction and sagged wearily in the saddle, letting Spur make his own way. When the sun did rise, their shadows once more stretched long in front of them and Jessica realized they were completely turned around. And when she saw the familiar shape of the butte looming ahead, she knew they had made a complete circle. Despair flooded over her, and at that moment, all she wanted was to die. She would die anyway, and her bones would be bleached to nothingness by the desert sun. Why not lie down and let the sun claim her now? Why struggle and prolong the agonizing path to the inevitable end?

With her last remnant of courage, Jessica fought off her impulse to surrender and instead made her way wearily to the butte and the life-saving shade it had offered her the day before.

All that day they rested, the mustang nibbling at the sparse grass, Jessica collapsed in the shade. They moved only to shift their position as the shade circled the butte with the sun's path. Jessica was lightheaded from the heat and the glare, and had to fight off dizziness every time she stood up. She no longer thought of food, but visions of water haunted her. She wondered if she would ever again see it flowing freely, surrounded by grass and bright flowers and tall, cool trees.

When night came, she knew she must try again. She struggled up and gave Spur a little of the precious water, saving it for him and only barely wetting her own lips, which were now swollen and dry. Then she mounted and headed back across the desert.

She no longer knew where she was going and made no effort to follow the direction of the moon or sun. All she knew was that she must move or die. She would probably die anyway, but until then she would wander this faceless and hostile waste, this desert of despair that, like a siren in the shining distance, had called her to her own destruction.

Dawn found her heading west again, not caring about her

direction. As the rising sun sent long fingers of shadow from each bush and tuft of grass, Jessica's hopes rose briefly. Just ahead, as dry and gray as the tumbleweed piled up against it, was a split-rail fence, zigzagging its way into the distance. Her hopes quickly fell again, however, as she drew nearer and saw that the fence was collapsing from neglect.

Nonetheless, she turned her course to parallel the frail structure, unwilling to leave the only sign of human life she had seen in two days. Perhaps it would lead her to something—if not to another human face, then perhaps to an abandoned dwelling which would provide shelter, or even to some source of water.

As the sun climbed, a desert wind sprang up, harsh and hot. It blew stinging sand into Jessica's eyes and seemed to suck the moisture from her very bones. She pulled her hat low to shield her face, blessing the sturdy little horse that plodded so stoically beneath her. It was only Spur's fidelity and endurance that now stood between her and death.

The fence ended abruptly, its disappearance as mysterious as its beginning. A faint, rutted track appeared just beyond, continuing into the distance, and Jessica followed it. A little farther, this road gave out. Beyond stretched a prairie-dog town, its holes and humps dotting the desert surface as far as the eye could see. Fearful that Spur might break a leg in one of the holes, Jessica dismounted so that she could lead him through the treacherous maze. She pulled her rifle from its scabbard. Perhaps she could manage to shoot one of the maze's occupants as it stood, stretched tall, on the observation post of its mound. She had no idea how prairie dog would taste, but surely it would provide some nourishment.

Her weakened arms could barely raise the heavy gun, and before she could get a bead on one of them, the little animals took alarm and loped off with their peculiar, long-legged gait.

A little farther on, near the end of the prairie-dog town, she came upon more signs of life—and death. In their path lay the carcass of a small, dark animal, some sort of goat-like creature, its sun-hardened skin stretched taut over protruding ribs. Two buzzards were feeding on the rotting entrails. They flew

off on reluctant, heavy wings as Jessica drew close. Nearby
stood two gray-and-white owls, squatters at abandoned prairie
holes. They swiveled their heads as Jessica went by, staring
at her with round, yellow eyes. She stared back, wondering if
she were beginning to hallucinate under the fierce sun. Surely,
owls did not sit outside like this in the daytime. There was
something eerie about their fixed, predatory gaze. Were they
waiting for their turn, she wondered, at the buzzards' gruesome meal?

The stench of the rotting carcass struck her like a blow as
she passed. Gagging, she hurried on, and then paused to look
back, compelled by a morbid fascination. That was what she
would look like in another few days, and the buzzards and
other scavengers would mysteriously appear out of this seemingly lifeless desert to gnaw at her flesh and bones. She
shuddered and turned away.

The day dissolved into a shimmering blur as she stumbled
on. There was no point in stopping, for there was no shade to
shelter them from the fierceness of the sun. Jessica led Spur
and gave him the last of the water. She would spare the poor,
drooping mustang as well as she could, although she was
convinced that neither of them would survive the desert.

At some point she staggered and fell, lying crumpled against
the hot earth for she knew not how long, before Spur gently
nuzzled her into consciousness again. On shaky limbs she
rose, and stumbled on, and fell again, and rose once more, her
skin chafed and burned by the sand and the sun, her mouth
parched and swollen, her eyes dry and aching from the dust
and wind.

She no longer remembered where she was, or who she
was, or how she had gotten there. She marched in pain-filled,
sun-blistered space, across a vastness that was the entirety of
any world she had ever known, could ever recall. Somewhere
just beyond her vision loomed dark clouds of death, and she
welcomed their approach and the release that they would
bring. She hoped they would come quickly and blot out the
fierceness of sun and sand. But perhaps they were only
another deception of the desert, like the shimmering mirages

that danced on the horizon and then disappeared as she drew near, tantalizing her with their suggestion of the water she knew was not there.

Gradually, she became aware of another vision in the distance. At first it seemed just a dark wavering dot. Then she saw that the dots were people, straggling in an uneven line across the desert. As they drew closer, she could see that they were Indians, men and women, their dark faces weathered an even deeper bronze by the desert sun. They wore feather-decorated cotton tunics over deerskin leggings, and shell-and-feather necklaces. Most of them carried packs upon their backs. She watched in fascination as they filed by, taking no notice of her. To her heat-fevered brain it did not seem strange that they did not see her. She realized that she must already be dead and no longer of their world. There was something sad about the faces of these desert travelers. A great weariness seemed to lie over them, and a sense of loss. No one spoke. One man lingered at the end of the caravan, stopping to gaze back into the distance, as if the horizon exerted some great pull which he had difficulty in breaking.

They filed past her and then gradually grew distant in the east. A great, swirling, yellow cloud had risen, obscuring the horizon. The marchers disappeared into the approaching storm as the cloud rolled across the sky.

The wind howled all around and the sky grew dim. The yellow cloud marched toward them, fell upon them, and the storm-driven dust sucked up the world, blotting out the sky and sun, filling the air with fury. The flying sand stung Jessica's skin, filled her nose, eyes, and mouth, and sifted down inside her clothing. She wrapped her kerchief around her mouth and nose, and shut her eyes against the blasting dirt. Her skin was chafed and raw. She felt smothered, drowned, beaten down by the maelstrom. She clung to Spur, who stood stoically, his back to the wind, his head down. She buried her face in his mane, seeking comfort and support from the only other creature visible in the hellish, stinging eternity of the storm. But her weakened legs could no longer hold her, and she slid to the ground. The swirling sand spread over her.

Though the sun was hidden, a strange light filled the air, as if each grain of sand glowed with its own reddish-yellow luminescence.

As she lay there, pressed against the hard drum of the desert floor, stunned and barely conscious, some sound, some vibration communicated itself to her. It was as if something moved, thumped, marched toward her. The sound grew closer. She struggled to rise against the weight and fury of the sand and wind. Raising her head, she saw a line of men moving toward her, out of the yellow clouds. They wore helmets and breastplates and carried swords and spears, the armor gleaming dully in the storm-burnished light. Their footsteps were heavy, grim, and weary, and as they approached, their leader turned toward the men, seeming to exhort them with words and gestures. Their faces lay in the shadow of their curved helmets, and Jessica could not see their features. The thudding of their measured tread grew closer, a counterpoint to the howling of the storm. Then, as they drew abreast of her, they turned their faces fully to hers. Jessica saw that each helmet was filled, not with a human face, but with a gleaming, grinning skull.

She heard her own voice screaming, raw and broken, somewhere in the distance, before it was sucked into the storm. Then she sank into oblivion, no longer aware of wind or sand or heat or of the marching of alien steps across the desert.

Jessica fought off consciousness as it returned, pushing it from her as it nudged the edges of her mind. She wanted no more of the desert, of sun and thirst, of heat and horrible visions. But some force within her persisted, pulling her toward life, refusing to let her give in to the death her exhausted body craved. She opened her eyes to see that the storm had passed and the sun was setting, red and angry, below a bank of dark clouds.

With her last remaining bit of strength, Jessica managed to stand up, clinging to Spur's mane to support herself, as the world whirled around her and threatened to spill her to the ground again. She felt as dry and weightless as a withered leaf. Fine grit covered her hands, hair, and face, and rubbed against her skin inside her clothes. Her eyes were swollen slits in her sunburned face. The canteen was hanging from the pommel of the saddle, and she grabbed it and shook it, hoping against hope for a few remaining drops, even though she knew she had emptied it long ago.

For a moment she stood, uncertain, and then, gathering her determination, she grasped the saddle horn and lifted her foot to the stirrup. With a body-wrenching effort, she dragged herself up into the saddle. She would ride as long as she could, giving Spur his head. She had no particular direction. Perhaps the mustang, with his keener senses, would smell water or trees or people before she herself could sight them. In any case, at least they would keep moving. They might find nothing as they wandered, but then there was nothing where they were.

The night was very dark, with only occasional glimpses of moon floating between the clouds. In the distance, the sky was aglow with flashes of lightning. Jessica could hear the faraway roll of thunder. Would the storm reach them, she wondered. She worried about flash floods and the danger of lightning, but she also thought of rain. One never knew what to expect with desert storms. They could pour torrents of water down in one place, and yet a few miles away the land would remain dry and parched. She tried not to hope, fearing disappointment and further despair, and yet only hope could keep her going, heading in the direction of the storm.

It reached them about an hour later, its fury building as it came. Spur nearly bolted, as lightning forked to earth only a few hundred yards away, and the tremendous crash of thunder on its heels almost knocked Jessica from the saddle. As she fought to bring her mount under control, she smelled the reek of sulphur in the air. There was another flash, farther away this time, illuminating the desert with an eerie silver light before the darkness rolled in again. And then the clouds broke.

Like everything else Jessica had experienced in the desert, the storm was extreme in its fury. Where there had been no water, now there was almost too much. It descended in punishing torrents, which beat against the ground so hard they made a layer of foaming spray, stretching out around them like a sea. Jessica raised her face to the rain, opening her mouth to the welcome moisture, letting it wash the dirt from her face and soothe her swollen, painful skin. The drops hurt as they pelted her, and she had to close her eyes against their sting, but she didn't mind. To be drenched in water, however punishing its force, seemed miraculous after her days of wandering in the desert.

Then she remembered Spur. The little mustang stood with his head bowed beneath the downpour. Unlike her, he could not lift his head to drink of the rain, and once the storm passed, the water would soon be gone, absorbed into the thirsty desert. Jessica dismounted and removed her sombrero. Although not completely watertight, it would hold the rain long enough for Spur to drink. The mustang slurped greedily from this makeshift basin, and then Jessica managed to fill the canteen by making a funnel of the brim. As the rain began to lighten, she drank her own fill from the hat and allowed Spur another ration. She watched the rivulets run off across the desert hardpan. There was no way to hold onto it, she thought in despair, no way to save it for future need. It all came at once, more than she could use, and then it was gone.

The storm had passed them now, and the rain had nearly ceased. Behind them, thunder continued to mutter, and brief flashes lighted up the sky, but overhead the clouds were beginning to break apart, and the silver face of the moon slid out. Jessica's clothes were completely soaked and she shivered a little in the night air. But she knew that soon—all too soon—her garments would be dry again. Nothing in the desert stayed wet for long.

Spur had been revived by the storm. If not entirely his usual energetic self, he was at least not as drooping and dispirited as he had been in the blistering heat of the day. Although weak from hunger and exhaustion, Jessica also felt somewhat revived, and her earlier dark despair, if not ban ished, was at least pushed for the moment to the edges of her mind.

As dawn began to lighten the sky's rim and gray light crept across the desert, Jessica noted some sort of change, some irregularity in the landscape ahead of them. Her hopes began to rise. Had they reached the edge of the desert, or at least arrived at some break in its pitiless expanse? As if he sensed her own change of mood, Spur began to trot, carrying them more rapidly toward the distant line on the horizon.

Dawn broke behind them, and the sun's rays began to stretch across the desert. They were close enough to see clearly what lay ahead. At the edge of what appeared to be a riverbed stood several clumps of stunted trees. Beyond, the landscape changed as the flat desert gave way to a low ridge of jumbled red and yellow rock.

Jessica felt disappointed as they rode up. She had hoped for something more dramatic, some real change in the pattern of the desert, but the dry riverbed and the rugged area beyond were still part of the same harsh life-denying landscape over which she had been wandering. Still, the sparse trees offered shade from the sun, and perhaps there was water to be found in the riverbed. As they rode up, a jackrabbit bounded off from its disrupted morning meal. And further down the bank a grouse suddenly flapped out of the bushes and disappeared.

Cheered by these signs of life, Jessica dismounted and tethered Spur in the shade of the trees. Then she scrambled down the steep, short bank. The riverbed was a wide, flat-bottomed channel, its banks lined with boulders which suggested powerful torrents of water. But there was no water now, Jessica discovered, as she dug futilely in the sand at the bottom. The storm of the night before had apparently left this river's source untouched. Not a drop of moisture seeped into her attempted water hole.

Well, she consoled herself as she toiled up the bank again to the shade of the trees, at least they still had water in the canteen, and perhaps somewhere else along the river's course they would find more. It was something—a mark, a guide in the trackless desert. Later, when the sun's heat began to fade, she would explore the rocky area on the other side of the river. And then, after that . . . She refused to let her mind go further. She would decide that later. Right now, she would rest.

She stretched out on a patch of dry grass beneath a tree and fell into an exhausted sleep.

Chapter 17

When Jessica awoke, the sun was low, and lengthening shadows softened the harshness of the desert day. The landscape was suffused with a strange sense of peace.

For a while she lay there, staring up at the dark branches outlined against the pale blue sky. Her sleep had refreshed her, though she knew she was still very weak. The grove of stunted trees, the river bed, the rock formations, and the desert all seemed dream-like and far away, as if she were already partly in another world.

She could hear Spur moving nearby, chomping languidly at the sparse clumps of grass. At least he had found some nourishment, meagre though it was, to sustain him in the desert. She remembered the rabbit and the grouse she had surprised earlier. She should make some attempt to hunt, before her strength gave out completely. But although she knew abstractly that she should eat, Jessica no longer felt hungry. Soon she was going to die, and her body seemed already to have separated itself from its own needs.

Here, in the vast peace of the desert did not seem a bad way to die. Certainly there were worse. She could have been

thrown from Spur the day of that first wild ride and cracked
her skull against the hard-packed earth of the ranch yard. Or
she could have died violently at the hands of some perverted
stranger, as Annunciata had.

There was no malice in her fated end. The forces of the
desert were impersonal; she, Jessica, simply did not matter.
She would vanish into nothingness in the vastness of sand and
sky, a shrinking pile of flesh and bones, sucked dry by the
sun. In a way, it felt good to have all passion, concerns, and
fears behind her. It gave her a curious sense of freedom and
of strength.

Jessica stood up and stretched. The movement caused her
heart to pound furiously, and she paused a moment for it to
calm down. It seemed to her that she could actually hear the
blood coursing through her veins, could feel every tiny speck
of the life within her, which soon she would lose.

She saddled Spur, then led him down the steep riverbank
and up into the rock formation on the other side. A flat-
bottomed crevice in the rocks opened into the red-walled
depths like a pathway to another world. No longer caring
about her destination, but compelled by some unknown force,
Jessica gave Spur his head and let him pick his way through
the maze of barren stone. They appeared to be following a
well-worn trail. Whether it was made by animals or human
beings, she could not tell, for she saw no signs of life, past or
present.

As the high, red walls cut off the rays of the late afternoon
sun, Jessica lost all sense of time. Had they wandered through
this rocky wilderness for half an hour? Or was it longer? The
rocks, themselves, blank and unvarying, gave no clue to their
progress.

Then, suddenly, they emerged from the maze of red stone
and found themselves at the edge of a cliff. The trail plunged
abruptly at their feet, zigzagging toward the bottom, and then
disappeared between the stone outcroppings on the cliff face.
Jessica reined in Spur and paused to stare down at the scene
below.

They stood on the rim of a wide canyon, almost a valley,

across which the sinking sun cast long, distorted shadows. In the distance, a tall, yellow butte jutted up from the canyon floor like a sentinel. The rest of the canyon was an expanse of pale yellow sand, dotted with clumps of brush and dry grass of the same color. Here and there rose mounds and jumbles of rubble and rocky outcroppings, thrown into a confusion of light and shadow by the slanting rays of the sun.

But Jessica noted little of this. Her eye was caught by the long, lush line of green trees which wound through the center of the canyon. Their presence spoke of water and of cool, welcome shade. Was this what had drawn her through the maze of rock behind her? Had the grove and the water which nourished it touched her desert-sharpened senses, pulling her forward with their tantalizing promise of life?

A futile promise, she thought, and for a moment she felt a strange reluctance to descend into the canyon below. This oasis would not save her, but would only prolong her inevitable death, for she could not survive forever in the desert, even with an endless supply of water. Was she always to be lured on, to be given hope just when all was hopeless, so that she could expend a little more of her almost nonexistent strength, and postpone for another hour, another day, that end which eventually must come?

Spur shifted restlessly beneath her, as if he could already smell the water in the canyon below them. Or perhaps it was simply that, untroubled by human doubts and despair, he sought only to survive and would keep moving as long as there was strength in him to do so. A little ashamed of her own hesitation, Jessica urged the mustang forward and they began the descent.

The trail was steep, but her little mount had carried her down worse slopes than this, and had no trouble keeping his footing. Once again, Jessica had the feeling that others had preceded them. The trail, though eroded and rubble-strewn, did not appear to be a natural path, but had been shaped by the hands and feet of men. Steps had even been cut, though they were now broken and treacherous. However, there were no recent signs of passage. Whoever had made and used the path must have done so a long time ago.

When she reached the foot of the cliff, Jessica paused once more to survey her surroundings. A vast quiet lay over the canyon. Nothing stirred; even the desert wind was still. The vast rock formations cast sharp shadows longer than themselves across the yellow sand. A cricket chirped briefly in a nearby clump of grass and then was abruptly still. The silence was almost brooding, and despite the late afternoon warmth, Jessica shivered.

The line of trees was farther away from the cliff than it had seemed at first. As they passed by one of the strange masses of rock huddled at the base of the cliff, Jessica turned to regard it curiously. It was the same yellowish hue as the cliff itself, but there was something unnatural about its outlines. She reined Spur to a halt, struck by sudden understanding. These were not piles of rock tumbled from the cliff, but the vast ruins of ancient buildings—abandoned, crumbling buildings, their broken walls fashioned from blocks of pale yellow stone, which blended with the sand around them. It was these ruins, Jessica realized, that gave the valley such an eerie, brooding air.

She stared at her discovery for a moment, and then started forward again, moving slowly so she could gaze at the ruins as she passed.

In some places, the walls had collapsed into piles of rubble, but in others they stood several stories high, jutting like jagged towers against the face of the cliff. Weeds sprouted between the stones, and tumbleweeds had piled into the corners, blown by the wind. Windows and doorways stared like dark, blank eyes. Jessica shivered again and quickened Spur's pace. An air of abandonment and death hovered over the ruins. They were the bleached and empty bones of some past people, and they spoke of her own fate.

Near the river, another cluster of buildings squatted like a shadow town, and Jessica gave it a wide berth as she made her way down the bank. There was something oppressive about the huddled ruins, and they seemed to deny the promise offered by the oasis which bloomed nearby.

At the bottom of the bank, Jessica paused to gaze at the first standing water she had seen for several days. The river was not deep or swift, but it stood in welcome pools, rippling here and there, and so clear she could see its sandy bottom. Rocky beaches stretched out on both sides of the river, testifying to times of fiercer and more voluminous flow. But at the moment, the stream was placid and unthreatening.

Jessica let Spur drink first, giving him a little water in her sombrero before letting him lower his head to the stream. She postponed her own first sip, savoring the thought of the luxurious abundance of water which confronted her. Then she drank slowly, rinsing her dusty mouth before letting the coolness trickle down her throat. When she had finished, she splashed water on her grimy face, not caring that it ran in little rivulets down the front of her shirt.

In the depths of the pool she caught a glimpse of her reflection. It was as if a stranger gazed at her. Her skin was brown from the sun, and the high cheekbones were prominent in her thin face, so that she appeared even more Indian than before. Something gleamed a brilliant blue between the tangled strands of hair, and Jessica reached up to her ear, realizing that she still wore the turquoise earrings Ross St. John had given her. How long ago that fateful evening seemed now. Pushing aside the masses of hair, she tried to restore some order to their tangle. But they were too matted from wind and dirt, so finally she simply pulled them back from her face and tied them up with her kerchief. With the band around her head, her sunburned face, and earrings, she really did look like a native of the desert. She stared a moment longer at her reflection and then abruptly stood up, disturbed by what she saw. It was as if she had entered another time and place and no longer was the person she had once known.

Leaving Spur to graze on the plentiful grass, Jessica climbed slowly up the slope toward the ruins nestled under the oak and cottonwoods at the top of the bank. Although they repelled her with their brooding air, she was drawn by their mystery. The buildings were a puzzling variety of shapes, some square-walled, others rounded, all joined together in one vast complex and surrounded by the protective ring of a crumbling stone wall. The yellow stone had turned a soft, grayish pink in the fading light, making the ruins even more eerie.

Cautiously, Jessica stepped over a low wall and found herself in a large, circular courtyard. Weeds grew in clumps in the dusty rubble beneath her feet, and small clusters of purple flowers glowed faintly in the dusk. Owls and bats must nest here in these ruins, she thought, but she did not see or hear any signs of life. Moving slowly, she headed across the courtyard toward the dark rectangle of a doorway. The rounded end of a log beam protruded through the wall above it, but the doorway itself was framed in large slabs of stone. Jessica crossed the stone lintel and found herself in a small roofless room. Its walls reached two stories high on either side, and above the beams she could see a pale blue patch of sky, rapidly turning to indigo as the sun faded. Beyond lay another room, with a tiny doorway one would have to stoop to enter.

Who had lived here? she wondered. The rooms were so small. It was hard to imagine furniture, household objects, or people in such a crowded space. Were they some lost race of the desert about whom she had heard so many tales? The broken walls, towering blankly above her, gave no clue.

She could take shelter tonight in these ruins. They would at least offer some protection from the desert wind and rain. But the thought was not appealing. Better to face the elements than to sleep between these walls, so heavy with some unknown and tragic past.

She turned to go and then stopped abruptly, her heart leaping in sudden fear. A man was leaning in the framed rectangle of the doorway, his form silhouetted against the gray dusk. His face was dark under the brim of his hat, but Jessica could see the rifle cradled in his arm and the revolver at his hip. Despite his seeming casualness, there was something lean and dangerous about his pose. His body was coiled and alert like a cat ready to spring.

Jessica tried to still the rapid pounding of her heart. Why, she thought despairingly, had she left her own rifle behind with Spur? She cursed herself for this bit of carelessness.

They stood in silence for a moment, and then Jessica finally summoned her courage and spoke.

"Who are you?" she asked, hoping her voice would not betray her fear. "What are you doing here?"

The man in the doorway straightened up, pausing a moment before he replied.

"I might ask the same of you," he drawled. "And I might ask why a woman like you is all alone in the middle of the desert." His voice was deep, with a hard edge to it.

Jessica stood uncertainly, not knowing how to reply.

The man bent to light the cigarette he held between his lips. In the brief flare of the match, she caught a glimpse of a lean, hard face, with two sharp lines, like parentheses, around the mouth.

"Well," he continued after a moment, "reckon it's none of my business why you're here. I'm camped up at the far end of the wash. If you'd like to join me for supper, you'd be welcome." His glance ran over her briefly. "Looks to me like you could use a little grub."

He turned abruptly and disappeared as quietly as he had appeared. Jessica stood for a moment, trying to collect herself and to calm the frantic beating of her heart. After so many days alone in the desert, it was a shock to encounter another human being. As she left the ruins and made her way down the bank to the river, she heard the faint sound of hoofbeats, fading into silence in the distance.

Spur was reluctant to leave his grazing, but she urged him up the bank, and then mounted, hesitating for a moment, uncertain as to what she should do. Finally, she turned up the canyon and headed in the direction of the hoofbeats. She would accept the stranger's invitation. She had nothing to lose. What did it matter, after all, if she were raped or even murdered? Without this man's help, she would die anyway.

She might as well take what he had to offer and hope that he meant her no harm.

At first she could see no sign of his camp. "The far end of the wash," he had said, but where was that? Did he mean all the way up the canyon? She wasn't certain she could find it in the dark. Then she saw that the river swerved, heading away from the main part of the valley and up into a small box canyon faced with square, broken stone walls. She could see the flicker of a campfire, and her nostrils were assailed with the smell of frying bacon, almost overwhelming in its intensity. The smell of the food and the light of the fire were invitations to life.

As she drew nearer, Jessica saw that the man had built his greasewood fire in an open area just beyond the bank of the river. He was kneeling beside the blaze, his face illuminated by the glow. From the grove of trees near the river came the faint nicker of a horse, as if in welcome. The man glanced up briefly as Jessica approached and then turned back to the bacon he was stirring in a pan.

"You can tether your horse down by the river," he told her. "There's plenty of grass, and he should be safe."

Wordlessly, she dismounted and followed his instructions. Two other horses were already grazing peacefully along the bank. One looked like a packhorse; the other was a well-groomed, chestnut mare with strong, graceful lines. She unsaddled her mount but did not have the strength to carry the heavy saddle up to the campsite. She dropped it down beneath a nearby cottonwood, and taking her rifle with her, climbed slowly back up toward the fire. She seated herself on a rock next to its flickering warmth and watched her host.

Saying nothing more upon her return, he continued his cooking, looking up at her occasionally. Jessica could detect no threat or malice in his manner, but something about this man told her that even if he intended her no harm, he was someone to be feared.

How did she look, she asked herself. Bedraggled and unappealing, most likely. Perhaps he even took her for an Indian, she thought, recalling her startling reflection in the river. Well, her ragged, dirty appearance should at least offer her some safety. Who, after all, would want her now?

Her companion had roasted some sort of a small bird over the flames and he cut off a portion of the meat and put it on a plate for her, along with bacon and several biscuits. Jessica sat for a moment, breathing in the unaccustomed aroma of food before she began to eat. As when she had stood by the stream, putting off her first drink of water, she felt a curious reluctance to partake immediately of the life-sustaining substance before her.

"Take it easy," the man told her as he knelt beside the fire with his own plate. "Eat slowly and don't eat too much at first." It must be obvious, Jessica realized, that she had been a while without food.

But his advice was unnecessary, for she could eat no other way than slowly, and the ravenous appetite which had overcome her when she first smelled food was quickly appeased. After a few mouthfuls, she felt almost uncomfortably full.

They ate in silence, and Jessica wondered at the oddity of her situation—that she should find herself here, sharing food with a stranger in the middle of the desert after so many days of wandering alone. Yet in a way it did not seem strange. It was part of her journey into another world, a journey which had begun with her waking up that afternoon, or perhaps even before that, with the storm in the desert. For a moment she imagined the man in front of her to be an emissary from beyond, come to guide her into that other world, following the footsteps of those figures she had seen marching across the desert. The thought did not frighten her. Rather, it gave her a strange sense of peace. She would follow where she was led and give herself up to whatever awaited. Beyond the circle of firelight, the bushes and trees grew dim, and the shadows wavered in long columns across the sand. The man's features shone in the reddish glow of the fire, taking on an almost diabolical cast. Jessica began to feel very warm. As the world around her started to fade, her head nodded, pulled irresistibly toward sleep.

"I don't suppose you have a bedroll with you."

The stranger had risen and Jessica jerked awake at his words. They were more a statement than a question, for it was obvious that she had wandered across the desert cruelly unprepared.

"I've got an extra blanket you can use," he continued. "Might make the ground a little less hard."

To Jessica it sounded as luxurious as a featherbed. He took a rough wool coverlet from a pack by the tree and spread it on the ground a short distance from the fire. Despite having slept all day, Jessica was very tired. And the food, which she had thought might revive her, had only made her sleepy. Her companion stood by the fire and watched her as she lay down, a cigarette burning lazily between his fingers. Jessica had a moment of unease. It seemed very intimate to lie down to sleep like this in front of a stranger. And what would happen when she was no longer awake? She drew her rifle closer, laying it alongside her body as she tried to make herself comfortable. If the man noticed her action, he made no sign. Later when she opened her eyes for a brief moment, he was kneeling by the fire, watching its dying embers with a distant look in his eyes. She shut her own, and drifted back to sleep.

When Jessica awoke, the sky was barely gray with dawn, and the chill air was fragrant with the smell of coffee and the smoke of the greasewood fire. She could see the shadow of her companion moving about the camp. Throwing back the blanket, Jessica stretched her limbs, stiff from days of riding and sleeping on the ground. The sky over the rim of the canyon was suddenly suffused with pink, and as if on signal, there burst forth a wild baying chorus somewhere high on the mesa. It echoed across the canyon and hung for a moment in the clear desert air, and then ceased as abruptly as it had begun.

The man smiled at her startled expression.

"Coyotes," he explained. "They're greeting the rising sun."

Jessica was thrilled. She had never before heard anything so glorious or so primitive. It seemed a good omen.

She sat up and attempted to straighten her disheveled clothes. It was hard to believe that not too long ago she had worn a cream satin gown and fine jewelry. Her stained and ragged riding habit seemed almost part of her. What would all the St. Johns' fine guests think if they could see her now?

The man brought her a plate of beans, along with some of the meat and biscuits from the night before. He handed her a tin cup filled with coffee. Steam from the coffee rose in the cool morning air.

He cut short her thanks.

"I don't usually eat breakfast, but I figured you'd need something to get your strength back."

Jessica found that she was able to eat more this morning. She emptied her plate and then sat sipping the coffee slowly. Though things still had a dream-like air, her surroundings were gradually beginning to seem more substantial. Bit by bit, the world was returning to her—or she to it.

Her companion had put out the campfire and rolled up his bedroll. Then he came over to her, rifle in hand.

"I'm going to do a little hunting," he told her. "If I were you, I'd take the blanket and move down by the river where there's shade. You might as well take it easy today. You won't be going anywhere for a while."

His words were not a threat but a simple statement of fact.

Jessica rose and began to fold the blanket. Then she paused. Suddenly it seemed odd to be camping with a stranger and know nothing of him at all.

"Who are you?" she asked. "I don't even know your name."

"It's Reno."

"That's all?"

"That's all you need to know." His tone was not unfriendly, but there was a finality about his words which discouraged further probing.

"My name is Jessica," she offered when he didn't ask. "Jessica Howard."

"I know."

"You know?" Although his response startled her, at the

same time it seemed inevitable. His knowledge of her name was part of the fate that had guided her to this remote canyon. But his next words deflated this romantic thought.

"I've seen you before, with the St. Johns," he continued. "Many people know who you are."

"Oh." With this prosaic answer, some of the mystery of the place and the man began to fade, and the world she had left behind began to draw closer.

But where exactly had he seen her? As they walked together toward the river, Jessica remembered that day in Las Vegas, the day of their departure, and the man she had stumbled against—the gunman with the hard face and the revolver, who had brushed against her as she passed. She cast a furtive glance at the man beside her. Was he the same person? The thought made her uneasy. It was one thing to camp with a mysterious stranger, a being of her destiny rendered not quite real by a flickering fire and the light-headed dreams of a desert-induced trance. It was quite another to confront a real person in the sober light of day—a gunman, perhaps a murderer, or worse.

They continued their walk in silence. As they approached the grazing horses, Spur looked up and gave a little whinny of welcome. Jessica put her arms around his neck, comforted by his familiar presence.

"That's your horse?" The man's incredulous tone reminded her of Ross St. John's reaction, and she immediately became defensive.

"What's wrong with him?" she asked.

"He looks as if he would bite your head off. I've seen tamer-looking horses in herds of wild mustangs."

Jessica glanced at her mount. It was true that Spur was not looking his best. Not that he ever looked exactly beautiful, but several days of riding in the desert with no proper food or grooming had left him looking shaggier and more disreputable than ever. From underneath his rough coat, his ribs protruded.

"He saved my life," she said, and she knew that it was true. "Without him I would never have made it through the desert." She rubbed Spur's muzzle affectionately. He took a mock nip at her hand as if to confirm his critic's words.

Reno gazed at her a moment, a faint smile tugging at the corners of his mouth. Jessica knew they must make quite a pair, she and Spur, two desert rats—but just as tough. Together they had survived.

After Reno had watered his horses, he saddled and mounted his mare and rode off, leaving Jessica alone by the river, with her thoughts. She spread the blanket underneath a cottonwood tree and stretched out. The day was beginning to get hot and she was grateful for the shade and for the knowledge of cool, life-giving water so close at hand.

She spent her day there, sometimes dozing, sometimes simply lying quietly, letting her thoughts wander. With the immediate dangers of her sojourn in the desert banished for the moment, other concerns came tumbling into her mind, and many of them were painful and unpleasant. Ross St. John filled both her sleeping and waking dreams, his image so strong and forceful that it seemed to Jessica that he must really be there beside her. She thought of him with a mixture of longing and guilt, anger and despair. Would she ever see him again? And what did he think of her now? Would he understand why she felt compelled to leave, or would his pride be hurt because she had made love with him and then run away? And Jeffrey—she tried to conjure up Jeffrey's image in her mind, but he was a blur. Grief and guilt flooded her. Jeffrey loved her so much, and she had failed him, failed everyone, including herself. Her world had been rich and full of promise, and she had destroyed it.

It was quiet in the canyon. During the morning, birds sang in the trees above her, but by midday the heat hung over the valley like a pall, and even the birds fell silent. Only the occasional shrill of an insect broke the stillness. At one point, Jessica heard gunshots far up the canyon. Assuming that it was Reno hunting, she did not let the sound disturb her.

As the afternoon wore on, she fell into a deep sleep. Once again she dreamed of Ross St. John. This time she was back on the Running J, riding up to the ranch house. And this time, Ross, instead of greeting her tenderly, turned away from her, his expression cold and unfriendly. He walked away across the pasture and she went running after him. But no matter how fast she ran, he kept moving farther and farther away until he disappeared into the distance. She called his name and heard the faint echo of her own voice across the mountains.

When Jessica awoke, the shadows were once again long with late afternoon, and Reno was kneeling beside her. A pair of dead grouse lay beside him on the grass. Tears had seeped from the corners of her eyes as she dreamed, but if he noticed them, he gave no sign. He stood up and extended his hand to help her to her feet. As she took it she noticed that his hand was not that of a cowboy. His fingers were slender and smooth, and gripped hers tightly. A gunfighter's hand. Even in hunting he wore the revolver strapped against his hip.

She turned and followed him silently toward the camp.

Chapter 18

The next few days passed quietly. Jessica gave no thought to her own future, but instead surrendered to the timeless serenity of the canyon. Reno seemed to have no plans to leave, so she let the rhythm of her days follow his. After her desert brush with death, she was content simply to savor life. Each day brought both repetition and newness: the constant play of color, light and shadow as the sun moved across the canyon; the wildlife that ventured forth, unafraid, as she sat motionless in the shade of the cottonwood by the river; the evenings by the campfire with her silent companion. Most of all, however, she was drawn by the ruins, and spent much of her day in exploration.

Reno, who seemed content to let their days run parallel, did not offer to keep her company, but did caution her to watch for rattlesnakes.

"The canyon's crawling with them," he told her. "And they like high sunny places especially, like the tops of those walls."

Forewarned, Jessica proceeded carefully, but she saw nothing more dangerous than jackrabbits, which fed alongside the

walls and bounded away on long legs at her approach. Occasionally, something would scuttle off into the darkness as she
entered one of the windowless interior rooms, and she would
back out quickly, content to leave the chamber to its unknown
occupant.

The valley was filled with these ruins, small fragmen-
tary towns which blended deceptively with the desert sand.
More than the desert itself, they called to her in a mysterious
voice, haunted and haunting. If only she could understand
what they were saying, she might understand some secret of
herself.

She tried to imagine the size of these towns when they had
stood, complete and whole, with high walls, courtyards, and
tier after tier of tiny apartments, and she tried to envision the
people who had lived, worked, and died here. At one time,
these towns must have had thousands of inhabitants. How did
they make a living from this barren canyon with its tiny
ribbon of river?

She touched everything, as if to absorb from the stones
themselves the secret of their past, and she marvelled at the
skill of these ancient builders. She ran her hand over the
yellow stone walls and leaned her cheek against their smooth
mortarless surface. Each stone fit precisely into place, and the
wall ran straight and true. Many of these outer walls had no
windows, or only the smallest of openings, high above the
ground. Had these towns been at war with each other, she
wondered, and raised these walls for defense? Or had some
outside enemy threatened them, perhaps driving them from
the canyon forever?

In the dry desert air, nothing rotted, and although the
buildings had been abandoned long ago, many of the materials of which they were constructed had survived. The great
beams that held the roofs and ceilings were still sound, as
were the peeled branches of willow, which overlaid them,
and which, covered with packed earth, formed the floors of
the rooms above. Jessica fingered the weathered logs, thinking of the treeless desert she had crossed. Where did these

great trees come from? Did forests once exist across the mesa? But the idea seemed absurd.

Here and there she found bits and pieces of the past: scraps of pottery painted with black, geometric designs, several beads made of shell, broken arrowheads—all scattered among the ruins. And once she came across a small, exquisitely shaped turquoise bead. She rubbed the dust from it with a moistened finger and then stared at it in the palm of her hand. Thinking of the stones she wore in her own ears, she felt a kinship with the past. Jewels of the desert—to her they seemed more beautiful than gold.

In the paralyzing heat of midday, Jessica rested in the shade of the great stone walls and let her thoughts wander. How easy it was, she reflected, to accept the importance of your own life and to assume that the things which filled it would always exist. Once, this canyon had hummed with life. For the people who lived here, it must have seemed the center of the world. But now the canyon was a crack lost in the desert, and no one knew or cared about its past inhabitants. She closed her eyes, trying to picture the towns filled with people, children playing in the courtyards, families gathering in the doorways to gossip, women strolling to the gardens by the river while the men returned from a successful hunt. As the afternoon shadows grew long around her, softening the ruins to a burnished glow, a vast stillness crept over her. Nestled in the remains of this unknown and long-vanished past, time no longer had meaning, and Jessica felt her own life slow and stop, suspended in the canyon's timeless peace.

"There are ruins like this all over the desert," Reno told her in the evening by the fire. "I've seen them set into the sheer faces of cliffs, and come across big, round, stone towers built like castles at the edges of canyons. The Navaho call them the Anasazi. That just means 'Ancient Ones.' Even they don't know who these people were, or where they came from, or where they went."

"But don't the Indians of the pueblos build towns like this?"

He shrugged. "Yes, but not as tall or vast. Whoever these

people were, they had a civilization of their own here in this canyon.''

Later he pointed out to her the walls of the round rooms, some built into the structures of the buildings, some set into the courtyards. Most of them were small, but others were forty feet wide or more and lined with bench-like shelves. Reno told her these were probably *kivas*, sacred structures such as those used by the Pueblo Indians for their ceremonies. Jessica found it hard to imagine these rubble rings as the site of colorful rituals and religious mystery.

Occasionally, Jessica hunted. Although she did not succeed in bringing down one of the grouse which so startled her with their sudden rushes from cover, she did bag several rabbits which were added to the meals she and Reno shared in the evening. She felt no repugnance at hunting here. It was not a sport but a necessity for survival, and she enjoyed depending upon her skill and wits.

Reno showed her other ways of surviving in the desert: how to dig for roots by the water's edge; where to look for berries and nuts; how to draw moisture from the fleshy body of a cactus and use its sticky, cool liquid on her sun-blistered hands. Jessica was impressed by his knowledge, but Reno did not seem to consider it remarkable.

She thought sometimes that perhaps she was intruding on his solitude, but he didn't seem to mind her presence. He made no demands, nor did he disturb her time alone. Pondering his presence in the canyon, Jessica wondered if Reno's solitude was self-imposed. One evening as they sat in companionable silence in front of the fire, she decided to ask.

''Are you wanted?'' Her question sounded blunt and she feared for a moment that he might take offense, but he only smiled.

''Not by anyone I know of,'' he replied. ''And how about you? Are you on the run?''

''Only from myself,'' she admitted, then hesitated. ''I guess maybe from someone else, too.'' Then, surprisingly, she began to talk about herself, haltingly at first, and then, as she was caught up in her own story, the words began to tumble out. She told him about her childhood in Texas, about her engagement to Jeffrey and her coming to the Running J, and finally, having said too much now to be embarrassed, she told him about Ross and what had happened the night of the fiesta, and about her own flight into the desert.

By the time she finished, the fire had dwindled into a glowing bed of embers. Reno, who had been lying on his back while she spoke, stood up and added a dry pine log to the fire. As he knelt to stir the blaze, the flames cast a copper glow across the chiseled planes of his face.

"It must be hard to be beautiful," he remarked laconically, keeping his eyes on the fire. "Not"—he added, a smile playing at the corners of his mouth—"that I've ever had that problem, myself."

"What do you mean?" Jessica asked, somewhat deflated by this casual response.

"There's a lot to you. You're courageous; you're strong; you've got a sense of honor and determination. But because you're beautiful, sometimes that's all that people see. And for that reason, too, men won't leave you alone."

Jessica didn't know whether or not to be flattered by this flat, almost disinterested appraisal. She noted that Reno didn't seem to include himself among such men, and for some reason she was piqued by this thought.

"I can't have looked too beautiful when I arrived here," she murmured, thinking of her reflection that evening when she gazed in the pool.

Reno smiled lazily at her over the flames.

"You looked like a lost, starved kitten." His smile faded and he rose and came over to where she was sitting. Kneeling down, he put his finger under her chin and lifted Jessica's face to his. Turned away from the fire, his eyes were dark pools without light. Jessica felt a shiver go through her at his touch.

"Do you love Ross St. John?" Reno's voice was soft but demanding.

"I . . . I don't know." Jessica felt tears start in her throat at this direct question. She had tried to think as little as possible about Ross in the last few days and it was painful now to have him filling her thoughts. "I think I do, but I don't know."

"A man forces you into his bed, violates his own son's fiancée, and you still think you might love him?" Reno's tone was harsh. Jessica turned her head away from his gaze.

"He . . . he didn't. I mean, I wanted . . . I . . ." Shame washed over her and she was unable to continue.

Reno rose and turned back to the fire. "Your problem, Jessica," he said as he absently stirred the coals with a stick, "your only sin, perhaps, is that you don't really know what you want." He gave a short, bitter laugh. "We're two of a kind, you and I, wandering the desert looking for heaven knows what. Ourselves, maybe." He turned to look at her again. "For me, beauty gets in the way, sometimes. I have to work to see through it. And so do you, I think."

With these ambiguous words, he left her and went to spread out his bedroll. Jessica sat staring into the flames for a while before she, too, rolled up in her blanket to go to sleep. As she gazed at the panorama of stars spread above her, she reflected on the odd, impersonal intimacy she shared with Reno. They ate, talked, slept together at the campfire, and yet they were apart.

Sleep came slowly. Her outpourings to Reno had released for Jessica the floodgates of memory and feeling. Reno was wrong, she reflected. Not knowing what she wanted was not her only sin. She had wronged Jeffrey. After all her running away, it was a realization she must face. Her wrong lay not so much in her passion for Jeffrey's father—terrible as the consequences of that had been—but rather in the way she had loved—and not loved—her fiancé. She had been in love more with what Jeffrey represented than with the man himself. Certainly she had been drawn to his gentle, courteous ways and intrigued by his artistic interests, but more than that, she had fallen in love with the idea of escaping the restrictions of her city life. And then, as they journeyed west, she had been captivated by the idea of becoming mistress of a large and prosperous ranch. Had she not been so blinded by this vision

of her future, she would long ago have realized that her own
passionate nature was at odds with Jeffrey's quiet and more
restrained ways.

Remorse swept over her as she contemplated how little she
knew herself. Never would she have thought she would know-
ingly hurt others. Yet she had betrayed two men with her
passions and cut herself off irreversibly from both, for Ross
was as unattainable for her now as Jeffrey. She thought of
Ross with anger, guilt, and longing. He had coaxed her to his
bed with his experienced intuition of her nature and her
needs, but she had followed all too eagerly. Even now, her
body remembered the feel of his and called out for a love she
knew could never be. Tortured by these and other thoughts, it
was a long time before Jessica fell into the oblivion of sleep.

Several days after her talk with Reno, Jessica decided to
climb the butte. She had been fascinated by it since her
arrival. Standing like a sentinel at the end of the canyon, its
colors constantly changing—from pale yellow to red to grayish
pink—in the canyon's continual play of sun and shadow, the
butte seemed to call her with an urgent voice. On this particular morning, Jessica had awakened before dawn, while Reno
was still asleep. Gathering her rifle and canteen, she tiptoed
away from the camp and toward the river. She saddled Spur,
plump after several days of grazing, and set out for the butte.

As she drew closer, it seemed even more massive. Then, as
the sun rose behind her, its face suddenly flamed with rosy
color. Jessica dismounted at the base and stared up at the
lofty stone walls. The lower part of the butte sloped gradually, but the face rose abruptly toward the flattened top.
Here and there were clinging clumps of brush, but in many
places the rock walls were sheer and bare. There was no sign
of any dwelling near the butte, and Jessica wondered what
part it had played in the lives of the ancient canyon dwellers.
She tethered Spur to a bush at the base, and began to climb.

The sun rose quickly, and the heat soon became oppressive, but Jessica continued her scramble up the brushy slope,
unwilling to turn back. When she reached the bottom of the

sheer rock wall, she started to circle the butte, looking for some way to ascend farther. At first such ascent seemed impossible and she was about to give up when she discovered a narrow rock chimney, little more than a treacherous cleft in the butte's face. It would be hard work to climb, but since the cleft faced north, it would offer some protection from the sun. Jessica paused a moment to gaze up, suddenly envisioning herself plunging down the narrow crevice of rock to the stony slope below. Then, gathering her courage, she began to climb.

The going proved even more difficult than she expected, and Jessica soon realized that her leather boots were not made for climbing. In several places she slipped, and for a heart-stopping moment, she seemed about to fall. Each time, she had to pause for several minutes to let her breathing return to normal. She began to regret her rash impulse, but as she looked down the narrow chimney, going on seemed preferable to trying to descend. Perhaps once she reached the top, she could find some easier way down. She clenched her teeth and resumed her climb.

Once she reached the top, Jessica found a narrow ledge upon which she could rest and let her shaky legs regain their strength. She could also contemplate the scene below her, and the dangers and difficulty of her climb were momentarily forgotten in her awe at the view.

She could see the whole length of the canyon, the winding line of trees along the river, the clusters of ruins—even more numerous than she had thought—which stretched into the distance, this arid expanse of land that once had supported a whole civilization. In the distance, the mesa was tinged with pink, and a line of fluffy clouds floated on the horizon. She sat there for a while, reveling in the magnificent vista which her climb had revealed.

Once rested, Jessica began to work her way along the ledge toward the southeast face of the butte. She had forgotten Reno's warning, and as she rounded a jutting pillar of rock, she suddenly came face to face with a large rattlesnake basking in the morning sun. It coiled menacingly and shook its rattle at her, the dry buzzing harsh in the still air. Jessica

jumped back and almost fell, sending a shower of stones
down the face of the butte. Heart pounding, she pressed
herself against the cliff. The rattlesnake, seeing the intruder
momentarily at bay, slithered away into a crevice at the edge
of the ledge.

After that, Jessica proceeded more cautiously, rounding
corners with care, and watching where she stepped. She came
upon two more rattlers, a little sluggish in the morning sun,
and paused to let them retreat, a rock clutched in her hand for
defense. If she were looking for clues to the ancient life of the
canyon, she reflected, she had been foolish to come up here,
for surely no one would ever have struggled up that narrow
chimney to challenge the rattlesnakes in their high kingdom.

But she was wrong. A little further along the ledge, she
came upon three sandstone slabs leaning against the face of
the cliff. At first they seemed to be simply an odd natural
formation, but as she came closer and peered between the
slabs, she saw two spirals, one larger than the other, painted
upon the rock. Strange designs, she thought, for someone to
have engraved in this remote, high place. She would have
expected something more in keeping with the vastness and
mystery of the civilization in the valley below.

As she watched, a dagger of sunlight burst into the vertical
space between the slabs, and inched like a bright finger across
the rock. It passed a few inches from the center of the larger
spiral, and then slowly traversed the entire circle and disappeared, leaving the painted finger once more in shadow.

Jessica straightened up and gazed out across the canyon at
the sun, shading her face with her hand. It was late in the
morning, she judged, perhaps near noon. She glanced back at
the reddish-yellow slabs behind her. Their position against the
cliff seemed casual, as if someone had carelessly laid them
there to rest and then forgotten them. But the shaft of light
suggested a deliberate effort to mark the sun's passage. Her
discovery of this device, continuing to keep time long after its
inventors had disappeared, aroused in Jessica a feeling of
kinship with the people who had inhabited the barren valley
below.

She sat for a moment on the ledge, her back against the cliff, drinking in the view and enjoying her sense of distance from the world. Then, tearing herself away from thoughts of the past, Jessica faced the present reality of having to descend the butte. There seemed to be no way down other than the chimney she had climbed, and she realized she would have to retrace her steps. Still alert for snakes, she returned to the chimney, and after pausing, panic-stricken, for a brief moment at its edge, she cautiously began to lower herself.

The descent was more terrifying than the climb, for now the bottom of the chimney looked painfully far beneath her. At some points she had to use her entire body to lower herself, bracing her feet against one wall and her shoulders and arms against the other. Occasionally, dizziness washed over her and she had to stop and close her eyes for a moment, struggling to regain her control. By the time she finally reached the bottom, her limbs were shaky and all her muscles ached, but the scramble down the rock and brush-strewn slope at the foot of the butte was easy compared to the rest of her descent, and Spur was placidly waiting for her at the bottom.

When she returned to the camp, Reno was sitting under a nearby tree, cleaning his revolver, the parts spread neatly on the blanket beside him. He glanced at her as she rode up and dismounted, his slightly raised eyebrows the only sign he gave of any curiosity about her long absence.

Jessica unsaddled Spur in silence and led him down to the river. When she returned, she helped herself to some cold beans, left over from the night before, and a handful of dried apples. Her climb had given her an appetite. She sat down cross-legged next to Reno and watched him work while she ate. She knew that she was dusty and disheveled. There was a time when she would never have let a man see her in such a state, but now she did not care. Was it the man she was with that made her feel that way, she wondered, and the fact that her appearance seemed to be of no interest to him. Or was it simply that the events of the past week or so had made such things as her personal appearance, no longer of any great moment.

She noted the deftness with which Reno reassembled his weapon, the long fingers moving almost caressingly along its surface. The revolver seemed an extension of his hand rather than a separate object. Watching him, Jessica reflected that her knowledge of his profession no longer caused her any fear or apprehension. It was not that she did not know him to be dangerous; the cool detachment which was reassuring in their own relationship would make him all the more formidable as a gunman. But this danger was part of another life, one which was, for the moment at least, unreal and remote.

Jessica contemplated her companion, who worked seemingly oblivious to her attention. How different he was from other men she had encountered, as sure of himself as Ross St. John, as quiet in his own way as Jeffrey, and yet unlike either of them. His hands fascinated her. She recalled the way his smooth tapering fingers had twined briefly in hers that evening by the river and she shivered. From her initial fear of being alone with him, she had passed to feeling herself drawn to him, in spite of—or maybe because of—his making no move toward her. She found herself watching his lean compact body as he moved around the campfire at night, and when she thought he wasn't looking, she studied his sun-bronzed face, wondering what thoughts lay behind it. Yet he sat beside her now, working quietly, ignoring her. Irritation rose in her. Was there something wrong with her, Jessica wondered, that he paid her so little attention? Or was something wrong with him?

As if sensing her annoyance, Reno looked up, an enigmatic smile playing at the corners of his mouth.

"Where did you go today?"

But now that he had finally inquired, Jessica felt reluctant to speak of her experience. She gestured in the direction of the butte.

"I went over there—just to explore a little."

"Did you go all the way to the top?" His question was casual, as if he referred to a stroll down the canyon.

"Yes," she replied briefly.

He stood up and holstered his gun.

"Next time, better take a rope. You're lucky you didn't break your neck."

He walked off, leaving Jessica uncertain if she had been rebuked or paid a compliment. Was his offhand treatment of her exploit a way of saying that what she had done was no more than he expected of her?

Jessica leaned back wearily against the tree and closed her eyes. What did it matter, after all, what he thought of her? She was on her own now, with no one to answer to but herself. It was better that way, she decided. All she had brought to other people was pain and trouble. Jessica tried to summon up thoughts of the Running J and her life there, but everything seemed far away and unreal. All the passions which had once possessed and impelled her had been purged by the desert, and all her concerns for social and material position rendered trivial by the immensity of the ruins. Here in the canyon, strewn with the remains of a long-gone people, the land seemed to mock the idea of being owned by anyone.

Tired from her climb and the midday heat, Jessica began to doze. The sound of gunfire jerked her awake. For a moment she sat in confusion, thinking she was back at the Running J and that, once again, it was being attacked. Then she realized that the sound had come from the direction of the river, and that Reno was practicing.

Chapter 19

Jessica sat on the river bank, tugging at her tangled locks, and for the hundredth time wished she had a comb. She had tried to fashion one out of a piece of thorn, with little success. She gazed down at the pool into which she had stuck her feet, still raw and sore from yesterday's climb up the butte. Her appearance, which had been of so little concern recently, had suddenly begun to bother her. She felt dusty and unkempt and her clothes stuck to her skin. And her hair . . . Jessica reached up once more to pull at it. Maybe she would have more success if she removed some of the grime deposited during the long days in the desert.

She stepped out of the water and knelt on the sandy bank, bending her head to the pool. Her hair floated on the surface like a dark fan. But the position was awkward, and besides, the front of her shirt was getting wet.

Well, why not wash that too? In fact, why not wash all her clothes? They certainly were dirty enough, their original colors almost indistinguishable beneath a layer of dust. Jessica glanced around. Reno had gone off somewhere down the canyon. Usually he did not return from his excursions until late afternoon.

She unbuttoned her shirt and slipped off her riding skirt, hardly more than rags now, she reflected, as she lowered them into the stream and began to scrub them against a rock. The water felt cool and inviting, and she splashed it against her naked skin. Then she looked down at the pool. It was shallow and there were no strong currents. There was no reason she could not bathe her body while her clothes dried. And once in the water, she could more easily wash her hair.

She wrung out her garments and laid them on a bush overhanging the stream. Then she slipped into the water. It felt silky smooth and refreshing against her skin. Jessica thought of the days in the desert when just a few drops of water seemed more precious than gold. She had never before appreciated the luxury of being able to immerse her entire body in this life-giving liquid.

She scooped a handful of sand from the bank and began scrubbing the layers of grime from her body. How filthy she was! She seemed to have carried a good part of the desert with her into the canyon. When she had finished scrubbing, Jessica lowered her body into the water and immersed herself entirely, letting her hair stream out behind her in the current. Then she took more sand and scrubbed her scalp, running her fingers through her hair. The flowing water and the action of her fingers helped lift the dirt and made her tresses more manageable. She stood up, and lifting her wet hair, she wrung it out and then braided it into a long rope which she let hang down her back.

Then she splashed herself once more with water and waded to the shore.

Her clothes were still damp, so she dried herself with her kerchief. She had lost weight, she noticed, as she glanced down at her white body, though her breasts were still full and rounded. She cupped them in her hands, watching the nipples harden into little pink buds as the air cooled them. She liked her body the way it was now. It was leaner, harder, tougher. It had taken her across the desert, she had climbed the butte, and lived for days eating sparse and simple food and sleeping outdoors on the ground. She felt confident and self-sufficient.

Jessica wrapped her long braid, now nearly dry, around her head and secured it with the kerchief. Then she pulled on her riding skirt and her boots. Plucking her shirt off the bush, she held it up for a moment. Even more than the skirt, it had suffered from the journey. It was ripped under the right arm, one sleeve was torn in several places, and a button was missing in a potentially embarrassing spot. Soon she would be as good as naked. She wondered if Reno had any spare clothes he might lend her.

She wasn't certain exactly what it was that caused her to look up, but when she did, Reno was standing above her on the bank, leaning against a tree. His gray eyes regarded her intently. She froze for a moment, and then instinctively clutched her ragged shirt to her chest to cover her bare breasts.

How long had he been there, she wondered. Had he seen her bathing in the river? Her momentary fear gave way to a little surge of annoyance. Not only had Reno been watching her all this time, but he had done so without making any move. Could he really be so indifferent to her beauty as to see her naked like this and not attempt to take advantage of her state? Was she really so unattractive to him? But, then, why was he watching her like that?

They stood by the river for a long moment, their gazes locked. Jessica was dimly aware of the gentle rippling of the stream behind her, and of the desert breeze rustling the leaves of the cottonwood trees. But these sounds seemed distant. Once again she felt she had entered another world. Slowly, as if toward her destiny, she moved up the bank, and into Reno's arms.

Later, lying beside Reno in the shade, her head cradled on his shoulder, Jessica felt at peace, the restless passions which had driven her finally stilled.

Reno turned on his side to look at her. He smiled, and this time the smile reached his eyes. Lazily his finger traced the smooth curve of her throat, and her flesh tingled at his touch.

"Why did you wait so long?" she asked. Then, surprised at the boldness of her question, she lowered her gaze and blushed.

Reno laughed and tilted her chin up with his finger, forcing her to look at him again.

"I was waiting for you to come to me," he replied. "You were at the end of your rope when you wandered in here. And it was a man who pushed you there. You needed time, and I decided to give you all the time you needed."

So Reno had not been quite as indifferent to her as he had seemed. The thought was comforting to Jessica's vanity.

"You startled me when you first arrived," Reno continued.

"I startled you?"

"You were like a ghost wandering in the ruins. Like an ancient part of the desert come alive."

"Oh." The description was hardly flattering.

"Then I realized who you were and wondered what had brought you here. I needed time to find that out and to decide what to do about you. And time to get to know you."

"And do you now?"

"A little. I know, for one thing, you're someone who does things the hard way."   .

"What do you mean?"

"You're headstrong and passionate and sometimes that doesn't take you in the best direction."

"You mean it takes me running off across the desert."

He smiled again.

"You're as crazy as I am." He rolled over on his back and lay looking up at the sky, visible in pale patches through the leaves of the tree. "What exactly do you want, Jessica?" he asked.

It was the same question Ross St. John had asked her so long ago in the barn the day they returned from Las Vegas. Jessica hesitated.

"I don't know," she confessed. But she knew that whatever it was, it was not what she had wanted before. Much about her had changed since that day she fled the ranch. "And what about you? I don't think I know you at all," she said, though she felt in her heart that this was no longer entirely true.

Reno ran his fingers along the curve of her shoulder and then moved his hand further down her body.

"Well, I reckon we'll just have to do something about that. Not," he added, "that there's all that much worth knowing."

Jessica doubted that, but she did guess there were things about himself that Reno was unlikely to tell her.

They slept, wrapped in each other's arms, in the dappled shade beneath the tree, and when they awoke, they went together to hunt for their supper, wandering in companionable silence in that softened and fading light which made this Jessica's favorite time of day. Reno bagged the inevitable jackrabbit and they carried their prize back to camp to be roasted over the brushwood fire. Jessica skinned the rabbit, following Reno's instructions and using his long-bladed hunting knife. She felt as if they were an ancient Indian couple, sojourners from the canyon's past, preparing their meal by the fire.

"Do you suppose the people who used to live here ate as much rabbit as we do?" she asked.

"Could be. But they had bigger animals to hunt. I once found the skull and antlers of a deer behind one of the ruins."

"Where did they come from?" Jessica had seen numerous deer around the Running J, but they seemed unlikely inhabitants of the desert.

Her companion had no answer.

Watching Reno as he tended the fire, Jessica was drawn to him as she had been so often before. She wanted to reach out and touch him, but she now felt shy. She was embarrassed that he had forced her to make the first move, making her reveal to him her own longing before he would touch her.

Reno in turn treated her much as before. But his detachment, the way he moved parallel to her, never impinging, now seemed a kind of intimacy rather than indifference. No words or gestures were needed to confirm their bond. But in the midst of her peace, Jessica felt a small stab of fear. What they enjoyed was something out of time, and she knew it could not last. Resolutely, she put such thoughts out of her mind. After all, she had learned all too painfully how impossible it was to know what might lie ahead.

After supper, Reno was restless, and when Jessica had curled up in her blanket, he came over and knelt beside her to say he was going for a walk. She felt disappointed in his leaving. She had been looking forward to lying in his arms and savouring the warmth and comfort of his body as she fell asleep. But she was reassured by the way he smiled at her in the firelight and the way his hand lingered for a moment against her cheek before he stood up to leave.

When she awoke, Reno was shaking her shoulder gently. Jessica had no idea how long she had slept, but she saw that the fire was dead. The breeze of afternoon had turned to a fierce dry wind, howling down the sides of the box canyon, blowing sharp gusts of sand into her bedding. Lightning flickered faintly at the far edges of the mesa, and Jessica could hear the distant muttering of thunder.

"A storm's coming up," Reno told her unnecessarily. "I think maybe we'd better take shelter. I've already moved the horses up near the cliff."

Jessica, remembering the downpour which had overtaken her in the desert, lost no time in jumping up and folding her blanket. She followed Reno toward the cliffs. The horses were tethered at the base, their backs turned patiently to the stinging wind. Spur looked up as she approached and gave a nicker of welcome. She marveled that her mustang had let Reno handle him. He was usually not willing to be led by strangers.

The shelter of which Reno had spoken was a series of shallow caves set in the cliff. Although apparently natural formations, they had been modified, for human purposes, with low crumbling walls running partway across the openings. Reno went in first, carrying a brush torch and a long stick, to make certain they would not be sharing their dwelling with any rattlesnakes. Jessica, her experiences on the butte still fresh in her mind, was quite happy to let him precede her. They were not the first to seek shelter in the caves, she noticed. In a corner near the wall, some creature had gathered bits of leaves, fur, and twigs into a crude nest, now abandoned, and bones were scattered in several places.

When Reno had determined that the cave was safe, they spread their blankets on the uneven floor and sat down to watch the storm. With the cave wrapped above and around them, and the stone wall in front, Jessica felt secure and snug. And when Reno slipped his arm around her waist and drew her against his shoulder, it seemed as if nothing could harm her.

The storm had drawn closer, and flashes of lightning brightened the broken cliffs across from them with a bluish light. The wind had picked up, sending leaves and scraps of brush scurrying across the sand. Jessica loved watching the play of elements across the sky and seeing distant storms approach. Spaces here in the West were so vast and beautiful, not like the closed horizons of the East. She voiced her thought to Reno.

"I can't even remember what it's like back east," he responded. "I've been out west so long."

Intrigued by this volunteered scrap of information about his past, Jessica sought to gently press him.

"Where was your family from?" she asked.

"Pennsylvania. My father was a farmer till the gold fever hit him, and in '59 he headed for Pike's Peak. I was just a kid at the time, no more than seven or eight, I guess. He dragged me and my mother along, certain he was going to make a big strike. He never did, of course, and it was my mother who supported us, doing laundry for the miners. Finally, she left in disgust, going back to Pennsylvania and leaving me with my father."

"What happened then?"

Reno lit the cigarette he had been rolling in the dark, and then sat quietly for a moment. The cigarette smoke drifted lazily toward the entrance of the cave, where it was suddenly sucked out into the night by the wind.

"Oh, we wandered a lot, my father and I. There was always a new strike somewhere, a new chance to make a fortune. Colorado, Idaho, Montana, Nevada, the Black Hills—we were always moving on to the next big place. Finally, my father began to drink. I think he knew by then he was never going to strike it rich, but he couldn't face up to the fact, couldn't give up his dreams. The drink killed him, I reckon, or at least I think he was drunk when he was placer mining in Montana and fell into the stream and drowned. Maybe it was the gold that really killed him."

He fell silent. There was a lull in the storm, and Jessica could hear Reno's steady breathing and feel the beating of his heart against her own. Then, unexpectedly, a streak of lightning broke the sky over the mesa, followed almost immediately by a peal of thunder that seemed to rattle the walls of the cave. In spite of herself, Jessica jumped.

Reno laughed and pulled her closer.

"I'm not afraid," she defended herself. "It just startled me." But she let him enclose her in the comforting circle of his arms.

"I used to see storms in Montana more spectacular than this. You can see farther there than any place I've ever been, and sometimes the sky would look like it was covered with sheets of lightning. And the winds. They could sweep up the canyons like a flash flood. Trees would topple just like matchsticks when they came."

"I've never been to Montana. Is it very beautiful there?"

"It's very beautiful. There's the wide sky and rolling hills and grassy plains. And the mountains—more rugged than anything here in New Mexico." He paused a moment, and when he continued, Jessica sensed in him a subtle change of mood. "But it's lonely country, bitter and cold and lonely in the winter. And winter comes quickly and stays long. Sometimes it's hard for a man—or a woman—to take."

"Did you live there long?" Jessica asked softly.

"Too long." His voice was low. "Too long and not long enough."

Jessica waited for Reno to go on. The tip of his cigarette was a glowing dot in the dark. A flash of lightning lit up his face, and Jessica could see his eyes, dark and intent, staring into the storm. She knew they were not seeing what lay before him, but were focused on some other place, far away in distance and time. Outside, the first drops of rain spattered tentatively in the dust.

"I had a ranch there, a horse ranch. The horses were my pride and joy. I loved them better than most men love their children. Almost better than I loved Sarah, my wife, though not quite. Or did I? Sometimes I wonder."

Jessica held her breath, willing him to go on, but not daring to speak.

But Reno seemed compelled to continue, and Jessica did not even know if he was aware of her anymore. Engrossed in his story, he had pulled away from her and sat with his arms wrapped around his knees.

"We had been there two years, two lonely and difficult years. But Sarah had stuck by me. She was strong as any man, and more patient. Good with the horses—and with me. And the horses—I would go down to Texas every spring and buy the colts and bring them up to fatten in Montana. I picked only the best. I had an eye for them. And the cream of the crop I kept for myself.

"In the fall of the third year, we had an early blizzard. It was only the beginning of September, but the wind blew strong and the drifts piled up around the house. My prize stallion picked that moment to jump the fence and wander off, and I insisted on going after him, even though I couldn't see a foot in front of me in the snow.

"Sarah didn't want me to go. She wasn't normally the nervous type. She didn't mind being alone, and once she had even shot some wolves prowling around the stable while I was gone. So I should have known she wasn't just being skittish when she asked me not to go. Maybe she sensed something. She was like that sometimes. She knew things other people didn't. But I was stubborn, and it was my prize stallion that was gone. So I left. She stood in the doorway and watched me go. It was the only time I ever saw her cry.

"I was five days tracking that stallion. He was still half wild and determined not to be captured. I followed him

through the blizzard and then over the hills when the snow
stopped, and finally I cornered him in a box canyon. He gave
up, then, and let me put a bridle on him. It took me only a
day and a half to get home.''

Guessing what was coming next, Jessica drew closer, but
Reno did not seem to notice.

"When I got back to the ranch, Sarah wasn't there. The
ranch door was wide open, the fire was long dead, and there
were snowdrifts still piled inside the doorway. And tracks—
there were several sets of tracks in the melting snow. I'm
good at tracking. I learned it when I used to hunt for meat
while my father searched for gold. And I followed those
tracks through the hills like a starved man tracks a deer—I
followed them day and night—until I found Sarah.''

The rain was coming down in wind-whipped sheets now,
beating the ground into a froth and blotting out their view of
the canyon. Reno flipped the stub of his cigarette into the
downpour and sat for a long moment before he continued, his
voice low.

"They had beaten her to death—raped her and beaten her
to death. She must have struggled; she wasn't the kind not to,
but there had been three of them, and she hadn't had a
chance. By the time I got to her, the wolves had found her
body.

"I buried her there, under a pile of stones, and then picked
up the tracks again. I trailed them for three days—they had
gone all the way to Virginia City. I lost their tracks in town,
but I hung around, and watched, and asked questions. And
then, when I was sure I knew who they were, I bought a gun.
I had hardly ever used a revolver before, didn't even own
one. But I practiced a little, and I suppose it helped that I
didn't care whether I lived or died. All I wanted was revenge,
and that's what I got. I surprised all three of them in a saloon
one night, and when I finished, they were all dead. I was
almost sorry, though, that I was still alive.''

He paused again, and in the dim light, Jessica could see a
small grim smile playing at the corners of his mouth.

"The irony of all of it is that one of the men was a

notorious gunman, and in killing him, I not only got revenge, I acquired a reputation. People began to call on me. They wanted my services, or they wanted to call me out, to take away my stolen reputation. It didn't matter to me any more. I didn't want to go back to the ranch. Killing seemed as easy as anything. I practiced. I wandered. I hired myself out. I've made a name for myself now, and there's hardly anyone who knows it who doesn't treat me with respect—or fear. And none of it really matters.''

Jessica leaned against his shoulder and Reno wrapped her in his arms, burying his face in her hair.

''What does matter,'' he continued in a low voice, ''what bothers me the most is that I left Sarah all alone there in that grave in the hills.''

They sat for a long time in silence, not moving, even though the rain had stopped and the clouds above the canyon were beginning to break apart. Jessica could think of nothing to say. What comfort could she possibly offer? Her own history, her own story and problems seemed petty beside Reno's. She understood now his desire for solitude and the detachment with which he viewed the world. And the hard lines in his face which had so frightened her at first—she saw them now as the imprint of the life, both forced and chosen, that he had led.

At a loss for words, but needing to tell Reno how she felt, Jessica leaned her head against his chest, pressing her hand to his heart. Its steady rhythm was reassuring. Despite all that had happened to both of them, they had survived, and were here, together, alive, in this desert refuge. Was it just their common bond of time and place that had drawn her so strongly to this man? Or was it some deeper force? Right now she felt she loved him both for what he was and all that he once had been.

Reno took her hand and raised it to his lips, kissing the palm and then each finger in turn. His kisses were warm and hard against her skin and each kiss sent longing for him pulsing through her veins. She wanted to be part of him, to share and absorb his pain, to soothe his grief and her own

with her body and with his. Reno cupped her face between
his hands, tilting it up toward his. His eyes searched hers and
Jessica caught her breath, overwhelmed by the longing she
saw in their depths. He bent to kiss her lips, and she parted
her own eagerly, letting his tongue explore the warm moist-
ness of her mouth. They clung together with their lips as if
each sought to draw from the other not simply comfort but the
very breath of life itself.

Breaking away, Reno gently eased her back against the
blanket and then bent to kiss her on the throat, his lips
lingering against the soft skin, his tongue making tingling
circles with each kiss. His deft fingers found the buttons on
her shirt and her nipples hardened in anticipation of his touch.

"Reno. . . ." Her voice was a sigh as she closed her eyes,
as she surrendered to his caress. His hands—those gunfighter's hands—were so soft, so gentle, as they touched the
intimate places of her body, moving slowly, touching lightly,
causing her to moan with longing.

She helped him remove his own garments, her fingers
clumsy from anticipation, and then in wonder ran her hands
over the hard, compact surfaces of his body, moving unafraid
to touch places she had never before touched, knowing by his
response that she was pleasing him. His breath was hot
against her cheek as he whispered her name, his voice lingering over each syllable as sensuously as his hands lingered
over the curves of her body.

Although his probing fingers told him she was ready, he
delayed, prolonging his caresses, so that when he finally
entered her, Jessica found herself moaning and biting his
shoulder as his rhythmic strokes brought her to an ecstatic
peak, where she trembled for a moment, exploded and then
fell. She held Reno tightly as he plunged deeper and deeper
inside her until he, too, shattered in release.

As she clung to him afterward, Reno gently wiped away
her tears and then held her tightly in his arms.

Chapter 20

The desert days passed slowly, perfectly. Jessica felt as if she had crossed over into another life, another world, where Reno had been waiting, fated, just for her. Other men and other passions had been left far behind, and since the evening in the cave, each drifting day brought more contentment than the last. Jessica marveled at the peace that she had found in this remote and wild canyon, and with the man she had found there waiting for her. He was a man who had nothing, seemed to want nothing, asked nothing of her. Yet he gave her so much, walking with her in the shadows of the ruins by day, talking with her quietly in the glow of the fire in the evening, loving her with gentleness and passion as she lay in his arms at night. Here, far away from everything she had once thought important, certain that she had lost all that counted in her life, Jessica had found a contentment she had never hoped to attain, and a bond stronger and more profound than she had ever thought to know.

She had entirely lost track of time. Then, one morning as she awoke, it intruded once again. This morning was not like the others. Something was different. Something was wrong.

Jessica lay for a moment, wrapped in her blanket, trying to determine what had given her this feeling. At first everything seemed normal. Reno was moving about the camp in the gray light of morning as he usually did. She loved to lie and watch him as he worked, recalling the feel of his body against hers as they lay together in the warm intimacy of the night.

But as she watched him this morning, she realized what was wrong. Instead of simply folding his bedroll and throwing it beneath a tree, Reno had rolled it tightly and tied it into a compact bundle. And the packs and saddlebags lay scattered around the camp, their contents stacked beside them. Reno was breaking camp. Jessica's sense of peace suddenly fled as she realized that their sojourn in the canyon was coming to an end.

Reno came over to kneel beside her.

"You're leaving?" She tried to make the question casual, but her voice quivered.

"We're leaving," he replied. "I have to go. I've been here longer than I planned, as it is. And I can hardly leave you here alone in the desert."

The "we" was somewhat reassuring, but Jessica still felt forlorn.

"What are you going to do?" she asked.

"I have a job to finish. And then, after that . . ." He shrugged and left his sentence unfinished.

Of course, Jessica thought. I'm forgetting who—and what—he is. A gunman, a drifter like Reno was hardly going to drag a woman around. Their stay in the canyon had been only an interlude for him, something pleasant to pass the time—nothing more.

As if reading her thoughts, Reno bent to kiss her gently on the forehead. Tears sprang to her eyes, and Jessica tried to blink them back. If she and Reno were to part, she was not going to let him know that it mattered.

Not noticing her tears—or choosing to ignore them—Reno rose and returned to his preparations for departure. Dispiritedly, Jessica got up and folded her blanket. She had little to pack. It was only through Reno's bounty that she had survived. She took her borrowed blanket over to where he knelt beside a pack, and dropped it to the ground. He stood up and put his arm around her, and despite her resolution to hide her feelings, Jessica leaned against him and hid her face against his shoulder.

"I'm sorry to leave the canyon." Let him think that was the cause of her sadness.

"It will always be here," he replied.

"I think I could stay forever."

He laughed and pulled away, holding her at arm's length. His eyes were affectionate and amused.

"You'd find it gets a bit cold in the winter."

"I wouldn't care." With him, and a fire, and some place to shelter, Jessica thought, she would want nothing more.

"What are you going to do, desert lady, once you leave here?"

It was a question which Jessica had avoided during her days in the canyon, content to let time flow by. Nonetheless, the answer came readily to her lips, and she realized it must have long been at the back of her mind.

"I'm going to return to the Running J."

She felt him stiffen.

"And how long will you stay?"

"Only long enough to make my peace. I was a coward to run away like that. It wasn't fair to Jeffrey, or even to Ross. I owe some apology, some explanation, at least, before I leave for good."

"And after that?"

After that? Jessica didn't know. As far as the future was concerned, her mind was blank. What sort of life could she have now? What sort of life did she want?

She stepped back and gazed into Reno's face.

"Reno . . ." Her hand rested tentatively on his arm.

Almost roughly he removed it.

"I'm a killer, Jessica." His voice was harsh. "I kill other men for a living. You know some other things about me, but that's what you need to know most because that's who I am."

Jessica bowed her head before the dark bitterness of his words.

"I swear to you, though, that I've only killed others like myself—people who've tried to kill me, people as lawless as I am. I've never killed in cold blood."

She raised her head to look at him again.

"You don't have to swear to me, Reno," she said softly.

He turned away, his shoulders sagging.

"Always till now I've been good enough—or lucky enough—to not get killed myself." He was staring toward the mesa, where the horizon was rapidly turning pink. "But that's what lies ahead of me—to be killed, myself, someday. Unless I stop." He turned back to her. "And I will stop. I'll stop soon—if I don't die first."

His words hung in the dawn air like a promise, and Jessica moved into his arms, uncertain who was holding whom, her feelings a mixture of sadness and hope.

They decided not to leave until late afternoon, when they could cross the scorching expanse of the desert in safety. After they had breakfast, Reno finished packing, and then headed down the canyon, as if to say his good-bye to this place that had sheltered them so long. Jessica spent her morning prowling restlessly through the nearby ruins, searching for some final message, some bit of wisdom she could take to guide her when she returned to the world she had left. But today the stone walls told her nothing. They were the crumbled remains of a forgotten people—nothing more.

Despondently, Jessica made her way back to the campsite and spent the afternoon resting by the river, saving her strength for the evening's journey. As she lay there, listening to the shrilling of the insects, the dry breeze in the trees, the contented chomping of Spur and the other horses as they gorged themselves on one final, grassy meal, Jessica felt some of the former tranquility the canyon had offered her. And by the time Reno returned, she felt at peace again, and almost looked forward to their journey.

As the sun began to slip toward the west and loosen its hold on the day, they loaded the horses and filled their canteens. Then, with the mounts in tow, they headed out of the canyon.

Their route up to the mesa was different from the one which Jessica had used in her descent. When they reached the top, she paused to look back. The canyon stretched behind her, the shadows of the ruins long and stark across the sand. The setting sun glinted behind the butte, turning the rocky pillar into a column of darkness against the sky. It was strange to think this place would stay behind her as she had found it, timeless and deserted. For a brief moment the world around her faded, and Jessica felt she was another person looking back, all the people who had ever stood there looking back, regretting their inevitable going. A tremendous yearning gripped her and it was with difficulty that she turned away and, mounting Spur, followed Reno across the desert.

Their trip, unlike her own wanderings, was swift and certain. There was no moon, but Reno seemed to have cat's eyes and an uncanny sense of direction, for he moved rapidly across the shadowy landscape. At times, Jessica had to press Spur to keep up with the pack horse and Reno's long-legged mare.

Shortly after dawn they reached Cabezon, a shabby but bustling town of reddish adobe buildings, dominated by a nearby peak which jutted from the desert. The peak's stone cap had been visible long before the town itself, and had guided them on the last part of their journey.

They left their horses in the livery stable and checked into the hotel. The clerk, a wizened man with several missing teeth, eyed them suspiciously as Reno registered, and later, up in their room, Jessica looked in the mirror and realized why. With her sun-browned face, tangled hair, and ragged clothes, she could hardly have looked more disreputable. No one could call her beautiful now, she thought, as she ran her fingers across her high, prominent cheekbones and down her thin cheeks. But Reno seemed to see no defects in her appearance. Coming up behind her as she gazed in the mirror, he reached his arms around her and began to unbutton her blouse. She turned and their mouths met hungrily, as if it had been days, not hours, since they touched. With urgent hands he pulled her down beside him on the sagging bed.

Afterward, Jessica lay listening to the sounds of other people around them: the footsteps in the hallway, the creaking of beds, the clatter of wagons in the streets, the muffled voices in the halls. It felt strange to be enclosed by walls and hard to believe that only a few hours ago she had been in a place that had gone for perhaps hundreds of years undisturbed by human sounds.

Jessica was hungry, but she decided she wanted a bath before she ate. While she soaked in the unaccustomed luxury of soap and hot water, Reno went to do some errands. When she returned to their room, he had laid his purchases—a pair of men's pants, a checked cotton shirt, a pair of new leather boots—across the bed.

"For you," he said briefly. "A couple more days in the clothes you've got on, and you'd be absolutely indecent. Not," he added, drawing her into his arms and kissing her, "not that I myself would mind. But I thought you might want to return to the Running J a little better dressed than you are now."

Jessica found herself deeply moved by his thoughtfulness.

"I . . . I have no way to repay you for this," she stammered.

"It doesn't matter. It's nothing, really. Now, why don't you get dressed while I go bathe."

Jessica shed the ragged garments that had served her in the desert, and put on her new clothes. As she pulled on the pants, she thought of Ross St. John, who so long ago had advised her to wear just such clothing for her riding in the mountains. What would he think when he saw her again? The thought aroused a good deal of trepidation. She remembered his volatile temper and the hurtful force of his anger. She also remembered his passion for her, and she shivered.

She was glad when Reno returned. He ran his eyes over her new attire and smiled.

"You look almost civilized," he told her. "But not too much."

In addition to his other gifts, he had brought her a comb,

and Jessica gratefully used it to restore some order to her long-neglected hair. She looked like an Indian boy, she reflected, as she regarded herself in the mirror. But the rounded breasts beneath the cotton shirt gave the lie to that impression.

She noted that Reno strapped on his gun when they went out. Gone was the relaxed air of the time in the canyon when, although always armed and alert, he had nonetheless seemed at ease. For Reno, it was not the desert that was dangerous, but the world of men.

It was early afternoon now, and despite the heat of the day, the streets were crowded. Jessica stayed close to Reno, nervous at this unaccustomed press of humanity. She noticed several Indians as they walked, shabbily dressed and seemingly intoxicated. She thought of the magnificent ruins in the canyons and of the people who had made them, and felt sad.

In the restaurant, Jessica made up for the sparseness and simplicity of her desert diet, to Reno's amusement.

"You won't be skinny for very long if you keep that up," he told her as she finished off a large piece of apple pie, and then settled back with her after-dinner coffee.

She smiled at him over her cup.

"Well, if I get too fat, I'll just have to go back into the desert."

"Do you think you can find your way this time?"

"I doubt it," she laughed. "You made it seem so easy, but I'm sure I'd just get lost again."

"Then I guess you'll just have to wait for me." Reno's expression was serious now and Jessica's heart leaped as she drank in the significance of his words. Hesitantly, she reached out to lay her hand on his. As his slender fingers closed over hers, she thought once more of the gun hanging at his hip, and she felt her happiness dissolve as she realized that much still lay ahead before they could hope to be together again.

They spent the afternoon in bed, talking, touching, dozing in each other's arms. In the evening they went out again to eat, and then, after a brief sleep, rose well before dawn to continue their journey. Reno would not tell Jessica his own destination, but he promised to leave her off on the road to the ranch. Her heart was heavy as they set out, the thought of their imminent parting at the forefront of her mind, and it was with mixed feelings that she watched the Sangre de Christo mountains come into view on the horizon. Their wild beauty never failed to stir her heart, yet she knew they were the signal for the separation of her path from Reno's and for the approaching confrontation on the Running J, which she was trying to gather the courage to face.

They reached the main road about mid-morning, and with the sun beating down upon them, began the laborious climb through the foothills. Several times they stopped to water the horses at the stream by the road, and Jessica noted with concern that the water was even lower than she remembered it. Either the storms she had encountered in the desert had not reached here, or they had left too little water to make any inroads on the drought.

Finally, as they reached the point where the piñon and juniper began to give way to yellow pine, Reno reined Felicia to a halt.

"This is as far as I go," he said. "You're on your own now, Jessica."

The significance of his words hung in the air between them. Blinking back her tears, Jessica extended her hand and Reno took it in his.

"Thank you for everything, Reno," she whispered. "I owe you my life."

"Perhaps we're even on that score." A smile curled the edges of his mouth but his eyes were sober. "You have a lot of courage, lady of the desert, and I wish you well." He paused a moment and then went on. "When you leave the Running J, or if you ever want me, just go to the livery stable in Bernalillo and ask for Pete. They'll know who you mean, and you'll be safe there till I can get to you."

She nodded, unable to say more.

"Good-bye, Jessica."

She turned to go, the trail blurred by tears as Spur resumed his ascent. She wiped her eyes and turned to look back, but Reno was gone.

Part III

*Sangre
De Christo*

Chapter 21

Reno stood for a moment, gazing after Jessica as she headed up the road. He had been alone for so many years now, he reflected. Why then did a feeling of such great emptiness come over him as he watched her ride away? It was as if some part of himself were leaving, some part he hadn't known even existed before. Or perhaps it was a part that had long been missing and only recently restored.

For a moment he was frightened by his feelings. Not since Sarah's death had he felt he had anything to live for, so he had never cared particularly whether he lived or died. And that had always been an important weapon in the kind of life he led. Where other men might lose their nerve, the thought of their own death making them cowards for a fatal moment, such a thought had never concerned him. And so he had never hesitated—and never failed. But now—now he had some glimpse of a different life, and he didn't yet know what that meant.

He wheeled Felicia and, with the pack horse trotting behind them, left the road and headed up the hillside. Although he could not risk riding with Jessica any further along the road to

the Running J, he was not yet ready to leave her. He would
cut across to the ridge overlooking the road, where he could
keep an eye on her progress and make certain that she arrived
safely at her destination.

Reno was uneasy about Jessica's plan to return to the
ranch, even though he understood her reasons. He knew she
had to settle her affairs with the St. Johns, both father and
son, face to face. She would never feel right until she had
done so. And yet, if it had been up to him, he would have
liked to keep her safely away somewhere until the whole
messy business was over. But of course Jessica would never
stand for that. She was not the kind of woman to be wrapped
in cotton wool. She would always insist on doing what she
had to do. And it would take more courage for her to confront
the St. Johns, he reflected, than it took to do most of the
things he himself had ever done.

Well, at least she should be well clear of the ranch by the
time things began to happen. Kincaid was not ready to move,
not quite yet. He was still waiting for his friends in Santa Fe
to act. Nonetheless, the whole situation made Reno uneasy.

There was something else making him uneasy, he thought,
as he made his way along the ridge. That something was Ross
St. John. The rancher was not a man to easily give up
something that he wanted. And he undoubtedly still wanted
Jessica. That was probably clearer to Reno than it was to
Jessica. After all, what man would readily give her up? Reno
doubted that Ross would accept Jessica's decision to leave the
ranch. He was afraid of the inducements—and pressures—
Ross might be able to bring to bear. It was not just Reno's
interest in Jessica which made him afraid. Ross was not good
for her. Or was it Reno's own hopes that made him feel that
way?

She was in view, now, making her way slowly up the
mountain on that ratty mustang. Reno smiled as he thought of
her attachment to her mount and her ready defense of its
virtues. He had to admit, however, that at least in one respect
she was right. Spur was a tough little creature. Not many

horses could have made it through the desert as he had. Perhaps she was right, she owed him her life.

As he moved along the ridge, Reno reflected on the irony of his vigil. Only two months ago—had it really been so short a time?—he had traveled this same route, trailing Jessica and Jeffrey St. John. He remembered how he had watched them with detached interest, wondering what would happen to them on the ranch. Never had he thought that Jessica's life would so directly touch his own. And yet when she had appeared that evening in the canyon, looking like an ancient Indian maiden, he had known right away who she was, and her presence there had seemed both remarkable and inevitable. How hard it had been to stand back the way he had and quietly watch her soul and body recover from her ordeal. And yet, he had enjoyed that watching, enjoyed her. She was strong and not afraid to be alone. That was how Sarah had been, and he, himself.

Abruptly, Reno reined to a halt and reached back to draw his rifle from its sheath. There were riders coming down the road below. Though they were still invisible to Jessica, he could see them clearly from his own position on the ridge. He urged Felicia forward again. He needed to get closer, and yet he had to be careful to keep to cover so that he would not be seen. They were coming around a bend now, almost directly below him. Soon they would see Jessica. Reno reined in Felicia again and rummaged in his saddlebag for his binoculars. Even from where he stood, the horsemen looked familiar, and he had a hunch they were Running J hands. But he had to make certain before he left Jessica in their care. He raised his binoculars and scrutinized the men below.

They were definitely from the ranch. He recognized at least two of the four men—a tall, thin fellow named Doan, and the foreman, Riordon. Satisfied, he lowered the glasses and nudged Felicia down the far side of the ridge, the packhorse tugging at the lead behind him. There was no use lingering where he might be spotted. Jessica would be safe, and that was all he was concerned about. What happened to her now would be up to the masters of the Running J—Ross and Jeffrey St. John. There was nothing more he could do for her.

Turning back onto the road, Reno headed toward the Burnt Cedar ranch. Kincaid would be angry with him for staying away so long. But no man stayed angry with Reno Hayden for long—at least not to his face. A grim smile playing around his mouth, Reno gave Felicia her head, and they sped down the trail.

Chapter 22

Jessica watched the riders approach, her feelings a mixture of apprehension and anticipation. Hugh Riordon was not exactly the person she most cared to encounter first thing on her return. On the other hand, maybe one of the cowboys could keep her company the rest of the way back to the ranch, giving her an opportunity to learn something about what had been happening at the Running J and preparing her for what she would find.

The men drew to a halt as they came abreast, and stared at her. Jessica, a little embarrassed by their scrutiny, did not know what to say, and there was a long, uncomfortable moment of silence, broken finally by Riordon.

"Well, well," he drawled, his eyes traveling over her insolently and taking in the men's clothing she wore. "If it isn't the wandering lady come back to honor us with her presence. And all decked out like a boy. Not that anyone'd ever mistake you for one," he added, his lip curling under his mustache.

Disconcerted by this insolent reception, Jessica glanced at the other cowboys, seeking some friendlier response, but they were all regarding her impassively. She turned back to the foreman.

"I'm on my way back to the ranch," she told him stiffly. "Perhaps you would be so kind as to spare a man to escort me."

"Oh, we'll escort you all right. Don't you worry 'bout that." Riordon chuckled. "But it might not be quite like you were plannin'. Jack!" He called to one of the men behind him. "Get her for me."

The cowboy rode up beside her, and before Jessica realized what he was about to do, he had leaned over and, wrapping one arm around her waist, lifted her from the saddle. As he deposited her unceremoniously on the ground, another man dismounted and, grabbing her, pinned her arms behind her back. Jessica recognized him as one of the cowboys who had flirted with her at the fiesta. But now his face was unsmiling and he gripped her arms painfully tight.

Struggling against her captor, Jessica sputtered her protests. "How dare you! Let me go! What do you think you're doing?"

"Just makin' sure you get back to the ranch safe and sound like you wanted," the foreman replied. "Only this time we ain't gonna have no runnin' away."

The man holding her had taken a rope from his saddle and, with swift brutal skill, bound her hands behind her back. Then he pulled her roughly toward Riordon. Shaken and a little frightened by this handling, Jessica nonetheless stared defiantly up at the foreman.

"Wait till Ross St. John hears about this!" she threatened. "He'll fire all of you for treating me this way."

"Ross St. John probably wouldn't mind if we threw you over the nearest cliff. However, we should get a nice little reward for bringing you to him. And we didn't even have to work hard for it. Wait till he hears that, after all this, you just walked neatly into our arms."

Jessica's heart sank. Ross must be even angrier with her than she had dreamed.

"Hand her up here," Riordon ordered. The man holding

her grasped Jessica by the waist and hoisted her so that
Riordon could grip her under the arms and pull her onto the
saddle in front of him. "You boys go on. I'll take her back to
the ranch. Reckon I should be able to manage by myself. She
can't cause too much trouble tied up like this." He grinned,
but the faces of the other men remained serious. Jessica was
confused by their hostility. Whatever Ross St. John's quarrel
with her, why did his men share it so thoroughly?

Riordon glanced over toward Spur. The little horse had not
moved since his mistress had been hoisted so unceremoniously from his back.

"Bring that mangy mustang over here. I might as well take
him back with me."

But as the cowboy approached, Spur shied nervously, and
when the man reached for the reins, he reared up and struck
out with his hooves. The cowboy ducked and attempted to
grab the reins again, but Spur would have none of it. He
snorted and backed away.

"The hell with him!" Riordon growled. "He's a vicious
beast anyway. Go ahead and shoot him and we'll be on our
way."

"No!" The threat to her beloved horse tore the scream
from Jessica's throat. "Run, Spur! Run!" she called desperately.

She didn't know whether he understood her words or whether
he simply sensed the impending danger, but the mustang
wheeled and took off down the road. The bullets from the
cowboys' rifles made little spats in the dust behind him as he
ran.

"Let him go," Riordon ordered, as one of the cowboys
mounted his horse to give chase. "He's not worth the effort.
A mountain lion'll probably get him anyway."

Despite the foreman's prophecy, Jessica felt her heart lift
as the little horse disappeared around a bend in the road. For
the moment, at least, Spur was safe.

Her own predicament, however, was more difficult. Tied
up as she was, there seemed no chance of escape from her
captor. And as if to make doubly certain that she was secure,

Riordon wrapped one thick arm tightly around her as they headed up the road toward the ranch. The cowboys rode off in the opposite direction, and Jessica had a sinking feeling in the pit of her stomach. Hostile as they had been, she felt safer in their presence than she did alone with the foreman.

They rode in silence for a while, Jessica lost in her own fears and doubts, afraid to ask any questions of the man with whom she was riding, and certain that in any case he would not give her the satisfaction of answering them. He seemed to take a cruel satisfaction in her dilemma, which she had difficulty understanding. She remembered that it had been he who had presented her with Spur, certain that the mustang would throw her.

Riordon was holding her tightly as they rode, more tightly than was necessary to simply keep her in the saddle. Jessica felt the warmth of his broad chest through the back of her shirt, and the feeling repulsed her. She tried to lean forward to avoid contact with him, but he pulled her back.

"No use wigglin' around, little lady. You ain't goin' anywhere."

He tucked his hand more firmly around her so that she felt it pressing up underneath her breast. Almost casually, his other hand stole around, and he slipped his fingers inside her blouse. Jessica struggled against his touch, sick with humiliation and rage.

"How dare you!" she gasped, trying to pull away, as his rough fingers explored the round contours of her breast. But Riordon held her in a firm grasp.

"No need to get so excited. I'm not doin' you no harm. You look a little skinnier than you did when you left. Just want to make sure there's enough left of you in the places that count. I'm sure Mr. St. John wants you back in good shape."

Then, as Jessica continued to struggle, he suddenly gave her nipple a rough tweak, sending a stab of pain through her breast. She gasped, fighting back tears.

"See. That's what happens when you don't sit still."

"Wait till Ross St. John hears about this!"

But her protest sounded weak, even to her own ears.

"You'll be lucky if he doesn't do worse to you himself."
Riordon's voice was grim. Then, as Jessica ceased her struggles and subsided into silence, he unbuttoned the top two buttons of her shirt and ran his entire hand over her breasts. She closed her eyes and helplessly endured his caress until, finally, seemingly tired of his play, he buttoned her up again and, putting his mount into a canter, rapidly covered the rest of the distance to the ranch.

Jessica thought she glimpsed Old Tom at the far end of the ranch house as they rode up, but when they clattered to a stop in front of the house, the yard and porch were deserted. Jessica was glad that there was no one there to witness her humiliation, but the quiet emptiness seemed ominous.

Riordon dismounted and helped her down. With her hands tied, she lost her balance and tumbled into his arms. He held her a moment, leering at her, before setting her upright. She turned toward the house. Ross St. John was standing on the porch, watching.

They stared at each other for a long moment. He looked older, she thought, with more fine lines around his eyes than she remembered, and more streaks of gray in his dark hair. His eyes regarded her coldly, as if she were some species of wild animal that Riordon had managed to capture and drag in.

"Brought you a present, boss." Riordon glanced at Jessica with a certain satisfaction, as if she were indeed a prize he had bagged.

"Where did you find her?" Ross's voice was hard, and Jessica's heart sank. Why was he so angry with her? she wondered. Even if her running away had upset him, even if his pride had been hurt that she had fled from his embraces, it hardly explained the way he was looking at her now. His unwavering gaze was filled with an almost palpable hatred. And Jeffrey—would he hate her, too? She looked around, but the younger St. John was nowhere in sight.

"She just walked into our arms, pretty as you please," Riordon was saying. "Riding up the road as if she owned the place. Hardly put up a struggle when I brought her in."

"You did well. I'll take care of her now. You go on and
get back to the long meadow with the boys."

As Riordon rode away, Ross stepped off the porch and
gripped Jessica by the arm, his fingers digging painfully into
her flesh.

"Ross . . ." She was hurt and bewildered by his reception
of her, and longed for some explanation of his hostility.

But Ross ignored her, and tightening his grip, dragged her
toward the breezeway at the far end of the house. She stumbled, trying to keep up with his long stride, unable to keep
her balance because of her bound hands. He pulled her through
the breezeway and down the long hall. Flinging open the door
to her room, he shoved her inside and slammed the door
behind him.

"Ross," she pleaded, close to tears now. "Why are you
treating me like this? Please, what have I done?"

"You bitch! You filthy, worthless little bitch!" he hissed
at her, his face contorted.

Jessica recoiled from the shock of his words and from the
suppressed fury behind them.

Then he struck her, a brutal blow with his open hand which
sent her staggering. Struggling to keep her balance, Jessica
backed away, but Ross was advancing on her, his hand raised
to strike again.

"Ross, please! Don't!" Her voice sounded thin and faint in
her own ears.

Ignoring her pleas, he struck again. The blow fell on the
side of her averted head and Jessica sprawled against the bed,
striking her shoulder painfully against the far wall. She lay
there for a moment, cringing in the corner of the bed, terrified. Her ears rang so badly that Ross's angry voice came to
her as if from a great distance.

"You worthless slut! You killed him! Just as sure as if you
put a gun to his head, you killed my son!"

"Jeffrey? Jeffrey's dead?" The shock of Ross's words
began to penetrate her fog of pain and fear. What was he
talking about? How could Jeffrey be dead? He was alive
when she left. And why was Ross blaming her?

"Yes, Jeffrey. My son." Ross was shaking her now, gripping her tightly by the shoulders, shaking her so fiercely she feared her neck would snap. "Jeffrey, your fiancé, little that you cared for him, you bitch. You just ran off and left him. He spent days looking for you, but you rode off without giving him a thought. I told him good riddance but he insisted on finding you."

Tears sprang to Jessica's eyes. Jeffrey! How loyal he was. How grief-stricken he must have been when she left. But how could he be dead?

"He rode all over the ranch looking for you, searched every scrub-filled arroyo, every inch of back trail." Ross had turned away from her now and was staring out the window. Jessica lay on the bed, not moving, every one of Ross's words a stab more painful than his blows. "One morning while he was out, his horse stumbled on a rattlesnake. Jeffrey was thrown and broke his neck." Ross turned back to her, his voice rising to an angry sob. "It's your fault my son is dead! You've brought a curse on the Running J. I should have known you were bad luck the moment I first saw you."

He towered over the bed, his fists clenched, but made no move to hit her again. Jessica struggled to sit up, trying to frame some words of comfort, longing to ask for forgiveness. What Ross had just told her couldn't be true. Not Jeffrey! Better that she herself be dead than that he should die because of her.

Ross shoved her roughly onto the bed again. Jessica fell sideways, striking her head against the bedpost. She heard the door slam and realized that she was alone. Numb with shock, grief, and fear, she made no further effort to rise. What would happen to her now? There was no one to defend her, no one to protect her from Ross's rage. As she tried to lift her head, a sharp pain shot through her skull. Everything grew black around her, and she fainted.

When Jessica awoke, it was late afternoon and the sun was streaming in dusty rays through the curtains. For a moment, she was confused by her surroundings. Why was she here between these walls? Why could she not smell the campfire and the aroma of coffee brewing? Then, gradually, she remembered where she was and, at the same time, became aware that someone had removed her bonds and dressed her in a nightgown. No longer was she sprawled across the bed, but instead lay between the sheets.

Tears sprang to Jessica's eyes as thoughts of Jeffrey flooded over her. In her shock at Ross's anger, her own grief had not sunk in. Ross was right; she had killed his son. If she had not run away, Jeffrey would not have died. How much better if Ross had killed her, she thought. He would have been right to do so. Her selfish and impetuous behavior had cost him his only son. And now she could never ask Jeffrey's forgiveness for what she had done. Jessica buried her face in the pillow, stifling her sobs. Then, as the afternoon sun began to fade, her grief and pain-racked body sought solace in sleep.

When she awoke, it was dark. Her mind was clearer now, and she realized that she should think about leaving. There was no longer anything to keep her at the Running J. But getting away might not be easy. Though she was no longer bound, she sensed that Ross did not plan for her to leave.

Jessica reached up and gingerly touched her face where Ross had struck her. His blows had been hard, and the flesh was tender to her touch. If she wished to escape, she would have to plan carefully. No mad dash through the mountains this time. In his present unforgiving mood, weighed down by his own grief and guilt, Ross might very well react violently to any attempt at escape. After his assault on her today, Jessica had not the courage to take the risk.

Maybe it would be better to just wait. Ross could hardly keep her here forever. Perhaps if his anger were spent, he might even listen to reason and let her go. Surely her presence could only be painful to him, a reminder of Jeffrey and everything that had happened since her arrival. And he obviously had nothing but hatred for her now. The desire, which had once caused sparks to fly between them, had, for Ross at least, turned to bitterness and contempt.

And on her part . . . ? During all her wanderings in the

desert, Jessica had tried to keep memories of Ross from her mind, for any thought of him was too painful to bear. When she did think of him, she recalled the passion of their love-making and the tenderness of her desert dreams in which Ross came to her across the barren wastes and took her lovingly in his arms. Her reception at the ranch had been a complete reversal of all that she had remembered and imagined. But, after all, her dream had been just that—a dream—for it had ignored the reality which made their love impossible. And it ignored the reality of Ross St. John, for she had dreamed only of the tender, passionate side of Ross and ignored the wilfulness and violence which were equally part of him.

Jessica sank back onto the pillow. She felt that not just one but two men she had cared about had died—not just Jeffrey, but also Ross St. John. Jeffrey, dead, came between her and Ross even more finally and absolutely than Jeffrey, alive, had done. Even if Ross's passion for her had not been transformed to hatred, it could never surmount the tragedy of his son's death. Whatever Jessica had hoped to achieve by her return to the ranch—some resolution, some reconciliation with the two men she cared about, which would have allowed her to part from them, if not as friends, at least without rancor—all of this was now impossible. Jeffrey was beyond the reach of her apologies, and so, in his own way, was Ross.

Jessica heard the click of the door latch and stiffened. A long rectangle of light shot across the floor and a masculine figure was silhouetted briefly before the door closed again. Muffled footsteps moved across the carpet toward the table where the lamp stood.

Was Ross returning? A shiver of fear shot through her. What did he want with her now? Jessica slid further down into the bed, pulling the blanket around her.

A match flared briefly and then the lamp was lighted. As the man by the table replaced the glass chimney, Jessica saw to her horror that it was not Ross St. John who had entered, but Riordon, the foreman.

"What are you doing here?" she demanded, sitting up, the covers clutched to her chest. "Get out! Get out right now!"

Riordon merely smiled, his teeth gleaming under the curve of his mustache.

"You're still the little spitfire, aren't you? I would have thought some of the starch would have been taken out of you by now."

"How dare you come in here like this? You have no right to be here."

"No use you kickin' up a fuss. There's no one to hear. And no one to care, anyway. Didn't I tell you St. John would just as soon we'd thrown you over the nearest cliff?"

"He wouldn't . . ." Jessica began to protest. But her voice carried no conviction.

"But you aren't goin' to give me any trouble, are you?" Riordon continued as if she hadn't spoken. He reached out to touch her bruised face. "You know what happens when you cause trouble, don't you now?"

His voice was soft but menacing. Jessica shuddered as his fingers brushed her cheeks, and tried to pull the bed covers protectively around her shoulders. But Riordon seized the edge of the blanket and jerked it out of her grasp, and then, almost gently, pushed her back against the pillow.

This can't be happening, Jessica thought in horror. She should struggle, scream for help. But what help would be forthcoming? This house, which had once been a place of warmth and refuge, was now alien and indifferent.

Riordon seated himself on the edge of the bed and reached up to touch her hair.

"No!" Jessica tried to twist away, but he pulled her back, pinning her arms above her head with one muscular hand. She was no match for his stocky strength, and Riordon seemed to take a cruel and deliberate pleasure in her helplessness. Keeping her hands pinned, he grasped the edge of her nightgown with his free hand. His eyes on her face, he tugged at her gown, inching it up her legs. Then he swept his gaze insolently down her body as he exposed first her thighs, then her white stomach, then her full breasts. He left the gown bunched around her shoulders and moved his hand down to caress her nakedness.

"My, you are a pretty sight." Pinning her legs with his, he pulled her thighs apart, his fingers probing the tangle of dark hair, running across her stomach to her breasts. "I like a woman who looks like a woman. No skinny sticks for me." He kneaded the firm flesh of her breasts between his rough fingers, pinching her nipples until she winced. "With tits like that, I bet men fall all over you, don't they?"

"Please . . ." Tears of humiliation sprang to Jessica's eyes.

Riordon deliberately mistook her plea.

"This is what you want, isn't it, you little vixen? I knew it from the first time I saw you. A little she-fox in rut, that's what you are." His body lay half across hers now, and Jessica could feel the hardness of his erection against her thigh. She shuddered and closed her eyes. If only he would hurry and be finished with her and stop tormenting her like this.

"Open your eyes!" he commanded. Afraid to disobey, she did. His gaze was mocking and triumphant. He laughed and sprang up off the bed. He ran his glance contemptuously over her body for a moment before throwing the blanket back over her nakedness.

"You're a prime piece, all right," he grinned down at her. "And all ready for it, too, despite your high and mighty manners. Well," he added, as he turned to go, "I guess you won't be quite so high and mighty in the future, now that your lover boy's gone. Things are going to change a lot around here, miss former queen of the Running J. And the sooner you get used to it, the better. And you're certainly going to be seeing a lot more of me."

Jessica lay there after he left, not moving. Her body felt sticky and unclean from Riordon's touch; her mind recoiled from his words. But there was something else—something urgent she must remember. The sound of his voice, the feel of his stocky body, his eyes and hands—all this had happened to her before, some other place, some other time. But where and when? Or was it just some awful remnant of a dream?

Then it all came flooding back—the night in the woods, the

night the ranch was raided. The man who chased her and attacked her—could it really have been Riordon? She tried to imagine those eyes above a mask, the feel of the body which had pinned her to the forest floor. She knew she was right. Riordon had been the masked attacker in the woods. But what had the foreman of the Running J been doing attacking his own boss's ranch?

Jessica closed her eyes as a shudder passed over her. Riordon, the raider of her nightmares, frightened her even more than Riordon, the arrogant foreman of the Running J. What would he say, she wondered, if he knew she had guessed who he was? What would he do to her?

Slowly Jessica sat up and pulled down her nightgown. Then, climbing out of bed, she went over to the dresser where a basin and a pitcher of water stood. She wanted to wash away the feel of Riordon's touch which still clung to her skin like a fine, dirty film. She wet a cloth and lifted her gown, working in a kind of daze. Yet part of her mind was active, poring over her discovery.

Was she right in her guess about the foreman? And, if so, what did it mean? Was Riordon working for Kincaid? Or was he involved in some scheme of his own? Had he been the one who had raped and killed Annunciata? There were so many horrifying possibilities, Jessica did not know how to sort them all out.

One thing she did know—she must tell Ross. She had to warn him that there was a traitor in his outfit, an ally of his enemy, or, at least, someone playing a devious game of his own. With a sinking heart, Jessica then realized that such a warning would be futile. Ross had often expressed to her his confidence in Riordon, and told her how much he depended on the foreman in the daily running of the ranch. Now that her own standing with Ross was so low, what chance did she have of convincing him that her suspicions were right?

And Riordon—what would he do if he found she had voiced such suspicions to his boss? Once again, Jessica thought of the brutal murder of Annunciata. The foreman might be capable of anything, including doing away with her, if he thought she presented a danger to his plans.

Jessica blew out the lamp and settled back into bed. All around her the ranch house lay silent. How long ago it seemed that she had left. And how long ago her return this afternoon now seemed. Her thoughts churning, Jessica tossed restlessly until, finally, she was claimed by sleep.

It was morning when she awoke. Although the house was quiet, she could hear the chatter of birds outside, and the noise of hooves and cowboys' voices from the yard. Jessica lay still for a moment, drinking in the familiar sounds, re-membering happier times. Her sleep had refreshed her and some of the horror of the previous day had faded. She would get up and find Ross, talk to him about when and how she would leave the ranch. And she would speak to him of her own grief and guilt and ask his forgiveness. If they could not part friends, at least they need not be enemies.

Yes, that's what she would do. Resolutely, Jessica climbed out of bed. The first thing to do was get dressed. She went to the wardrobe to get some clothes.

The clothes she had been wearing when she rode to the ranch were nowhere to be found, so she took a serge skirt and a white, high-collared blouse from the wardrobe and rum-maged in the drawers for some undergarments. Once dressed, she washed her face, and then, picking up a comb, she went to the mirror to arrange her hair.

Her reflection shocked her. Not that she hadn't expected the marks of Ross's blows to show; but she hadn't thought one side of her face would be so red and puffy, or that the area over her cheekbone would be quite so blue-black with bruises. Ross must have struck her harder than she thought. Gingerly, she touched the injured flesh with her fingertips.

One thing was certain; she would hardly want to venture out with her face like this. Everyone would know what had happened to her. And even if she could get to Reno, she wouldn't want him to see her looking as she did. Ross, on the other hand, was a different story. She hoped that when he saw the damage he had inflicted, he would feel some stirrings of remorse.

Jessica pinned up her hair, securing it with several of the tortoise-shell combs that were lying on the dresser. Most of her things seemed to be still here, even after her several weeks' absence. Had they been expecting her back, she wondered, or had they simply not known what to do with her abandoned belongings? It gave her a strange feeling to see her possessions awaiting her like that—familiar and yet somehow alien.

Then she noticed the tray on the table by the window. It held a small earthenware jug, a cup and saucer, and a plate of bread and jam. Someone must have come in while she was still asleep and left breakfast. Once again Jessica's thoughts turned to Serafina. Had it been that young woman's hand behind those few acts of kindness she had experienced since her return—the nightgown and fresh sheets, the water for washing, and now this? But if so, why had Serafina herself not appeared? Was she embarrassed at Jessica's situation, or concerned that Jessica might be ashamed to see her? Or maybe Ross had forbidden her to come.

Jessica crossed over to the table and laid her hand on the earthenware pot. It was still warm. Whoever had left it had done so not very long ago. She poured some of the hot chocolate into the cup and raised it to her lips, savoring the aroma before she sipped. How comforting was this familiar brew that had begun so many of her days in New Mexico. She sat at the table and poured a little more, then broke off a piece of bread and spread it with blackberry jam. Although she had little appetite this morning, she felt she should eat to keep up her strength. She would need it to face whatever lay ahead.

Her eyes fell on the writing materials which lay nearby on the table—the neatly boxed stationery, the bottle of violet ink, the pen and blotter—and she felt a pang of guilt. Her mother—she really should write to her mother. The last time she had written, she had been full of plans for the wedding. Had anyone written to her mother recently, she wondered, to tell her of Jeffrey's death and her daughter's departure? How difficult it was going to be to write. And how much more difficult since she could not tell everything. And how could she explain that, even though she was not to marry Jeffrey St. John, she still planned to remain in New Mexico?

For she would stay, Jessica reflected, as she gazed out of the window at the ranch yard, deserted now except for the chickens scratching in the dust. She would not let Ross St. John, or Riordon, or anyone else drive her away. New Mexico and the West were in her blood, and she would never leave.

She was feeling a little odd. Her head was very light, and the scene outside the window seemed to have dimmed. Had the sun gone behind a cloud? Why did her limbs suddenly feel weak? She broke into a sweat and then almost immediately began to shiver. Something was wrong.

Alarmed, Jessica stood up. Now, spots were dancing in front of her eyes, and the room was beginning to waver. She clutched the back of the chair for support. She was sweating again, and she knew she was about to be very, very sick. She turned and stumbled toward the basin. But before she could get there, her knees gave way and she slipped into a roaring, swirling blackness.

Chapter 23

She wandered through a long, dark tunnel. Somewhere ahead of her lay the end. Occasionally, she could even glimpse a glimmer of light. But then she would turn a corner and it would disappear. She knew she must reach that light soon, and she hastened her steps, but always it remained far away. If only she could get there. Something awaited her—some key, some solution to a puzzle, some answer for which she had been searching. But she did not know what it was. She only knew that if she did not hurry, did not get there soon, it would be too late.

The walls of the tunnel were of glistening black stone. All along these walls ran ledges set with skulls. The skulls had gold teeth which grinned as she hurried by. But she didn't mind these skulls. She was not afraid. They were all dead. They couldn't hurt her. But something else could, unless she reached the end of the tunnel.

Suddenly a gaping hole appeared at her feet. Frantically, she tried to pull back. But the momentum of her hurrying steps propelled her. She teetered on the edge and then pitched forward. She was falling, head over heels, down a deep, dark shaft. . . .

*   *   *

Jessica opened her eyes. The room around her was suffused with a soft, late daylight which lent a slightly hazy air to everything. Where was she? Hadn't she died? Maybe she had, and this was what it was like.

There was a hand lying in front of her on the cover, gaunt and thin under a fading tan, the blue veins standing out like tiny snakes against the flesh. With a shock she realized the hand was her own. She tried to move the fingers, but the effort was too much.

She heard movement nearby and the swish of skirts. Suddenly, Serafina was leaning over the bed. Jessica felt a sudden stab of fear. Serafina! Hadn't the Mexican woman done something bad to her? Hadn't she tried to harm her? She tried to think but could not remember.

The face of the person bending over her was pale and drawn with concern, and a small smile of relief flitted over it when she saw that Jessica had opened her eyes.

"*Madre de Dios!* You are alive. I was afraid you would never look at me again."

"What . . . what happened?" Jessica's mouth had difficulty framing the question, and the words were weak and faint.

"Sssh! Don't try to talk. Evil things have happened here, but you're safe now. Here, drink this." She lifted Jessica's head and brought a glass of water to her lips. "You need lots of liquids. You've been lying here in a fever for days."

For days? Weakly, Jessica laid her head back against the pillow. How could that be? She had just arrived at the ranch yesterday. And then she had become ill. What was Serafina talking about?

But the effort to think was too much for her, and she drifted back to sleep.

Every time Jessica woke, Serafina was there. The other woman bathed her face, gave her water, and propped her up with pillows so that she could scoop food into Jessica's mouth.

"Don't worry," she said, as she dipped a spoon into a

bowl of cornmeal pudding and carried it to Jessica's lips. "I have been making all of your food, myself, from scratch, so everything is safe."

What is she talking about? Jessica wondered. But she was still too weak to ask.

She had little sense of time. Days slipped by but she didn't know where they ended or began. She drifted in and out of sleep, her dreams and her awakenings running into each other. Sometimes she was in strange places, in the desert, trying to follow Reno across the scorching sands. But her limbs were too weak to keep up, and she fell behind, desolate and lost. Then she was on the ranch, and there were people all around her. She could hear voices and see figures moving back and forth, but could make out no faces. Weakly, she reached up to pull someone closer, but her hands would not move.

Little by little, however, her strength began to return. She began to sit up in bed, and then, with Serafina's shoulder to lean on, she took a few steps around the room. She was very thin, and the gaunt face in the mirror, still marked faintly with bruises, hardly seemed to be hers. But gradually her appetite increased and, with it, her spirits. During this time she had seen no one but Serafina, and finally she pressed the Mexican woman to tell her what was happening.

At first, Serafina was hesitant.

"You are not strong enough yet," she said. "All of this can wait till later. There is no need for you to be concerned with it right now. At the moment you are safe."

"But didn't someone try to kill me? Someone tried to poison me?"

Reluctantly, Serafina nodded.

"Who was it?" Jessica persisted. "Was it Ross?" Yet she knew as she spoke the words, it had not been he.

Serafina shook her head.

"I am ashamed, very ashamed to tell you," she said, her voice low. Jessica remembered her initial suspicions. Had it in fact been Serafina, now repentant, who had made this attempt on her life? But the girl's next words made her ashamed of such thoughts.

"It was my mother, Donaciana. She put poison in your chocolate and brought it in here that morning on the tray. I knew nothing of it. If I had seen her, I would have been suspicious, because she has never had much kindness for you, and like Ross St. John, she blames you for Jeffrey's death."

Jessica leaned back against the pillow and closed her eyes. So much hatred. Never before in her life had she been the object of so much anger and hatred.

Serafina had jumped up and was now pacing the room as she spoke, echoing Jessica's thoughts.

"This house is now full of hatred and evil. I can almost feel it in the air. Bad things have happened, and you have become their victim."

Jessica opened her eyes. A wave of guilt flooded over her.

"It is because of me they have happened," she replied. "It would have been better for everyone if I had never met Jeffrey, had never come here."

"No!" The vehemence with which Serafina spoke caused Jessica to jump. "No! It is very easy to blame you. That is what everyone wants to do. But it is not you who have caused all this to happen. It is passion and greed and willfulness. It is bearing grudges and hating. These are to blame."

"I don't understand."

Serafina sat down on the edge of the bed and looked at Jessica for a moment. Then she spoke again, her question blunt.

"He seduced you, didn't he?"

Jessica recoiled at the word.

"What . . . what do you mean?"

"Ross. He seduced you the night of the fiesta."

"He . . . he didn't . . ."

Serafina interrupted her firmly.

"Call it what you will, that's what he did. He dishonored you and himself. And he has paid for it, as we all have."

"How . . . how did you know?"

"I found your dress—your beautiful satin dress—torn to

shreds and stuffed in the back of the closet. There was blood on it and on the petticoats and towel you had hidden with it. It was very clear to me what had happened to you, and clear to me that it was not something Jeffrey would have done. And if it had been, that would certainly not have caused you to run away, since you were engaged to be married to him. In fact, such passion on his part would probably have been welcome to you.''

Jessica blushed at the other's perceptiveness. Serafina pretended not to notice.

''And if a stranger, or even someone at the fiesta had attacked you,'' she continued, ''you would hardly have run away then, either. You would have told Ross St. John or Jeffrey. So I knew it could only have been Ross himself who had done it, because only that would have caused you to flee as you did, in the middle of the night, leaving a letter that only Jeffrey read. You are a good person. I knew you would not have left Jeffrey like that unless you felt deeply ashamed of something, something you felt was so dishonorable you could not even tell him about it.''

''No!'' Jessica felt compelled to protest Serafina's characterization of her. ''I am not a good person, not at all. I . . . I wanted him. I wanted Ross. But not like that. We . . .''

''Yes, I understand,'' Serafina interrupted. ''I sensed right away that you and Ross were more *simpático* than you and Jeffrey were, that you would strike sparks with each other, even though you would also fight like cat and dog. But you, I know you. You would have kept your word to Jeffrey in spite of that. You would have married him if Ross hadn't forced himself upon you.''

Jessica wanted to believe the other woman's words, to absolve herself of guilt, but she was suddenly overcome with grief and remorse.

''How I must have hurt him,'' she murmured, closing her eyes again.

Serafina understood her.

''Jeffrey was very grieved when you left, and very puzzled. But he always felt there must have been some overpowering reason for you to do what you did, and I supported him in that belief, even though I never let him know what I knew."

"He was such a good person, and always so kind to me. I think maybe I never really appreciated how good he was."

"Sometimes I think he was too kind, too nice," Serafina said. "It was almost too easy to take him for granted, and I don't think any of us really bothered to know him."

Jessica hung her head. What Serafina said was true. Good, gentle Jeffrey. He had always been there, always been kind to her. But how much had she really understood him? Always she had been more concerned with her own feelings, her own hopes and ambitions.

"He saw in you a source of the strength he sometimes felt he lacked," the other woman continued, "a person who would be an inspiration for him, who would bring out the passion which I think lay buried deep within him."

"And I failed him."

"Not only you. We all did, including Ross St. John, including me." She laid a gentle hand on Jessica's shoulder. "Do not blame yourself. The two of you were not right for each other, I think. Neither saw the other clearly."

"You are so kind to me!" Jessica burst out, suddenly overwhelmed. "So understanding."

Serafina folded Jessica's thin hands in hers.

"I love you, Jessica," she said. "I love you as I would a sister, a very dear sister. When I first heard that Jeffrey was engaged, I was very worried. I had always been treated like a member of the family, and I was used to doing what I wanted in this household. I was afraid when you came that, like many *gringos*, you would look down on me, you would despise me for my dark skin, and I would be for you just another Mexican servant girl. But from the very beginning, you were nice to me. You accepted me, talked to me, listened to me. You were not too proud to ask me for advice, or to learn from me. You made me your friend. Aside from Jeffrey, you're the only real friend I've ever had. I was very unhappy when you left, and when I thought my own mother had killed you, I felt I, myself, could die from grief."

Jessica felt the tears spring to her eyes at the other woman's words and, unashamed, let them spill down her cheeks.

"I love you, too, Serafina," she whispered. "And right now, you're the only friend I have."

They clung together for a moment, locked in mute, mutual emotion and then, briskly, Serafina stood up, brushing her own eyes with the back of her hand.

"Well," she said, "no more talk now of the past. Right now we need to think about what you will do."

"What can I do?" Jessica asked with a touch of bitterness. "I'm still too weak to move, and besides, Ross St. John seems to be keeping me prisoner."

"Don't worry about Ross. I will keep him away from you. What happened to you scared him a little, I think, though he won't admit it. So he listens to me when I tell him you are too weak to see anyone."

"I doubt if he wants to see me anyway."

"Don't be so sure of that," Serafina replied enigmatically. "But for now, you stay under my care. When you are well, I will help you do whatever you want to do. But we can talk about that later. I think I have tired you enough as it is."

Jessica had to admit that she was feeling weak and drained. There were so many thoughts and emotions she had to cope with, and she had so little energy to do it. She made no protest when Serafina closed the curtains and, gathering up the dishes from the meal she had brought, left Jessica to sleep.

The next several days passed slowly but not unpleasantly. Jessica spent her time resting, reading, and restoring her lost weight with Serafina's cooking. She saw no one else, though she could glimpse other members of the household from her window. Several times she saw Ross striding across the yard wearing his riding gear. Once, she saw Riordon giving orders to several of the cowboys by the barn, and then, later, as he headed toward the house, she quickly withdrew behind the curtains, fearful lest he catch a glimpse of her. She had not told Serafina about the foreman's visit to her room or voiced her own suspicions about him to anyone.

Serafina had filled her in on the news of the ranch. There had been no more overt moves from Kincaid, but there had been a number of incidents and skirmishes—cattle rustling, cut fences, once a running battle between the Running J hands and a group of masked men at one of the line camps. Serafina thought that perhaps Kincaid, for all his bluster, was uncertain that his legal maneuvers were going to succeed and was trying to get what he could from the Running J by other methods. Or perhaps he meant to weaken Ross St. John's position through constant petty attacks, in preparation for some kind of takeover by force. What Ross St. John thought, Serafina didn't know, for he had apparently said little to her, or to anyone, in the last few weeks. He had much to preoccupy himself for, in addition to Jessica's disappearance and Jeffrey's death, they were suffering from lack of rain. If the drought did not end soon, it might very well finish off those cattle that had not already succumbed to rustlers.

Listening to Serafina's recital, Jessica felt that indeed some evil had descended on the ranch. And despite the other woman's reassurances, she could not help feeling that she herself was somehow to blame. Everything had been going well until she arrived, and since then, so much had gone wrong.

However, confined to her room as she was, in a weakened state, still, and with no company but Serafina, Jessica found that she had a sense of distance from the ranch and its troubles. No longer was her own future bound up in that of the Running J. But where, then, did it lie? She thought of Reno and his parting words to her, and she had a moment of panic. She had been at the ranch about ten days now, and had lain unconscious in her bed for almost four of them. Would Reno already have finished the mysterious job he had spoken about and then, hearing no word from her, have simply gone on his way? They had spoken of no time by which they would meet, but she knew she had given him the impression that she would not be long at the ranch. But how long was that? One week? Two weeks? More? Would he have expected her to have left by now? She had no way of getting him a message and she could not leave yet. She could only hope he would wait.

Jessica was able to write to her mother, however, and Serafina promised to see that the letter was mailed. Jessica did not ask if this would be accomplished with or without Ross's knowledge. It was difficult to compose the letter; she felt she had to leave out so much, and to distort what she did write. Omitting the story of her flight from the ranch, she simply spoke of Jeffrey's accident, and tried to explain her own decision to stay.

> . . . *everyone has been very sympathetic and supportive, and Mr. St. John has urged me to consider the ranch my home for as long as I wish. I find that there is much to occupy me here, and even though there are constant reminders of Jeffrey, the beauty and peace of the mountains are healing to my spirit.*
>
> *Please do not worry about me. I am doing well. I will write later to let you know when I will be returning to New York.*
>
> *Your loving daughter,*
Jessica

She was unhappy about what she had written. She longed to tell her mother more, to share with her the bitter lessons she had learned and seek her mother's advice. But it was impossible to do by letter, perhaps impossible to do so at all. Isabelle Howard was not a worldly woman, nor did she share her daughter's passionate nature. How could Jessica explain that her engagement to Jeffrey had been a mistake and that the things which drew her to Jeffrey—his manners, his kindness, his education—were not sufficient to cement a marriage. And how much more difficult to explain the passion which had flamed between herself and Ross, leading to her own downfall and to Jeffrey's death. No, as much as she hated to deceive her mother, better the half-truths she had written than a true account of all she had been through.

At least, she was beginning to look better. The swelling in her face had gone down, though one blue-black bruise, turning an ugly yellow around the edges, was still visible. Her face, thin and gaunt after her days of unconsciousness, was beginning to fill out, and except for the dark circles under her eyes, the ravages of her illness were scarcely visible. Still, Jessica thought as she contemplated her reflection in the mirror, she looked anything but beautiful. Would even Reno want her now?

Soon she would have to speak to Ross. She sensed that both of them had been avoiding a confrontation, using her illness as an excuse. But that could not last indefinitely. Jessica would have to tell him that as soon as she was strong enough, she would be leaving. And if he told her he would not let her—then what would she do? But surely there was no reason for her to stay. She was an embarrassment to him and a painful reminder of his son.

Well, whatever Ross said, one way or another, she was determined to get away. And when she did, she would find Reno. She didn't know what her future could be with him— perhaps there was none. But at least she would try. In the darkness of the last week and a half, only thoughts of Reno and of the days they had spent together in the canyon had sustained her.

The next day, Jessica began to carry out her resolution, sorting through her clothes, trying to decide what to pack. She could not take everything, and what she did take would have to be altered, for she was thinner now than she had been when she first arrived at the ranch. Among her clothes was the outfit Reno had bought for her. Serafina had returned it, everything cleaned and pressed. She also brought a broad-brimmed, black felt hat, trimmed with a turquoise and silver band. Jessica recognized it as the one she had tried on in Las Vegas that day long ago when she and Serafina had gone shopping.

"Here." Serafina handed her the hat. "Jeffrey bought this

for you as a present, but he never had a chance to give it to you. I know he would want you to have it now.''

Too moved to say anything, Jessica took the hat and tried it on in front of the mirror. It was as beautiful as she remembered. Dear Jeffrey. How hard he had tried to give her everything she wanted.

The hat now hung on the edge of the mirror, and every now and then Jessica paused to finger the brim and run her hand over the silver band. Then she touched the turquoise studs she still wore in her ears. How odd that both father and son had picked such appropriate gifts. She no longer felt shamed and guilty when she looked at the hat. It seemed to her that with it Jeffrey had reached out to her across the chasm of death and told her of his love. She sensed that he, at least, had forgiven her. Would his father ever do the same?

The sound of hoofbeats drew her to the window, and she pulled back the curtain just in time to see one of the Running J cowboys, reining his horse in front of the house, sending up a swirl of dust and scattering the protesting chickens. Serafina came onto the porch, wiping floury hands on her apron, and Jessica saw Ross St. John striding over from the direction of the stable. He broke into a run when he saw who the rider was and bounded up onto the porch. Jessica could see the cowboy gesturing excitedly, and then Ross called out something in the direction of the barn, bringing the foreman hurrying over, but she couldn't tell what they were saying. She lifted the window, letting in the drifting dust, in time to hear Ross say ''. . . Kincaid and a bunch of his men. Tell Shorty to break out the rifles and get the men lined up here on the double.''

Was this it? Jessica asked herself. Was this the showdown they had all been expecting? Or was it simply another of Kincaid's acts of harrassment? They had been waiting for him to make a major move for some time now. Perhaps the time had finally come. She wondered how many of the Running J hands were around at the moment. She knew several had ridden out just that morning to relieve the crew at one of the line camps, so it was likely they were somewhat shorthanded.

She wished she had her own rifle with her, but it had disappeared with Spur when he ran away.

She stayed by the window, keeping out of sight behind the curtain, but positioning herself so she could peer out. Ross had sent Serafina back inside. Jessica hoped he would not see her by the window and order her out of the way. She wanted to see what was going to happen.

Ross St. John was waiting on the porch and several men with rifles were standing behind him when Kincaid came riding in. The other rancher had brought only half a dozen men, though they all seemed to be heavily armed. Kincaid reined to a halt in front of the porch. There was a tense moment of silence, broken only by the restless shuffling of horses' hooves. Then Kincaid spoke.

"This don't look like a right neighborly reception, Ross," he remarked, glancing over the men on the porch. "I'm not here to cause any trouble. Just dropped by for a friendly visit."

"Those two words don't go together where you're concerned, Kincaid," Ross replied. "No visit from you is ever friendly."

"Well, I'm sorry to hear you say that, Ross," Kincaid responded in mock grief. "It does pain me to think we can't be on more cordial terms. On the other hand, you won't have to worry about me bein' your neighbor for too much longer."

"What do you mean?" Ross growled suspiciously.

"Why, Judge Denton handed down a decision in Santa Fe yesterday regardin' the land grant for the Running J. Seems like, just as I suspected, there's a few, shall we say, irregularities in it. Like somebody didn't draw the boundaries too careful-like and kinda slipped over onto land that's rightly owned by the Burnt Cedar. In fact, some of the Running J claims are downright invalid, includin' the land this here house is standin' on. You'll be glad to know, however, there is some of it still belongs to you—some of the land down by the village, and part of the back country. Not quite as big as you're used to, maybe, but you might be able to manage. I got the survey right here, if you'd care to see it.'' He gestured toward his saddle bag.

"I got no interest in your crooked surveys, Kincaid, nor in your crooked judge. Say right out what you've come for, and then get the hell off my land.''

" 'Tain't your land anymore, Ross. That's what I come to tell you. Most of it's mine now, and I'm orderin' you to get off.''

"The hell with you, Kincaid. You aren't ordering me anywhere, and you know it.''

"I was afraid you'd be like that, Ross. But I just want it known that I tried. If I got to use force, it'll all be legal-like.''

"Don't bet on it. You aren't the only one with friends in high places.''

"I'll give you a couple weeks to get out, Ross. After that''—the rancher shrugged—"I'll do what I have to, to get my own.''

Jessica stood glued to the window, listening and watching. What would Kincaid do now? Of course he had known Ross wouldn't quietly hand over the ranch. So he must be prepared to take it by force, using the land grant decision to put the law on the side of whatever means he might use. And for his part, Ross St. John was prepared to fight, whatever side the law was on. The long-awaited range war seemed imminent.

As Kincaid wheeled to go, Jessica ran her eye over the men who had come with him. They certainly were a hard-looking bunch. One, in particular, a young man with a thin, pinched face, looked quite vicious. And the man riding next to him . . .

Suddenly Jessica stiffened and drew in her breath. She had not noticed the other man before. He had kept in back of the others. But now that they had all turned to go, she glimpsed a familiar figure. That hard body, the easy way he sat in the saddle—if only she could see his face. But his hat was pulled low on his head, casting his features in shadow. She recognized the horse, however, a chestnut mare with delicate and distinctive lines. There was no doubt now. It was Reno. It was Reno who had just ridden off. Jessica felt her knees begin to buckle, and she sank weakly into a chair near the window.

Reno! What was he doing riding with Kincaid? But she knew the answer to her question. Her heart turned cold and for a moment everything around her grew dim. She heard a murmur of voices outside on the porch and was vaguely aware that Ross was sending his men back to their duties. Then she heard Ross's footsteps in the hallway. Abruptly, she jumped up and ran to the door of her room.

He looked up in surprise as she emerged into the hall. She reached out her hand to halt his passage. They stood for a moment staring at each other, and Jessica realized that he had not seen her since the day she had returned to the ranch.

"Who were those men with Kincaid?" she demanded.

Ross seemed startled by the vehemence of her question. He glanced down to where she had laid her hand on his arm, and she realized she was clutching his sleeve tightly. For a moment she thought he was going to shake her off, but instead he turned his gaze back to hers.

"Those were just some of Kincaid's tough boys," he replied. There was a patient, almost reassuring note in his voice.

"But who exactly *were* they?" she persisted.

"A couple of cowboys from the Burnt Cedar, riffraff mostly, drifters. And a couple of gunmen Kincaid hired from outside."

"Which ones were those?"

"One of them was a young punk named Rutledge, Jack Rutledge I think his full name is. They say he's a Billy the Kid in the making. And the other was Reno Hayden. He's got a reputation as one of the most vicious and deadly hired killers around. I've heard Kincaid intends him for me." Ross gave a grim little laugh. "I'm afraid he gives too much credit to my ability with a gun."

Jessica had dropped her hand at his words, feeling all the life go out of her. Ross stared at her curiously.

"Well," he said finally, "if you're finished with me, I'll be going. I've got to write a letter to my lawyer in Santa Fe to find out the details on this business, and also get in touch with Sheriff Towers in Bernalillo. I'm sure Kincaid's not going to let himself be stopped by any legal maneuvering on my part, but at least I can put myself on the right foot with the law when he tries anything."

Lost in her own misery, Jessica made no reply to his words, and he turned and went down the hall to his room. She remained leaning against the doorway for a moment, and then turned back wearily into her own chamber and shut the door.

Reno! It was hard to believe he was working for Kincaid. And yet, after all, it was not really so strange. He had been honest with her about his profession. He had told her he had a job to do. It should have been obvious to her that it was something nearby, for he was familiar with the Running J and its inhabitants, and even knew who she was. He was one of Kincaid's hired guns. "One of the most vicious and deadly hired killers around," Ross had called him. Yet, that description did not fit the man she had known during those weeks in the canyon, the man who had shown her understanding and gentleness, who had offered her no violence, and left her alone to heal herself when she badly needed healing. The Reno she knew had buried his face in her hair and held her tightly when he spoke to her of his dead wife in her lonely grave. He was not the gunman who had been hired to kill Ross St. John. But it was that gunman she had seen today. It was that gunman who was the Reno she did not know.

Jessica collapsed onto her bed. She felt drained of all hope. It was the thought of Reno—the memories of their days in the canyon, the visions she had of their future—that had sustained her till now. She felt tears welling up inside her. Her shoulders shook with sobs, and for the first time since her return to the ranch, she gave way completely to grief and despair.

Chapter 24

As the door opened, Jessica looked up, expecting Serafina come to clear away the supper dishes, which lay on the table almost untouched. To Jessica's surprise, it was Ross St. John who entered. She regarded him dully as he walked over to where she was sitting. She felt no anxiety or fear at his presence. In her present mood, she was beyond caring what happened to her.

He paused a moment before he spoke.

"I'm glad to see you're feeling better." There was something stiff, almost formal about his tone, as if he were an acquaintance making a social call.

"I'm as well as can be expected," she replied in the same tone of voice, wondering if he noticed, or would acknowledge, the bruises that still marred her face. "I think very soon I'll be well enough to leave. I'm sure you'll be glad to have me out of the way."

"Leave?" He stood looking at her appraisingly. "Leave? I don't recall sayin' anything about you leaving."

"Well, you certainly can't want me around. I would have left sooner if I'd been able."

"There'll be no talk of leaving." Ross's voice began to take on some of its normal fire. "That's a decision I'll be making, not you. You're my responsibility now and I won't have you running around the countryside by yourself again. You'll leave when I'm good and ready for you to leave, and not before."

"And when might that be, Mr. St. John? Or do you intend to keep me here forever?"

"Maybe I do. We'll see." He bent over and gripped her shoulder tightly, ignoring her wince of pain. The lamplight highlighted the bronze planes of his face, and she saw his mouth harden. "You're not finished paying for what you owe me, not by a long shot. So don't you go making any plans for the future, because they're not yours to make." His expression seemed to challenge her, almost daring her to resist.

He likes this, Jessica thought as she looked up at him. He enjoys the power he has over people. He likes bending others to his will.

Something inside her seemed to snap. She was tired of this, tired of being threatened and pushed around. Jumping out of her seat, she shook loose from Ross's grip and turned to confront him.

"Who do you think you are?" she raged. "Do you think you own people? Do you think you can control everyone's life? Do you think we're all just like the cattle you run on your ranch, your possessions that you can do whatever you want with?"

Ross retreated a step, taken aback at her outburst. He opened his mouth to reply, but she plunged on, refusing to allow him to speak.

"You thought you could get everybody to do what you wanted, didn't you? You wanted Jeffrey to be the ideal son and carry on the ranch just the way you have. You didn't care what he wanted. And when you decided you wanted his fiancée, well, you thought you could just take what you wanted there too, didn't you? And then when things turned out wrong, you blamed the rest of us, not yourself."

"You little bitch!" Ross burst out finally. His voice was

low but rough with fury. "Don't you try to tell me what happened between us was all my doing. You wanted it as much as I did. You played coy, but you were begging for it. I didn't force you."

"Oh no, you didn't force me," Jessica replied. "You just pulled me inside your room and started pawing me, telling me how determined you were to have your way. Maybe I might have wanted you, Ross. I won't say that I didn't, that I wasn't attracted to you. But I never would have done anything about it. I would have stayed faithful to Jeffrey. You knew that. That's why you did what you did."

"If you were so unwilling," he sneered, "why didn't you call for help?"

"That's right. I should have screamed. And maybe brought Jeffrey so he could see how his own father betrayed his trust. I would have kept faith with Jeffrey, Ross. Whatever I felt for you would have been my secret, and my shame, and Jeffrey never would have known. But you, you had to have what you wanted, no matter what the price. You took advantage of my feelings and my inexperience. And you know that it was because of what we did that I ran away that night. You had shamed me so that I could no longer stay. And it was because of you that Jeffrey died."

Jessica stepped back and moved the chair between them as he came toward her. His eyes blazed and his fists were clenched, but she didn't care now what he did to her. She would have her say, whatever the consequences.

"You never really cared about Jeffrey, not about him as he really was," she went on. "All you saw in him was a link in your dynasty, and you despised him when you thought he was not strong enough. And it was your own lack of concern for him that caused his death. You know that, Ross St. John. You feel guilty about that. But you can't acknowledge your own guilt, and so you take it out on me, instead. You accuse me of killing him but it was your own ambition and your own passion that drove the nails into his coffin."

Ross's face had turned ashen, though his eyes still blazed.

"How dare you!" he choked. "How dare you say such things to me!"

She fully expected him to strike her, but instead he drew back a step.

"Somebody has to dare," she replied. "No one else seems to be willing to stand up to you and say what needs to be said."

Ross still glared at her angrily, his face pale, but she could see the grief in his eyes, and she knew that her remarks about Jeffrey had hit home.

"You have no right," he whispered hoarsely, "no right to talk to me about Jeffrey. He was my son, my only son. You most of all have no right. You can't know how I felt about him."

Suddenly remorseful, Jessica softened her tone.

"Please, Ross, can't we stop all this hating and anger. It can't bring Jeffrey back to us. We can blame each other all we want, and what good will it do? We both loved Jeffrey, we both miss him, we both feel guilt for his death. Can't we comfort each other, instead of being enemies like this?"

Ross slumped into the chair, his face drawn and tired. He propped his elbow on the table and leaned his head on his hand, closing his eyes. Suddenly he looked old.

"Ross . . ." Hesitantly, Jessica reached out her hand but did not dare touch him. She stood there a long moment before he finally looked up. There was a brief flicker of fire in his eyes and then it died. Without his anger to fuel him, he seemed suddenly lost and uncertain.

"I'm a fool, Jessica," he said, shaking his head. "Sometimes I don't know what gets into me."

Jessica sank down on her knees by his side, and he put his arms around her shoulders and rested his face against her hair. She felt a pang of grief as she remembered someone else who had once sought comfort from her thus, but resolutely she stilled it. Her time with Reno was past, now. All that was real was the present. And in the present was Ross St. John, in pain and needing her.

Ross raised his head, and putting his finger under her chin, he tilted Jessica's face up to his. Gazing into her eyes, he finally spoke.

"Jessica, forgive me," he said simply. "I was wrong—please forgive me."

She stared at him. Did he realize what he was asking? Did he understand the enormity of all he had done, or comprehend the anguish and humiliation she had endured? How could she ever find it in her heart to forgive him after all that?

And yet—did she not need his forgiveness too? It was true that Ross had acted thoughtlessly, swayed by his own passions, careless of others. But was she any better, herself? Her heedlessness had brought tragedy to them both. After all that had happened, forgiveness was the least she had to offer.

As Ross stood, she allowed him to lift her up in his arms and then pressed her body tightly against his as the gentle urgency of his embrace communicated to her his need for comfort. She made no protest when he drew her over to the bed.

In the morning, after Ross had left, Jessica sat up in bed, wondering what would become of her now. Serafina had been right. Ross still wanted her. There had been no anger or hatred last night, only a great need for her. But did she want him? Jessica recalled the enveloping warmth and strength of Ross's body and the way her own body had responded to his caresses. But was she really responding to him or simply to her own hunger for comfort and her need for his forgiveness?

Everything that passed between her and Ross St. John seemed to leap between extremes—violent anger, violent passion, hatred and love—nothing was halfway. She recalled Ross's hard, dark anger, his blows, and wondered if she could ever trust him or recover from the wound to her spirit. But then she thought of the way he had collapsed in remorse and grief, punctured by her own angry words, and how he had begged her forgiveness, and she knew that he still had the power to evoke some feeling in her—tenderness and pity at least, and perhaps something more.

What did he intend for her? she wondered. Would he regret

his weakness in front of her and would anger and pride assert
themselves again? Was he still determined that she not leave,
or would he be more willing to listen to her now? She was no
longer certain herself what she wanted to do. The clarity of
her vision in the desert seemed to have dissolved, and she felt
confused and uncertain. Perhaps that vision, like the man
with whom she had shared it, had been a mirage, and none of
the things she thought she had discovered—the sense of
peace, of knowledge, of destiny—had been real, after all.
Like Reno, they had turned their other face to her, and that
face was laughing at her in scorn.

Lost in her thoughts, Jessica didn't hear Serafina knock and
then open the door. With an almost guilty start, she looked up
as Serafina entered the room, bearing breakfast on a tray.

"Good morning. I trust you slept well." Serafina's tone
was neutral. As she set the tray on the table by the window,
Jessica realized that the dishes from the night before were still
there. Serafina had never come to collect them. Had she
known that Ross was in the room, and that he had stayed
during the night? Jessica felt herself blushing, and she turned
away, hoping Serafina wouldn't notice.

"Yes, quite well, thank you," she murmured. "In fact, I
am feeling much stronger today and I think I will soon be
completely recovered."

Serafina was stacking the supper dishes on the empty tray.

"Good," she said. She seemed to be choosing her words
carefully. "Maybe you should try getting out today, perhaps
take a walk around the yard, or in the woods. I would go with
you, but I have to go to the village on some errands."

"I would be embarrassed to have anyone see me, I'm
afraid." Jessica reached up to touch the still visible marks on
her face.

Serafina regarded her sympathetically.

"I don't think you need to worry about that," she said.
"There are very few people around today. The hands are in
the far pasture or posted as guards along the road. Besides, all
anyone knows is that you were sick, and that could account
for your looks."

"They know Ross was angry with me."

Serafina laughed, her reserve suddenly vanishing.

"It's nothing strange for Ross St. John to be angry. Everyone around here is used to his rages, and his other moods as well. You certainly aren't the first person he's been angry with, or the last, I'm sure."

Jessica pondered Serafina's words as she ate breakfast. It was true that she was going to have to face the world sooner or later. And Serafina's suggestion that she take a walk certainly implied that she was not a prisoner. As for the hands—did it matter what they might think of her? After all, she had been Jeffrey's fiancée, and for all anyone knew, she was still a guest of the ranch, under Ross St. John's protection. Then she recalled how she had been seized on the road and transported like a trussed calf, and she felt humiliation sweep over her once more.

Well, she decided, standing up, she couldn't stay in her room forever. She rummaged in her wardrobe for a skirt and blouse. At least she could step outside for a little while. Now would be a good time, before the midday heat. She could take a book and sit on the far end of the porch, away from the kitchen.

She saw no sign of Ross as she settled into the rocking chair, and there were no sounds from his room. She knew he sometimes spent the mornings in there, working on accounts for the ranch, but this morning he seemed to be busy with other chores.

The day was already warm, but not unpleasant, and Jessica was glad she had decided to come outside. She breathed deeply of the pine-laden air. The ranch yard was very quiet this morning. A few chickens clucked and scratched in the dust under the harried eye of a proprietary rooster. Horses grazed peacefully in the pasture. But the only sign of a human being was Old Tom, moving in and out of the stable, cleaning out the straw. He stayed at a distance, and Jessica was grateful for this. She would just as soon he didn't see her.

At first she had difficulty becoming absorbed in her book. It was one she had purchased in Las Vegas—Thackeray's

Barry Lyndon—one of the few books by that author she had not read. Her mother had considered it too risqué, a view that in light of her recent experiences Jessica now found laughable. At first, the book's subject matter seemed too remote, but then, gradually, that very remoteness began to engage her, and she lost herself for a while in the events of another time and place. When she finally looked up, the late morning sun was streaming across the porch. And a man was standing beside her chair.

Startled, Jessica gave a little gasp and let the book drop into her lap. The man was a complete stranger, not very tall, and of slender but wiry build. His face was brown and sun-creased, and a neat, dark mustache covered his upper lip. He carried a rifle in his hand.

"Do not be afraid, señorita." He knelt beside her chair and smiled up at her, both gestures seemingly intended to reassure. His teeth were white and pointed, reminding Jessica of a cat's.

"Who are you?" Strangely enough, she was not afraid.

"A friend. A messenger, if you will. My name is Amadeo. I have come to return a few things to you. Here, I believe this is one of them." He laid a rifle on her lap; Jessica recognized it as her own.

"Where did you get this?" She fingered the brass carvings on the stock. The gun looked as if it had been recently cleaned and polished.

"It was with your horse, which I have also returned."

"Spur? You have Spur?" Her spirits suddenly rose at this unexpected news.

The man nodded, obviously pleased at her relief and delight.

"Yes, he is tied up behind the stable."

"But I don't understand. How did you get here without anyone seeing you?"

He flashed her another grin.

"No one sees Amadeo if he doesn't want them to."

"But how did you find Spur?"

"A friend gave him to me to bring to you. A friend who also wishes to know how you are."

Jessica was aware that he was gazing at her searchingly, now, and she remembered the still visible bruises which lingered on her face. She tried to draw back into the shadows.

"It is rumored that you have been ill," he continued. "Is this true?"

"Yes," she replied stiffly, uncomfortable under his penetrating gaze. "Yes, I was ill, but I'm all right now."

"I see." He paused a moment. "Well, if you need anything, just let me know. I am at your service."

"And your friend?"

"He, too," Amadeo replied enigmatically, as he rose to go.

"Wait. I . . . thank you for bringing back my horse."

But he was gone, disappearing as silently as he came.

Jessica sat a moment, staring down at the rifle, her thoughts in turmoil. Who was this mysterious "friend" who had sent her rifle and her horse? For a moment she thought it might be Ross St. John. She remembered the conversation she had with Serafina about the stolen Running J horses and Ross's strange relationship with a horse thief named Amadeo. But Ross would hardly have asked how she was. Was it Manuel Valdez, perhaps, who had done this favor or someone else, unknown to her? Or . . . but she would let her thoughts go no further.

She jumped up. Spur was back. Tied up behind the stable, her mysterious visitor had said. She had better go take care of him, and also get him out of sight so that Riordon wouldn't spot him before she could talk to Ross.

She hurried toward the stable, keeping an eye out for Old Tom. He must have finished his chores, for the stable was empty now. Spur stood out in the back, concealed behind a pile of logs that were waiting to be split for fencing. He lifted his head and whinnied in greeting, and Jessica rushed over to him and buried her head in his mane, tears welling up in her eyes. How good it was to see him again. Here at least was one true friend.

Jessica would have liked to take the mustang into the

stable. Though he appeared to be in good shape, he could
have used a rubdown and a currying, and it would have been
nice to give him some oats. But that would have to wait.
Right now the important thing was to get him out of sight.
Quickly, she unsaddled him and led him over to the pasture
gate. He would be less conspicuous out grazing with the other
horses. She gave him a pat on the rump to send him on his
way and then fastened the gate behind him. Then she returned
to the stable and picked up the saddle. She would have to get
it out of the way, too.

She left the saddle in a far corner of the stable, with a pile
of discarded gear. Then she brushed the telltale pieces of
straw and streaks of dirt off her skirt and prepared to return to
the house. Maybe Ross would be returning at midday, and
she could talk to him then about Spur.

Lost in thought, Jessica did not see Riordon rounding the
corner as she stepped out of the stable, and she almost
bumped into his broad chest. She stopped and retreated a step
as he blocked her way. Had he seen her with Spur, she wondered, her heart pounding with fear.

"Well, well, look who's up and about. Glad to see you're
feelin' better."

Apparently he hadn't seen her, but her momentary feeling
of relief quickly gave way to further anxiety as she realized
that she was all alone in the ranch yard with the foreman.

"Excuse me," she murmured. "I was on my way back to
the house."

"Don't be in such a hurry." He had backed her into the
stable now, and she pressed against the side of one of the
stalls. He leaned over her, his hands resting on the wall on
either side of her, pinning her in, the corners of his mouth
curving up cruelly. A strong odor of horse and masculine
sweat emanated from his body.

"We ain't had a chance to talk at all since that night I came
to see you," he continued. "That ain't hardly friendly, is it?
However, I reckon now that you're feelin' better, we might
find time for another visit." He lifted his right hand, and ran
his fingers along the bare skin of her neck.

"No!" She flung away his hand. "Don't you touch me!"

He dropped his hands and straightened up. He was still smiling, but his eyes were hard.

"I wouldn't be so high and mighty if I were you, Miss Spitfire. And I wouldn't count on Ross St. John to protect you either. He may think he's a big man around here, but his day will soon be over. And when I get what's comin' to me, you're goin' to be part of it. So I suggest you start actin' nice and cooperative."

He stared at Jessica meaningfully for a moment. She wondered if he knew that she had guessed he was the man who had attacked her in the raid on the ranch. What would he do if she revealed her knowledge? She didn't like to think about it.

Abruptly, she turned and brushed by him toward the stable door. He made no move to stop her. She hurried across the yard, not looking back until she reached the porch. When she turned, he was still standing by the stable, watching her. Her refuge on the porch spoiled, Jessica picked up her book and her gun and sought shelter in the house. But the foreman's words haunted her, and she found it difficult to return to her reading.

Ross didn't return until late that afternoon. Jessica heard his heavy footsteps in the hall, but by the time she got to the door, he had already entered his own room and shut the door behind him. She was reluctant to disturb him there, so she decided to wait.

Shortly after that, Serafina came to tell her that Ross had decided to eat in the dining room that night and that he wanted Jessica to join him.

"Is that an invitation or an order?" Jessica asked.

Serafina shrugged.

"With him sometimes it's hard to tell. But if you would rather not, don't go. I will tell him."

"No, I'll go. Maybe at least it will make things seem as if they're normal."

"Sooner or later we all have to go back to living our lives as usual—if we can figure out what usual is."

Jessica was surprised at the bitter edge in Serafina's voice, but before she could respond to her words, Serafina had gone.

Jessica dressed herself carefully for dinner. She wanted to look pleasing to Ross, but she did not want to give him any excuse for accusing her of being provocative, or suspect her of trying to win him over. In the end, she settled for a dark skirt and high-necked blouse, the outfit she had rejected as too dowdy the first night she had dined with Ross. Perhaps, she reflected dryly, it would have been better had she worn that outfit after all. But she kept the turquoise earrings in her ears.

Ross looked her up and down as she came into the living room, an amused expression playing over his face, but he said nothing, and offered her his arm as they went into the dining room. She tucked her hand almost gingerly into his elbow, still uncertain of his touch.

"Well, I see your ratty little mustang made it back," Ross remarked casually, as he cut into his roast beef.

"How did you . . . when did you find out?" Jessica was uncertain as to how much of her own knowledge regarding the horse's return she should reveal.

"Riordon spotted him in the pasture this afternoon. I wonder how he got back?"

"A friend of yours—at least I think that's what he is—returned him," she murmured, lowering her eyes.

Ross chuckled.

"Figured that's what happened. Guess he must have told you about it, too. You don't seem very surprised." Before Jessica could reply, he went on. "Riordon wanted me to have him shot. Claims he struck out at one of the men the day you were brought in."

Her heart pounding with anxiety, Jessica opened her mouth to plead for her horse, but before she could say anything, Ross relieved her fears.

"Don't worry, I won't let anything happen to him. I know you're fond of the little beast, though damned if I can figure out why."

Once again Jessica felt that she had to defend Spur.

"He's a good horse," she insisted. "He's loyal to me and he's strong. While I . . . when I . . ." She hesitated a moment. "When I was gone, I was lost in the desert for a while. Spur saved my life. If it hadn't been for him, I would never have gotten out alive."

Ross regarded her keenly for a moment. Then he shrugged.

"Well, I did wonder what you were doing all that time you were gone. Glad to know you were alone in the desert with your horse."

Jessica kept her gaze downcast, playing with her food, unsure how to reply. She could feel Ross's eyes on her, and she had no doubt about how the evening would end.

Later, she lay naked in his arms beneath the covers, and he stroked her body in long lingering caresses. As she felt his strong rough hands slide over her satin skin, she recalled other hands that had touched her, tapering fingers that had known just where to touch and probe, a body that had molded itself to hers, and she shivered. Ross drew her close.

"Jessica," he whispered, "don't be afraid. I won't hurt you, ever again, I promise." There was a long pause and she could feel his heart beating as he held her head against his chest. Then, his voice low against her hair, he murmured "I love you."

Those words—the ones she had thought, had hoped she had heard him utter the night of the fiesta when he had pulled her into his room, the words she had clung to as she wandered alone in the desert—those words now, for some reason, made her feel desolate.

"Ross . . ."

"It's like a dream having you here in my arms, Jessica. You don't know how I've longed for this, how devastated I was when you left."

"Ross, this isn't right. We can't . . . Jeffrey . . ."

"Jeffrey's dead, Jessica. Whoever was at fault, he's dead and nothing we do will alter that. And it would be foolish now to let Jeffrey stand in the way of our own happiness."

"But . . . I mean, what will people think if they find out you and I . . . if right after Jeffrey's death . . . it's not . . .

it's not . . . proper!'' As soon as she said the word, she knew
it was the wrong one.

Ross gave a low laugh.

''Proper! I hardly thought that was something you would
be so worried about, Miss Jessica Howard.''

For some reason, Jessica felt stung by his tone.

''I suppose you don't think it was any sense of propriety
that made me leave, that night of the fiesta.''

''Propriety? Perhaps. Fear, panic, being unwilling to admit
where your own feelings and passions were taking you.''
Abruptly, he rolled her over on her back and gazed down at
her, propping himself on his elbow. ''Don't worry. I'm not
going to suddenly appear in public and announce that Ross
St. John has appropriated his son's fiancée. At least not until
a decent interval has passed. And by that time it should
appear quite normal and natural.''

''You seem to be forgetting that I might like to have some
say in this,'' Jessica protested, annoyed at the cavalier way he
was making assumptions about their future together.

''Jessica.'' His voice was serious now. ''You don't know
how I suffered when you left, how I blamed myself. I moved
too fast and scared you away. But you don't know how much
I needed you, how much I still need you. Marry me, Jessica.
I promise I'll do everything I can to make you happy.''

''Marry you?'' Even though his words were not entirely
unexpected, Jessica was a little taken aback. ''I . . . I don't
. . . So much has happened, Ross, that I can hardly think
straight. Don't you think that . . . maybe . . . it would be
better if I went away for a while so that we could both think
this whole thing through?''

''I don't need to think it through,'' he replied firmly. ''I
know exactly how I feel. And so do you, if you'll only admit
it.'' He bent and kissed her, and then smoothed her tousled
hair back from her forehead with a gentle hand.

''You know my first marriage wasn't a happy one. And
I've always shied away from marriage since then. Guess I
never knew whether women were in love with me or with my
ranch and money. But with you, it's different.'' He regarded

her tenderly. "How about it, Jessica—what will it be? Yes or no?"

There was nothing but affection now in his eyes. Nor did she doubt his need for her. And what else did he have now, with Jeffrey dead? No son, no heir. He had only her. But with her perhaps he could have other children, and she could make up to him for all that had happened. As for herself— what did she have? Jeffrey was dead and Reno was beyond her dreams. Even if she no longer loved Ross as she once had, she still cared for him, and still felt—if she had to admit it—some remnant of their former passion. Perhaps together she and Ross could work to build a future that would help them both to forget the past.

"Yes." The tears sprang to her eyes as she whispered her reply. Ross bent to kiss them away and then lovingly moved his hand down the curve of her body. She wrapped her arms around him, hungry for comfort, and gave herself up to his embrace.

But later as she lay listening to Ross's heavy breathing beside her, she remembered a fairy tale her mother had told her as a child. In it the hero had been granted three wishes. But although each wish came true, it did so in some horrible and unforeseen fashion, leaving the hero regretting the fulfillment of his desire. She remembered her fantasies about Ross on the return trip from Las Vegas, her dreams of a future as his wife. Her first wish had come true. She hoped she would never make a second one.

Chapter 25

Jessica paused as she stooped to pick several sprigs of the lupine which grew near the edge of the clearing. She added them to the bunch of late dogtooth violets clutched in her hand, and then stood up. Across from her lay the cemetery, a single row of roughly carved tombstones beneath the pines. One of these tombstones was Jeffrey's.

It was not until today that Jessica had the courage to come here and confront the reality of Jeffrey's death. She had put off this final visit for days, but that morning she had awakened feeling the need to come. She had put on her black skirt and jacket and turquoise earrings, and then, with a pang of guilt and grief as she remembered his thoughtfulness, she placed the hat Jeffrey had given her at a rakish angle on her head. She reached up to the hat brim now, tilting it forward to shield her face from the sun, and drawing a deep breath, crossed the clearing to the graves.

Only three of the tombstones in the cemetery had been kept up—Jeffrey's and two others which lay close by. Jessica paused a moment to read the inscriptions. The larger of the two stones bore the name of Jeffrey's mother, Reina Bowman

St. John. Beneath it were the dates, "January 7, 1844–August 18, 1873," and beneath that, "Beloved wife of Ross St. John and mother of Jeffrey Bowman St. John."

Beside this stone was another, smaller one. Jessica had to stoop to read it: "Cecelia Margaret St. John, April 13, 1873–July 19, 1873."

A daughter—Ross St. John's daughter. Neither Ross nor Jeffrey had ever mentioned this baby to her. How sad to think of this tiny child who had died just before her mother. Had that hastened Reina St. John's own death? Jessica wondered. The girl would have been eleven years old now, had she lived. Would she have been like Jeffrey? Or would she have taken after her father, instead, giving Ross St. John what Jeffrey had not—a child just like him in spirit and temper?

Jessica moved on to the next grave. The freshly carved stone read "Jeffrey Bowman St. John, March 15, 1863–July 11, 1884." The rectangle of dirt was still fresh. Jessica knelt by the grave and laid her flower offering at the base of the headstone.

Jeffrey! It was still hard for her to believe that he was dead. He had been a living person, loving her, making plans for their future. How could he so suddenly cease to exist. And yet . . .

To her sorrow, Jessica realized that Jeffrey had already become a shadowy figure in her mind. She recalled Serafina's words: "None of us really knew him." Though Jessica had been engaged to him, she had never really tried to understand Jeffrey's feelings and ambitions. Like his father, she had concerned herself more with how Jeffrey might be persuaded to go along with her own plans than with what might make him happy. And yet, to the very end, apparently, he had faith in her, never doubting she had some good reason for having run away.

"Good-bye, Jeffrey," she whispered, tears in her eyes. "I'm sorry—for everything."

She knelt for a long time, lost in her reflections. Then, brushing the tears from her cheeks, she stood up. How very final death was, she thought. And yet sometimes it seemed

welcome for its finality. She recalled her days in the desert,
when death had seemed close and inevitable, and not unpleasant. How had Jeffrey felt when his own death came? Had he
been afraid, or had he wanted it, or had it been too sudden for
him to feel anything at all? She, Jessica, had escaped and he
had not. Perhaps it should have been the other way around.
But she would make it up to him, to the St. Johns who lay in
their graves around her. She would make certain their line did
not die. And then—she glanced around at the peaceful, sunny
clearing—when her own time came, her bones would lie here
with the rest. She brushed the dirt off the front of her skirt
and turned to go.

Then she saw him. He was standing at the edge of the
clearing, near the path which led to the house. His hat was
tilted back on his head and she could see his gray eyes
clearly. He had appeared before her as quietly and catlike as
he had that first night in the canyon.

Jessica's heart turned over at the sight of him. She stood
frozen in the middle of the clearing. He watched her a
moment and then moved forward, stopping a few feet from
where she stood.

"Hello, Jessica." His voice was low and even.

"Reno . . ." Her voice was choked. "What are you doing
here?"

"I was worried about you. I came to see if you were all
right."

"But why . . . why should you be worried?"

"Spur came to me—a couple days after I left you, still
saddled, with the rifle in the sheath. I thought something had
happened to you, but then I heard you'd made it back to the
ranch. After that it was rumored you were sick. I began to be
afraid something was wrong. I had to see you."

"You came . . . the other day."

"I had to come. It was part of the job to come. But I also
hoped I might catch a glimpse of you. I thought maybe if I
stayed in the background and kept my hat down, you wouldn't
recognize me, but I guess I was wrong."

Jessica hung her head, not trusting herself to speak.

"When I didn't see you, I decided to send Amadeo back with your horse. I figured if anyone could get in to see you, he could."

"And what did he tell you?" Her voice was low, and she kept her head down, not daring to look up.

"He thought something was wrong. Is that true?"

Again Jessica said nothing. Reno stepped closer, and putting his fingers under her chin, he tilted her face up to his. She knew there was no way she could hide the traces of her illness or the fading bruise mark on her cheek.

"Did Ross St. John do this to you?" He touched his finger to her cheek.

"Yes," she whispered, unable to lie to him.

"I'll kill him for that." His tone was flat and matter-of-fact.

"No!"

He dropped his hand and regarded her for a moment.

"You still love him, then?"

She shook her head.

"No . . . that is, I don't know. . . . I don't want him killed. He did hit me, but he was angry, over Jeffrey. He blamed me for Jeffrey's death. But that's all over."

Reno was silent for a moment, weighing her words.

"I'm sorry about Jeffrey," he said finally, his voice gentle.

She felt tears welling in her eyes and quickly blinked them back. She was not going to break down, not now, not in front of Reno.

"There's no reason, now, is there, for you to stay here." It was as much a statement as a question.

"I can't leave . . . not . . . not just yet," she stammered.

"I want you, Jessica," he continued, ignoring her response. "I've been thinking about you a lot these last weeks. I want you to come away with me, away from everything that's happened here. I want to marry you. I know I haven't much to offer—only myself. But we can make a life together, I think, if you're willing. There's some land I can get in California, or in Colorado, or Wyoming, if you wish."

Tears of anger and despair came to her eyes as she listened to his words.

"I don't understand you. How can you talk to me like that? How can you ask me to go away with you when you've hired yourself out to an enemy? Why didn't you tell me before who you were?"

Reno regarded her speculatively for a moment.

"It seemed of no significance out there in the desert. And I didn't try to deceive you about who I am. I am not your enemy."

"But you're Ross St. John's . . ."

"And his enemies are yours? I would have thought you'd no longer be concerned about the Running J, especially after all that's happened."

"I . . . I'm going to marry Ross," she blurted out.

It was as if she had struck him. Reno stiffened and drew back, his eyes hard. There was a long pause, the silence tense between them.

"I see," he said finally, his voice harsh with scorn. "I should have guessed."

"What do you mean?"

"I suppose the lure of being mistress of the Running J is just too strong for you to resist. And if you can't marry one man to get what you want, you'll marry another."

"Reno, please . . ."

"And you don't care that the man you marry seduced you while you were still engaged to his son, that he brought about his own son's death, that he has beaten you and kept you prisoner. You don't care that Ross St. John is a man who takes what he wants with no thought for others. I would have expected better of you, Jessica."

Although she had said many of these same things, Jessica felt moved to defend Ross.

"He's a good man," she protested. "He cares about the ranch and the people on it. And how dare you talk to me of whom I should and shouldn't marry, after you deceived me the way you did." Her voice rose in anger. "Why didn't you tell me you were working for Kincaid? Why didn't you say he had hired you to kill Ross St. John and take over the Running J?"

"Have you no faith in me, Jessica?" His words were spoken quietly and they stemmed her impassioned tirade. She stood trembling, gazing into his eyes, remembering the feel of that hard mouth on hers, the warm strength of his arms wrapped around her. She knew that what she wanted most of all was for Reno to take her in his arms and carry her away, overwhelming her doubts and anguish in the strength of his embrace. If he took her, she would go, despite everything she had just said. But she knew that he would not. He had always let her make her own decisions, ever since that first night she encountered him in the canyon. She stood frozen in despair and stubborn pride, unable to act.

"Well," Reno drawled, finally. "Reckon I made a big mistake. Maybe several, though I haven't quite figured out which was the biggest." He reached out and touched her briefly on the cheek. "Good-bye, Jessica," he whispered. And then he was gone.

She stared forlornly after him for a minute and then made her way slowly down the path to the house. She felt as if she had just been granted her second wish.

Chapter 26

Gradually, Jessica's life on the ranch began to assume some outward semblance of normality. Her strength came back and she was more active, helping Serafina with the chores and taking short walks in the woods behind the house. She even rode Spur. Ross forbade her to go on any excursions, however, and she confined her riding to the pasture. She was happy enough to obey Ross's orders, not because she feared some attack by Kincaid's men, but because she had no desire to run into Riordon. She always waited until the foreman had left or was occupied in some task, before she went out by herself, and by such means she had avoided any further encounters.

Spur was frisky after his long period of inactivity, and he had fattened up on the Running J grass. He was impatient with their restricted lopes around the pasture and Jessica sensed that he wanted to be off again, into the mountains or across the desert.

"Some day," she whispered in his ear. "Someday we'll really ride again, just the two of us. I promise." But she didn't know where or when.

Every time she saw Spur, she remembered that Reno had been responsible for the mustang's return, and despite her anger at his deception and the pain of his scornful parting words, she felt grateful for his thoughtfulness. After running away, her horse had gone to Reno. She marvelled at that and wondered what it meant. Spur at least had sensed a friend. Sometimes it seemed to Jessica that it was Spur and the warm mutual affection she and the horse gave each other that gave her the courage to go on.

Amadeo, the horse thief, had also handled Spur. Strange how that little man served both Reno and Ross St. John. He was a link between them, just as she was. Jessica grew cold thinking about that. Reno had been hired to kill Ross, and given Ross's treatment of her, Reno had even more reason to carry out his charge. Or did he no longer care?

How unfair Reno's parting words had been! He didn't understand what she owed Ross. It was her regard for Ross and her disillusionment with Reno that had led to her decision—not the desire to be mistress of the Running J. Or was it? Deep down, Jessica feared that Reno was right and that she was making the same mistake with Ross that she had made with his son—seeing the ranch first and the man second.

Underneath the surface of daily life, things were not as they had once been. Before, Jessica had enjoyed riding with Ross to watch the cowboys at work, but now she avoided the hands as much as she could. She also stayed away from the kitchen and back yard, where Donaciana worked. Ross had pried from a reluctant Serafina the true story of Jessica's illness, and he had wanted to send Donaciana away. But Serafina had persuaded him to let her mother stay, and Jessica had wondered about this. Serafina, though still friendly, had become somewhat distant. She always seemed to be very busy, bustling around the house, having little time for the sort of intimate talk they had enjoyed when Jessica was ill.

Ross St. John was the most normal member of the household. Assuming that their future together was now mutually agreed upon, he seemed relaxed and almost cheerful in his dealings with Jessica. He came to her room nearly every night, and they lay together and talked for hours. Or rather, Ross would talk, telling her of his plans for the ranch, for themselves, and discussing the day's events.

"What about Kincaid?" Jessica asked at one point. "What is he going to do?"

"Try to drive me off the ranch, one way or another," Ross laughed.

"Aren't you worried?"

"Of course—a little. I'll feel better when he actually makes some move. This hide and seek we've been playing is getting on my nerves. But he knows he's going to have to confront me sooner or later. What bothers me sometimes," Ross continued, "is not that Kincaid wants the Running J. Anyone in his right mind would want the ranch. What bothers me is that Kincaid is no rancher. He just wants to get what he can out of the place, as quickly as he can. He has no notion of how to handle land and cattle—or people. He'll suck the place dry."

"What about the gold mine?"

"Gold mine?"

"The one Jeffrey talked about. The one Don Octaviano is supposed to have known about. Do you think Kincaid is after that, too?"

"So Jeffrey sold you on the gold mine business." Ross chuckled. "Well, maybe he was right. It would explain what they wanted from Don Octaviano. I'm beginning to wonder if Kincaid wasn't behind that, after all. Maybe they found out what they wanted, too. I'll tell you, though, if there's a gold mine somewhere on the Running J, I sure wouldn't mind knowing its whereabouts right now."

"Why?"

"Between the cattle rustling and the drought, my losses have been so bad this year, a little extra money would sure help."

"You're not in danger of losing the Running J, are you?" Jessica asked, suddenly anxious.

He laughed and rumpled her hair.

"No way I could be in danger of losing it, at least not now. No, I'm just going to be a little short this year, that's all. My big worry at the moment is Kincaid, but I'm not afraid of him."

"What about that man he hired—the gunman? Hayden, you said his name was."

Ross shrugged.

"He's dangerous. And I hear he's good. I'd just as soon not tangle with him, but if the time comes, I'll do what I have to do."

Unable to share Ross's apparent nonconcern, Jessica lay awake for a long time after he left. Unbidden images of the meeting between Ross and Reno passed through her mind, and she grew sick with anxiety. Over the last few weeks, she and Ross had woven a bond of mutual understanding and affection and even cautious trust. She did not wish to see him hurt or killed, but neither did she wish harm to Reno. If there ever came the promised confrontation between the two men, she feared she would be torn in two.

In bed, Ross was passionate, intense, and insistent. Jessica let herself be swept along by his ardor, trying not to be concerned if her passion did not always match his. Sometimes he would come in after she had gone to bed, slipping, naked, under the sheets and lying next to her a moment before taking her in his arms. At other times he would come in earlier and stand with her in front of the mirror so that she could watch him undressing her and then see herself naked in the lamplight, as his hands explored her body. And yet, despite all these attentions, Jessica felt something was missing. What was it Serafina had said to her about herself and Ross? That they had struck sparks from each other, that was it. But now, although affection and warmth were there, the sparks were gone.

As August wore on, the days grew increasingly hotter, and there was no relief from the drought. Occasionally, dark clouds piled against the peaks at the far end of the valley and distant mutterings of thunder reverberated in the mountains. But no rain fell in the valley itself, and very little elsewhere. The stream behind the house was a trickle of its former self and Serafina said she had never before seen it so low.

Jessica had taken to sitting out on the veranda, where it intersected with the breezeway in front of Ross St. John's room. Here, when the sun was at its highest, she could find shade and occasional stirrings of air to relieve the oppressive heat. She brought mending, or a book, to pass the time, and she could also watch the comings and goings in the yard.

One day—a day which she would have sworn was the hottest yet—sultry and still, with the leaves hanging limply from the trees—she found herself unable to concentrate on even the simple sewing in her lap, and she leaned her head against the back of the rocking chair and closed her eyes. Somewhere near the edge of the porch, a cicada churred dispiritedly for a moment, rising to a high pitch, and then stopped abruptly. Jessica was vaguely aware that someone had joined her on the porch.

"Señorita."

Jessica's eyes flew open and she found herself staring up at the dumpy figure of Donaciana. She felt a sudden rush of alarm. She had not seen Donaciana since her return to the ranch. What did she want now?

But there was no malevolence or hostility in the other woman's eyes. Instead, Jessica read a look almost of fear, and the brown, creased face was knit into a frown.

"Señorita," she repeated, the words rushing out. "I have come to ask your forgiveness. It was a bad thing I tried to do to you, a very bad thing, a sin. It was wrong. I should never have done it."

Jessica was taken aback by this unexpected apology. She had the odd feeling that it was not she, herself, who had inspired Donaciana's repentance, but some other person or force that had humbled the Mexican woman. Her religion perhaps? Had she recently been to see the priest and made confession? Was this her penance?

"I, too, am at fault," she murmured, suddenly realizing that she had never made any effort to penetrate Donaciana's initial reserve and hostility. It had been, she knew now, an almost fatal error on her own part.

Donaciana hurried on, ignoring Jessica's words.

"You do not need to fear, anymore. You will be safe now. No more harm will come to you. You are promised that." Her eyes darted sideways a moment, as if she feared someone were watching, and then, before Jessica could make any further response to this surprising speech, she waddled off down the porch toward the kitchen.

Jessica sat there for a moment, staring after her. Then she stood up and walked to the far end of the porch. She was disconcerted by Donaciana's sudden appearance and by her words. So many things, she reflected, had turned out not to be what they seemed when she had first arrived on the ranch— including herself. What she had wanted seemed so simple, then, and so easily obtained. Now, she didn't even know what she wanted, let alone how to attain it.

"No more harm will come to you," Donaciana had said. Had she meant simply that she herself would make no more attempts on Jessica, or had there been some deeper, more general significance to her remark?

Well, what more harm could come to her, in any case? Surely, enough had happened already. Still, Jessica felt something oppressive and threatening hanging over the ranch. Donaciana's sudden appearance and her words, rather than alleviating any of Jessica's anxiety, had only served to augment it. There was a sense of waiting and of tension in the air. Even the animals felt it. The horses in the pasture were both listless and restless, their heads hanging in the heat, their tails and ears twitching nervously.

Perhaps it was just the sultry weather. Far to the east, dark clouds were piling up against the peaks of the Sangre de Christo, though the sky overhead was still pale and clear. If the storms did move up the valley, perhaps they would bring relief from the oppressive heat.

With a sigh, Jessica turned back to the rocking chair. But she found that she was unable to get to work again, and she sat rocking, waiting for the day to pass.

Chapter 27

Jessica was awakened by the thudding of boots in the hallway outside her door. As she struggled to open her eyes, she heard someone pounding on the door of Ross's room. She peered at the face of the clock, barely visible in the faint moonlight streaming through the window. It was the middle of the night.

Alarmed, Jessica jumped out of bed. Throwing a wrapper over her nightgown, she ran to the doorway to peer down the hall. Ross had just emerged from his room and was hurrying down the steps of the breezeway, still buttoning his shirt. Just behind him trotted one of the cowboys. One glimpse of the man's anxious face told Jessica that something was very wrong. She ran after Ross, but his long strides had carried him too far for her to catch up. She reached the side of the cowboy and caught his arm.

"What's happening?" she asked breathlessly.

The cowboy, a young Mexican named Tomás, turned to her, his dusty, sweat-stained face tense in the moonlight.

"Forest fire. Down past Bolita Canyon, headed this way. Probably set by lightning."

For the first time, Jessica became aware of the distant

rumble of thunder and the faint blue light flickering on the horizon. As Tomás hurried after his boss, she felt a cold wave of fear wash over her. Forest fire! The woods were tinder-dry from the drought. The entire valley—the pastures, the ranch, everything—would go, if the fire swept this way.

Ross was returning, and behind him, the bunkhouse lights were aglow, casting yellow rectangles into the night. Several of the cowboys were already running toward the stables, fumbling with shirt buttons and belts as they ran.

Jessica accosted Ross at the breezeway steps.

"Let me go, too," she urged, her hand on his sleeve. "I want to help."

He shook her off.

"No, it's too dangerous. I want you to stay here."

She grabbed his sleeve again, pulling on his arm and forcing him to look down at her.

"You'll need every hand you can get. I'm strong. I can do lots of things as well as a man. And besides," she added, "if you're there, I want to be too. I can't just sit here at the house while the ranch is in danger."

Ross regarded her for a moment and then smiled thinly.

"All right, you can come. I'm going to leave some of the hands here to guard the ranch, so we'll need all the extra help we can get. Go put on some pants and boots and bring leather gloves. Also a couple wool blankets. Saddle Spur and tell Serafina and Donaciana to put together some food and a couple canteens of whiskey while they're at it."

Jessica ran to do Ross's bidding, darting into her room to pull on her pants and a cotton shirt and tying a scarf around her head before hurrying toward the kitchen.

Serafina and Donaciana were already bustling around the kitchen. They packed loaves of bread, cold beef, and other items of food in large baskets, and Jessica helped fill several flasks of coffee. Remembering Ross's instructions, she took the decanter from the sideboard in the living room and filled another flask with whiskey.

The yard was a hubbub of activity, with cowboys running between bunkhouse and stable, saddling horses, and yelling orders to each other. The buckboard and wagon were pulled up to the house, and men rolled barrels to fill at the pump behind the kitchen. Axes and shovels were thrown into the back of the buckboard, along with bundles of burlap bags tied with rope, and Jessica piled on top of these the blankets that Ross had requested. Then she helped Donaciana load the baskets of food, before running off to saddle Spur.

The mustang was waiting for her at the fence, his head up and alert. Jessica led him into the stable to be saddled, adding to her gear a spare hatchet, a length of rope, and an extra blanket she found near one of the stalls. She wasn't certain exactly how one fought a forest fire, but to judge by the preparations being made in the yard, it looked as if a variety of equipment might be called for. It couldn't hurt to have a few extras.

She brought Spur outside and mounted. Already the laden wagons had begun to roll down the road by the pasture, accompanied by several hands on horseback, leading extra mounts. Jessica urged her horse forward to join them. Ross was not yet part of the cavalcade, and Jessica glanced back to see him still in the yard, mounted on his strawberry roan, giving last-minute orders to those who were waiting behind. Serafina stood on the porch, a lantern in her hand, anxiously gazing up at him. Her features were pale and drawn in the lamplight, but her stance was resolute, and she nodded firmly when Ross turned to say something to her before he whirled and took off after the wagons clattering down the road.

He pulled up alongside Jessica for a moment, slowing his mount to a canter.

"Be sure to keep a firm rein on Spur as we get close to the fire," he warned her. "Horses have a tendency to panic when they catch a whiff of smoke." Then, before Jessica could reply, he had spurred the roan forward, ahead of the wagons.

Jessica gave Spur a pat on the neck, a little ruffled by Ross's words. Had Spur not carried her safely through the hardships of the desert? He certainly was not going to panic at a mere forest fire.

They turned east onto the main road. Several other riders,

late receivers of the news, caught up with them as they rode, their horses lathered, their faces grim, and halfway down the valley they encountered one of the cowboys from the closer line camp. He had spotted the fire from the high slope where his cabin stood and was on his way to the ranch with the news. Ross had him change mounts and then join them.

The only sounds as they rode were the pounding of hoof-beats and the jingle of harnesses. No one spoke, and everyone concentrated on the road ahead. Overhead, the sky was darkening as clouds began to roll across the valley, slipping across the silver face of the full moon.

Maybe it will rain and put out the fire, Jessica thought as she once again heard the distant mutter of thunder. But the air around them was dry and still, with no promise of relief. As they approached the far end of the valley, she caught a whiff of smoke, acrid in her nostrils, and as they rounded the foot of the mountain that guarded the valley's eastern edge, she could see an orange glow on the horizon where the fire tinted the east like a monstrous dawn.

Despite these forewarnings, Jessica was unprepared for the sight which greeted them as they broke through the forest and had their first clear view of what raged across the mountains ahead.

It seemed at first that the entire Sangre de Christo was ablaze. The inferno was sweeping down the slopes of the mountains, consuming the tinder-dry forest in a huge roaring cloud of fire and smoke, eclipsing the night sky. Even from where she stood, Jessica could hear the crackling of the pines as they blazed like torches and toppled to the ground. In the blackened swath where the fire had already passed, trees still smoldered and here and there a branch flared in a final burst of death.

It was difficult to tell how far away the fire was, for the leaping flames distorted the distance, devouring the sky. Was it a mile away? Five miles? Whatever its distance, it would soon be upon them, for the breeze that touched Jessica's cheek, warm and ash-laden, was directly from the east.

To the left of the road was a meadow, stretching to the foot

of the slope that enclosed one side of the valley's end. Across
the meadow ran a river, only a trickle of water, now, because
of the drought, and just beyond the river the forest began
again, descending steeply down the mountainside. On the
other side of the road, the river plunged into a deep ravine;
Bolita Canyon it was called. Jessica remembered traveling
alongside it as they made their way down the mountain on
that long-ago trip to Las Vegas.

It was here, at the gateway to the lush valley where the
ranch house lay, that Ross had closen to fight the fire.

He ordered his men across the meadow and toward the
stream, the wagons lumbering behind. At the water's edge,
they dismounted and began unloading equipment, piling the
axes, shovels, feed bags, blankets, water barrels and other
gear onto the ground. Jessica dismounted, too, and then stood
indecisively, feeling useless. Everyone else already seemed to
know what to do. Some men had already seized axes and
shovels and were wading across the stream.

Ross strode by leading the roan and abruptly shoved the
reins into Jessica's hands.

"Here," he said. "Take the horses over to the other end of
the meadow and tether them by the trees. When you're
finished with that, you can come back and help pile brush."

Grateful to be given a task, Jessica led Spur, Ross's roan,
and several other horses to the spot Ross had indicated. Spur
was calm under her hand, but several of the other horses,
scenting the fire, had become wild-eyed and skittish. She had
difficulty trying to control all of them and was grateful when
Tomás came to give her a hand. The horses' fear seemed to
communicate itself to her and she felt overwhelmed as she
looked out toward the burning sky. Surely there was no way
they could stop such an inferno. It would sweep past their
puny efforts, and roar up the valley, destroying the forest, the
pastures, the ranch house, themselves. For the first time, she
realized that if the fire trapped them here, they would die in
it, a horrible, searing, painful death. She began to regret her
rash impulse to come with the men. She had no business
being here. She was helpless, useless—and terribly afraid.

Tomás had stopped beside her to gaze at the blazing mountains, and his face reflected the same awe and fear that Jessica felt. They stood for a moment and then he tugged gently at her sleeve.

"Come," he said. "We must go to help."

Ashamed of her own fear and weakness, Jessica trotted beside him across the meadow. She could see the other hands working frantically among the trees on the far side of the stream and hear their shouts and the ring of an axe on wood.

"What are they doing?" she asked Tomás, still confused about exactly how one fought a forest fire.

"They are digging a trench and cutting trees and brush to start a backfire," he explained to her.

"They're going to *set* a fire?"

He nodded.

"If they can get a fire going toward the other fire, they will have a barrier to it, a burned out area that it cannot cross. Then the fire will sweep off in another direction, away from the valley. At least, that is what we hope."

"But isn't that very dangerous? I mean, what if the fire you set starts toward you instead of in the other direction?"

"Yes, it is very dangerous," he replied. "It is very tricky to do, and you must be on your guard for sparks and burning branches. That is why we have the blankets and the extra water, and why we dig a trench."

Just as they reached the wagons, there was a tremendous crash in the brush just upstream and Jessica looked up just in time to see a large buck leap the stream. It stood poised on the bank a moment, staring at them, its fear of men banished for the moment by a much greater fear. Then it bounded off across the meadow.

Ross had just come up to the wagon to get one of the flasks, and he stared after the deer for a moment.

"God only knows how many cattle are being fried in there," he muttered. He turned to Jessica, his eyes searching her face, as if he were trying to fix a memory of her in his mind.

"Once we've set the backfire, I want you to go get Spur

and hightail it out of here, pronto,'' he told her brusquely.
"Understand? I don't want you waiting around to see if our
break holds.''

Jessica nodded, mute.

"You head straight back to the ranch. Serafina's got everything there ready to evacuate if we need to. And I want you
to be one of the first ones out if the fire heads up the valley.
Now, let's get to work.''

Jessica followed him across the stream. She was a little
piqued by the harshness of his tone. Well, she would show
him that she could do her share and make good her boast that
she was as useful as a man. He would not regret that she had
come.

She had little leisure to think in what followed. All along the
edge of the forest, on the far side of the stream, the men were
clearing a wide strip, cutting down trees and digging up
bushes to create a buffer zone to contain the backfire. Jessica
set to work dragging brush from this strip to the edge of the
forest where the fire would be set, piling it up against the
trees, and helping to haul logs lassoed with ropes. Her arms
and back soon ached from the unaccustomed effort and Jessica was glad she had followed Ross's orders to wear her
leather gloves. Even so, her hands were raw and scraped from
all the tugging and pulling. Every now and then she took a
break to carry water to the dusty, perspiring men, but such
breaks were rare, for no one could pause for long in their
frantic efforts.

The fire was closer, advancing up the mountainside. Every
now and then a shift in the wind gave them a moment of
hope, a few more minutes in their race against time. But then
the wind would back around to the east again. Overhead,
black clouds had completely blanketed the sky, and away to
the northeast, lightning forked. But, so far, there was no hint
of the promised rain, and the lightning itself brought the
threat of further fire.

Though no more deer came crashing through the woods, a
myriad of other scurrying creatures rustled through the grass
and brush. How many little animals would be caught between

the two fires when they set the backfire going, Jessica wondered. She felt heartsick at the destruction of the forest and all
the wildlife she loved. The air was thick with ash and Jessica
wet her bandanna and wound it around her mouth and nose to
keep from choking.

Ross seemed to be everywhere, encouraging, exhorting,
bullying. At the same time, he worked as hard as any of the
men. As she watched him, Jessica began to see what made
him such a respected leader. He was willful, even headstrong,
but he was also courageous, powerful, and fair. Jessica had no
doubt that his men would have taken no more risk and
worked no harder had it been their own ranch that was
threatened. And, she reflected, in a way it was, for Ross St.
John saw all those who worked for him as part of the ranch in
a way most ranchers did not.

As Jessica crossed the stream to fetch another canteen of
water from the wagons, a movement near the far edge of the
meadow caught her eye. She looked up to see a group of
horsemen standing by the road. One of them had just broken
away from the others and was trotting across the meadow. It
was difficult for Jessica to be certain in the dark, but the
horseman looked suspiciously like Stuart Kincaid. She dropped
the canteen and ran back to where Ross was working.

"I think we've got visitors," she told him breathlessly.

Ross swore and checked his gun. Then, pausing to give an
order to Riordon, he strode across the stream to confront the
rider.

It was indeed Kincaid.

"Come to make sure your property's all right?" Ross
growled as the rancher rode up.

But the other man refused to rise to the bait.

"We're all in this together, Ross," he replied. "I brought
a few of the boys along with me. Figured you could use some
help. If this fire heads up the valley, we're all in trouble."

Jessica could see that it was on the tip of Ross's tongue to
refuse, but then common sense got the better of him. Any
help—even Kincaid's—could be crucial for them right now.

"Get to work further down the stream, near the canyon,"

Ross ordered. "We're almost finished up here and we need to get the backfire going as quick as we can. I got more axes and shovels in the wagon if you need them."

"We got our own. Give us a yell when you're ready to go." Kincaid wheeled his mount and headed back across the meadow to where his men were waiting. Jessica saw them scatter toward the far end of the creek. She wondered if Reno was among them, but she couldn't see his familiar figure in the dark. He probably hadn't come, she decided. Kincaid wouldn't risk his prize gunman fighting a fire. Or did he have in mind some sort of ambush or trick? Well, they would all be too busy with the fire for a while, for him to try anything.

As Jessica resumed her labors at the firebreak, she reflected on how odd it was that they were all working together, united by a common danger. Even Riordon did not seem threatening to her, and he treated her no differently from any of the others. She had even brought him the whiskey flask at one point, at his request, and he had wiped his mouth on the back of his sleeve and returned the flask, not even glancing at her as he did so. For the moment, at least, all individual animosities, differences, and concerns were buried in the face of overwhelming danger.

Then Jessica heard Ross's voice booming across the night. They were ready to set the backfire and he was ordering everyone away from the line of debris piled at the edge of the forest. Several men doused the brush with kerosene, a step that seemed to Jessica unnecessary, given its tinder-dry state. The rest of the men stood by tensely, with buckets of water and wetted feed bags and blankets at hand to control the fire should it decide to spring in the wrong direction. Jessica grabbed a blanket and dipped it into the stream, turning it over in the shallow pool so that it would be thoroughly soaked. The stream itself, which might have provided a barrier to the approaching inferno, was now barely deep enough to wet the blanket. It was even too shallow to effectively fill the buckets; the water barrels from the ranch had been pulled close to the bank for this purpose.

The brush piles blazed, shooting orange tongues of flame into the air, and then the fire ran rapidly down the line of

piled debris, leaping into the forest beyond. Trees turned
instantly into flaming torches, and Jessica could hear the
hissing of boiling pitch and the popping of exploding branches.

She had no time to watch, however, for she and the others
stationed along the line were soon kept busy stamping out
sparks and burning bits of debris blown across the protective
strip of clearing and into the grass and brush beyond. Flailing
the heavy, wet blanket, she dashed at the circles of flame that
spread with frightening rapidity throughout the grass, wherever a spark or cinder landed. Nearby, a dead bush exploded
into flame, and almost instantly two of the cowboys were
upon it, dousing it with bucket and blanket.

They had set their backfire just in time, for the vast expanse of burning forest had almost reached the tip of the
valley. The wind, which whirled around them, was dry and
searing, scorching skin and eyeballs with an almost unbearable heat. The noise of the two fires drowned out all else, and
Jessica could no longer even hear the thunder, although flashes
of lightning still emblazoned the sky overhead.

Their line held and the fire they had set rushed eastward to
meet the inferno that engulfed the lower slopes. Would its
own swath be wide enough now to deter the larger blaze, or
would the forest fire leap easily over it and rage on up the
valley? The line of men along the creek stood tense, waiting.

Jessica felt a hand gripping her arm and looked up to see
Ross, his face stained with ash and sweat, bending over her.

"Get to your horse," he ordered. "You've done all you
can and I want you out of here—now."

Before Jessica could reply, he had moved on down the
line, giving orders to the other men, who began to pick up
buckets and tools and make their way back across the creek.

Reluctantly, Jessica left her post and crossed the meadow
to the tethered horses. She untied Spur's reins from the
branch where she had looped them and mounted. But instead
of heading toward the road, she turned around for one more
look. How could she leave before she knew whether or not
their efforts had been successful and while others were still in

danger? She would wait just long enough to see if the fire-break held.

Across the meadow was a scene from hell. The entire sky seemed to be ablaze, and against the flaming background of the fire darted the frail silhouettes of the Running J hands, loading equipment into the wagons, beating out the last stray sparks. Then, as if on signal, they all turned to gaze at the inferno behind them. The two fires had merged. The twin walls of flames licked in a towering embrace, hesitated a moment, and then raced off to the south, up the mountain and away from the valley. The break had held. Above the roaring of the fire, Jessica could hear a faint cheer from the men across the meadow.

Weak with relief, she dismounted and led Spur back toward the wagons. It was all over. They had won. Whatever further destruction the fire would wreak, the valley at least was safe. There was no point now in her returning to the ranch. She might as well help pack up and leave.

As she came up, Ross was giving orders, arranging for the loading of the rest of the equipment, and posting men along the break to check for stray fires and burning debris. The forest ahead of them was mostly black now, but here and there a branch still blazed. A few trees, their tops still intact, stood like ghostly survivors amidst the blackened rubble.

While the men worked, Ross anxiously surveyed the horizon.

"We aren't safe, yet," she heard him say to Riordon. "If the wind shifts again, it could send the fire right back down the mountain at us." He glanced overhead at the dark clouds. "Maybe, if we're lucky, that damn rain'll come and dampen things down a bit."

As if in response to his words, a flash of lightning illumined the meadow, and thunder rattled between the mountains, echoing down the valley. For a moment Jessica thought she felt a change in the breeze, a touch of coolness, a whiff of moisture. But it was probably only her own imagination, for no rain fell.

Ross was just about to give the order for the buckboard to

move out, when a rider, bent low over his horse, galloped up
from the far end of the meadow.

"What the hell!" Ross growled.

As the rider drew closer, Jessica recognized him as Kincaid's
foreman.

He reined his horse abruptly to a halt in front of them,
kicking up clods of grass, but he didn't dismount.

"The fire!" he yelled at them. "It's jumped the road and
it's doubling back up the canyon and heading this way." He
wheeled and was gone before they could respond.

Jessica felt cold fear welling up. Just when they thought
they had the fire beaten! The canyon would act like a funnel,
and the fire would roar up its narrow depths, right back into
the valley. There was no time now for another firebreak. All
they could do was flee. The fire had defeated them.

Ross was already frantically yelling orders as the cowboys,
drawn by the sight of the urgent rider, clustered around the
wagons.

"Cut the horses loose and get the hell out of here. Leave
the wagons, leave everything, just get the horses." As the
men rushed to do his bidding, he turned on Jessica. "I
thought I told you to leave. Get going! Now!" His face was
contorted with anger and defeat. Jessica did not argue but
quickly mounted Spur and headed across the meadow.

Just before the road, she stopped. Several of the hands
surged on by her and down the road. Others had just finished
cutting the horses loose from the wagons and were driving the
animals before them across the meadow. One horse had gone
charging back across the stream, and someone had ridden
after it. Jessica could hear the shouts, the frantic neighing of
the horses, and somewhere, faint but ominous in the distance,
the muffled roar of the fire. She glanced toward the far end of
the meadow where the stream plunged into the narrow canyon. Bolita Canyon was a brush-choked cleft running down
the mountainside, so narrow in spots that a horse could easily
have jumped from one side to the other. Who could have
known that it would become a funnel of death?

There was a tremendous crash from the direction of the

canyon's mouth. As Jessica turned to look, a steer lurched up the bank and onto the level surface of the meadow. It paused a moment, its eyes wild, its nostrils flaring. Then it pounded off in panic down the bank of the stream.

One of the lucky ones, Jessica thought, as she watched it disappear into the darkness. How many head would the Running J lose tonight?

Well, she had better get out of here if she did not want to become a victim herself. Already, the rest of the hands were well down the road, driving the extra horses in front of them. The wagons stood in lonely abandon in the meadow. She couldn't see Ross anywhere. He must have gone ahead. Jessica turned Spur toward the road and urged him forward.

The frantic hoofbeats thudding on the dry ground behind her caused her to turn. At first she thought it was one of the runaway wagon horses that was galloping, riderless, past her toward the road. Then to her horror she saw that it was Ross St. John's strawberry roan, still saddled, flying by. She spurred her own mount forward, hoping to catch the other horse, but it twisted its head away as she came alongside. Its eyes were wide with fright, and Jessica's efforts to grab the reins only increased its panic. It wheeled and dashed past her into the woods on the far side of the road.

Ross. Where was Ross? He would never have turned the roan loose to find her own way. And she was still saddled. He must have been thrown or injured for his mount to be loose like that.

Her heart beating frantically, Jessica wheeled Spur and headed back toward the stream, trying to remember where she had last seen Ross. She could see no one by the wagons, and there was no sign of a body lying along the bank by the stream. Could it have been Ross that she saw pursuing the fleeing horse? That rider had crossed the stream and then headed along the firebreak toward the mouth of the canyon. Jessica urged Spur in that direction. The little mustang caught the scent of the approaching fire and tossed his head, but then obeying the urgent pressure of her thighs against his flanks, he plunged through the brush along the bank.

Here and there, charred branches from the backfire still smoldered and Jessica carefully guided her mount around them. She could see no sign of Ross in the darkness. She was risking her own life staying behind like this, and it might very well be for nothing. But if he was here, if he was helpless or injured or even just on foot, she could not leave him to die.

Then, as lightning flared briefly above her, she saw him. He was lying face down near an unburned stand of pine and brush. Swiftly, Jessica dismounted, and tying Spur's reins to a nearby branch, she hurried to Ross's side and bent down.

She couldn't tell if he was still alive. His eyes were closed and she could detect no signs of breathing. Frantically, she lifted one of his arms and tried to roll him over. His heavy, limp body resisted her efforts until, with one final, desperate heave, she managed to turn him on his back. A long dark smear of blood ran across his forehead. She fumbled with the buttons on his shirt and slipped her hand inside. Yes, there, she could feel it. His heart was beating, slowly but regularly. He was still alive.

How was she to get him out of there? It would not be long before the fire was upon them. And there was enough un-burned timber around so they would be consumed themselves once the fire reached this spot. She thought for one wild moment of trying to drag Ross into the already burned area, but there were too many smouldering timbers and half-burned trees ready to catch fire again and fall. Ross was so heavy, she could barely move him, let alone heave him up onto Spur to carry him out of danger.

Then she remembered the rope she had thrown across her saddle when she left the stable. She ran back to where Spur was tied. Yes, it was still there. She grabbed it and hurried back to where Ross was lying. Maybe if she could loop it around his chest, under his arms, then at least Spur could drag him out of this patch of woods and out of the direct path of the fire. And after that? . . . well, she would worry about that later. The first thing was to get him out of here. Then maybe she could find some way to protect both of them from the approaching flames.

Jessica had no idea about how to tie a knot, but after several fumbling efforts, she managed to tie one that would hold, running the rope twice around Ross's chest and under his arms. Then she looped the other end over her saddle horn and urged Spur forward. The mustang seemed to understand what she was trying to do, for he moved slowly and carefully, jerking his dragging burden as little as possible. Jessica winced as they pulled Ross along over rocks and fallen limbs. She knew that she was hurting him, but she didn't know what else to do. Better a few scrapes and bruises than for him to die in the fire.

Gingerly, she maneuvered her burden across the stream and then stopped beside the abandoned wagons. Could she take the buckboard, she wondered? But all the harnesses had been cut. There was no way to hitch up Spur. And she wasn't certain she could manage to lift Ross into the back. She thought for another wild moment of remaining where she was. Perhaps they could wrap themselves in dampened blankets, take buckets of water and wet the grass around them. But then she glanced beyond the far end of the meadow, at the yellow tongues of flame licking up from the canyon. The wind had shifted for the moment, slowing the fire's progress, but she knew that it could quickly shift again. She had only a minute or two at most, to decide what to do.

She would have to get Ross up onto Spur. There was no other way. She led the horse over to where Ross lay, and he stood tense but quiet while she struggled to raise the rancher's shoulders. If she could only get Spur to kneel, then perhaps she could get Ross partially upright. He could fall over the saddle so he could be carried.

Though she had never demanded it of him before, Spur, experienced cow pony that he was, readily obeyed her commands and knelt beside her. Her breath came in short painful gasps as she bent all her strength to trying to lift Ross's limp weight into the saddle.

She didn't see Reno until he was standing right beside her. Startled, she stared up for a moment into those familiar gray eyes, and then, letting her burden fall back to the ground, she stood up to face him.

"What are you doing here?" she demanded.

"Seems like you're always asking me that," Reno smiled. "I thought this time I'd be welcome. Especially since I stayed behind just so that I could make certain you were all right."

They stood in silence for a moment and Reno glanced down at the body at her feet.

"Is he alive?"

"If he weren't, I wouldn't be here trying to move him like this," she replied testily. She waited, but the other man made no move.

"Give me a hand with him, Reno," she said finally. Her voice was flat, but it held a challenge.

"Is there any reason I shouldn't just leave him here to die?" He spoke coldly.

"Yes." Her eyes met his. "Yes, because you're not that kind of a man."

A look almost of pain seemed to pass across his face. Then he smiled again, the deep lines at the corners of his mouth turning up.

"All right, Jessica, you win. You're a hard woman to resist."

He bent to help her, and between them they managed to lift Ross into the saddle. Then, working deftly and quickly, Reno took the rope and tied him securely in place.

"I think that's about as much of a burden as Spur can handle," he told her. "You get up behind me on Felicia and then let's get out of here before we all get fried."

He mounted his mare and then gave Jessica a hand up behind him and they headed across the meadow at a trot. As they reached the road, Jessica glanced back in time to see a line of flame shoot from the mouth of the canyon and run along the unburned edge of the stream. At the same time, something wet plopped onto her forehead and she heard other heavy drops splatting in the dust around them.

Reno glanced up.

"Maybe we'll get a little rain, after all," he remarked. "Though it'll have to be a lot to do us any good right now."

He put Felicia into a canter, and Jessica glanced back to make certain that Spur and his burden were all right. What would Ross say if he knew that the man who had been hired to kill him had just helped to save his life? And what would Kincaid have said to know that one of his own men had performed such a deed?

The rain was coming down harder, now, and beginning to soak through her cotton shirt—the shirt Reno had bought her the day they rode to Cabezon. That day she had let herself hope there might be some future with him, before she had understood what divided them. She contemplated the strong, familiar back in front of her. How she longed to lean against it and wrap her arms around his waist, sinking into the comfort of his body. She would give anything to lie in his arms again, to spend hours in quiet talk, as they had those times in the canyon. But, instead, she sat straight in the saddle, allowing herself only to lightly grasp Reno's belt to steady herself. There was no use dreaming about what could not be.

Reno had slowed his pace as the rain increased. Jessica glanced back again. Although she could still see faint flickers of fire against the horizon, the rain appeared to have already dampened the flames. At least the valley would be saved. This part of the Running J was safe.

And its owner? She cast another anxious glance at the body slung over the horse behind her. How badly had he been injured? Had she risked her life to save him, only to have him die? She closed her eyes and uttered a silent prayer. He's got to be all right, she told herself. He's got to be. The idea of the Running J without Ross St. John was unthinkable. He was an invincible presence. He could not die.

Suddenly Reno reined Felicia to a stop.

"Riders coming," he told her. "Reckon I'll leave you off here and be on my way before they arrive. Sure as anything they're from the Running J."

Jessica had heard nothing above the beating of the rain, but she did not doubt Reno's word. She slid down from the saddle. Reno dismounted and stood beside her.

Why does he always manage to see me at my worst? Jessica thought. She had been disheveled and half-starved when she met him in the desert, bruised and gaunt that day in the cemetery. And now she was drenched, her face streaked with soot, her hair hanging in damp tendrils around her face.

Reno reached out and gently touched her wet cheek.

"You've got courage, Jessica," he said softly. "I hope it brings you what you want."

She shivered at his touch. How was it that such a man could be so gentle, gentler in some ways than anyone she had ever known before. And yet, in other ways . . .

"I love you," he continued, dropping his hand. "Don't forget that."

"I won't," she promised. And it was a promise.

Abruptly, he turned and mounted, and before she could say anything more, he had wheeled Felicia around and disappeared into the forest. Jessica stood in the rain, staring after him. Then, gathering Spur's reins, she headed toward the ranch.

Chapter 28

Riordon was leading the caravan that came around the bend,
Ross's strawberry roan in tow. He pulled to a halt beside
Jessica, water streaming from the brim of his hat and dripping
off the corners of his mustache. She couldn't see his eyes but
his mouth was grim. Is he disappointed? she wondered. Did
he hope that Ross had perished in the fire? She remembered
her last encounter with the foreman on this mountain road and
felt a momentary rush of fear.

But this encounter was different. No sooner had Riordon
dismounted than they were surrounded by the rest of the
rescue party, half a dozen cowboys who had turned back
when they were overtaken by Ross St. John's riderless mare.
Jessica was vaguely aware of a flurry of activity around Spur
and some discussion as to whether Ross should be left as he
was and carried to the ranch or if someone should be sent to
fetch the abandoned buckboard. One rider galloped off toward
the ranch house to alert them to what had happened and
to send to Bernalillo for the doctor. Jessica was helped up
onto a strange horse and someone—she thought it might have
been Tomás—threw a slicker over her shoulders. She appreci-

ated the thoughtfulness of the gesture, even though it was of little use, since she was already soaked to the skin. Almost as much attention was being paid to her as to Ross, and Jessica realized she had become a hero. While everyone else rode on, she had stayed behind to save the boss's life.

The ride back to the ranch was a blur. Now that the danger was over, all the efforts of the past few hours caught up with her. Arms and shoulders ached from the work on the firebreak, eyes and nostrils burned from the smoke, and several spots on Jessica's neck throbbed painfully where burning cinders had landed. The rain seemed to have soaked through to her very bones, and she was shivering uncontrollably by the time they rode into the ranch yard.

Serafina hurried out to meet them, her rebozo thrown over her head against the rain, her face anxious and drawn. She hurried over to where the cowboys were lifting Ross off Spur. Urging them to be careful, she accompanied them as they carried their burden toward the porch. Donaciana was waiting by the breezeway with a lantern, and Jessica watched the light disappear as they carried Ross into his room.

Jessica led Spur to the stable to unsaddle him and rub him down. After all his efforts and bravery that night, he deserved a little care. Tomás came in while she was at work, leading several of the other horses

"Here, señorita," he said gently, taking the brush from her weary hand. "Let me finish this. You need to change clothes and get some rest."

Jessica started to protest that Spur seldom allowed anyone else to groom him, but the mustang seemed to be content under the young man's hand, so she relinquished her task gratefully and made her way back to the house.

Serafina was emerging from the door of Ross's room as she stepped up to the porch.

"How is he?" Jessica asked.

Serafina shook her head, her face pale.

"He has had a bad blow on the temple. He was thrown from his horse, I think?"

Jessica nodded.

"That is his main injury, it appears," the other woman continued. "There are a few others, not as serious. He is still unconscious, and his breathing is very rough. We have sent for the doctor, but it will be many hours before he can get here."

"Is there nothing we can do?"

"Keep him quiet and warm. And pray. For now, that is all."

Suddenly, she noticed Jessica shivering in the draft of the breezeway.

"Here. What are you doing standing here all wet? We do not need two sick people." She put her arm around Jessica's shoulders and propelled her firmly toward her room. "Go take those clothes off and put on something warm. I will bring you some hot chocolate. Then you must try to sleep. You have done enough for one night; you can do no more."

Docilely, Jessica obeyed. Once in her room, she shed the dripping slicker and stripped off her wet clothes. Then she toweled herself dry and slipped on a flannel nightgown and her robe. She found that she could not stop shivering. She didn't know if it was simply the rain that had chilled her to the bone, or if the fear and excitement of the night had also left her weak and shaken. She was grateful when Serafina appeared with a pot of hot chocolate and some bread and jam, and she curled up in the chair by the window, sipping the liquid slowly and letting its warmth seep gradually into her limbs.

It was still raining outside, pouring in sheets off the roof of the porch, turning the ranch yard into a muddy sea. At least they would have no more worries about fire that night. And perhaps this rain signaled the end of the long drought. If so, that might offset some of this night's loss—if anything could begin to compensate for those many acres of ruined, bare mountainside.

She tried not to think about Ross. Serafina was right. It was out of her hands now. She had done what she could. The rest was up to God—and to the doctor, when he came, if he came in time.

But he couldn't die, could he? Not Ross. He was too strong, too vital. What if he lived, but as a cripple? That would be worse. But he wouldn't die. He couldn't.

And what of herself? Without thinking she had risked her own life to save Ross St. John's. Did that mean that she did love him after all? She had fought that night for both Ross and the Running J, and in her mind they were somehow inseparable. One could hardly survive without the other. But where did she, Jessica Howard, fit in?

When she had finished her hot chocolate, Jessica blew out the lamp and lay down on the bed. It was almost dawn. She knew she was bone weary and should get some rest. But it was difficult to sleep. She was too aware of the man lying unconscious in the room down the hall and alert for every footstep that passed by her door on the way to his. Several times she rose to peer out. She could see the crack of light underneath the door and hear a murmur of voices from the room. But she could not hear Ross's voice among them. At one point, Serafina emerged from Ross's room and, meeting Jessica's eye, shook her head.

The rain had stopped and the pale gray light of dawn was breaking under the clouds when Jessica finally drifted into an exhausted but uneasy slumber. When she awoke several hours later, the yard was sunny, and she could hear the chickens scratching and clucking near the porch. She sat up with a start. She hadn't meant to sleep so long.

She tumbled out of bed and quickly changed into a skirt and blouse. Then she opened the door of her room and gazed in some trepidation down the hall. Serafina was coming from the direction of the kitchen, bearing a pitcher of water.

"How is he?" she asked fearfully.

"No change. He is still unconscious, but his breathing is more regular, I think, and his color is good. The doctor should be here soon. Maybe he can tell us more."

"Can I see him?"

"Why don't you wait," Serafina replied kindly. "There's nothing for you to see right now. He doesn't know anyone yet. Why don't you go on down to the kitchen and get some breakfast? I promise we'll call you if anything changes.''

Almost relieved not to have her request granted, Jessica made her way to the kitchen. It was a little frightening to see Ross St. John helpless.

When Jessica entered the kitchen, Donaciana was bending over the stove, frying bacon in an iron skillet. As she looked up, Jessica realized with a start that this was the first time she had invaded the Mexican woman's domain since she had returned to the ranch. Donaciana regarded her with bright eyes.

"You would like some breakfast?" For the first time since Jessica had known her, Donaciana addressed her pleasantly.

"Just some coffee, please." She knew she needed food, but her stomach was still knit with anxiety and she doubted she could eat.

"You sit down." Donaciana indicated a chair at the table. "I get."

Before Jessica could seat herself, the other woman came over and threw her arms around her. She gave her a brief hug and then drew back.

"You saved his life. They told me. You pulled him out of the fire after they all had left. You saved his life." She shuffled off to fetch a china mug from the shelf by the stove, wiping her eyes with her apron.

Jessica sat down, embarrassed by Donaciana's sudden emotion. It was hard to believe this dumpy, pleasant-looking woman had once tried to kill her. How her own status in the household had changed!

Donaciana had no sooner poured her a mug of steaming coffee and placed the sugar bowl next to it, than Jessica heard the pounding of hooves in the yard. She ran to the window to peer out, just in time to see Doan and a man carrying a small satchel disappear in the direction of Ross's room. Their lathered horses stood by the hitching rail, swishing their tails languidly.

Jessica abandoned her coffee and hurried down the hallway

toward Ross's room. Serafina was standing outside the door, with Doan beside her looking drawn and weary after his long night's ride. Serafina was trying to urge him to get breakfast and rest, but he stubbornly refused to leave.

"Ain't goin' nowhere till I find out if the boss's all right," he said. "I haven't ridden all this way just to trot off to bed now."

As Jessica came up, Serafina turned toward her with a thin smile.

"Dr. Crawford won't let anyone in while he's examining Ross," she said. "So I guess we'll all just have to wait out here for his verdict."

Jessica noted Serafina's pale cheeks and the tiny lines around her eyes, and she realized that between the fire and Ross's injury, the Mexican woman had been up all night. Impulsively she put her arm around the other's waist. To her surprise, Serafina leaned against her and buried her head on her shoulder. When she raised her head again, there were tears in her eyes.

"He can't die," she whispered brokenly, echoing Jessica's own thoughts. "He just can't."

After almost an hour, the door to Ross's room finally opened and the doctor emerged. Dr. Crawford was a portly individual with ruddy, jowled cheeks and a drooping, gray mustache. He glanced solemnly at the three people who waited tensely for his verdict, and then cleared his throat.

"Well, I must say, Mr. St. John is a lucky man. It also helps that he has the stamina of a bull. He got a nasty blow on the head, but there's no concussion. He needs a week or so in bed, though I suspect you might have a little trouble keeping him there. Other than that—a few cuts and bruises, nothing serious."

"Santa Maria!" Serafina let out a long breath. Jessica felt her knees go weak with relief.

"Is he . . . is he conscious yet?" she asked.

The doctor nodded. "Yep. He's awake. And already giving orders." He glanced from one to the other. "Which one of you is Jessica?"

"I am."

"Well, he's asking for you. You can go on in and see him. But only for a few minutes, mind. We don't want to tire him. I'm going off to tend to a couple of burns over in the bunkhouse, but I'll check in on him before I head back."

"Why don't you stay, doctor," Serafina suggested, accompanying him down the steps. "We could put you up overnight with no trouble. You could head back in the morning."

"I'd love to, Miss, but I got a patient expecting, and it could be any hour now, so I'd better . . ."

Their voices faded behind her as Jessica stepped inside and shut the door. Her heart was pounding, and she realized she had not set foot in Ross's room since the night of the fiesta. As the light was dim, she paused a moment while her eyes adjusted.

"Hello, Jessica." Ross's voice was weak and she could barely make out his form against the pillows. She made her way over to the bed and sat down. He reached out and laid his hand over hers.

"I understand I owe you my life."

"Anyone else would have done the same." For some reason, his gratitude embarrassed her.

"Don't give me that, my dear." His face was pale and lined, but the bandage around his head lent him an almost rakish air and the half-mocking smile he gave her was that of the old Ross St. John. She felt a rush of relief.

"You're far too modest," he went on, squeezing her hand. "It took more than a little courage to head right back toward the fire to find me. And I still don't know how you managed to hoist me up onto your horse."

"It wasn't easy," Jessica replied evasively. "I guess fear must have given me extra strength."

"Well, you told me you'd be useful as a man if I took you along. In fact you were about ten times better. Best decision I ever made."

"Aren't you glad I didn't obey your orders to leave?" she asked impishly.

"Little bitch. I suppose I should have you horsewhipped

for defying me. But thank God for a woman with a mind of her own. Speaking of horses," he added, "I reckon I owe that little mustang of yours an apology. That damn roan of mine—I had the devil of a time getting her to cross the stream to make sure everyone had cleared out. Then when that steer came charging out of the brush, she went wild. Couldn't control her, and she threw me. First time a horse's ever done that to me."

"I told you I was a good judge of horses."

"I should have listened to you. Sure am glad I didn't have that nag of yours shot, after all."

He sank back weakly into the pillows and reached for the glass of water beside the bed.

"You'd better get some rest. You need to save your strength." Jessica rose to go, but Ross tightened his grip on her hand.

"Jessica," he said, his voice serious now. "I just want you to know that whatever debts you might have had to the Running J, you have more than repaid them."

He released her hand and she bent over and kissed him on the forehead. Then she slipped out of the room.

Serafina was waiting for her.

"How is he?" she asked.

"I think he'll be all right. But he's still weak."

"We'll take care of him. And I think the doctor's right. The hardest part is going to be keeping him in bed until he gets his strength back."

"Why don't you do something about getting your own strength back," Jessica suggested, noticing that the other woman was swaying on her feet. "You haven't had any rest. Your mother and I can take care of things for now, and the doctor will look at him, too, before he leaves."

Serafina nodded.

"You are right," she said. "I will sleep, but not too long. There are many things that need to be done, and we must make certain that everything is in order so that Señor Ross has no excuse to get up before he should." She started down the hallway toward the kitchen, and then turned back to give Jessica a hug.

"Thank you," she whispered. "Thank you for saving him." And then she was gone.

Jessica stared after her for a moment. She felt overwhelmed by the gratitude heaped upon her, and a bit guilty. She had only done what she had to, and she knew that even then, without Reno's help, she and Ross might both have perished in the meadow. Thoughtfully, she made her way toward the kitchen. She would have Donaciana make a little broth. Ross would protest such weak fare, but perhaps she could persuade him to eat some. The sooner he was on his feet, the better for everyone, including himself.

Later that afternoon, after Serafina arose, Jessica went to bed and slept around the clock.

Chapter 29

"An excursion? What sort of excursion?"

"I suppose you might call it a pilgrimage." Serafina stood by the buckboard, watching Tomás hitch up the horses. She was wearing her best skirt and jacket and carrying gloves and a rebozo. She looked sprightly and fresh and only the tiny, faint lines around her eyes testified to the long days and nights she and Jessica had spent tending Ross St. John.

"I am going down the mountain to the little church—you have seen it, I think? The one with the cemetery behind it. I would like to light a candle to Our Lady, since I have much to give thanks for. Will you come?"

"Me?" Jessica glanced down at her dusty skirt. She had spent the afternoon exercising and grooming Spur and her clothes showed the effect of her activities.

"We have time for you to change. And you don't need to dress up to go."

Still, Jessica hesitated.

"I don't know," she said, glancing back toward the house. "Ross . . ."

Ross St. John had been confined to his room for almost a

week, and as the doctor predicted, he was becoming increasingly impatient with his bedridden state. It had taken the combined persuasion of Jessica and Serafina to prevent him from plunging back into his normal duties.

"Ross will be all right," Serafina replied firmly. "My mother can look after him. Besides, he is nearly recovered now. He doesn't need us to watch over him every minute. Come," she added impatiently, as Jessica still hesitated. "It is only for a little while, and I would like your company. Besides, it is a nice day for a ride, and we have both been too much in the house."

Sensing something more important in Serafina's request than a simple wish for company, Jessica finally agreed and went into the house to change clothes and rearrange her hair. When she returned to the buckboard, Serafina was already perched on the high seat, the reins in her hands. Tomás was nowhere in sight.

"We aren't going alone, are we?" Jessica asked.

"I can handle the buckboard," Serafina replied. "And we will be in no danger. Don't worry. It is better that we go alone."

Despite her companion's reassurances, Jessica felt uneasy as she clambered up to take her seat. Maybe Serafina had some good reason for her confidence, but she knew that Ross would be angry if he knew they were to be traveling by themselves.

The day was hot and clear, with tiny puffs of cloud rimming the horizon. Jessica's misgivings began to fade and her spirits rose as they headed down the road. The fragrance of pines, the cawing of crows, the warmth of the sun, even the swirls of dust stirred by the buckboard were all welcome, for they spelled the outdoors, open spaces, movement—things she had been denied since her return to the Running J. Serafina was right. She had been too much indoors.

The two women said little during the trip. Serafina seemed preoccupied, and Jessica gave herself over to enjoyment of the outing, thinking of nothing save her immediate surroundings, glad to be able to forget, if only for a few moments, the burden of the past and the unanswered questions of the future. Occasionally they had to stop to clear a path through the rockslides washed down the hillside by the torrential rains of the week before. Fortunately, most of the slides were made up of small rocks which they could easily roll aside, and they were able to maneuver the buckboard around the larger boulders. Neither woman complained about the delay or the effort, for the rains which had caused their path to be blocked had also saved the ranch from destruction.

As they threaded their way down the mountain, Jessica glanced at the stream which wound through the ravine below. Although it had flowed muddy and swollen after the rains, it was now low again. The storm that had thundered over the mountains on the night of the fire had not really relieved the drought. Too much water or too little—Jessica reflected on the truth of Ross's words.

As they descended, the pine began to give way to juniper and scrub. It was hotter here and even drier than in the mountains above. Although the desert was not visible to them, Jessica could sense its barren presence in the distance.

It was a wonder that people survived on this land at all, she thought. As the little whitewashed adobe church came into view around the bend, stark against the bare hills, it seemed to her an appropriate symbol of the often futile human effort to find some source of strength against the brutalities of nature.

Serafina drove the buckboard into the bare dirt yard, and dismounting, she tied the horses to a weathered hitching rail. Jessica hopped down and followed Serafina toward the church. Sagging, wooden double doors, their panels freshly decorated with bright blue paint, fronted the little building. Serafina pulled her rebozo over her head and, pushing open the doors, entered. Somewhat nervously, Jessica followed.

The cool, dim interior was a welcome relief from the glare of the afternoon sun. Several votive candles, burned almost to stubs, still flickered in the candelabrum near the doorway, and the faint scent of incense perfumed the air. Jessica lingered by the door while Serafina lighted a fresh candle from a dying one and stuck it in an empty holder. Then the Mexican woman circled the church, crossing herself in front of the faded, gilded icons, before kneeling at a wooden pew near the altar and bowing her head in prayer.

Uncertain about what, if anything, was expected of her, Jessica remained near the door, slightly uncomfortable in the face of Serafina's devotions. Except for their discussion of the *Penitentes* the day Jessica had first seen Serafina's uncle Manuel, Serafina had never brought up the matter of her religion or her feelings about it. As far as Jessica knew, Serafina did not attend church regularly, and she seemed scornful of what she regarded as religious excess. Yet Jessica had the feeling that Serafina's religious feelings ran deep, so deep that they were simply taken for granted, an essential part of her, which she did not need to discuss or explain. Her faith was as unassuming and tenacious as this church, and well-suited to the harsh life of New Mexico.

Jessica gazed at the high, whitewashed arch above her. Sunlight streamed through the narrow window, casting intricate patterns on the flagstone floor. Outside, she could hear the soft cooing of a dove which had made its nest somewhere in the eaves. She wished she could find the peace and solace in this simple place that Serafina did. How long since she herself had known such spiritual comfort? She could not remember. The church she and her mother had attended in New York seemed distant in her memory, its lines severe and cold, the sermons hard and uncompromising. It had never cast a spell over her as did this humble adobe building with its scents and candles, its chipped gilt and its blue paint, its doves and sunlight and whitewashed arches.

Finally, Serafina rose. Crossing herself one last time, she made her way slowly down the aisle to where Jessica was standing.

"You are very patient," she said, smiling. "This must all seem strange to you, but sometimes it eases my heart a little to come here to pray."

"I don't mind waiting," Jessica replied, feeling a little guilty about her own discomfort.

"Sometimes we forget," Serafina continued. "We forget

that we must be grateful to God. It is easy to think that we are masters of our own destinies. I come here to give thanks and to remind myself that all things come from Him." Her voice was serious now. Jessica remained silent as Serafina took one last look around the church. Then they stepped outside, shutting the sagging doors behind them.

"This is a very old church," Serafina explained. "It was built by the Franciscan missionaries who came here to convert the Indians. The church was burned down at least once, maybe by the Indians. I don't know for certain. Some Indians still come here to mass, and some of the herders. The priest lives in the village." She grabbed Jessica's hand, leading her across the yard's bare earth, striped with the long rays of the late afternoon sun. "Come. I will show you the cemetery. All the early missionaries, and some of the Indians, were buried there."

Jessica was in no hurry to leave such a peaceful place, and she willingly followed her companion to the grassy area behind the church where the cemetery lay. The gravestones were shrouded in weeds and neglected, but Jessica was able to make out a date here and there. Some of the stones were over two hundred years old, and she paused to marvel that people had lived and struggled here so long ago. How wild and alien this land—and its people—must have seemed to these early Spaniards. And what courage it must have taken to live here. Was it faith and conviction alone which drew them, she wondered, or had they found some other reward, something in the land itself.

A broken adobe wall ran along one side of the cemetery. It looked as if it had been part of a building.

"That was the mission," Serafina told her. "The brothers lived there and they farmed this land. They even had sheep. There was an orchard on the slope that runs down toward the stream. You can still see the apricot and peach trees if you go down there, but no one has tended them for years, so they've run wild."

Jessica approached the ruined wall and saw that it enclosed a large rectangular space, now filled with weeds and rubble.

She had seen so many ruins out here, so many ways of life abandoned. And two hundred years from now, would someone explore the remains of the ranch house and marvel at the ancient people who had wrested a living from the land with their horses and cattle?

It would be getting dark soon, and Jessica knew they should be starting back. The road up the mountain was not one to be traversed at night, especially by two women alone. Yet Serafina seemed in no hurry to leave, and Jessica felt a curious reluctance to prod her. She had a sense that the other woman had brought her along to show her something, though she had not yet revealed what it was.

"Come." Serafina was tugging at her hand again. "There is still more to see, some of it not quite so old."

They threaded their way along the edge of the ruined wall, stepping over eroded heaps of adobe brick and grass-choked piles of rubbish, and then plunged into the thicket of brush and trees which lay beyond, following a faint path in the dirt. Jessica noted the twisted branches of what appeared to be old fruit trees, but it was hard to imagine that this tangled undergrowth had once been a cultivated orchard. The thicket sloped toward the stream, ending abruptly at the edge of a steep bank. Serafina led Jessica along the grassy rim until they reached a spot where the slope softened, and then she scrambled down the bank to the stream's edge. Hesitantly, Jessica followed. There was a path of sorts down the slope, but it was eroded and steep. She descended cautiously, afraid of losing her step. By the time she reached the bottom, Serafina had already started down the sandy beach.

The sun was quite low now, and the ravine through which the stream flowed was already shadowed by the hills, taking on a dusky purple hue. The smooth surface of the stream gleamed softly in the semi-darkness. Jessica glanced up at the fading sky, beginning to feel uneasy. Where was Serafina taking her? It would be impossible for them to get back to the ranch by dark. Surely the other woman knew that. Yet Serafina was striding ahead into the dusk. Jessica hurried to catch up.

Several hundred yards down the stream, a small bridge had

been constructed from two split logs and set high over the water to be out of reach of floods. Serafina crossed it with surefooted steps, which suggested she had been there before, and Jessica, her own steps more cautious, followed. From the other end of the bridge, a narrow path led through another thicket and up a slope. The two women emerged from the brush at the top of a rise, which looked down into a small hollow between the hills. Nestled in the hollow at the base of a jumbled mass of boulders was a crude adobe house, barely visible in the fading light. It had a wooden door, but no windows, and several large wooden crosses leaned against its front wall.

Serafina knelt in the dry grass at the top of the rise and motioned Jessica to join her. Puzzled, Jessica eased herself to the ground and gazed down into the hollow. Was this what Serafina had brought her here to see—this primitive little building hidden in the dry hills? What was so important about it? And why was Serafina behaving so strangely? Jessica opened her mouth to question her companion, but Serafina gestured her to silence and pulled her lower in the grass so that they were both lying almost flat, their heads barely sticking up above the dry tufts of grass.

Serafina stared intently into the hollow, and then, as if reassured, she sat up. Jessica followed suit and Serafina laid a hand on her shoulder.

She paused a moment before speaking, her eyes searching Jessica's face.

"I have a favor to ask of you," she said finally.

"A favor?"

"It is a favor mostly to yourself, I suppose, but also, in a way, a favor to us."

"What are you talking about?" Jessica was thoroughly confused now.

Serafina hesitated again. When she spoke, her answer seemed unrelated to Jessica's question.

"You have been here in New Mexico for only a short time." Serafina looked away, her hand playing with a stalk of grass. "Only a short time, and yet it seems to me as if you have always been here, you have so quickly become part of this land and its people. Many things have happened since you arrived, things which have changed your life and ours. Some of these have not been good, but for everything, I think, you have forgiven and been forgiven. Except for one thing.'' Serafina looked up again. ''You have not yet forgiven yourself.''

''I don't understand. . . .'' Jessica was a little frightened by the other woman's intensity.

''The favor I have to ask is this—I want you to stay here tonight.''

''To stay? But why?'' Jessica stared at Serafina in amazement. Surely she was joking? How could she stay out here alone in the hills?

''You will be safe. Just lie low and make no sound. Above all, do not move from this spot.'' She gave Jessica a reassuring pat on the shoulder. ''Do not be afraid. Nothing will happen to you.''

But Jessica was far from reassured.

''Won't you at least tell me what it is I'm supposed to do here?''

''You need do nothing. But you will see something tonight that is very important. It may seem frightening—it will certainly seem strange. Yet if you try to understand it, perhaps it will help to open your soul and enable you to find the forgiveness and the peace which you still seek.''

''But I can't . . .'' It was on the tip of Jessica's tongue to simply refuse and to insist that Serafina take her back to the buckboard.

''Please. Please do this, as a friend.'' Serafina's eyes held hers and Jessica was unable to look away. ''I promise, you will come to no harm.''

Jessica sank back onto the grass, still reluctant, but swayed by the other's insistence. After all, Serafina was her friend. Would she have brought Jessica here if it were not important?

Serafina stood and unwrapped her rebozo, placing it around Jessica's shoulders.

''Here. This will keep you warm while you wait. It can get

chilly here after the sun goes down. And its color will help to keep you hidden.'' Turning toward the path leading down the hill, she paused a moment, glancing back over her shoulder as if seized by a moment of doubt. Then she gave Jessica a last encouraging smile and disappeared into the thicket. As Jessica heard her footsteps fade away down the path, she had an impulse to jump up and follow. Then, compelled by her own curiosity and the urgency of Serafina's request, she lay back down in the grass and settled herself to wait.

Darkness had settled over the hills, with only a faint glow marking where the sun had set. Though it was not yet cold, Jessica shivered and drew the rebozo tightly around her. She felt lonely and uneasy lying on the hill. Remembering Serafina's command that she not be seen, she wriggled lower in the grass and peered over the hilltop at the adobe building which lay below. Whatever it was that she was here to see must surely center around that building, for there was nothing else anywhere nearby. Her stomach was knotted with anticipation and anxiety, and Jessica hoped that something would happen soon to ease the strain of waiting.

She had been there only about an hour, though it seemed much longer, when she became aware of some movement in the grove of trees at the far end of the hollow. Her heart beating in anticipation, she lifted her head slightly to obtain a better view, but it took a few moments before she was able to distinguish a line of men filing slowly out of the woods. There were perhaps ten or twelve of them, and they gathered in a knot at the edge of the clearing before moving together toward the building. All the men seemed to be Mexican, dressed in loose cotton trousers and shirts, and they all wore broad-brimmed hats. They moved in eerie silence toward the adobe house. Jessica ducked her head, afraid of being seen.

When they reached the building, one of the men stepped forward and fumbled a moment with the door. Then it swung open, and one by one, the men shuffled into the dark interior. Only one remained outside, squatting by the doorway, the tall silhouette of his rifle stark against the pale adobe wall. Jessica could see nothing of the interior, even though the wooden door had been left open.

Then someone lighted a lamp, its flame flickering across the whitewashed adobe walls. There were objects hanging on the walls and something else barely visible at one edge of the doorway, but from where she lay, Jessica could not make them out. The sound of muffled voices reached her across the still, night air, and although she could tell by the cadence that Spanish was being spoken, she could distinguish no words.

In sudden determination, she rose from her prone position to a kneeling one. She would move closer, she decided, so that she could have a better view of the interior of the hut. If she had been brought here to see something, she wanted to be certain that she saw it, and from her present position she could see very little. She began to crawl cautiously along the edge of the rise, moving toward a point almost directly opposite the lighted rectangle of doorway. She kept a careful eye on the guard, but for the moment, at least, he was staring toward the forest and not looking in her direction. Even from her new vantage point, however, her view was obscured by the height of the hill. She would have to inch her way lower if she really wished to see. She squinted in the darkness, trying to make out what lay below her on the slope. There was a mesquite bush about twenty yards away. If she could get to it, she would be sheltered from view of the men and be better able to view their activities.

She wrapped Serafina's rebozo tightly around her, drawing part of it across her face so that the whiteness of her flesh would not show in the darkness. Then she slowly began to ease her way down the slope.

The moon had not yet risen, and although this aided Jessica's concealment, it also obscured the obstacles in her path. The edge of her skirt caught on a jutting point of rock. As she tugged to set it free, she sent a tiny shower of pebbles down the hill. The guard jerked his head in her direction, staring intently into the darkness. Jessica held her breath, her heart pounding wildly. But the guard apparently decided he had only heard some small animal, and turned away. It was a moment or two before Jessica had the courage to continue her descent. Then, as she resumed her crawl down the slope, she pressed her hand against the sharp spine of a plant and had to bite her lip to keep from crying out in pain.

Finally, she reached the mesquite bush, and with a small sigh of relief, she settled herself behind it. She could see perfectly from here. It was about thirty yards from her hiding place to the doorway of the building, yet she was well-hidden behind the branches of the mesquite.

At first, all that she could distinguish inside the adobe hut were the dark silhouettes of bodies moving between her and the lights within. A thin chanting rose into the night air, eerie in its cadence. Then the bodies parted and she glimpsed a crude platform, draped in black, above which hung a wooden figure of a crucified Christ. A skull, seemingly cut from white cloth, decorated the draperies of the altar. On a nearby shelf stood a candle, a real human skull, and what appeared to be several statues crudely decorated with paint and gilt. The building below her must be some kind of church. But the sinister air created by its remote location, the secretiveness of its congregation, and its gruesome ornaments gave it an air which seemed to Jessica completely opposite to the spiritual peace of the little church she had visited that afternoon.

Suddenly the chanting ceased. There was a long silence, during which Jessica could hear faintly the rushing of the stream far behind her and the furtive rustling of some tiny creature in the brush. Then from the interior of the little chapel came a sound that made the hair on the back of her neck stand on end.

It was a high-pitched wailing that sounded at first like the keening of some wild animal. It rose and fell and wavered on the night air. Jessica felt shivers run up her spine at the sound. It wove itself around the night, mysterious, inexplicable, something from another world. And then, as the men began to emerge from the building below her, she realized that what she heard was a flute, some sort of strange exotic flute, expertly and expressively played.

The men were filing into the clearing, one by one, the flute player in the lead, their way lighted by pine torches, which several of the men held above their heads. They had removed their shirts and wore only their white cotton trousers and small, black cloth caps, and their bare torsos gleamed with sweat in the wavering light of the torches. Several men carried in their hands what seemed to be long whips made of clusters of strips from a fibrous plant. To the plaintive wailing of the flute were added the rattling of chains and the rhythmic clanging together of tin cans.

Only one man, besides the guard, did not form part of this procession which now began to circle the clearing. He had emerged from the hut last and was leaning against the wall near the doorway. He still wore his shirt, and stood with his arms folded across his massive chest. He wore no hat, and in the guttering light of the torches, Jessica recognized the broad, pockmarked face of Manuel Valdez. Though his face was familiar, his presence at this strange ritual was anything but reassuring. His own mysteriousness was heightened by the sinister aura of the gathering, and Jessica wondered what his role was and what he would say or do if he knew she lay concealed on the hillside above. For if it had not already become evident to her that what she was witnessing was a ceremony of the utmost secretiveness and solemnity, the drama that now began to unfold would have proved it beyond any doubt.

As the men shuffled along, those with the long, fibrous whips in their hands raised them and slowly and deliberately began to bring them down across the backs of those who marched in front of them. Then, just as deliberately, they reversed their blows, sending the stinging strands back across their own shoulders, never breaking their shuffling gait, never faltering in their steps. The flute player continued his wild melody, seemingly undisturbed by the lashes on his back. Jessica heard the dull smacking of the whips on flesh. The backs of most of the men were already crisscrossed with

scars, like those she had seen on the back of Manuel Valdez.
Soon, long trickles of blood began to ooze from the newly
inflicted wounds. They ran down the backs of the flagellated
men, soaking into the white fabric of their trousers, which
were soon stained with dark streaks of red.

Jessica watched the scene below her in horror, unable to
tear her eyes away. It was like a vision of hell, with the lurid
glare of the torches, the sobbing melody of the flute, the
blood gleaming on the backs of the men as they circled,
whipping themselves and others in a steady, plodding beat.
And Manuel Valdez seemed to be the Devil himself, watching impassively from his position by the door.

And yet, despite its horror, there was something compel-
ling about the scene. This was the other side of the serenity
that Jessica had glimpsed in the little whitewashed church.
This was the deepest, darkest part of the soul with all of its
nightmares and sins. It was inner torment made external, and
a reminder of the frailty and temporariness of the flesh and its
desires. The eerie melody of the flute echoed her own soul's
anguish, speaking to her of all suffering, all sorrow, all loss.

The men trudged on in utter silence. Though blood flowed
freely down their backs, and though occasionally a man
would stumble or fall and have to be helped up by his
comrades, not one man moaned or cried out. Jessica recalled
her own mindless march toward death as she struggled through
the vast indifferent spaces of the desert. Was that the meaning
of this harsh ritual, she wondered, to show the pain and
suffering of our common journey to the grave? Was this what
life was about, this death in life itself? She felt smothered by
a heavy despair, pressing her down like the wings of some
dark bird, shutting out the light. She prayed that soon the
spectacle below would stop—surely it must stop soon. The
bodies of men could sustain for only a short time such torture
as this. Yet, the procession continued, though the footsteps of
the worshippers began to flag, and the flute became faint and
ragged.

Then, finally as the torches burned low and began to gutter
in the cool night breeze, the flagellants lowered their whips,

and one by one, they shuffled back into the adobe hut. Manuel Valdez entered last, shutting the door behind him. Only the guard remained outside, and Jessica could see the glowing orange dot as he lighted a cigarette.

Feeling nearly as drained as the participants must be, Jessica sank weakly to the ground, burying her head in her arms. So dazed was she that it was not until she tasted the salty drops upon her lips that she realized that tears were streaming down her face. It was as if the bloody rites she had witnessed had released some force deep inside her, broken down a wall that held back a torrent of guilt, despair, and grief.

She had no idea how long she lay there, but gradually she was aroused from her half-conscious state by the sound of voices below her and by the decisive slamming of a door. She lifted her head and peered down into the clearing in time to see a line of white-clad figures disappearing into the woods. The guard also appeared to have departed, and the door of the adobe hut was tightly shut.

Jessica waited until the men were completely out of sight, and then she stood up. Her legs felt shaky and her limbs were cramped from the hours spent crouched behind the bushes. She stretched, attempting to relieve the stiffness. What was she supposed to do now? she wondered. Would Serafina return, or should she try to make her own way back to the churchyard? She hesitated to leave her hiding place, afraid both of losing her way in the dark and of being seen by anyone who might have stayed behind in the hut. And again she asked herself why had she been brought here in the first place. What was the reason for having her witness such bizarre and secret rites?

Puzzling over these questions, Jessica wrapped Serafina's rebozo more tightly around herself and settled down as comfortably as possible, to wait. A tiny sliver of moon was rising over the mountains when she finally fell asleep.

When she awoke, it was barely dawn. Standing above her, silhouetted against the pale sky, was Manuel Valdez.

Jessica sat up, startled and somewhat frightened. Manuel

knelt down beside her, his broad face creasing into a gold-toothed smile of reassurance.

"*Buenos días*, señorita Jessica. I hope you slept well."

Was he joking with her? Flustered, Jessica did not know how to respond. Behind his genial manner she could see the torch-lit countenance of the man who had presided over the evening's bloody rites.

"I . . . I didn't really intend to sleep," she replied awkwardly.

"No reason you shouldn't have. It is perhaps not the most comfortable of beds, but you were quite safe here."

"You . . . you were here? You stayed all night?"

"Yes, I was here." Abruptly he stood and extended his hand to Jessica. She grasped his strong, broad fingers and awkwardly rose, stiff from her night on the ground.

Self-consciously, Jessica brushed bits of grass and twig from her skirt, and smoothed her hair. Then she arranged the folds of the rebozo around her shoulders. Ill at ease, she stood for a moment, waiting for some explanation, unable to ask the questions which would elicit it. There was something intimidating about Manuel Valdez. Perhaps it was the way he seemed to see right through her and his air of knowing more than he chose to reveal.

He was looking at her now, and his penetrating gaze made her uncomfortable.

"What you saw last night was something not many *gringos* see," he said finally. He paused for a moment before continuing. "It is not forbidden to view our rituals, but our own church withdrew its support from the *Penitentes,* the Brothers of the Light, some years ago. And since the coming of the white man in great numbers to our land, we have preferred not to make of ourselves a public spectacle for the curious. That is why we have moved our *moradas* to places like this." He gestured toward the adobe hut below.

"Usually," he went on, his eyes still on the clearing, "we perform the ritual which you saw only before Easter, in imitation of Christ's sufferings. But lately, many evils have befallen us—violence and drought and fire. Such disasters are God's punishment for sin, and we must do penance." He turned back to Jessica. "I know that these are not your beliefs, but we feel that suffering comes from sin and it is to rid ourselves of this burden that we torment our bodies. It is said that a man who dies in our rites dies cleansed of all sin."

"And you," Jessica finally felt emboldened to ask, "What about you? You did not take part last night."

"I am the *hermano mayor*, the president of our chapter, so I oversee the rituals but do not participate." He regarded her keenly. "This is not your faith, and it probably seems bloody and barbaric to you. But it is our own faith, born of our own land, and I know that you will understand that. Perhaps you, too, have sinned. I know most certainly that you have suffered. Perhaps we have taken some of the burden of such suffering for you, and maybe it can make you better understand what we do and believe."

"And is this why you have brought me here?" Jessica was stung by his perception and frightened by the truth of his words.

"Yes, that is why. It was my decision to do so. Serafina was opposed, although I finally persuaded her. She does not approve of our rituals, but I thought perhaps you would understand. You have learned that in the heart of life there is death, and that in death there is life. That is, of course, what our religion teaches us, but it is also something that is revealed to all of us in our hearts, as well."

"But why me? Why does it matter if I understand?"

Manuel regarded her for a moment before he spoke.

"You are an unusual person, Jessica. You have had many difficulties, yet you have responded to them with courage, not only physical courage as when you saved Don Rosario from the fire, but other kinds of courage as well. What you saw last night was only a prelude to what I wish to show you today. Come." Manuel turned and strode toward the path leading downhill to the stream. Although she hurried after him, Jessica was apprehensive. After the events of last night, she was not certain she wanted to see whatever else Manuel had to reveal.

They climbed to the top of the rise and then descended to the water's edge. Instead of crossing the bridge, however, they continued along the bank, working their way upstream. The sun had not yet risen above the hills and the little ravine through which the stream ran was shadowed and cool. The path was faint, almost imperceptible in places, but Manuel Valdez kept up a good pace, pausing only to hold back branches so that Jessica could pass.

After they had gone about a mile, Manuel turned abruptly and began to climb the hill above the stream, following a path or marker visible only to himself. The hill was very steep and in places Jessica had to grasp tree limbs or small outcroppings of rock to pull herself up or to keep from sliding down the hill. The sun was up now, burning into her back, and her lungs felt about to burst from the effort of the climb. The effects of her long night's vigil were beginning to tell, and she was acutely aware that she had eaten neither supper nor breakfast. With each step, her annoyance at the Valdez family and their mysterious errands increased. At one point, after she had induced Manuel to stop so that she could catch her breath, she turned on him.

"Is it too much to ask," she demanded, "that you give me some idea of where we're going and why you insisted on bringing me here?"

Manuel smiled at her almost apologetically.

"You must forgive us our peculiar ways," he replied. "I'm afraid it has become almost second nature to work secretly and to say little. I suppose it is the nature of conquered peoples. We learn to be devious, sometimes even when it is not really necessary."

A little abashed, Jessica lowered her gaze.

"What I want to show you, however, really is a secret," Manuel continued. "Come, we have only a little farther to go."

He turned to continue the climb and Jessica reluctantly forced her weary legs to follow.

They worked their way up through a stand of pine, the carpet of fallen needles making their ascent even more slippery and treacherous. Then they emerged into a small clearing, bordered on its upper end by an outcropping of jumbled rock, the base of which was choked with mesquite and stunted juniper. Manuel led her across the clearing to the outcropping, and then, choosing his steps carefully, began to climb again, using each boulder as if it were part of a zigzagging series of steps. Hesitantly, Jessica followed, not daring to look down as she ascended the treacherous rock face. Near the top of the outcropping, Manuel paused at what seemed to be a broad natural ledge jutting out from the slope, and turned to look back. Jessica, panting from her exertions, clambered up to join him, and after pausing a moment to catch her breath, she, too, turned toward the vista lying below them.

They had climbed further than she had thought, and could see over the hills below them to the jutting peaks of the Sangre de Christo. Far below, the stream wandered invisibly in its ravine, and Jessica thought she could see in the distance the old church and graveyard she had visited the day before. Had Manuel brought her here just to see the view? It was quite spectacular, but it hardly seemed to warrant either the rigorous climb or the aura of mystery with which Manuel had surrounded it.

But Manuel had turned away from the view now, and was moving toward a clump of mesquite growing at the far end of the ledge. He motioned to Jessica to follow.

"This is what I wanted to show you." He knelt down and pulled aside some branches.

At first, Jessica saw nothing. Then, gradually, she could distinguish an opening in the face of the stone wall, and then the weathered timbers which framed it, sagging wearily under the weight of the mountainside and undermined by the roots of the encroaching bushes. Rubble lay piled in the mouth of the opening, and even as she watched, a trickle of gravel disturbed by Manuel's movement slid from the hillside above and clattered across the rocks and into the dark-framed depths.

Jessica could hear the faint echo of its passage reverberating in the mountainside before it faded away.

"What is it?" she asked her companion. But even before he replied, she already knew the answer to her question.

"A mine. *The* mine, I suppose I should say. The gold mine that legend says is to be found on the lands of the Running J."

"Then it really exists."

"It really exists, has existed almost since the first coming of the Spaniards. Maybe even before that, the Indians used it. Who knows? But it is very old."

"And you have known about it all along?"

"Ever since I was a child. My father brought me up here one day to show me, and told me it was a Valdez family secret, something I should know. He showed me all around—the mine shaft, the little road that had been built on the hillside and then covered by landslides, the place by the stream where he thought there had been a sluice, now all washed away by floods. He told me it was a Valdez family secret, to be passed on from father to son. Unfortunately there were others who knew of the secret—or at least others who knew that we knew."

"Then, Don Octaviano . . . that was the reason why he . . . they . . ."

"Yes, he was killed for that. But he never gave away the secret. And so his murderer came to me." Manuel chuckled grimly. "That was his mistake."

Something in his tone made Jessica shiver. She turned to gaze at the hole in the hill behind her. The thought that men had shed blood over what lay within gave it a sinister air.

"But I don't understand why you are telling me all this." She turned back to Manuel, but he was not looking at her. Instead, he was gazing across the distance at the mountain peaks. He stood silent a long moment before he replied.

"As I said, the secret has always been passed on from father to son. There are no sons in the family now. Perhaps it is time to take the burden of the secret and pass it on to someone else." He turned back to look at Jessica. "I spoke earlier of sin and suffering and the release from our burdens. This mine has been a burden to the Valdezes from the very beginning, a curse which has brought nothing but trouble. It has caused the death of many men, including my father. We don't even know if there really is any gold there, yet we have clung to it, guarded its secret, partly out of greed, but also from a kind of stubborn pride. When my father lost the ranch, this secret was the one thing we still owned. Despite all that had happened to us, we had not learned the vanity—and the danger—of clinging to earthly things.''

"But why me?'' Jessica persisted. "Why not tell Ross about the mine? After all, it's on his ranch.''

Manuel looked back over the hills, an odd smile playing around the corners of his mouth.

"It was my father's wish,'' he said. "He told me that if ever the time came to pass on the secret, it should go to you, and you would know what to do with it. Perhaps it was just the whim of an old man—I know my father was much taken with you. Or perhaps he truly saw something in you, some bond with the land, some deeper understanding which made you the right person for this task.''

"And Ross?''

"Ross St. John is a strong man, in many ways a good man,'' Manuel responded thoughtfully. "The ranch has been in good hands under him and he has treated us fairly. Yet he is ruled by pride, and is prone to passion and violence. He sometimes forgets that no one really owns the land. It owns you. He thinks he can bend the world to his will and does not understand the necessity for humility and patience.'' He turned back toward Jessica. "We, the Valdezes, are part of the land, of the Sangre de Christo. Someday, in the course of time, it will return to us. In the meantime, we stay and we wait.''

"And what am I to do with this secret you have given me?''

"That is entirely up to you.''

"But you—you and your family—why did you never do anything with the gold?''

"Perhaps we felt no need for it. Perhaps we were simply afraid. We have seen too much of what gold can do to men. And yet at the same time, we could not bring ourselves to give it up."

Jessica felt uneasy and dissatisfied with his answers. The burden of the secret weighed upon her. They stood a moment in silence and then Manuel laid a hand on her shoulder, transfixing her for a moment with the black depths of his eyes.

"I must go now," he said softly. "I will leave you alone to sit and think. Let yourself be one with the land and your own heart, and they will tell you what to do. When you are ready, you can find your way back to the church. Serafina will be waiting." He removed his hand and turned to go. Then he paused a moment to look back over his shoulder. "*Hasta la vista,* señorita Jessica. I hope we meet again."

Jessica sat for a long while on the ledge, lost in thought. Ahead of her, the mountains and hills wavered in the heat, and the sun beat fiercely on her perch, but she was oblivious to her discomfort.

The gold mine—so it existed after all—an almost invisible brush-covered hole in the hillside behind her. Jeffrey had been right. And it was for this mine that Don Octaviano—and maybe many others—had died.

Right now the gold mine belonged to Ross—and yet it didn't, for it would not become his until she told him of it. Despite his opposition to mining on the ranch, Ross would undoubtedly welcome her revelation of this secret. Its wealth could help him recover from the damages of rustling, fire, and drought. The Running J would be more prosperous than ever. She and Ross would preside over this prosperity and share it with their children. Why, then, did she feel such a reluctance to tell him of the mine's location?

"The land will tell you what to do." Her thoughts kept returning to Manuel's words. She recalled the vastness of the desert, the canyon with its long-abandoned ruins, the visions she had as she staggered on the edge of death. She also remembered the peace and freedom she had experienced by living with nothing, there in the middle of nothing. She thought of the Spaniards, drawn to a sun-scorched death in their quest for gold, and of Reno's father and his own futile, fatal search.

Manuel was right. The land owns you. It can bring you peace; it can drive you mad; it can kill you. And the desire for the treasures which lay beneath its surface was the most fatal obsession of all. Was Ross St. John immune? Was she herself immune?

She thought back to what she had witnessed last night, to the *Penitentes* and their bloody rites. They believed they were taking their sins—and hers—upon their shoulders, staggering beneath the cruel blows of their own whips. In their rejection of the flesh, they sought peace for the soul.

And, lastly, her thoughts turned to Jeffrey. He had loved the land, but he knew not to be trapped by it. Perhaps that was what he had tried to tell her, was telling her now, reaching out to her across the desert of death. Was that not what Serafina and Manuel were also trying to tell her—that without peace with the world beyond and those who dwell there, one cannot have peace with one's self?

Jessica looked out across the mountains. The rich and wild lands of the Running J stretched as far as she could see. She knew what Jeffrey would tell her—not to be trapped by illusions or pride or by the expectations of others, but to have the courage and confidence to create her own life. He had that courage. So would she.

Resolutely, she stood up and contemplated the ramshackle entrance to the mine. She knew what she had to do, but she was not yet certain how she was going to do it. She glanced at the hillside above the shaft, crowned with a precarious jumble of boulders, and remembered the trickle of gravel which had greeted Manuel's steps. Cautiously, she crawled up the hill, working her way around and above the mine shaft, testing the outcroppings of rock with her foot as she went. Since several of them were loose, she chose her steps with care.

At last, she reached the top of the outcropping, directly above the shaft. Below stretched an expanse of jumbled rock, while above stood a thicket of juniper, pine, and mesquite. Gingerly, Jessica tested one of the smaller rocks. It shifted slightly at her effort, but it was too heavy for her to lift. She cast around for some tool to aid her, and spotted a bleached dead branch lying a few yards away. It made a perfect lever, and she wedged it under the boulder, pushing down with all her strength. At first, all she loosened were several showers of small stones, but then, as she gave a final push, the rock tilted, teetered, and then suddenly came loose and plunged down the hillside, carrying with it several of its neighbors. More boulders were exposed now, and Jessica pried at another. Though it was not large, it seemed to have been holding back a large portion of the hillside, which gave way after it.

Barely in time, Jessica jumped back from the avalanche she had created, clinging to the rough trunk of a yellow pine to keep herself from sliding down the hill. With a tremendous roar, the wave of rock gathered momentum and swept away the rocks and bushes below, overwhelming the ledge and burying the shaft of the mine beneath a stream of rubble.

Her heart pounding, Jessica clung to her perch and surveyed the destruction below. A cloud of dust rose from the rockslide, and a few stray pebbles were still bouncing down the hill. Above her, in the branches of a pine tree, a crow squawked loudly protesting to the disturbance of his peace.

Carefully, Jessica worked her way up into the thicket above her, and then circled around the landslide down to the clearing below the mine shaft. When she looked back up to where she had been, she could see no trace of the mine. Even the thicket that had obscured the entrance was completely buried by the slide. It was gone completely and, she hoped, forever. All that could be seen now was a fresh landslide, not an uncommon sight in the mountains.

As she stared up the hillside, Jessica recalled Ross's words to her after the night of the fire: "Whatever debts you might have had to the Running J, you have more than repaid them.'' He was wrong, she thought. Only now did she feel she had repaid her debts, but in a way that Ross would never know, and probably never understand. And in doing so, she had reached an important decision about her own life.

Slowly, Jessica made her way down the steep hill, and then headed back to the church.

Chapter 30

Parked under an oak tree near the church was the buckboard, with Serafina sitting patiently on the high seat. She smiled as Jessica arrived, but her smile was a little tentative, as if she were uncertain as to how Jessica would respond. Jessica placed the folded rebozo in the back of the buckboard and climbed up. She and Serafina stared at each other for a moment, and then Jessica leaned over to give the other woman a hug. Some of the tension seemed to leave Serafina's body, and she returned the hug warmly before turning to pick up the reins. Urging the horses forward, she headed out of the churchyard and down the road toward the ranch.

They rode in silence for a while, and then finally Jessica spoke.

"I've decided to leave the ranch."

If Serafina felt any surprise at this abrupt announcement, she did not show it. Instead, she merely nodded.

"I thought you might not stay."

"Why do you say that?"

"It is difficult for you to be at peace here now. Too much has happened, and there are too many memories."

"And yet it's hard to leave." Jessica took a deep breath and stared out over the dry hills. "I had thought I could make up for the past, erase the memories. But now I know it cannot be done. And yet if I go, I must break a promise, and that makes me afraid."

"What do you mean?" Serafina turned, her dark eyes curious.

Jessica lowered her head and stared down at her folded hands.

"Ross asked me to marry him, and I said yes."

She felt Serafina stiffen.

"I . . . I did not know that." The other woman's voice was controlled, but Jessica sensed some tension behind the words. "When did he ask you?"

"A few weeks ago. I don't know exactly why I agreed. Maybe I felt guilty about Jeffrey's death. I thought if I married Ross, I could make up to him the loss of his son, maybe give him another one."

"But you don't love him?"

"I don't really know." Jessica paused, searching for words. "I do care for him. I think I might even have loved him, once. But, as you say, too much has happened. There is too much between us now for us to ever be happy together."

"Then why are you afraid to leave?"

Jessica looked up into Serafina's eyes. There was something veiled, almost guarded in the other's expression.

"It is because of Jeffrey. I left the son—and now the father."

Suddenly Serafina smiled. She reached over to pat Jessica on the knee.

"I understand. But don't worry. Ross is not Jeffrey. He won't die if you leave. He will be angry and hurt, but he will live."

"Still, I feel terrible about what I must do."

"It would be more terrible if you married him when you did not love him. To marry him out of guilt and obligation would truly be wrong, for both of you."

"I suppose you're right." But the thought of confronting Ross pressed down on Jessica like a weight.

"Where will you go when you leave?" Serafina's question interrupted Jessica's gloomy thoughts.

"I don't really know. I don't want to go back to New York. Perhaps I could have my mother wire me some money until I can find a job. I could teach, or keep account books, or sew, or even look after horses, I suppose. I should be able to find something."

"No need to write your mother," Serafina said briskly. "I have a little money saved. I can lend you whatever you need."

Tears of gratitude filled Jessica's eyes.

"You're very good to me," she said huskily.

"Not good at all," Serafina replied. "I hate to have you go, but you must do what you have to do. And what are friends for? After all you've done for us, it's the least I can do in return." Whatever constraint Jessica had sensed earlier between them now seemed to have completely disappeared, and the two women rode in companionable silence the rest of the way back to the ranch.

As they rolled up the driveway toward the house, Jessica noticed several strange horses tied at the hitching rail in front of the porch.

"Looks like we have company," she remarked. She was suddenly aware of her own dirty and disheveled state. Maybe she could sneak into the house and change clothes before anyone saw her. She could use something to eat, too. For the first time since they had left the church, Jessica became aware of how hungry she was.

Serafina seemed to read her thoughts.

"I'm afraid the Valdez family has neglected you," she laughed. "Let's turn the buckboard over to Tomás and see if we can't find you some food. Then I'll have Maria heat water for a bath." Her expression sobered as they drew up by the house. "That looks like Sheriff Towers's horse," she remarked. "I hope nothing is wrong."

As they were dismounting from the buckboard, Ross St. John emerged from the main doorway of the house, the lanky figure of Pete Towers behind him. Ross scowled as they came up.

"Where the hell have you been?" he demanded. "This is a fine time to be running around the countryside."

"As my mother told you, we went to stay with my aunt in the village," Serafina replied firmly. "And as for you, you know you aren't supposed to be out of bed yet. You need to stay put until that wound on your head is healed."

Ross's scowl deepened at her scolding, but the sheriff's mouth curved up in a wide grin under his sandy mustache.

"You're a lucky man, Ross, to have two pretty nurses lookin' after you."

But Ross was not amused. He turned to Serafina.

"The sheriff's got word about Kincaid," he told her. "He's comin' here with a party of armed men, probably sometime early tomorrow morning, ready to take over the ranch."

Serafina turned to Pete Towers.

"You're certain about this?" she demanded. "It seems very bold of Kincaid."

"I'm almost positive, ma'am," he replied. "And Kincaid does hope to take you by surprise. But I think his plan is to pick off Ross, here, maybe using one of his hired gunmen, and then hope that with Ross gone, the rest will be easy."

"We'll show him," Ross growled. "None of it's going to be easy. The bastard will find that out soon enough."

"You brought men?" Serafina was still questioning the sheriff.

"All I could on such short notice. Two deputies from Bernalillo and a couple of kids from the village. If it comes to a pitched battle, the odds are pretty even. But I would hope to avoid that. A lot of men could get killed. And some women, too," he added, his glance sweeping from Serafina to Jessica. "In fact, I've been tryin' to persuade Ross to send both of you, and Donaciana, too, down to the village until all this blows over."

"Not a chance," Ross chuckled, his good humor suddenly restored. "If you knew these two any better, you wouldn't even mention the idea. They're both stubborn as hell, and they've each probably got twice the guts of any man on the place. What's more, there's no man that can stand up to them if they're determined on something. I don't think anyone but the two of them could have managed to keep me off my feet and in bed all week."

The sheriff grinned at these words and seemed about to say something. Then he apparently thought better of it and gave Jessica a big wink instead. She blushed, but whether from the risqué comment which the sheriff had refrained from making or from Ross St. John's rough praise, she was not certain. Ducking her head to hide her flushed cheeks, she started toward the kitchen. Serafina made some further remark to the sheriff, and then caught up with her.

"First we feed you," Serafina told her, putting her arm around Jessica's waist. "Then we'll worry about this other business."

"What about Ross?" Jessica was worried that the rancher had risen too soon from his sickbed.

Serafina shrugged.

"There is nothing more we can do for him. He's hardly going to stay in bed now. He seems strong enough for the moment, and the sheriff is here to help him. Once it's all over, he can worry again about taking care of himself." She turned suddenly to Jessica. "But you. It is different for you. What the sheriff says is right. You should leave. This is no longer your quarrel. You have done enough for Ross and for the Running J. There is no use risking your life."

"Perhaps you are right," Jessica replied slowly. But she was not certain she could leave just yet.

For the rest of the day, Jessica saw Ross only at a distance, as he busied himself preparing the ranch for the expected attack. She sensed that he was glad to be out of bed and to have something to do. Despite the possibility of a fight with Kincaid and his men—or perhaps because of it—Ross seemed almost cheerful as he conferred with Pete Towers, gave orders for the heavy shutters (usually reserved for winter storms) to be put up on the ranch-house windows, chatted with the Mexican boys from the village, and once more took charge of the ranch.

Jessica watched all these preparations with a sense of distance, as if they were for some event which did not involve her. And yet, despite the calm which such distance promoted within her, there also ran by its side a current of apprehension. Perhaps it was because of the bloody scene she had witnessed the night before, but death and violence no longer seemed to her distant possibilities, things that happened only to others, but very real and possibly imminent occurrences in her own life.

Jessica excused herself immediately after dinner, to Sheriff Towers's obvious disappointment, and retired to her room, leaving the men in the dining room to talk. She needed time alone to think and to decide what she should do.

Perhaps Serafina was right. She should leave soon, maybe tomorrow, before Kincaid and his men arrived. Jessica had brought in her saddlebags earlier in the afternoon, and halfheartedly she began to pack. If she did leave, it would not be because she no longer saw the quarrels of the Running J as hers. Rather, it was that she could not bear to be at the ranch when Reno arrived, nor to see him confront Ross St. John in what might be a fatal shoot-out for one or both of them.

Would Ross be angry with her for leaving? Considering his speech to the sheriff, he would probably regard her departure as desertion. Well, let him be angry. It might make the parting easier and his recovery from it more rapid.

Jessica went to bed early, tired from her sleepless night and the long day which had followed. She would rise early and carry out whatever decision the morning might bring. She fell asleep quickly, but her rest was disturbed by vivid dreams. She was crossing endless deserts and mountains, hillsides and streams, all inhabited by a grotesque confusion of wild animals, great herds of horses—and people, all kinds of people, some dark-skinned and others light, some with bloody faces, some friendly, others hostile. It was difficult to tell what all these people wanted, though many of them seemed to be speaking to her, trying to tell her something. As she wandered among them, she began to lose all sense of who she was, and she became the people who accosted her, the animals who roamed the hills, the very mountains themselves, and her body began to dissolve in the dry mountain air and to shrivel like a corpse in the desert.

Jessica awoke in a cold sweat, and lay a long time awake, her heart pounding, burdened by a great and nameless fear. Who was she, and what was to become of her? The questions she could face with courage during the day became overwhelming and unanswerable in the night. It was a long time before she could allow herself to fall asleep again.

When Jessica awoke, it was not yet light outside, though she sensed that dawn was close. She threw back the covers and arose, savoring for a moment the still darkness of the room, the smooth pine boards beneath her bare feet, and the illusory sense of peace that hung over the ranch. She glanced around the small room that in such a short time had come to contain so many memories, both pleasant and painful. So much had happened to her here. But now, she knew, it was finally time to leave.

Quickly, she slipped off her nightgown and dressed herself in trousers and cotton shirt. She pulled on her boots and then laid her saddlebags, hat, and jacket on the bed, ready for her departure. Before she left, however, she would fortify herself with something from the kitchen. Maybe if Donaciana were up, there might be a little coffee. Then she would find Ross and say good-bye. Facing Ross would be the hardest part of leaving, but she was determined to do it. This time she would not sneak off unnoticed in the night.

As she emerged into the dark hallway, she was startled to hear the sound of loud, ragged snoring issuing from Jeffrey's room. Then she realized it was the sheriff. He had been given the spare room for the night. She tiptoed past, not wishing to wake him or to face his questions and scrutiny.

The heavy shutters on the windows made the house very

dark, and Jessica had to pick her way carefully through the living and dining rooms as she made her way to the kitchen. The back window of the kitchen was open, letting in the first pale light of dawn, and the soft breath of the early morning air mingled with the faint murmur of the creek below the house. There was no one up yet, so Jessica fanned the coals in the cast-iron stove, adding slivers of kindling and then a few split logs before she placed the remains of the evening's coffee in the enameled pot on the stove to warm. Then she cut a large slice of bread from the loaf on the shelf, and went out on the front porch to eat it while she waited for the coffee.

The yard was still and peaceful. Even the chickens were not yet astir, and Jessica could see the horses huddled together near the far end of the pasture, dim shapes in the not yet faded dark. The sky overhead was rapidly growing light but the forest, outbuildings, and pastures were still dark. Jessica could see wood smoke drifting from the direction of the bunkhouses, its acrid scent teasing her nostrils, and she knew that at least some of the cowboys were up. Then a door slammed, and Ross emerged from the breezeway at the far end of the house and strode across the yard toward the stable.

Well, at least she would not have to wake him. Jessica turned back toward the kitchen to check on the coffee. Maybe Ross would come in seeking breakfast, and then she would have a chance to talk to him privately.

The sound of hoofbeats caused her to turn back toward the yard. Someone—it looked like one of the Running J hands—was riding up the road toward the house. Ross had also heard the sound, for he emerged from the stable, and the rider reined in beside him and jumped down, the dust of his haste swirling around them. The cowboy conferred urgently with Ross, and then mounted again and rode off, while Ross turned back toward the house, his stride long and determined.

Thoughtfully, Jessica shut the kitchen door and went to the stove to pour herself a cup of coffee. Had she delayed her departure too long? she wondered. Perhaps Kincaid was already on his way. If so, she could not leave now.

Her question was answered as she made her way down the hall, coffee in hand, just in time to encounter Ross pounding on the door of the sheriff's room. Pete Towers, still clad in his underwear, appeared in the doorway, squinting sleepily at Ross in the dim light, only slightly disconcerted to see Jessica standing there, too.

"Kincaid's got an early start," Ross told him curtly. "He and his boys are on the way. I sent Doan out to pull in the pasture guards and I'm on my way to rouse the bunkhouse."

"Got you." The sheriff was wide awake now. "I'll get dressed and be out in a jiffy. Glad things are breakin' quickly," he added, as he started to close the door again. "Saves a lot of waitin' around."

"Let's hope it's not too quick," Ross responded grimly. "My men are still pretty scattered."

As the door shut behind the sheriff, Ross turned to Jessica. For a moment their eyes met, and Ross's held a peculiar gray light. Jessica expected him to tell her to stay safely out of sight and she was ready to protest his paternalism. But his actual words surprised her.

"This isn't your fight, Jessica," he said, echoing Serafina's words. "There's no call for you to risk yourself."

"I guess I'll be the judge of that, Ross," she replied quietly.

He laid his hand gently on her shoulder and gazed down at her. She had the sense that he was about to say something more, but he just stared at her for a moment. Then he dropped his hand and turned toward the door at the end of the hall.

"Go get Serafina up," he told her, "and tell her to get out the extra rifles and have them loaded."

Jessica went off to do Ross's bidding, but found Serafina already up and stirring around in the kitchen. The homey aroma of frying bacon filled the air. Serafina merely nodded when Jessica told her what was happening. Deftly, she fished the bacon out onto a platter and cracked several eggs into the skillet.

"Here." She handed the spatula to Jessica. "You turn these when they're ready. I'll go get the guns."

Jessica, watching the edges of the eggs bubble and then turn lightly brown in the hot grease, smiled to herself to think that here on the morning which was to have marked her final and perhaps dramatic leave-taking from the Running J, she found herself instead in the kitchen frying eggs. She flipped her charges over, let them cook a moment more, and then lifted them to the platter.

"Hmmm! Smells mighty good."

Sheriff Towers had come into the kitchen while she was at work, and Jessica seated him at the pine table while she served him bacon and eggs and coffee. This was no time for formality, she reflected, as she sliced some bread and then snatched a piece of bacon for herself, eating it with her fingers. But it did seem an odd way to eat what might be her last meal at the Running J.

Despite his jocular greeting, Pete Towers was regarding her seriously.

"I wish Ross had listened to me," he told her. "I'd like to see you out of here right now. I could have sent you back to Bernalillo with a couple of my men for guard. You'd be much safer there."

"I prefer to stay here," Jessica replied, a little stiffly, forgetting for the moment that she had in fact been about to leave.

"Well, Ross is right about one thing. You sure got backbone and spirit. I heard about the way you pulled him out of the way of that fire. Sounds like he owes you his life. Still," he went on, "you can't hardly blame folks for bein' concerned about you and wantin' to protect you. And I'd still feel better if you were out of here."

It was not until she had left the kitchen and was on the way back to her room that it occurred to Jessica to wonder exactly what "folks" the sheriff was talking about.

Once in her room, she paused, uncertain what to do next. Her things lay ready on the bed, but there was no question of

leaving right now, not with Kincaid and his men on the way.
Jessica lifted her rifle from its pegs on the wall. She would
have her weapon loaded and ready to go, just in case. When
she had finished that task, Jessica went to the window and
peered through the shutters into the yard. Several cowboys
hurried across her field of vision and then she saw Ross
walking with Riordon toward the stable.

Riordon! In all the confusion and excitement, Jessica had
forgotten about the foreman. She had not seen Riordon for
several days and had never said anything to Ross regarding
her suspicions.

She stood for a moment in an agony of uncertainty, watching the two men. Should she say something to Ross? But
right now was a difficult time to do so. With Kincaid coming,
Ross's attention was focused on the upcoming confrontation.
How likely was he to have the time and inclination to listen to
her? And yet she had no doubt that Riordon was dangerous,
although she did not yet know why or how. She should at
least *try* to say something to Ross, whether he would listen to
her or not.

She glanced out of the window again. Riordon was gone
and Ross stood by the stable door, conferring with one of the
Mexican boys from the village. Jessica saw the youth nod
vigorously and then duck into the stable, his rifle clutched
tightly in his hand. Ross stood thoughtfully for a moment,
staring down the road. There was still no sign of Kincaid.
Had he changed his mind? Or were they not headed toward
the Running J at all, but bent, instead, on some other errand?
Jessica prayed that the whole matter was just a false alarm.
She noticed that Ross had a revolver strapped in a holster at
his side. It was the first time she had seen him so armed.

Now was her opportunity to talk to him. But before she
could act, Sheriff Towers strolled across the yard from the
kitchen and joined Ross by the stable. The two men stood
talking, and then the sheriff lighted a cigarette. She could
hardly tell Ross about Riordon's visit to her room and his
threats and her suspicions under the sharp-eyed gaze of Pete
Towers. Or could she? After all, what did her personal em-

barrassment matter in light of Riordon's possible danger to the ranch?

Still, she hesitated. The sun had risen now, sending long, slanting shafts of shadow and light across the bare, packed earth of the ranch yard. Except for the two men by the stable, the yard was deserted and deceptively still. Jessica knew that Ross's plan was to keep most of his men deployed but out of sight around the yard and buildings, as well as in more distant outposts, in case the confrontation on the ranch should be a deception on Kincaid's part, designed to divert attention from some mischief or attack elsewhere.

Then she heard, still faint in the distance, the thudding of horses' hooves on hard ground, unhurried, almost leisurely in their approach. The long curve of the road leading to the ranch was beyond her view, but she could see Ross and the sheriff stiffen and turn to stare into the distance. Then they both ran toward the house, Ross calling something toward the bunkhouses as he went. The two men disappeared along the porch, and Jessica heard a door slam. Then both Ross and the sheriff emerged again, rifles in hand, to stand at the edge of the porch. Riordon and two of the sheriff's men, similarly armed, joined them.

Her stomach knotted in fear and anticipation, Jessica strained to see, her vision frustrated by the shutter. Gingerly, she raised the window and eased the shutter open a crack to give herself a better view. She was afraid for a moment that Ross would turn and see her at the window and order the shutter closed again, but he was intent on the scene before him. She peered through the crack between the shutters and saw Kincaid and his men trotting into the yard.

They looked grim and ready for battle—all except Kincaid, who had a pleased, almost genial air about him. The rancher's thin, blond hair was slicked back under his hat and his face was ruddier than ever in the early morning light. Jessica did not have to look hard this time to spot Reno. He and the other gunman rode flanking their boss, their weapons hanging low and businesslike at their sides. Reno's face was shaded by his hat, but Jessica got a glimpse of the hard line of his jaw and the familiar scarlike lines on either side of his mouth. One hand held Felicia's reins with an easy grace, while the other rested in seeming nonchalance at his side, just above his holstered gun. The other gunman, the young one Ross had called Rutledge, was tense with excitement, his eyes darting eagerly toward the men who faced him, his mouth drawn in a tight-lipped grin.

Jessica's heart began to pound at the sight of Reno. Kincaid had certainly gathered a formidable group of men around him, she thought, and she felt weak with foreboding.

There was silence for a moment in the yard. If Ross felt any fear or misgiving, he gave no sign. He stood tall and resolute, his rifle cradled in his arms, waiting for Kincaid to speak. The dust raised by the horses still swirled in the air, glinting in the slanting sunlight. In a pine tree by the house, a squirrel scolded angrily and then was still.

"Well, Ross"—Kincaid finally broke the silence—"I see you're still here on the ranch—my ranch."

"You think I'd run from the likes of you?"

Kincaid's glance moved to the sheriff. "Sure didn't expect to find the law takin' sides like this."

"Sometimes the different parts of the law don't agree with each other, Kincaid," the sheriff replied smoothly. "I'm here to try to make sure no violence is done."

"You couldn't express my own wishes more clearly." Kincaid's glance moved back to Ross. "However, your friend here seems a mite stubborn. He refuses to give up when he's clearly lost. Can I help it if he makes me resort to force to get what's mine?"

"What's yours is only what you can take and hold, Kincaid. And all the crooked judges in the world aren't going to make me give up the Running J. So let's stop playin' games and get on with it. You want a fight, you got one. I assume that's what you came for."

"Not at all." Kincaid seemed to be enjoying himself. He sat nonchalantly in the saddle, and his voice was unruffled. "Why, a fight is the last thing I want. No use your boys and mine shootin' up each other. What good does that do anybody? No, I got a deal to offer you, instead."

"What's that?" Ross growled suspiciously.

"How 'bout we make this one-on-one—a gentleman's way of settlin' this little disagreement."

"Just me and you, you mean?"

"Just you and one of my boys—or one of my boys and one of yours, if you'd rather. Doesn't matter to me." Jessica knew that of course it did matter; Kincaid wanted Ross dead, not one of Ross's men. But Ross would never let another man stand in for him, whereas Kincaid had no such scruples. And, she thought with mounting dread, she could guess who that man would be.

"Winner takes all," Kincaid continued. "No further bloodshed. Everybody's happy—except the loser, that is."

"You know I'm no gunman, Kincaid. And if you weren't so lily-livered, you'd face me yourself."

Kincaid shrugged, unperturbed.

"That's my deal. Take it or leave it."

Jessica wanted to cry out to Ross to say no, but she knew that Kincaid had judged his opponent with diabolical cleverness. There was no way Ross St. John could refuse such a challenge. Even if he were hopelessly outgunned, even if he knew he would die, he would face whomever Kincaid brought against him, for his own honor and the honor of the ranch. And the fact that such a confrontation would avoid the shedding of others' blood, the blood of those whom Ross, the *patrón*, had under his protection, would only be further incentive for him to accept Kincaid's challenge.

Why doesn't somebody stop him, Jessica thought wildly. But the men on the porch stood silent, intent upon the unfolding drama, and even the sheriff made no move to persuade Ross to refuse.

"All right, Kincaid," Ross said calmly. "I'll accept your deal. But how do I know you'll abide by your terms if I win?"

"How do I know your men will go along with it if you

lose?'' Kincaid countered. ''Guess we'll just have to trust each other. But my men will put all their guns away, and yours can keep theirs out, if it'll make you feel any better.''

He's very confident, Jessica thought. But then he had Ross's sense of honor on his side. Ross would not go back on his word and take advantage of his opponent's offer. On the other hand, she could put no similar trust in Kincaid.

''All right then. Who's your man?''

Kincaid beckoned to Reno.

''Reckon you know Hayden here, at least by reputation.''

''I certainly do,'' Ross replied grimly.

And so do I, Jessica thought, remembering the loving and expert way Reno cleaned his gun, the practice sessions by the river, the long smooth fingers of his gunman's hand. She felt cold horror seeping through her, but she stood frozen by the window, unable to tear herself away from the scene in the yard.

Ross had handed his rifle to the sheriff, and he stepped forward, adjusting his gunbelt. He seemed calm, almost unnaturally so, and Jessica, like everyone else watching, knew that he faced death.

Reno was still mounted, and Ross paused in front of Felicia and looked up.

''I'm no match for you with a gun, Hayden,'' he said. ''You know that.''

''I know it, Ross St. John,'' Reno replied softly.

''But I'll do the best I can, and I'm not afraid to face you.''

''I know that, too.''

''Let's get on with this.'' Kincaid was beginning to sound impatient. ''Hayden, you get ready. The rest of you men, scatter and give them some room.''

Ross began to back away across the yard, his hand poised above his gun, his eyes wary. The men on the porch stood tense, their rifles clutched expectantly. True to his word, Kincaid's men kept their own weapons holstered, though their postures were alert and ready for action. Rutledge brought his horse closer to Kincaid's, his mount's restless dancing feet

mirroring his own eagerness as his eyes flicked over the scene
before him. Kincaid had dismounted, and Reno drew Felicia
closer to the porch and then swung easily to the ground, one
hand held in purposeful nonchalance just above his holster.

Jessica closed her eyes. She could not watch. She could not
bear to see this duel whose only outcome could be death. She
was aware that everything in the yard had suddenly become
still. She could imagine Reno turning toward Ross, the men
around them backing away to give them space. Her stomach
knotted as she waited for the fatal shots, and she found
herself praying, but she did not know for whom. There was a
seemingly interminable moment of silence.

It was broken abruptly by the sound of Reno's voice.

"Well, I think maybe it's about time we called a halt to
this little game." His words were almost casual, but his voice
was penetrating in the stillness.

Jessica's eyes flew open in surprise. In front of her in the
yard, an unexpected scene was unfolding. Reno had drawn
his gun, and Jessica could see, from the corner of her eye,
that Ross, several yards away, had begun to go for his. But
he had halted in midair, his hand poised above his holster.
Reno could easily have killed him, Jessica realized, for his
draw had been as lightning fast as his reputation claimed. But
instead of taking aim at his opponent, Reno had turned his
weapon on Kincaid, and the barrel of the gun was pressed
meaningfully against the rancher's ribs.

There was a long moment of shocked silence. Then Kincaid
began to sputter in indignation and dismay.

"You dirty double-crosser! What the hell do you think
you're doing?" He had started to reach for his gun, but a hard
poke in the side from Reno's own weapon made him think
better of it. Reno reached around and pulled Kincaid's revolver from its holster, tossing it to the ground. Kincaid's
men, several of whom had dismounted, stood frozen, watching the scene uncertainly.

"Let's see you get your hands in the air." Reno prodded
Kincaid with his gun and the rancher reluctantly obeyed.

Ross, still wary, had drawn his own gun now and moved

back to join his companions on the porch. Reno propelled Kincaid in their direction, turning momentarily to warn back Kincaid's men.

"Just take it easy," he said pleasantly. "One move and it's all over for your boss. Keep your distance and get back to your horses, and we'll all be happy."

"Do as he says." Kincaid's voice was hoarse, his ruddy face drawn and gray.

"Guess he's all yours, sheriff." Reno halted with his prisoner in front of the party on the porch. Pete Towers started forward, his mouth creasing into a grin of satisfaction beneath his long mustache.

"Not so fast!"

Jessica's glance, like that of the other onlookers, swung around suddenly to this new speaker. To her horror she saw that Riordon had slipped up behind Ross and, drawing his gun, shoved it against Ross's side, holding him just as Reno held Kincaid. Ross's weapon clattered onto the pine boards.

Kincaid halted, suddenly relaxed, and a little smile played around his lips.

"Well," he drawled. "Looks like I ain't the only one who's got a double-crosser on his hands. Quite a little stand-off we got here, gentlemen. Wonder what's going to happen." He lowered his hands but prudently refrained from moving away from Reno's gun, which did not move from its position against his ribs.

Ignoring Kincaid, Riordon loooked directly at Reno.

"What's it going to be, Hayden," he demanded. "You going to put away your gun? Or are you going to watch Ross St. John die? Maybe you didn't have the guts to shoot him, but it wouldn't bother me one bit."

Don't do it, Reno! Jessica cried out silently, desperately. Don't put away your gun. He'll kill Ross no matter what you do. And he'll kill you, too.

But Reno, hesitating at first, lowered his gun, and then, reluctantly, holstered it. Kincaid, a grin of satisfaction spreading across his face, bent to pick up his own revolver from the dust.

"That's it. Now just move away. Keep your hands out, away from your sides. The rest of you men, move in closer. Jake, you get up here on the porch and take everybody's guns. I want everyone to move slow and easylike, no sudden moves."

"Do as he says, boys." Kincaid's command reinforced the foreman's, but his words were unnecessary. Riordon, until now a shadow in the background, was suddenly in charge, and the men around him moved quickly to obey his orders. The man he had indicated approached the porch cautiously, but no one made a move toward Reno, who still stood to one side, his hand held conspicuously away from his gun.

Jessica drew back from the window. Unless she moved quickly, all would be lost. She had no doubt that Riordon would not hesitate to shoot Ross in cold blood. And without Ross, the Running J could not win any battle with Kincaid's men. She did not dare think what her own fate would be with Ross dead, and doubtless Reno, too, and Riordon and Kincaid in charge of the ranch.

She grabbed the rifle from the bed, checking once more to make certain it was properly loaded, and then ran down the hall toward the breezeway at the far end. Cautiously, she opened the door and peered out. Nothing of the drama in the yard was visible from here, and she knew she herself could not be seen. She moved through the breezeway and peered around the corner of the porch. Riordon had his back to her, as did the rest of the men on the porch. The attention of those standing in the yard was riveted by the scene in front of them, and the shadows of the porch helped conceal Jessica from their gaze. Crouching low, she worked her way along the outside wall of the house, using the chairs and benches for concealment. She knew she had to be quick, yet she could not afford to be seen.

"I don't know what your game is, Riordon." Ross's voice was steady. "But you'll never get away with it. My men will cut all of you to ribbons if anything happens to me."

"I don't know what men you're talking about, St. John." There was a hint of a sneer in Riordon's voice, and though his back was to her, Jessica could almost see the cruel eyes and the mocking curve of his lips.

"If you mean the men I was supposed to post behind the bunkhouse and in the woods," Riordon continued, "they're all out in the far pasture, instead, where I told them Kincaid would be heading. I doubt they'll be able to get here quick enough to do much good."

Ross swore.

"You really are a double-crossing bastard, Riordon."

"It won't be something that's going to concern you too much longer, *Mr.* St. John." There was a savage edge to Riordon's voice.

Jessica dropped to her knees behind a pine bench. Moving slowly so as to attract no attention to herself, she raised the barrel of the rifle and propped it across the edge of the seat. Her hands were trembling and sticky with perspiration as she sighted along the barrel. She took a deep breath to steady herself. She had to stay cool. Her shot must count, for she would not have a chance to make another. Slowly, that was the key. She must do everything slowly, even though her fear and her racing heart urged her to be quick. She must sight carefully, squeeze the trigger slowly, hold the gun steady so her shot would not fly high at the last minute.

For a moment a red haze floated in front of her eyes. She was dimly aware of Reno, edging away from Kincaid and toward the porch, and of the sheriff, his revolver confiscated by Kincaid's men, backing toward the pillar where Ross's rifle was propped. She must move, now. She blinked her vision clear and steadied herself.

Everything happened at once. With a movement almost too swift to follow, Reno dropped to one knee, his revolver leaping out of his holster and into his hand. At the same time, the sheriff faked a stumble backward and grabbed for the rifle. Jessica fired.

The crack of the rifle was startling in the close confines of the porch. Riordon straightened up suddenly, as if at the sound, and for a horrible moment, Jessica thought she had missed. Then his body arched backward grotesquely, his gun falling from his limp hand and clattering to the ground. A bright stain spread across the back of his shirt before he crumpled abruptly to the ground.

Her knees suddenly weak, Jessica leaned back against the wall of the house. Then she quickly flattened herself against the floor as gunfire broke out all around her.

The sheriff had spun around at her shot, his eyes widening in surprise as he saw her kneeling there, rifle at her shoulder. But Ross, not even turning to see who had rescued him, immediately dived for his rifle. The sheriff, recovering quickly from his surprise, scooped up Riordon's fallen gun and then dropped to his knees behind one of the porch chairs. At the same time, Kincaid had gone for his own revolver. His men had scattered, drawing their weapons and seeking cover around the edges of the yard. Jessica heard the crack of a rifle from the direction of the stable and knew that the young man whom Ross had stationed there had opened fire. There was an answering volley from behind a pile of logs near the house, and a bullet hit the wall above Jessica's head with a dull thunk, embedding itself in the pine log. Only one man remained standing in the open, seemingly oblivious to the bullets splattering around him, and that was the young gunman, Rutledge. He had turned meaningfully toward Reno, and there was a momentary halt in the hail of gunfire as the two men faced each other.

"What about it, Hayden? Are you game to take me on, or have you lost all your nerve?"

Reno's answer was to move out into the open, away from the porch where he had sought shelter. He holstered his own gun and then stood, his hand poised, his face composed and hard.

Jessica held her breath.

But it was over very quickly. Reno's draw was too fast for her to see, and the other man's gun was hardly halfway out of his holster when he spun around under the savage impact of his opponent's bullet, and crashed into the dust. Then Reno, much to Jessica's relief, dove for cover behind a water trough as the gunfire broke out again across the yard.

The battle was soon finished. With both Riordon and Rutledge down, and Reno no longer on their side, Kincaid's men lost heart. Despite the rancher's exhortations, several managed to mount their horses and gallop off. The others, Kincaid included, their escape cut off by the sheriff and his men, surrendered. The young Mexican in the stable emerged cautiously, his rifle still held ready, and several of Ross's men were running across the yard, guns drawn, alerted to Riordon's deception by the sound of gunfire. They surrounded the prisoners and began helping to tie them up. One of the sheriff's men had been grazed on the shoulder, and one of Kincaid's had suffered a leg wound, but no serious injuries were incurred.

"You got no call to take me in, sheriff." Kincaid was protesting, even as the handcuffs were being put on him. "I done nothin' wrong. Everything's legal. I was just tryin' to get my own rightful property."

"We'll see about that," Sheriff Towers replied grimly. "We got a judge in Albuquerque who says your property's not quite so rightful as you claim, and I also got some evidence that some of your other doin's ain't been too legal, either. Like takin' a few head of cattle here and there that ain't yours, and such like."

Reno had holstered his gun, and he now came up toward the porch, leading Felicia by the reins.

"And what about this man?" Ross demanded. "He was hand in glove with Kincaid till the end. Till he lost his nerve and turned on him."

Pete Towers grinned.

"First time I ever heard anyone suggest Reno Hayden might lose his nerve," he replied. "Good thing for you he's on your side."

"What do you mean, on my side? Kincaid had him handpicked just to gun me down."

"You got Reno to thank for all the evidence we got on Kincaid, and for the early warnin' he was comin' today. Reno and I are old friends. We knew each other in Montana, way back when. And we've worked a few deals in New Mexico, here and there. He was plannin' to retire, but I talked him into doin' a couple little jobs for me before he hung up his gun. This one—gettin' himself into Kincaid's gang—was to be his last.'' He glanced down at Riordon's body. "What neither of us figured on was Kincaid's pullin' the same sort of trick. He sure stayed closemouthed about that one. Even his own men didn't know who Riordon was.''

"He was my brother,'' Kincaid burst out suddenly, all his composure gone. "My half brother. We had the same mother. He . . . he and I, we had it all worked out, this deal, to get the ranch, split everything. . . .'' He stopped, his shoulders sagging, and lapsed into silence.

Jessica had drawn back into the shadows, listening intently to the sheriff's words. She seemed to have been momentarily forgotten, and she sensed that Ross still had not realized that it was she who had shot Riordon. She watched as he stepped off the porch and approached Reno, his hand extended.

"Reckon I owe you an apology, Hayden.''

"No need,'' Reno replied evenly. But he did not take the other's hand. "I have to admit you've got guts, St. John. Glad I didn't have to kill you.''

"So am I,'' Ross grinned, taking no offense.

Jessica backed up toward the breezeway. Her quiet departure went unnoticed. It was all over, she thought, and there was nothing more to hold her.

Back in her room, she closed the door and leaned against it for a moment, feeling suddenly shaky. It sank in for the first time that she had just killed a man. The fact that it was a man she hated, a man who had tried to rape her and had threatened Ross St. John's life, did not entirely balance out the horror of it. She felt worse, still, as she realized the significance of the sheriff's words. All along, Reno had been working for Ross. And although Reno had begged her to have faith, she had rejected him with harsh words and sought to banish him from her heart and mind. Instead of listening to him, instead of

trusting him, she had let her own pride and hurt overcome the
love that had blossomed between them in the desert. And
now—would he want to have anything more to do with her?

Resolutely, Jessica straightened up and gathered her rifle
and saddle bags. She had sown and now she must reap—they
all must reap—the harvest that had come. She was leaving—
that was all she knew. What came after that she had no way
of foreseeing. She pulled on her hat and went out into the
yard. At least when she said good-bye to Ross, she could also
say good-bye to Reno, and find some way to let him know
she was sorry she had doubted.

Everyone was still gathered by the porch, and no one
noticed her as she skirted the yard and moved quietly toward
the pasture. She called Spur to her and saddled him. Then,
fastening her saddle bags securely, she took the reins and led
him across the yard toward the house. He seemed to sense
some adventure in store, for his hooves danced restlessly and
his tossing head jerked the reins in her hands. But Jessica did
not share his excitement, and her heart felt leaden as she
approached the porch. Serafina had joined the group and was
talking animatedly to the sheriff, but Reno was no longer
there.

Ross looked up as she came, his eyes sweeping over her
attire, taking in Spur and her bags slung across the saddle. He
knows, she thought. Perhaps he has known for a while, now,
that it would eventually come to this. His face registered
concern, a little anger perhaps, but no surprise. He stepped
forward to meet her, and for a moment, the eyes of all those
gathered there were upon them.

"You're leaving?" It was a statement as much as a question.

"Yes." Jessica tilted her chin resolutely and gazed up into
Ross's dark gray eyes. What did she read there, she wondered. Regret, perhaps. Sorrow, too? Perhaps also some slight
feeling of relief? She noted the many fine lines around his
eyes, the gray streaks along his temples. He looked older than
he had when she first met him. But there was still much life
and will in him, and she felt his vitality and strength radiating

toward her. She, too, had a momentary stirring of regret, but she quickly stilled it.

"There's too much that stands between us, Ross," she continued. "Too much, I think, for things to ever work out well."

He nodded, his gaze still locked with hers.

"Thank you, Jessica. Thank you for everything." His voice was hoarse, but with what emotion she could not tell. She could think of nothing more to say and wanted to reach out her hand to touch him one more time. But she was afraid that he would reject her gesture, just as Reno had rejected his. So she said no more, and simply turned away.

As she led Spur across the yard, she heard footsteps behind her, and turned to see Serafina running toward her. She stopped as she came up, and, breathless, flung her arms around Jessica.

"I will miss you," she said. "We will all miss you." She followed Jessica's glance as it moved back toward Ross, still standing by the porch. "Do not worry," she said. "He will be all right." She turned back to Jessica. "And you—I hope all will be right for you. I wish you good fortune, wherever you are, and whomever you are with. *Vaya con Dios*, my very good friend."

Tears in her eyes, Jessica embraced Serafina once more.

"I'll miss you, too," she said. "And I'll write to you. I promise."

The sheriff had mounted his handcuffed prisoners on their horses, and he and his deputies were heading them toward the gateway at the end of the yard. Jessica mounted Spur and caught up with them, and Pete Towers waved her over to him as she passed.

"Leavin' us, huh?"

Jessica nodded.

"Reckon I know why." He glanced meaningfully down the road. "He just left a few minutes ago. He'll be headin' down the road toward Bernalillo. But you'd better hurry, 'cause he won't be stoppin' there."

Jessica stared at him for a moment, but she was not really surprised that he knew. She remembered Reno's mysterious friend in Bernalillo, the one he had told her to turn to if she needed him. And Reno had obviously turned to him, too, and talked of her. Her heart rose in sudden hope.

"Thank you," she murmured.

"Thanks ought to go the other way, I reckon. Sure am glad you stuck around. But now you'd better get movin'."

Jessica pointed Spur toward the road and then paused to gaze back. Ross was standing on the porch, Serafina at his side. He was leaning toward the Mexican girl, and his hand was resting on her shoulder as he stared after Jessica. She remembered Serafina's words and she knew that Ross St. John would indeed be all right. And she knew, too, what it was that Serafina had been waiting for. She recalled Manuel's prophecy and she wished them both well.

With a lingering glance, she drank in her last view of the ranch. Then, turning, she urged Spur forward, giving him a short stretch to warm up before putting him into a gallop. The pasture fence swept by them, and she hardly paused as they made the turn onto the main road. Anxiety gripped her. Reno might just have left, but she knew that Spur, for all his endurance, was no match for Felicia's long legs. Reno would already have a good head start, too good for her ever to be able to catch up should he decide he was in a hurry. And why should he not be in a hurry? His job was done, and he was probably eager to leave the Running J far behind. She urged Spur to greater speed, and she could feel the little mustang stretch taut beneath her as he strove to comply with her commands. Dust rose in puffs behind them as they galloped up the road out of the valley. Though he was breathing hard, Spur did not slow his pace on the steep ascent. They topped the rise and then began the long, winding descent out of the mountains.

He was waiting for her as she rounded the first bend. She slowed Spur to a walk and came toward him, hesitant now. He was regarding her intently, unsmiling, his eyes shadowed beneath the brim of his hat.

But he had waited. She reined up beside him and then, pausing a moment, she stretched out her hand toward him and gathered the courage to ask for her wish.

"May I come with you?" Her heart was pounding as she waited for his reply.

Suddenly, his face relaxed into a smile, the sharp lines on either side of his mouth curving upward. He reached out to take her hand.

"You know you're welcome wherever I go," he replied simply. He raised her hand to his lips and gently kissed the palm. She knew whatever road she traveled now, she would no longer be alone.

About the Author

Jill DuBois grew up in central California where she acquired a lifelong taste for Mexican food and sunny skies. Now a resident of North Carolina, the author shares her small house with two white cats while teaching and waiting to strike it rich as a famous author.

When her schedule allows, Ms. DuBois loves to travel, and often uses background material from her trips in her novels.

She is currently working on her second historical romance, which will be set in Charleston, North Carolina and on the Kansas frontier.